A Body on Pine

Acknowledgements

Fortune is found in those you love and who love you. I am very fortunate.

I have to thank Jason Li, my closest friend, who believes in me, gives me confidence and critique, and is the best friend a person could ask for; my mom, Caroline, who has been an unfailing source of support and love; Michele Hyman who saw me through some dark times; Steve Berman whose friendship, guidance, and sense of humor has been invaluable; Barbara Ryan and Chuck Lyons, friends who provide loyal support, comfort, and who put up with a lot; Skip Strickler, a friend whose quiet wisdom is a comfort; Margaret Rohdy and Eric Mayes whose advice and critique have been so very helpful; Louise, Tom, Sal, Jody, Howard, Geneva, and a host of others who keep me grounded. There are some who I know are watching and guiding still, whose presence I miss: my father, Fred; my aunt Mary; Rusel; Harry L. and Harry M.; and most of all of these my late partner William Phillips. There are others. I am grateful and thankful and I'll never forget.

A Body on Pine

A Marco Fontana Mystery

Joseph R. G. DeMarco

LETHE PRESS
MAPLE SHADE, NJ

Published by:
Lethe Press, 118 Heritage Ave, Maple Shade, NJ 08052.
lethepressbooks.com   lethepress@aol.com

Cover by Niki Smith
Book design by Toby Johnson
ISBN 1-59021-345-9 / 978-1-59021-345-2

_____

Library of Congress Cataloging-in-Publication Data

DeMarco, Joseph R. G.
A body on Pine : a Marco Fontana mystery / Joseph R. G. DeMarco.
   p. cm.
ISBN-13: 978-1-59021-345-2
ISBN-10: 1-59021-345-9
1. Gay private investigators--Fiction. 2. Masseurs--Fiction. 3. Gay men--Violence against--Fiction. 4. Murder--Investigation--Fiction. 5. Philadelphia (Pa.)--Fiction. I. Title. II. Title: Marco Fontana mystery.
PS3604.E449B63 2011
   813'.6--dc22
                        2011013043.

For Jason Li

And for my mother, Caroline

Chapter 1

I tried forgetting Stinky and his sordid life as I climbed the steps to my office. Sometimes being a P.I. makes you feel as dirty as your clients. But, the Stankowitz case was over and done with. A long, hot shower would wash it all away.

Anton stood at the top of the stairs, arms folded across his broad chest, like a sentry on duty. Tall, blond, and square-jawed, he looked down at me and smiled. I hadn't seen him much in the past three weeks since I'd been on stakeout and I felt happy at the sight of him.

Anton is my right-hand when it comes to running StripGuyz, the male stripper troupe I own, so it was no surprise finding him outside my office at Bubbles, the bar we use as the troupe's base. The strippers and my work as a P.I. bring in enough money to pay the bills but both jobs keep me running. Having Anton manage the dancers and their schedules makes a big difference.

"Marco! You're early. Did you give up on Stinky?" Anton had dubbed my target "Stinky." It was a name that fit.

"You know me better than that." I reached the landing and every knotted muscle the stakeout had caused tightened painfully. "Stinky is history."

I took Anton in my arms and planted a kiss on his mouth. Surprised at first, he responded wrapping his arms around me and pressing me close. His warmth felt good and I wanted more but Anton had his rules and I had no choice. We stayed in each other's arms a while, then he gently pulled back. Turning toward the closed office door, he swung it open.

"The office is all yours."

Walking into the small room, I felt liberated after the long stakeout. It wasn't my regular office, which was bigger and lots more comfortable, but this one would do for now. I moved to the desk, dropped into the chair, and let out a sigh. The battered old desk chair felt like heaven after a couple of weeks bent behind a steering wheel or peering out the car's window. Sam "Stinky" Stankowitz, the sex-addled whacko, slipped into more places more quickly than anyone I'd ever followed. I was right behind him every minute, watching, taking pictures, and making notes.

"So, you're all finished with the Stankowitz case?"

"Stinky's not gonna give his wife a problem ever again."

"He's not… um… you know…?" Anton paused. "…is he?"

"The slime ball is still alive. But once his wife gets my report, Stinky will probably *want* to be on a slab somewhere." A sharp pain stabbed at my leg. Leaning down, I massaged my left calf which had a knot the size of Kansas. Grudgingly, the muscle relaxed. Eventually, it'd be back and with friends. "Think you can lend a hand and massage a kink or two out of my shoulder?" I smiled then winced feeling the pain in my calf again.

Anton tossed me a sympathetic smile, moved behind me, and placed his hands on my shoulders. He gripped them gently at first and I leaned back and sighed.

"Feel good?" Slowly he began to press and squeeze until I felt an exquisite but painful relaxation of the muscles. "Got yourself all scrunched into knots."

"F-feels…unh… feels great…," I drew a sharp breath when he hit a particularly sore spot. "Ow…"

"Sorry, big boy…"

"No… Feels… feels great… yeah… yeah… do that again." In seconds, my shoulder muscles turned from angry to blissful.

"Now that you've finished snooping and taking whoopee photos, you're turning them over to his wife? Poor woman." He gave me an extra hard squeeze to punctuate his remarks and I yelped. Anton knew the investigative drill but something about this aspect of P.I. work rankled him.

"Snooping is such an ugly word. I was gathering intel. Besides, Mrs. Stinky hired me and demanded color close-ups. She can have them. I'm glad I won't have to see Stinky's face again. I've had enough of him to last three lifetimes. I won't miss the little porker."

It'd be satisfying pulling Stankowitz out from under his rock, watching him blink in the sunshine. Satisfying but not much fun because everybody gets hurt. The wife, the kids, even Stinky himself, not that I had a speck of feeling for him.

Spying on cheating partners wasn't my favorite kind of gig, too much pain and trouble. But those cases brought in the dough. Since I'd moved my investigative offices to a newer building, I needed better cash flow.

"Until he comes after you for destroying his marriage," Anton said and massaged my shoulders more gently.

"Hey, *he's* the one who destroyed his marriage." I said. "When he decided to cheat on his wife with any and every man he could find, he made his marriage moot."

"You just took pictures to illustrate Stinky's drama." Anton smirked.

"It pays the bills. Anyway, his wife deserves a good settlement when they divorce. She'll have three kids to raise all on her own. Those illustrations will help her case. Stinky's a chiropractor with money coming out of his ass."

"I guess you know what you're doing, Marco." He gave my shoulders a few more gentle squeezes then stepped around to the front of the desk again.

"Guys like Stinky are slime. They want it all no matter who gets hurt. I'm helping him face reality."

"Here's some reality for *you*, boss man: there's a truckload of things going on right here at Bubbles. Maybe you remember us? Weeks staked out in your old BMW made you forget your responsibilities here, right?" Anton affected a world weary look.

"Like?" I played innocent but knew full well what was coming.

"The Campaign Express is rumbling through Bubbles and you graciously agreed to co-host the event. Hot politicians trying to get the gay edge in the primary are gonna be all over you. After *they* crawl out the door, there's the Amateur Competition."

"I only recall promising to play with the politicians." Stan, the bar's owner, had roped me into doing the political event. With the primary a few weeks away, some candidates were visiting the bars on their "I Love Gays" tour. That's what I called it. Love was the furthest thing from their devious political minds. Votes were what they craved. The sincerity behind their gay pub crawl wasn't high but it was better than having them ignore us completely.

"You're right, you didn't promise to help with Amateur Night. I've already got a host lined up," Anton said, a dazzling smile spreading across his face. "Good thing you put me in charge of scheduling and managing the guys. Especially since you spend so much time taking dirty pictures." He winked at me. Anton was as good at keeping the schedule running smoothly as he was at managing the StripGuyz dancers.

"The politicians are all I can handle tonight. Three weeks tailing Stankowitcz was torture. I never realized how cramped my car is. There's no way to get comfortable in that tin can."

"You could find other kinds of cases." Anton smiled innocently. "Or buy a bigger car."

"Not complaining. But I'm looking forward to the massage I scheduled with Brad tomorrow." I smiled thinking about Brad, who'd been my masseur for several years. I scheduled myself for a massage twice a month, which never actually happened twice a month because cases always got in the way.

Not only was Brad a great masseur, he was a good friend who was never bothered by my quirky schedule and last minute cancellations. I intended to keep this appointment no matter what. My screamingly knotted muscles would never forgive me if I cancelled. As if to remind me, the arch of my right foot developed a painful spasm, curling my foot and making me cringe.

"Brad again, huh? Sounds like you're getting more than a massage with him. I've known lots of masseurs. When they advertise a deep massage they're not just talking pressure."

"Jealous?" I winked at Anton who also knew Brad. "What happens at Brad's spa stays at Brad's spa. That's what I always say." I glanced at Anton and noticed a strange expression cross his face. "Don't worry. Brad and I are as chaste together as you and I."

"Why should I worry? You're a free man, tiger."

I didn't comment. Those words were loaded and I wasn't about to light that tinder box.

"Brad's totally professional with me. Whatever he does with other clients, I don't know and don't care. All I want is a good massage and that's what I get."

"All I know is," Anton said wistfully, "when you're on his table, he gets to see more of you than I ever have."

"Uh, correct me if I'm wrong, handsome, but I'm not the one holding out. Am I?" I looked up innocently. Anton wanted the whole package: monogamy, cozy nights at home, a white picket fence. Short of that, we could kiss and cuddle but that was all.

Settling down sounded so permanent but at the same time, appealing. Half of me wanted to dive right in but there were issues I needed to resolve and I refused to give Anton false hope. I had strong feelings for him but something stood in the way, something in me. Maybe I was a fool thinking he'd wait.

I kept having doubts, kept thinking about all the bad relationships I'd seen. I'd watched too many broken hearted guys trudge through my office. Did I want to create one more situation like that?

Even more important, did I love him? Strong feelings aren't love but maybe that's how love starts. Anton was important to me, more than important. I needed to know if I loved him before I did anything. And before Anton decided to move on.

"Let's not go there right now," Anton said. "We've got politicians to coddle."

"Who's on the Campaign Express?" I asked.

"I think Stan has a list. He'll fill you in."

On my way out, I took Anton in my arms again, felt his muscular form relax against me. Our lips were about to touch when someone knocked on the door. As we slowly pulled apart, the door edged open.

"Anton? Oh! *Pardon!*" Jean-Claude, one of our newer dancers, stood in the doorway. The yellow office light brushed his wheat-colored hair giving him a sleepy-soft, seductive look. Tall, muscularly slender, with light brown eyes, Jean-Claude was a transplanted French-Canadian who'd started work a few months back. "Oh, *desolé*. I will come back." Jean-Claude's French accent laced his words.

"Hold on, Jean-Claude. We've got to talk about the contest. Marco was just leaving," Anton said. "He's got politicians to meet." Glancing first at me then at Jean-Claude, Anton's demeanor shifted from wistful to welcoming.

"Right." I moved toward the door. "Can't keep the pols waiting. See you later?" I looked at Anton.

"I'll be here," he said. "If you need me, just call."

"Will do."

Jean-Claude moved into the office. Suddenly they were all business and I felt invisible.

"Try and have a good time, Marco." Anton said over his shoulder. "I'll be swamped with this contest. We've got a lot of wannabes coming in and..."

"You should pay this man more, Mr. Fontana." Jean-Claude looked admiringly at Anton. "He works too much."

Anton smiled at me. "See? Someone appreciates my work."

The sound of manipulation clunked in the background as I watched him try to push me into a pay-raise corner.

"Times are tough, Jean-Claude. Anton knows how much I value what he does... and him. See you guys downstairs later?"

"Uh, I... I don't think so, Marco," Anton said. "Got a lot to do before the contest."

"Me neither," Jean-Claude said. "I'll help Anton before I get ready to go onstage."

"I'll face the politicians myself, then." I laughed.

Anton and Jean-Claude quickly got back to work. Anton obviously needed an assistant, especially since I wasn't around enough, and Jean-Claude seemed more than willing. The way he looked at Anton, though, made me feel vaguely uneasy.

I closed the door, squared my shoulders, and got ready for the political parade downstairs. Stepping into the main bar, the music hit me like a jackhammer. People laughed and talked. An air of excitement suffused the place.

"Marco!" A short guy in an expensive gray silk suit, stuck out his hand. I had no idea who he was as we shook hands. "Hey, how are you?" I said noncommittally.

"You don't remember me, do ya?" He winked at me. "I was involved in that case you handled in South Philly coupl'a years back. The one with the widow…?"

"Oh, right. Right!" I remembered everything now. Shorty was a deep pockets businessman who'd been helping out a boy toy he'd taken under his wing. I presumed he'd dug into those same pockets to back one of the candidates tonight. "How's… um… your friend?"

"Y'know, I can't remember his name either. We split a while back." He didn't seem bothered by the break-up. "I'm here supportin' Nussbaum. Been in that seat a long time and I wanna keep him there." He winked again.

"He's got a tough young opponent, from what I hear."

"That's why I'm spreadin' some cash around."

"Gotcha," I said and moved off into the crowd.

None of the politicians had arrived and it was getting late. I wondered who'd organized this whole thing. I found Stan yuckking it up with some patrons, waving his hands like an old helicopter. He loved owning Bubbles and the high profile it gave him.

"Ready for the Attack of the Politicians?" I asked.

"The Campaign Express, Marco. We gotta play the game. It's not every day politicians come begging to gay voters."

"Yeah, like we really matter," said a guy I didn't recognize. He rebalanced himself on his barstool and gulped his drink.

"Who's supposed to be here?" I asked.

"Somebody named Nancy has a list, she's organizing it. Far as I know, most of the heavy hitters like Terrabito, Kelley, Nussbaum, Clarke and some newbies. Nancy what's'ername hinted some surprises might even show."

"And I'm supposed to do what?" I asked. Stan knew my feelings about political soirees. I hoped he also knew how much he'd owe me after this event.

"Turn on the charm with Nancy. Help her introduce the big dogs to us regular slobs. Schmooze with them. Let 'em see that gay people are real live voters, too. I'd do it but you're a hell of a lot prettier and you know more people."

"When's this happening, Stan?"

"Right about now." He glanced at his watch then peered at the entrance. A tall, neatly coiffed man entered accompanied by a small, grandmotherly woman. Helen Bell was the State Representative for the district. One of the few politicians I almost trusted. She was running unopposed but never missed an opportunity to meet constituents.

Some well-dressed guys trooped through the doors one or two at a time. Too stiff and slick to be patrons. I had to admit, though, some political types were attractive, even hot. I'd could enjoy the eye candy and ignore the hot air.

"Who are these jokers? I don't recognize any of them." I nudged Stan who shrugged.

One suit after another entered gazing around tentatively. All of them dressed in clothes that cost more than I made in six months. The older ones looked like lost sugar daddies, the younger ones seemed ready to bolt. They wore their suits like armor, ready to fend off unwanted passes.

"I don't know their names, Marco. Hell, I don't even know their faces. I was countin' on you…"

"Must be the advance team paving the way. Or staffers."

"You'll have to get their names, introduce them around. Where's Nancy? I don't see Nancy." Stan shot glances all around then gave me a gentle shove in the direction of the nearest suit, a dark-haired number, wide-eyed and nervous.

I stuck out my hand. "Marco Fontana," I said and smiled. His spicy cologne floated over the odor of stale beer but wasn't overpowering.

"Josh Nolan." He shook my hand. His palm was sweaty but his grip was firm.

"You're running for…"

"Running? No… funny. No. I'm Senator Terrabito's chief of staff. Got here ahead of him I guess. You haven't seen him, have you? I didn't get to the other bars. I thought he'd be here." The words tumbled out with an edgy quality.

"Never been in a gay bar before?" I asked as soothingly as I could. "How about a drink? That'll help." I signaled the bartender.

"Th-thanks. And no, I haven't ever been in a gay bar before." Despite the slight edginess, his voice was like thick honey.

"It's the same as any other bar except it's different. If you know what I mean."

The bartender slapped down a napkin. "What'll it be?"

"How about a Long Island Iced Tea?" I winked at the bartender.

"That should do it." Nolan seemed grateful for the suggestion.

"It'll settle your nerves." It'd more likely knock him for a loop. "On the house."

The bartender gave me a knowing smile. I knew from experience just how the powerful drink could sneak up on you after a while. I was betting Nolan knew it, too. Maybe he wanted to loosen up for some reason. If he could stand after a couple of Long Island Iced Teas, he might even have a good time.

"Comin' right up." The bartender turned and got busy.

"Been a long day," Nolan said. His eyes betrayed his attempt at seeming calm and nonchalant.

The bartender placed the drink on the bar and Nolan slipped him a five. Which raised him a few points in my book.

"When's the Senator getting here?" I asked, trying to relax him.

"Truthfully," Nolan glanced at his watch, then snatched his drink from the bar and took a long gulp. "I thought he'd be here by now. He said he had some business to clear up and would meet me here."

"He's not the only one who hasn't shown," said a stubby man who'd sidled up to us. His suit was as expensive as the others but looked like a cheap tablecloth marred by wrinkles and stains.

"Marco Fontana," I said sticking out my hand again. "You are..."

"Stu Henderson, on the Governor's staff." He turned to Nolan. "How you doin' Nolan? You're lookin' a little green around the gills." He laughed, a sandpapery sound, and it seemed he'd already had more than the legal limit. "Don't worry, kid. Anybody makes a pass at you, tell 'em I'm your boyfriend." He laughed louder this time.

Nolan said nothing, gulped more of his drink.

"You were saying, Stu... about Terrabito not being the only one?" I asked.

"Yeah, 'ats right. Uh, what was your name again?"

"Fontana."

"Yeah, Fontana. I don't see Nussbaum or Kelley or some'a the local boys?" Henderson got the bartender's attention. "Scotch, neat."

"We all agreed to be here by 10:30," Nolan said. He swiped a hand through his thick dark hair and finished his drink.

I wanted to be around later when that drink knocked him on his cute ass.

"Senator Terrabito will be here. He never breaks a commitment. The man is a machine," Nolan added.

"None of 'em break commitments. Never." Henderson laughed, a loud and uncontrolled sound. His wide-open Irish face was too blotchy-red and more than a little lined. "Unless they gotta break a commitment, that is. Right?" He elbowed the more elegant Nolan who edged away. When Henderson's Scotch was delivered he gulped the whole thing and motioned for another.

"The Senator never breaks commitments," Nolan said, obviously trying to maintain his cool.

"The Governor gonna be here tonight?" I asked not so subtly changing the subject.

Henderson's red face exploded into a smile. "Nah. I'm just here keepin' tabs. He likes to know what's goin' on."

Nolan rolled his eyes and motioned to the bartender for another Long Island Iced Tea. Boy, did I want to be around later.

As Henderson nursed his drink, a medium height, barrel-chested woman stared then approached me. Dressed in a peach-colored pants suit with a hunter-green silk scarf at her neck, she walked with authority and purpose.

"Nancy Gonzalez." Flashing a prefab smile, she reached out her hand. "StonewallVotes. We put this event together."

"Nice to meet you, Nancy. Where are the big names hiding?" I asked and watched her smile fade. "If your politicians get here any later, they'll end up in our Amateur Strip Contest."

"Amateur? There's a…?" Nancy looked confused. "Nobody said there'd—"

"Ha!" Henderson let out a honking laugh. "Good one, Fontana. Can you imagine some'a these political types in g-strings?" He inhaled his second scotch and snorted.

"We've got a contest every Friday, Ms. Gonzalez. It won't cause a problem and it can start late if necessary," I said.

"Well, I hope so." The phony smile didn't return, instead her lips stretched into a thin tense line.

At that moment Nussbaum, big-boned, and slovenly, loped through the doors followed by Clarke and Murphy both dressed to the nines.

"Where's Kelley and Terrabito?" I asked Nancy.

"Don't ask. They've been trouble all night. They refuse to appear together anywhere."

"I've heard about the rivalry. Intense." I may not like political events but I pay attention to politics.

"They're more like enemies. The party is backing Kelley. Terrabito is furious. He's been a state senator for twelve years. Thinks the party owes him."

Sounded to me as if StonewallVotes had taken sides, which wasn't so unusual.

"Whereas Kelley just thinks he owns the party because of his name, right?" I said. Kelley was the scion of a family of politicians spread across the state. His father was a one-term failure of a governor. One uncle had been Pennsylvania's only Democratic senator in the fifties and another had been Pennsylvania Attorney General. Kelley, himself, was an undistinguished state representative from a district spanning Philly's northern suburbs. He was rich though, and getting richer, from the businesses his family controlled. He had no trouble raising money while Terrabito struggled for every cent.

"Kelley's family has done a lot for the state and he's pro-gay down the line."

"Oh?" I needled her. "Did he change his position on gay marriage and I missed the announcement?"

Nancy tossed a dark look my way. "Come on, let's get this show on the road." She pulled me along to greet the politicians and introduced me to each one.

As we moved, I glanced back at Nolan to make sure he was still standing after all the liquor he'd downed and noticed one of our regulars sidle up next to him and conspicuously press an arm against the hunky Nolan. To his credit, Nolan smiled and nodded. Perhaps the Long Island Iced Tea was working its magic.

Nancy gathered her brood of candidates onstage where she introduced them to the patrons. Visibly tired, she finished her mercifully short speech with, "The candidates would love to discuss your concerns." Then she plugged StonewallVotes and exhorted people to get out and vote.

It took a while for the politicians to wend their way around the bar, chatting, shaking hands, and pretending they enjoyed themselves. I couldn't help but notice their nervous glances and the way they winced whenever anyone took their picture.

Around 11:15, State Senator Bob Terrabito rushed into the bar looking disheveled and out of breath. Josh Nolan, floating on the liquor he'd consumed, brought Terrabito to meet me. Middle-aged, balding, and swarthy, Terrabito—known as Senator Smiles because of the permanent smile on his moon-round face—gave a wan version of his signature grin and gazed around the bar. Like the others, he wore an expensive silk suit, accented with the almost-required blue tie. It should have looked good but it was a bit mussed and smudged. For a State Senator, he wasn't very imposing.

"Mr. Fontana. I'd like you to meet Senator Terrabito." Nolan's velvet voice was getting slurry.

The state Senator dutifully thrust out his hand and smiled.

"Great to meet you, Senator."

"Yes... uh... who can tell me what's going on here?" he asked a little shakily. There was an arrogance beneath the ruffled exterior. Terrabito turned to Nolan. "Can I get a drink or do you think that would look..."

"It would look like you're a human being," I said and waved over a waiter. Terrabito ordered gin. "Looks like you've had a rough night, Senator."

"Wha...? Nothing of the sort. Not at all. I've been up since three this morning. I'm still on the go. Politics isn't for siss..." he started, then caught himself. "Politics is tiring work and I've had a tough day. Now if you'll excuse me..."

Before I could speak, Casey Kelley, Terrabito's rival, stumbled through the door.

"What's *he* doing here? I should never have agreed to this nonsense." Terrabito glared at Kelley, then pinned Nolan with a stare. "I thought I told you *not* to let this—"

"But… you arrived…I—" Nolan stuttered.

"You bungled it, Nolan."

"Let's walk over there, Senator." Nolan steered Terrabito away from his rival.

I watched Kelley move around the bar peering at customers. He was younger than I'd thought he'd be, but disheveled and harried. The Senate wannabe gave the general impression of being gray, not because he was old and gray, which he wasn't, more like the gray of dull and boring. He stared tensely as if he had no idea where he was and expected someone to guide him through whatever it was he was supposed to do. When he spotted Nancy, a look of relief relaxed his features.

Nancy flew to his side and beckoned me over.

"This is State Representative Kelley," she said, all smiles and obsequiousness. "Mr. Fontana."

We shook hands and Kelley smiled weakly, looking distracted as if he'd lost something.

"Anything we can do for you, Mr. Kelley?" I asked. "A drink maybe? Need to freshen up?" He certainly appeared to need freshening up, as tousled as he looked.

"I'm fine, thank you." Kelley seemed annoyed. "Has anybody seen Shuster?"

"Your campaign manager?" Nancy asked. "He was with us earlier, I think. Yes. I remember seeing him at The Westbury."

"He should have been here by now. He lost track of me, of course. He assured me he'd call when Terrabito left here." His face took on color as his anger ramped up. "Terrabito's still here. Why didn't anyone let me know? Shuster had instructions. He should have called."

Nancy smiled, undoubtedly embarrassed. "Sticking to the schedule has been a challenge. Senator Terrabito arrived a moment before you," she said. "If Mr. Shuster were here, I'm sure he'd have called you."

"A competent campaign manager would be on top of things. If my father could see the sorry state of things and what a failure Shuster's been, he'd collapse."

"He'll be here," Nancy said, her voice soothing, her manner gentle.

"He'd better be," Kelley snapped.

"How about that drink?" I slapped him on the back. He was only a State Rep after all, you could slap them on the back. He looked up at me with his version of a withering stare. I found it comical coming from such a gray, ineffectual man.

I eventually left him in the company of the loud-mouthed businessman who'd talked to me earlier, whose name I still couldn't remember. They chatted cozily, though Kelley never lost the frosty expression planted on his face.

As I turned to get a drink for myself, someone banged through the front doors noisily and in a hurry. I recognized tubby Denny Shuster. Eyes wide, he lighted on Kelley immediately. Funny how these guys sense their masters. He moved swiftly to the representative's side and I edged closer to hear what they'd say. Hey, listening in is second nature to me. Never know when you hear the juicy.

"Where were you?" Kelley hissed.

"I-I must've lost track… I thought you were…"

"You thought…" Kelley noticed people subtly turning in his direction. "Let's hash this out elsewhere." He placed a hand on Shuster's back and turned him toward the doors. Outside, I saw Kelley's arms waving and Shuster looking like a whipped dog.

Eventually they returned, and I noticed Shuster gaze around the place until he spotted someone. I looked in that direction and realized Shuster was staring at Nolan across the room. Josh Nolan turned, looked at Shuster, then, as if embarrassed or afraid, quickly turned away. I wondered how that little affair would ultimately play itself out.

The rest of the night went off without further problems. Stan was happy with all the candidates and the crowd of drinking patrons. After the last of the politicians filed out the door, Nancy gripped my hand as she thanked me. I suddenly felt the weight of the long day dragging me down. I also felt relieved that I'd finally get to go home and sleep.

"I've gotta get outta here, Stan. Tell Anton I'll call him tomorrow."
Turning, I collided with Jean-Claude who looked at me questioningly.
"Jean-Claude, what's up? Need some help?" Not that I could contemplate
anything other than taking a long hot shower and slipping into bed.
"Uh, no… not… for the contest. I need to… to ask…," he fumbled.
Jean-Claude Favreau usually a no-nonsense guy, couldn't get his question
out. "A while back you said we could… have the talk… yes? About work?
This is still possible, no?"

"Sure, Jean-Claude. Right now I've got a date with my bed."

"It will not take long. I promise." Undeterred, he stared at me, his light-
brown eyes bright, expectant. Jean-Claude had performed as a stripper in
Montréal where guys knew just how to work a crowd for the money they
made in the strip clubs. He'd learned to be persistent without being pushy,
which isn't easy.

"We'll talk tomorrow. No interruptions. Whaddaya say?"

"You're sure you cannot talk now?" Jean-Claude battered my resolve
with the saddest hungry-puppy stare.

"What's this about, Jean-Claude?" I tried keeping the annoyance from
my voice.

"About working… for you. At your…"

"You already work for me."

"I mean in your P.I. firm. Like I have mentioned before. You remember
this?"

Jean-Claude had moved from Québec to study criminal justice at
Temple. He wanted a career as an investigator and was dying to work with
me as an intern. I was hoping to avoid complications.

"I haven't had time to think about it."

"But—"

"Tell you what. First thing tomorrow night, we'll discuss it. Deal?"

"*Oui*. Deal. I'll be here, Mr. Fontana. This is for real, no? You are not
just playing the games?"

"On the level, Jean-Claude." I smiled. "None of this 'Mr. Fontana' stuff."

Jean-Claude nodded, and I was out the door before anyone else could
stop me.

I walked slowly back to my building. I was too tired to enjoy the breeze kicking the air around and the pleasant drop in temperature that came with it. Tired as I was, though, I felt like I was floating and that everything was possible.

Grace was on the front desk in the lobby as I trudged through. I nodded a good night to her and headed for the elevators.

When I got to my apartment, I skipped the shower and headed straight for bed. The silence was bliss after hours of pounding music. I undressed in the dark, closed the vertical blinds, and fell into bed.

Chapter 2

The morning sun filtering into my bedroom roused me from a deep sleep. I stretched out enjoying the feel of the cotton sheets against my skin. Rolling away from the light, I tried falling back to sleep, then I remembered the massage I'd scheduled. I smiled, yawned myself awake, stretched again for good measure, and glanced at the clock. Enough time for breakfast and a long, hot shower.

Anticipating Brad's massage propelled me into the day. He'd worked magic before, when I'd injured my back on a case. He'd iron out all the knots Stinky Stankowitz had caused and flush the rat out of my system for good.

My usual oatmeal was more than enough breakfast. I read the newspaper and lingered over coffee, while keeping thoughts of work at a distance. That was step one according to Brad. He insisted clients free themselves of thoughts, worries, and desires. Step two was a long, hot shower to relax my muscles for the pummeling they'd get.

By the time I finished I was floating. I slid into a pair of jeans and my favorite Phillies t-shirt, threw on a light jacket and walked out the door as if I didn't have a care in the world. Which I didn't. With Stinky out of the way, I'd decided to wait until Monday before even thinking about work.

I hit the pavement with enough time for a slow stroll down Pine Street to Eleventh Street where Brad located his mini-spa. May was gently breezy and elegant, like Spring should be. I took a deep breath and ambled toward Broad. As I neared the Doubletree Hotel, I noticed Bob Terrabito, barrel-chested, neatly attired, his salt and pepper hair well-coiffed unlike the night before when he'd run into Bubbles so late. His signature smile on his face, he shook hands with voters and was the picture of a politician. Reputed to be tough, fair, and honest, if any politician could be said to be honest, he campaigned as if he was ahead in the polls and not hanging on by his fingernails and desperately trying to solidify his base.

Standing near him was Josh Nolan, whose slightly puffy red eyes were the only visible sign he'd had too much to drink the night before. This morning he looked as calm and confident as his boss.

Terrabito nodded and smiled as I passed by and, distracted by his charm display, I bumped into Denny Shuster, Kelley's whipping boy.

"Hey! Watch where you're…," Shuster exploded, then did a double take when he saw me. "Fontana. Prowling for cases?"

"You lookin' for a new job after your boss unloaded on you? Or are you thinking about jumping onto Terrabito's bandwagon?" Needling him was so easy, I should've been ashamed of myself. But I wasn't.

"Checking out the opposition, is all," Shuster said, avoiding my eyes. "Last night meant nothing. Kelley is high strung. This campaign's been rough on him."

"So you let him abuse you to take out his frustrations?"

"Listen, Fontana, why don'cha go twirl your g-string or whatever it is you do when you're not snooping into people's lives."

"You and Nolan both look like you could use a vacation. After watching you guys trying to keep up with your candidates last night, I know for sure politics isn't my game."

"I got Kelley squared away last night. That's all that matters." Shuster played things close to his vest. That's what campaign managers do. That, and spin like a top.

"Good thing you settled him down. Kelley was about to bust a gut."

"Whatever." Shuster moved off into the crowd.

I was about to continue toward Pine when I heard a commotion rumbling over the sidewalk toward the crowd.

Five people on Segway knock-offs rolled down the pavement followed by a small crowd chanting something I strained to hear over the traffic and street noise.

"Clean up the mess! No more hypocrisy. Clean up…" They went on and on.

Someone in the crowd tossed a roll of toilet paper which unfurled like a giant streamer through the air toward Terrabito.

Nolan caught it and threw it at one of the charioteers. The lead "rider" was Ricky "Dead Snake" Sorba, the city's longest-lasting, most outrageous radio talk show personality. Got his nickname because he often sent a dead snake to his enemies or people he just didn't like.

"Hey! Terrabito! Gonna clean up the mess your predecessor leaves when he goes?" Sorba's grating voice cut through the street noise and got Terrabito's attention.

The politician smiled and waved but said nothing. Terrabito's supporters turned and spat angry insults at Sorba, not realizing it was like mother's milk to him and they'd only fed his ego.

"Just so you know, you're in our crosshairs. We'll be watching." Sorba shouted. His followers cheered. "I only play hardball."

"Yeah, Dead Snake! Tell 'im!" came a growl from somewhere behind the rabble rouser.

Another roll of toilet paper sailed over the crowd as the Segway knock-offs trundled away. The ragtag followers shouted: "We'll be watching. No more hypocrisy. We'll be watching!"

Terrabito smiled and shook hands appearing unfazed. His crowd loved his non-response because they chanted his name as I walked toward Pine Street.

Politics. Gotta love it.

The closer I got to Brad's spa the better I felt. My muscles started singing the Halleluiah Chorus just knowing they'd be getting a massage. I turned onto Pine at Broad and headed for Eleventh three blocks away.

Pine is an edgy urban mix of residential and commercial properties like Giorgio's Restaurant tucked away on the corner of Juniper. Further down the Grounds for Coffee café caters to a crowd that some days looks like disaffected dissidents waiting for the revolution that'll never come, and at other times houses a tattooed and pierced artsy crowd. Today it was the revolutionaries. I sauntered by Giovanni's Room, the gay bookstore, and one block later, entered Antiques Row. On Pine, just past Eleventh Street, lined with old plane trees and stretches of uneven paving, I found Brad's DreamSpa.

The mini-spa occupied a four-story, red-brick commercial building. Pine Street has a laid-back, easy-going feel making it a perfect spot for a quiet, relaxing day spa. Opening the etched glass door of DreamSpa, I entered. A chime sounded when I stepped into the empty reception area. Brad didn't want a receptionist, choosing instead to greet his clients personally. He occasionally allowed other masseurs to rent space but he concentrated on building his own repeat clientele. No one answered the sound of the chime. Not unusual if Brad was with another client. My muscles, however, didn't care how busy he was and ached for attention.

Brad's appointment book lay open on the desk. He claimed, once, that having a computer at the front desk was a jarring note in a spa, so all his digital records were stored at his home. Quirky but that was Brad's way.

I took the opportunity to look at what he'd written. Leaving an open book in front of a P.I. is an invitation. There was no one listed ahead of me which made me wonder why Brad hadn't come out to meet me. On the page for the night before were sets of initials, but nothing other than my name for the morning. Brad probably hadn't heard me enter. He'd be out when he was ready.

I took a seat and waited. The only sound was syrupy new age music. A relaxing lavender scent floated on the air and had me wanting to drift off. I lazed on the couch anticipating the massage. Visions of Stinky dropping his pants in back alleys quickly faded into the recesses of my mind. Nothing mattered as I melted into the soft cushions.

Something shook me awake suddenly and I realized I'd dozed. I didn't like letting my guard down. I looked at my cell phone and saw that I'd only been snoozing a few minutes. Everything was still and silent. Brad was being unusually slow and I felt edgy. Looking around I noticed the reception desk was measurably better than the one that'd been there before. Polished cherry wood with brass fittings and an expensive lamp were luxuries I didn't think Brad could afford. It piqued my curiosity. So, after having waited fifteen minutes, I moved past the reception desk to the doorway leading to the massage rooms.

"Brad? Brad, you back there?"

No response. Not a sound. I felt the hair rise at the nape of my neck. Something wasn't right.

"Brad. It's Marco. You forget about my appointment?"

Nothing.

Slowly I moved through the doorway. Without my gun, I was extra cautious. At the first massage room, the door was ajar and I pushed it open. White walls, low lights, massage table at the center. But no Brad. I moved on. The second and third massage rooms were exactly the same. All of them empty, their dim lights shining.

A shiver ran down my spine as I approached the door to last massage room. The door was closed and the air smelled vaguely of something familiar. The odor was out of place in a spa. It was faint, probably hours old, but recognizable: the pungent odor of a gun having been fired.

I carefully edged my way against the wall to the door. This would be the largest of the rooms. Standing to the side, I placed a hand on the doorknob and turned slowly until it opened. Carefully I pushed it inward.

Silence and stillness.

"Brad?" I called his name before making myself a target in the doorway. There was no response. No movement. I had no choice but to enter the room.

When I did, a nightmare situation stopped me cold. A man lay dead on the floor. It appeared he'd been shot. Blood spattered the walls and pooled around his body.

It wasn't Brad.

Chapter 3

F ully dressed, the victim was an elderly man. It appeared he'd been dead for hours. Only the medical examiner could pinpoint a more exact time of death.

I knew I should call 911, but I needed to search the room. Brad was missing, maybe wounded or bound or… I didn't want to think about that. I needed to look around.

Two doors, both shut, were at the back of the massage room. I knew one was a shower room and the other a walk-in closet. I moved cautiously to the closet first and, standing against the wall, threw the door open. Except for sheets and towels and massage supplies, it was empty.

The showers would be more tricky, plenty of places to hide in there. Three shower stalls and a couple of sinks were what I remembered. I moved to the door, pounded on it, then pulled it open while standing to the side. Darkness. Antiseptic soapy odors wafted out of the room.

"Brad?" I listened for even the slightest sound. A weak breath, a faint murmur.

Nothing.

Feeling for the light switch, I remembered being on the left, I flipped it and fluorescents crackled to life. The room appeared empty but I checked each shower stall anyway. Everything was still. No one hid in the windowless room.

I decided to search the rest of the building before calling the police. Brad might be depending on someone to find him. I located a box of rubber gloves in the supply closet, and took two pair so I could search without leaving prints.

Turning to leave the room, I considered checking the body for ID. Technically I'd be disturbing a crime scene, but if I could to do it without the police noticing, then what they didn't know wouldn't hurt them. The dead guy lay face up. Moving the body would be noticeable. I stared at him. Gray-haired and dapper, the man's elegant features were ruined by the grimace frozen on his face. The blood pooled under him. He'd probably been shot in the back. I didn't need to feel for a pulse. I'd seen enough bodies to know this client was dead.

Though there were signs of a struggle, the dead man seemed to have been shot before the fighting occurred. Brad must've grappled with the intruder after his client was killed. The sequence of events wasn't clear but the evidence of a struggle was massive, making it look as if a tornado had ripped through.

The massage table was overturned, broken bottles of massage oils leaked their contents over the floor, a lamp and a small table had been tossed aside, and towels littered everything. Blood smeared the walls and floor along with the usual mess that accompanies a death.

The unreality of the scene was emphasized by utter stillness, as if someone had set up the violent, gory tableau for a lurid murder museum exhibit.

I can't say it didn't disturb me, but I was no stranger to a crime scene. What worried me most was that Brad was missing. That could either be good or it might mean something very bad. I didn't want to think about that yet. Instead, I surveyed the room once more, taking a few pictures with my cell phone.

I pulled on a pair of the rubber gloves, then searched the first floor again. Neither Brad nor anyone else was anywhere there.

Finding the stairs to the second floor, I stood at the bottom listening for something, anything. There was only silence.

I resigned myself to a quick search before calling the police, in case Brad was incapacitated somewhere.

Starting up the steps, I tried avoiding renovation debris. Brad had big plans: a dry sauna, a steam room, relaxation rooms, even living quarters. I was about to see how far he'd gotten.

On the second floor, I saw the changes Brad talked about had been nearly realized. Almost forgetting I was searching for Brad, I moved between a state of the art dry sauna through two sleek relaxation areas and into a steam room with elegant fixtures and intricate tiling. Where had he gotten the money, I wondered. The last time I'd visited he struggled to make ends meet. He seemed to have raised a lot of money somewhere. There was no one in any of the rooms. I moved back to the stairs. The two upper floors remained sealed off. There was no way up without breaking through a heavy door.

There was a basement, as I recalled, and I headed back down to check that before calling in the police.

Glaring lights turned on when I flipped the switch. The rickety stairway to the basement barely held me as I clambered down. There was nothing but an old heater and built-in shelving.

Sadly, I climbed the stairs back to the reception area. As I looked around I realized it had been given a subtle, rich-looking, and probably expensive facelift.

I suddenly remembered a back door leading to a patio garden which Brad had transformed so clients could relax with herbal tea after a massage, weather permitting. The door was open, one of its windows broken. Evidence that the conflict spilled through that door and onto the patio jumped out at me. I stepped into the pint-sized garden.

The struggle had wrecked the place. Every café table was overturned. Marks on the ground indicated someone had been dragged against his will to the rear exit. The wrought iron gate hung open. There was no sign of Brad or anyone else. A napkin trapped under a fallen table fluttered helplessly in the breeze. The fragrance of flowers scenting the air and the bright sunshine seemed incongruous.

Brad had obviously struggled like a demon with the intruder. He was strong. I'd often seen him lifting weights at the gym, heavy sets, and without strain. Whatever had happened at the spa, I was sure he gave as good as he got. It was obvious though that whoever attacked him must've won because Brad was gone.

Inside again, I gazed around feeling the helplessness that people experience in these situations. Except I didn't intend staying helpless. Before calling the police, I took out my cell phone and speed-dialed Brad just in case. His phone went straight to voicemail. Not a good sign.

I considered calling his sister Emily to see if she knew anything. They lived together and were as inseparable as twins. I didn't want to worry her. If Brad was at home, then it wouldn't matter. If he wasn't... I dropped the idea.

The only thing left was to call in the police and wait. Before I did, something told me to take another look at Brad's appointment book. Still wearing the rubber gloves, I turned a few pages. Names, times, and often cryptic notes along with them.

Flipping out my cell phone I photographed a few of the pages for future reference.

Then I slipped off the rubber gloves, pocketed them, and dialed 911.

* * *

Police sirens blared their way down Pine shattering the morning peace and replacing it with tension and fear. I'd told them the place was cleared, there was only one dead body, and I'd be waiting for them. There was no need for a splashy, all out, sirens-blasting entrance. But that's how they rolled in and I had a good guess who might be behind the display.

When Detective Gina Giuliani strode into the spa, I knew I'd been right. Gina wanted to make sure people knew she was on the job. Moving up in the ranks, she grabbed onto whatever helped facilitate her rise to power. Thing is, she was great at her job, more than competent, and just the kind of person you'd want heading up the force. She didn't need the showy stuff, she'd make it without that.

She also hated me but that was another story.

"Surprise, surprise," Gina said when she saw me, her brassy voice laced with contempt. "You turn up in the nicest places, Fontana."

"Strange. I always meet you in the same exact spots."

"Wise ass. You never change. Unlike your brother who changes with the wind," she said. "What've you got for me?"

"One stiff and a missing masseur. How's that for a peace offering?"

"The body I see, but how do you know the masseur is missing?" Riveted on me, she ignored the crime scene workers already processing the place, like carpenter ants swarming over everything. "You have an explanation?"

"Well, for starters, he isn't here." I couldn't help myself.

"Doesn't mean he's missing," she said giving me a cross look. "Maybe you'd better start at the beginning."

I opened my mouth to begin, "I got here…"

"And don't leave out a thing."

"You want everything. Even the…?" I teased, knowing it would annoy her.

"Even what you did once you had your pants off." She paused. "That's what this kind of place is all about, right?"

I ignored her. "I arrived for my ten-thirty appointment fifteen minutes early."

"Hungry for it, huh?"

"After sitting in reception for a while, I got this feeling…"

"Sounds familiar. Your brother got a lot of feelings, too."

"So, as I was sayin' I got this feeling. I called out to Brad who usually meets clients and takes them to the massage room."

"And?"

"And no answer. It was too quiet. I got suspicious."

"So naturally, you being the hero type, you went back to investigate."

"Naturally. I needed that massage after being on stakeout for three weeks. I wanted to see what the delay was."

"And you didn't?"

"Find him? No. I didn't. I called out, went from room to room, kept calling his name. Until I got to the back massage room and…"

"That's where you found the db."

"That's the long and short of it, Giuliani."

"Detective Giuliani," she snapped and looked at her watch. "You say you got here at ten-fifteen?"

"About then. Why?"

"Your call to 911 came in at ten-fifty."

"If you say so," I stayed nonchalant. I knew what she was getting at and I was ready.

"So, let me ask you, Fontana," she paused for effect.

I jumped in, refusing to give her the edge and maybe just to show her I wasn't as dumb as she hoped I was.

"You're gonna ask, why did it take so long to call it in? Right?"

"Make it good, Fontana." There was disappointment in her voice.

"Like I said, I waited before I called out to Brad. So, maybe it was ten-thirty before I went back there."

"Okay. That still leaves twenty minutes…"

"I searched the place. Slowly."

"It's not that big a joint, Fontana."

"Two floors and a basement, lots of spaces to search. I took it slow. When I found the body, I checked to see if the guy was still alive then gave the room a good once over. Then I searched again. In case Brad was hiding somewhere or hurt. I went back over everything. He was nowhere. I called his phone."

"Any answer?"

"Nope. I'm figuring whoever did this took Brad for some reason."

"Or, maybe Brad did the murder and ran," she smirked. "For some reason."

"You can't be serious." I looked her in the eye. "Brad couldn't do this. Besides there are signs of a struggle all around. He fought but he lost and they took him."

"Could also mean your guy Brad snatched a third party who was also here. Brad shoots one guy then takes the other against his will. They struggle, Brad wins."

"Why? What reason would Brad have? You're nuts, Giuliani."

"Who knows his reasons?" She looked up at me, her eyes intense. "Let me tell you, Fontana, when we find your friend, and we're going to find him make no mistake. If we discover the tiniest piece of evidence linking him to this, he's ours."

"I'm telling you there's no way Brad did this. It's just not in him."

"Everybody's got a dark side we never see. Until it's too late. Trust me. You've been around, Fontana, you should know this."

"Not Brad… he's…" I stopped and thought. I didn't doubt Brad but Gina had a point. I'd put a different spin on it, though. Everybody snaps when things get too much. Everybody has a breaking point. If that's what she meant by a dark side, then, sure. We've all got 'em.

"Maybe you don't know him as well as you think."

Before I could say anything, a uniformed officer arrived and stared at Giuliani, obviously aware she hated being interrupted. Young and innocent, his skin had that twenty-something, touch-me sheen. His eyes trained on Giuliani, he reminded me of a puppy waiting for a treat.

For a millisecond, he flicked his baby-browns at me then snapped them back onto Giuliani as if I were *verboten* territory.

Giuliani looked over at him like he was ruining her good time attempting to browbeat me. She nodded at the unie and he responded, eagerly moving to her side, his face still deadpan serious.

He leaned in to whisper something to her. I noticed Giuliani glance in my direction as he spoke, her expression remaining neutral.

The unie finished, nodded crisply to both of us, and turned to go.

Giuliani peered at me and I imagined she was carefully choosing her next barb. The light pouring into the reception room windows made her dark hair glisten. Her deep brown eyes held me in a stare.

"Your friend…"

I refused to give her a chance to implicate Brad without evidence. "Look, Giuliani, I'm telling you. Brad didn't do this. He couldn't have."

"I know."

"He's not that kind of… what?" I didn't think I'd heard her correctly.

"I believe you."

"That's a switch. What changed…" I stopped. I had a sickening feeling about what she was going to say.

"They just… Your friend is dead, Fontana. They just found his body a couple of blocks away."

"Dead? How?" It's what I feared. It's even what I figured would be the probable outcome, but hearing it didn't make it any easier to accept.

"He was beaten. Pretty severely. They shot him, too… just to make sure. Nice people, whoever they are."

"They…?"

"Question is, Fontana, why'd they shoot one without any fuss but take your friend and beat him before they shot him?"

"Makes no sense, does it?" I said, my mind running the possibilities.

"Does anything like this ever make sense?"

"Guess not. But I can't leave it at that."

"Let the big boys handle it, Fontana. This one is…"

"Detective?" One of her crew approached.

She turned to him. "What've you got, Doc?"

"Looks like that one's been dead twelve hours or so. Liver temp indicates at least that much but the AC is on and that's bound to affect things. We'll know better once we get him back to the morgue."

"Anything else?"

"The techs picked up some trace. They're still combing through everything. There's no weapon. Doesn't look like any of the shots were through-and-throughs, so we'll have to wait until we dig out the slugs."

"All right, Doc. Let's wrap it up here. You can move the body if you're through photographing. I'll get a couple of uniforms to tape off the place and post a guard." She turned back to me.

"He had a sister. She'll need to be notified. There isn't any other family." I took out my cell phone, brought up Emily's number, and handed the phone to Giuliani. "Her number."

"We'll handle it," she said making a note of the number. "She might need a familiar face, though."

"I'd like to go along when you…"

"Detective Shim," she called and a young man, looking newly minted, moved to her side. "This is Marco Fontana." She gestured to me with her chin.

"Mr. Fontana," Shim nodded, his dark hair tumbling into his eyes as he did. He brushed it back and smiled. A real looker and not even aware of it.

"I want you to notify the vic's sister. Fontana will accompany you. He's a friend of the family. She'll need someone she knows."

"Got it. We have an address?"

"I know where she lives," I said. "It's not far. We can walk."

"Let's get going," Shim gave a curt nod to Giuliani and headed for the door.

"We through?" I asked her.

"For now, Fontana," Giuliani said. "Just make sure we can reach you. This is a long way from over and you're right at the center of it. I want you close."

"That makes me feel all cozy," I said. "Be seein' you."

"Fontana?"

I turned back expecting another swipe at my character. "What? Not finished roasting me?"

"I'm sorry for your loss, Fontana." She stared for another second or two and I could swear there was a glint of feeling in her eyes, then she turned back to directing the crime scene techs.

I was caught off guard and couldn't respond but I was sure it was a momentary lapse on her part. She'd get back to hating me. For that moment, though, she was a lot like the old Gina I'd known.

Turning to the door, I saw Shim on the sidewalk staring at his wristwatch.

Chapter 4

S him looked up when he saw me open the door, then quickly glanced down at his notebook and wrote something.

Out on the sidewalk, I noticed a few people gathered a short distance from the spa. A woman in her forties, thin jacket around her shoulders, folded her arms over her chest and peered at the scene before her, a glassy look of fear in her eyes. She was accompanied by two or three others. All of them looking confused and worried. Across the street another gaggle of people watched the police come and go. A few stood alone gauging for themselves what might be happening. A woman dressed in a thin smock, shivered as she watched, one hand covering her mouth in obvious expectation of something horrible. A curly-haired young man with intense eyes and a scraggly beard, stared at me and Shim as if he expected us to burst into flames. He fingered a large camera slung around his neck and adjusted his bulky pocket-covered vest, but made no move to take a picture.

"Where to, Mr. Fontana?" Shim looked up at me without smiling. He was obviously determined to appear all business but I sensed something else under Shim's façade of efficiency. Was my gaydar oscillating?

"Emily lives a few blocks west and south of here on Fifteenth and Naudain. Familiar with that neighborhood?"

"Sure. A little shabby but improving. Where'd the vic live?"

"Brad and Emily shared the place. Neither of them made much money. Sharing a house made sense."

"Sucks for privacy, though." Shim walked next to me, matching my stride without a problem.

"True. But we make compromises."

"Too many sometimes." He let out a barely audible sigh which sounded to me like frustration.

"Doesn't have to be," I reminded him. "How long have you been on the force?"

"A few years. Just made Detective," he said. "Wasn't easy."

"Piece of advice?"

"Yeah?"

"Don't let the bozos make you doubt yourself. Does Giuliani believe in you?"

"Seems to. She gives me space to do my job."

"That's all you need, then. She knows her stuff."

"She's got it in for you, though. Told me to be careful around you."

"Yeah, well, there's a lot of history between us. Long story for another time."

"Got'cha," Shim said. "Heard you almost made it onto the force."

"A long while back. I'll tell you that, too, sometime."

"No problem." Shim stared straight ahead and kept walking.

He didn't say anything after that. Didn't take much to see he wasn't looking forward to delivering the bad news. Neither was I. Emily was strong but I've seen this kind of thing break the strongest.

"Not my favorite part of the job," Shim murmured as we approached Naudain.

Both of us had unconsciously slowed our pace as we neared the house, putting off the inevitable.

"I'll do the talking if you want. I know Emily."

"We're supposed to get used to this but…"

"It'll never be easy." I looked at him sympathetically. I'd never found an easy way to tell someone their life would be horribly changed forever. "At least she knows me. That won't change anything, but…"

"You're right about that." He glanced at the sidewalk. Then, squaring his shoulders, he asked, "Which house is it?"

"One of the newer ones there." I pointed. The neighborhood sat on the edge of dreary. A few houses lined Fifteenth, some neat and clean, others in need of more work than their owners could afford. A drab grey-stone church loomed over everything. Emily's house faced a mostly-empty parking lot. Still the center of town, this neighborhood seemed to belong somewhere else.

"That one." I indicated a three story building near the corner. Red brick and lots of windows.

"Think she's home?" Shim asked. I could tell he was grasping for an excuse to turn around.

"We'll find out." I strode across the street and climbed the steps. Shim followed.

When Emily opened the door, a smile broke out and lit up her face until she saw Shim, pad and pen in hand, standing behind me.

"Marco... what's going on, is everything all right?"

"Can we come in, Em?" I made a slight move forward and she edged back. The look on her face said she knew everything wasn't all right.

"Em..."

"Just say it. Something bad's happened. Just tell me." She backed up as she spoke and found herself against a wall. Small and thin, she looked helpless.

"It's Brad. He's... Listen, Em... there's no easy way, for me to say this. Brad is dead."

A small sound escaped her. She slid down against the wall until she sat on the floor and was silent. I dropped to one knee and took her by the shoulders which is when she began to sob.

When she was able, she looked up at me, tears streaming down her face. "H-how? Where?" A sob shook her and she gripped my arm.

"Near his spa," I said not wanting to give her the details right then.

"Did you... are you the one who f-found him?"

"No. The police found Brad." I winced at the stark pain in her eyes. "I'm so sorry, Emily."

"Why would anyone...?" She looked confused, bewildered.

"We're working on it, ma'am." Shim had finally found his voice.

"Johnny," Emily said weakly. Certainty seemed to replace the confusion that had marked her face. "Johnny did this. I know it."

I looked at her then glanced at Shim who stared at me as if I should know what she was talking about. I didn't.

"Em… who's Johnny?" I paused. "Em?"

Her eyes fluttered shut and, still in her sitting position, she dropped forward. She'd fainted.

With Shim's help I moved her to the sofa, got her to sit and lower her head to between her knees. In a few moments she came to and sat up unsteadily. The pained expression on her face made me powerless. I knelt on one knee in front of her and took her hand in mine.

"Feeling any better?" I asked her, then glanced at Shim.

"Do you need some water?" Shim asked.

"N-no. I'll be… all right. Give me a minute. "I can't believe this. Is it really true, Marco?"

"I'm afraid so, Em."

"What happened?" She didn't look at Shim, choosing instead to address me.

"No one knows just yet, Ms. Lopes. We're working on it," Shim answered.

"I don't trust the police, Marco. Don't you know how I feel about…?"

"The detective is gonna need your help, Em."

"I promise you we're doing everything we can, Ms. Lopes." Shim turned toward me as if asking for back up.

"You people didn't help Brad when he needed you. Now that he's dead you'll do everything you can? And you want my help?" The color returned to her face and she sat up straighter.

I had no idea what she meant about Brad and the police. I'd known Brad and Emily for years but her feelings about the police were new to me.

Shim appeared taken aback by her reaction. He was probably newer at this than I'd imagined.

"You sure you don't need some water, Em?"

"No. I need to know what's happened. That's what I need."

"We'd all like that," I said and nodded at Shim.

"We could use your help Ms. Lopes." Shim took my cue. "I know you don't feel like answering questions but... We're all in the dark here."

She looked from Shim to me. Her eyes welled up but she remained in control.

"I... I don't know what I can tell you. I didn't know every detail of Brad's life."

"Before you fainted, you said a name," I coaxed, trying to get her to be more cooperative. "You said 'Johnny.' It sounded like you think he might've hurt Brad. Who's this Johnny?"

Her face darkened with an expression of anger and disgust. I glanced at Shim and saw he was ready to take down whatever she might say.

"Johnny could have been a client of his. I don't know for sure. All I know is that Brad was afraid of something in the past few weeks and I think it was Johnny." She took a breath and calmed herself.

"Johnny harassed your brother?" Shim asked.

"Brad told me Johnny was a client, I think, who began stalking him a while back. He never said what went on between them except that Johnny hung around even after Brad asked him to stay away. Brad went to the police..." Emily paused and stared at Shim. "...but they claimed there was nothing they could do. Another opportunity you guys ignored. But now you want to help. Now that my brother is dead."

"Do you remember Johnny's last name, Em?" I asked.

"I can't think... my brother is dead and I can't remember if I ever told him how much he meant to me. He..." She lapsed into silence.

"He knew, Em," I said. "He spoke about you all the time. Said his world wouldn't be complete without you."

"What do I do now, Marco?"

"Just take care of yourself. I'm here if you need me," I said.

She was quiet.

"If you remember anything... anything at all...," I said reaching out for her hand, "Call one of us. Whenever you want."

"He's right, ma'm," Shim added. "You can call me." He handed her a card. "Any time. If I can help..."

"You guys…," Emily started to say something then obviously thought better of it and cleared her throat. "What else do you need? You want to know if Brad had enemies? Did he take risks? What else?"

"If you remember anything about this man Johnny, that's a place to start," Shim said gently. "Please don't take this the wrong way, but is there any reason anyone else would want to hurt your brother?"

"No. No! This is insane. He didn't have… no one would hurt Brad. His friends loved him, so did his clients. He always told me about the people in his life, about his business. That's how I know about Johnny. "

"Had anything changed for him lately?" Shim asked, sounding less tentative.

"N-no. His routine has been the same for a long time. He's been establishing his business. Renovating the spa. He didn't have time for much else…" She paused, placed a hand to her mouth as if thinking. "He had jury duty recently and couldn't get out of it which pissed him off. When you run your own business you can't take time off so easily."

"When was this, ma'am?"

"Last month. It wasted a couple of weeks. Brad wasn't happy. In fact, he was seriously agitated."

"Did he mention anything specific about jury duty?"

"Just that he was upset at losing so much work time. He'd put every cent he had into the spa. It was his dream. He resented any time away from it."

"I see," Shim murmured. "Did he ever talk about the trial?"

"He didn't care about trials or anything. He never talked about it."

"You can't think of anyone who might've wished your brother harm? Other than Johnny. Was there anyone in your brother's life? Was he in a relationship?"

"He had a couple of relationships, one of them bad, very bad. That was years ago. Brad hasn't been involved with anyone else."

"Do you remember the names of the men? Your brother's former partners? Do you have any idea where they might be?"

"One is dead. The other, I don't know. Out of state, I think. They broke up years ago. It was a bad time, and Brad wanted to forget."

"If you should remember anything…"

"I'm really tired. Can't we do this another time, Detective? Brad is gone... I can't think straight. Marco, do we have to do this now?"

"Of course not, Emily." I looked over at Shim. "Let her have some time. I'm sure she'll be willing to come in and tell you whatever she remembers. Will that work for you, Detective?"

"Sure, I don't see why not." Shim folded his notebook and stuffed it into his jacket pocket.

"That okay with you, Em?" I glanced at her.

Looking lost and broken, she nodded.

"Ma'am..." Shim looked at her. "If you need anything, just call. You've got my number. When you're ready you can arrange to come in. We'll do our best to find whoever did this to your brother."

She stared at him for a moment then gave a faint nod.

"I'm very sorry for your loss, ma'am."

His words didn't sound hollow. Shim seemed genuinely sorry. I liked that about him.

"Thanks for holding off," I said as we walked to the door. "I'll make sure she talks with you."

"Listen, I didn't want to mention this, and there's a little time, but we're gonna need her to..."

"To ID the body. Right, I know. I'm glad you didn't say anything."

"She'll have to, though."

I nodded. I'd have to be there with Emily. "Just give me a heads up. I'll get her there. And maybe she'll be able to talk with you then."

"You know the deal, Fontana. The more we know and the faster we know it, the more likely it is we close this case." He gave me a serious, I-mean-business, look.

"She'll be there, Detective. Keep me in the loop."

"I'll do what I can. Don't shadow us, Fontana," Shim said, maintaining the tough guy act. Didn't seem his heart was in it. He started to go then turned back. "Thanks for coming along. I wasn't sure I wanted you there at first. But I'm glad you were there." He took the steps slowly, as if he were trying to remember something, then started on down the street. Half a block away, he looked over his shoulder at me then turned away quickly as if he were embarrassed.

I shut the door and returned to Emily, face covered by her hands, weeping silently. I sat next to her on the sofa and waited while she cried herself out. Wiping away her tears with a handkerchief, she took a deep breath.

"Brad's the only family I have. You know?"

"I know. I also know Brad loved you very much."

She almost started crying again but took control and searched my face for answers.

"Th-they're sure it was Brad?"

"They found ID on his… in his wallet. They're sure."

"You didn't see him, then?"

"I had an appointment with him this morning." I told her the whole grisly story then, from my finding the dead client to the police stumbling upon Brad's body after I'd called them. "That's what we've got so far."

"Who'd do this? Who? Do you think this person Johnny might have…? I mean, Brad didn't have enemies. Could it have been a random crime? A robbery? A bashing? Brad was so open and out. Could it have…"

"It's possible. We've got to wait. When you can manage it, you need to try and remember anything you can. The sooner the better."

"Can you investigate, Marco?"

"The police will…"

"I don't trust the police. I never have. Considering Brad's occupation, how much time do you think they'll put in on this?"

"It's a double murder and in center city. It's too big to put on a back burner. The police will have to come up with answers."

"You think so? Because, I don't. They'll seem like they're doing something. Once they hit a dead end, they'll give up and the case will never get solved. You'd never give up."

"You want me to shadow their investigation?" I knew Giuliani wouldn't like it but it's what I was planning anyway. If Brad's sister was asking me to help, I'd feel better about getting in on it. Maybe I could even get Shim on my side.

"I want you to find out who did this to my brother."

"I'll need information. Whatever you can give me."

"Anything."

"Listen to me. The police need your help, too. Don't hold back. You don't trust them, fine. Help them anyway." The more eyes on the case the better.

"If you think so…"

"I do, Em. Now tell me about his friends. Places he likes. Things he'd been doing lately. That's a start."

"I can do that," she said. "What about his computer? You think you might find something there?"

"The police will need to take a look at that, too, Em. They'll want access to everything. Best to let them see what they want. It could crack the case open."

"You take a look first. Before they touch Brad's things… I'd feel better that way."

I was treading into deep water here but, hell, what the police didn't know wouldn't hurt me. Besides, there was no way in hell I'd stay out of this. Brad was a friend and Emily had no other family. I couldn't walk away.

"I'll do whatever I can. You know that."

"I don't want you doing anything that will…" She hesitated.

"Don't worry, Em."

"How do we… I mean, what do we do now?"

"Where's Brad's computer? Let's start with that." I knew there'd probably be client lists, an address book, maybe more.

"Upstairs. You haven't been here since we rearranged the place. Brad took the third floor for himself, leaving me the second floor which is nicer. Since we were kids he's looked out for me, was always so nice. I don't know why…"

"He loved you, Em." I took her hands in mine and squeezed. "You're gonna have to be strong, Emily."

She nodded struggling with herself for control. Then she stood and walked over to the stairs. Short, unlike Brad, and blond, also unlike her brother, Emily was delicately beautiful. Her pale coloring and long hair gave her an ethereal appearance. Brad had been the opposite, always solidly planted on the earth.

Moving up the stairs with a grace I'd only seen in dancers, Emily seemed to float through the house. When we reached the third floor landing she stepped aside for me.

The silence in the house was unpleasant. Maybe because Brad was gone and all that was left was silence. Emily would have to live with that and the only thing anyone could do was find out who did this and make them pay.

Standing there for a moment, I took in everything: sights and fleeting sounds, odors and shadows. I tried imagining Brad moving through the hall toward one of the rooms.

I moved slowly to the first doorway. His bedroom. Light poured in from a window bringing life to the room and a sense of expectation. It looked lived in but not messy. Brad kept it as neat and clean as his spa. His bed hadn't been slept in, of course.

"Was it odd that Brad didn't come home last night?" I asked. Emily stood in the doorway staring blankly ahead.

"Wha…? Oh. No. No, I didn't think anything of it. Brad often came in after I was asleep and usually left the house before I was up. He was intense about his business."

I started with the closets. Even though I didn't expect to find much I had to look. Filled with coats, jackets, pants, the closets were what you'd expect. Then I looked under the bed. You never know where people will store something important. There was nothing, not even a small dust bunny. My place was neat and clean but Brad's efficiency put me to shame. For some reason, that made everything seem even sadder.

I moved to the next room and Emily followed. This was where he kept his computer on a small desk. A bulletin board with a three month calendar spread across the top hung on the wall next to the desk. On the desk another appointment calendar lay open to the week leading up to this Saturday. He'd obviously been obsessive about making sure he never forgot an appointment, especially considering the appointment book at the spa itself. More records never hurt, especially in an investigation.

The room also held a large TV and a cable box. Opposite the TV was a recliner and a circular end table. That was about all the room could fit.

I patted my pocket, feeling for the flash drive I always carried. I wanted to download anything that looked important. I reminded myself that whatever Giuliani didn't know wouldn't matter and I didn't think Shim would object.

I also remembered the rubber gloves I'd used at the spa earlier which I'd saved. In case they decided to print the room for some reason, I had no intention of leaving fingerprints behind to complicate everything. I took them out of my pocket.

"You carry gloves?" Emily was wide-eyed.

"Sometimes. You never know."

The Spartan desk chair was what I'd imagined someone like Brad might have. Not that he disliked comfort but he didn't want to grow soft in a padded chair, surfing the internet. I sat and powered up the computer. Then I turned to Emily standing in the doorway, staring at the room probably seeing nothing but memories.

"Em?"

"It hasn't seemed real until now. You know?" She sighed. "I mean, it was all a little distant. Just words from you and that detective. It's so quiet here. There's no escaping it, is there?"

"It'll take time, Emily. A long time." I didn't need to tell her that nothing would ever feel the same again. She'd known that ever since her parents died. With Brad gone, her lonely place in the universe would seem even more empty.

"I miss him."

"Give me a hand with some of this," I said gesturing for her to step into the room. "We might find something to get the bastard who did this. How about it?"

"I don't know…" Her eyes were glassy with tears.

"Maybe you'll notice something that'll spark a memory. I know it doesn't feel right."

She stared at the floor. Taking a deep breath, she lifted her head and tentatively moved into the room. She looked around as if expecting her brother to appear, then came to stand behind me.

Before dealing with the computer I looked over the wall calendar and the appointment book. I swept the page of the book with my gloved hand as if I'd get some kind of feeling through the paper and ink. He'd had a full week of appointments. I slipped out my notebook and copied every name in the book for that week and the three weeks prior. There were only evening appointments for most of April. He had only a few names for the week following this one and I noted those also. Some listings had phone numbers.

I riffled through the rest of the appointment book. There were no loose papers, no more appointments past the next week, no other notations.

The bulletin board calendar held the broad outlines of Brad's life for April and the start of May. Massage appointments and construction schedules. I copied the names and times of clients and workers and took a picture of it with my cell phone.

"Looks like jury duty put a dent in Brad's work for April," I said nodding to the calendar.

"He hated the whole thing. Said it was a waste of time."

"No wonder, poor guy couldn't schedule day sessions for more than two weeks. Had to hurt financially."

"He complained but…" Emily stared at the calendar as if trying to remember something, or, was deciding to tell me something she hadn't been willing to share before.

"Is there something else, Em?"

"What?… Oh…" She brushed strands of her pale blond hair from her face, but they fell back.

"Emily, I've got to know what you know, even if you only suspect something. It could make a difference."

"Brad worried about something, but he wouldn't tell me what."

"What exactly did he say?"

"That's just it. He wouldn't say much. Just that something worried him. He didn't say who or what. I assumed it was Johnny. Maybe Brad was worried about finances. Do you think there was something…?" She paused. "Ohgod, do you think… maybe I missed something? Should I have pressed him more? Maybe this wouldn't have happened if I'd…"

"Don't do this, Em. There was no way you could've known."

She stared at me, her big eyes childlike and filled with pain. "I… I know… but, he only had me. I should have asked what was bothering him."

"What about the trial? What did he tell you about it? Any details or names?"

"He wasn't happy. He said there was some dangerous character on trial. It made him nervous."

"They weren't sequestered. Brad could take evening appointments."

"They were given strict orders not to speak about the trial, or read news in any form."

"So, he never told you about the defendant or anything?"

"No. When he mentioned the trial, he said that 'those people' that's how he referred to them…" She glanced away and to the right as if remembering. "He said 'those people' were frightening. The way the defendant looked at the jurors scared him."

"It can be intimidating. That's usually all it is."

"Brad said he should have ignored the jury summons and risked the fine or whatever they do when you refuse to serve."

I'd have to head down to City Hall and see what I could find out about trials in the past month. I needed to narrow it down.

"Did he tell you what the outcome was?"

"We had dinner the night the trial ended. Brad looked worried. He said the defendant had been convicted. That should've made him happy, right?"

"Sometimes jurors can feel the weight of the responsibility they had. Even if they make the right decision. They can also feel a let down once the trial ends."

"I suppose," she said.

"At least the guy will do some time."

"Brad was edgy. Maybe there was something else bothering him or someone else. I should have pulled it out of him."

"Brad's never edgy," I murmured. Which was why he was good at relaxing his clients. "He's always calm and collected."

"There must have been something I missed. Some other problem. I feel terrible."

"You couldn't know that at the time."

"Maybe not, but…"

"What is it?"

"Nothing," she said. "It's just…"

"What're you thinking, Emily?"

"None of it matters now, right? Brad is dead and none of this matters."

"Not true. Anything might help. His friends, his contacts. Even his clients. One of them may know something or could be the one..."

"The one who... killed him. Yes, you're right," she said, her voice a whisper.

I pulled open a drawer in the desk and found it full of mini-Three Musketeer bars, mini-Snickers, and other candy. I'd never have guessed Brad liked candy. His figure never showed an extra ounce. I felt uncomfortable and a little sad. There was probably a lot I didn't know about him.

Emily saw the candy and a wistful smile came and went on her face.

"I had no idea Brad was a sugar addict," I said.

"He loved candy. But he never touched it. He called that drawer his 'Resistance Control.' He said if he could open that drawer each day, look at the candy, and never touch it, he would be stronger for it. He *was* strong, I'd never resist."

I closed that drawer and continued rummaging. Another drawer held pens and writing pads. The third contained notes and letters. I was happy I'd used the gloves. If the police fingerprinted anything, it would be these notes, especially if any of them seemed suspicious. I pulled out the pile and plopped it on the desk.

"Hard to believe people still send anything through the Post Office," I said, spreading out the notes.

"You'd be surprised." She picked a birthday card from the pile. "I sent this two months ago. Of course, Brad would save it. He was always so sweet."

She held the card and stared.

"We didn't get to hang out enough, but he was one of the good guys." I fingered the notes on the desk. "I'll find out what happened, Emily. I promise. Why don't you go and relax downstairs? I'll be through here in a bit. Maybe you could make some tea?"

She nodded and without a word drifted out of the room, the card still clutched in her hand. I didn't think there'd be any harm in letting her have the card.

I went through the rest of the notes and letters and realized I'd been wrong. Most of them hadn't been sent through the mail, most of them were notes of appreciation for his massages undoubtedly left in the tip envelopes at the reception desk.

They were all praise and admiration. "You're the best, Brad." Signed "Kev." Or, "I've never had such a great massage. I feel like I'm floating." Signed, "Bob." Or, "I can hardly use this pen, I'm in a daze. You're fabulous." No signature on that one.

Most of the notes in the drawer ran that way. With one exception. "Must talk soon." The initial "M" appeared at the bottom of that one. I made notes and placed everything back in the drawer. The police might need all of this. I liked having a jump on Giuliani when I was on a case but I'd never obstruct her investigation.

Turning my attention to the computer, I clicked on Brad's work folder and it opened immediately. The computer wasn't password protected which figured. Brad was too trusting and never wanted to be bothered with passwords.

There wasn't much in the way of files. Client lists, an address book, a few game shortcuts, and some random files. I fished out my flash drive, plugged it into the computer and downloaded everything.

That was it. I needed to get back to my office and put things in motion. I'd start Olga searching, and I'd mine the files for information. As I finished up, Emily appeared in the doorway.

"I made that tea, want some?"

"You bet." I smiled at her. Then I remembered something I'd seen. "You happen to know who that is?" I pointed to a name and number tacked to Brad's bulletin board over the calendar.

"That's Charlie."

"Who's Charlie?"

"He subbed for Brad when there was a last minute problem or a flood of appointments. Sometimes Brad let Charlie use one of the rooms for his own clients. Is he important?"

"Don't know yet. Gotta check every name I come across. I'll give him a call."

"He's out of town. At least he was, which is why Brad couldn't use him while he was on jury duty. Charlie has family troubles somewhere out of state, I think."

"Worth a shot calling."

"I'll go pour the tea. Coming?" Emily left the room as if it were too painful for her to be there. It was easy to see how lost she felt.

I removed the flash drive, powered down the computer, then stood and peered around the room in case I'd missed anything. I'd done things like this a million times and never felt the way I did at that moment. Maybe Emily's presence had an effect on me. Maybe Brad's death had shaken me and I needed to get some distance on this if I was going to find his killer. I walked out of the room and down the stairs unable to shake the mood. The only way to get rid of the feeling was to find the guy who killed Brad.

"Hey," I said as I stepped into the living room. Emily held a photograph of her brother. A tray with teapot and cups sat on the coffee table.

"Find anything helpful?"

"Bits and pieces. You never know what's going to help. If I can put things together, who knows? It's a start."

We sat quietly having tea, or rather, I had tea, Emily let hers grow cold. Once or twice she looked at me and I could see Brad in her eyes. It was haunting.

"I should get going on this. Call me. Any time you need to. You hear?"

She nodded without much feeling and saw me to the door. I turned as I left and caught her looking off into the distance. No one felt Brad's loss more than she did and I wanted to do something to ease the pain she felt.

Outside in the sunshine, I felt alone. The sensation was enhanced by the dull gray church dominating the neighborhood. Nothing felt right and I resolved to do something. Giuliani had a humongous case load, the Department wouldn't move fast enough. Brad's case would take its place in line. I wasn't about to sit and wait for results. If this was going to get solved before everything went cold, I'd have to investigate. Giuliani wouldn't be happy but I wasn't born to make her smile.

The walk back to my office gave me time to plan a course of action. Brad's contacts would be the logical place to start. If I could get a line on the other victim, that would present leads, too.

Some days the world gets a little smaller. You see it happening right in front of you and feel powerless to do anything about it. I could at least find out what had happened to Brad and why.

I had a lot to work with. More than I could handle alone. I decided to call Luke and Anton to help. The faster we moved on this the better. I palmed my cell phone and dialed their numbers.

Chapter 5

My feet took me to my office more or less automatically. As I walked through the gayborhood, I was reminded of one of the last times I'd seen Brad. It was outside the Village Brew where he'd stood chatting with a friend. Cafés and shops had been busy then, too. In the presence of loss all the hustle and bustle was surreal. I've been down that path before, especially when Galen went missing. Everything around me rushed on as if nothing were wrong. That's how it is, the world keeps moving no matter who's gone. You either keep up or you don't.

I was glad Luke and Anton had agreed to help research the names I'd gathered. The unknowns were piling up and they'd help sort things out more quickly. Both Luke and Anton were detail oriented. What's more, I trusted them to do the job.

Aside from the lists there was that ghost of a name: Johnny. No last name, no nothing. Maybe we'd find him tucked away in Brad's notations. If we were really lucky, there'd be some other lead. It's no good going into a case with the feeling that you've got too much mountain to climb and not enough rope. You've gotta believe you'll find a lead or you're dead in the water. Whoever did the crime had left a trail whether he knew it or not. You've got to know how to read the signs.

But something felt just out of reach about these murders. I had a feeling it'd take more than extra sets of eyes to figure it out.

I looked forward to shutting myself in my office for a while before the others arrived. The new digs were miles better than the other building but I missed the old place. The new building was a tidy, newly-renovated five story structure on Spruce. Everything about the interior was sleek and modern. The stairs didn't creak, the doors didn't squeak, and there were no apartments with blaring TVs a floor below. This building, housing only offices, was empty and lifeless on weekends. I missed Drew and his video store in the old place and made a mental note to stop in to see him.

Sitting at my desk, I ran a hand over its rough surface. The desk felt like an old friend. It was good to have my furniture here even if the rickety pieces looked drab in the new setting. Olga complained about my hanging onto the old stuff, but I'd gotten her a new desk and she'd stopped grumbling for a while.

Before anything else, I picked up the phone and called Charlie, the person who sometimes subbed for Brad. As Emily predicted, the call went straight to voicemail. I left a message and told him I was a friend of Brad.

There were files on my desk reminding me I had other cases needing attention but Brad's face floated up in memory and my thoughts turned dark and angry again. I wanted to find whoever did this more than I needed to work other cases. The silence in the office amplified my anger keeping me from sinking into the abject helplessness that people feel when someone close is murdered. I told myself I wasn't helpless, that I had the tools to solve Brad's murder and had no intention of doing nothing.

Before I had another thought, Luke swept into the office, his beautiful, classically Chinese face set in a sad expression.

"You all right?" Luke placed his warm, gentle hand to my face.

"I'll feel better once we get going." I squeezed his hand then pulled him down for a brief kiss. "Sitting around, doing nothing drives me nuts."

"You looked so intense just now, I wondered if something else was wrong." His movement around to the front of the desk was smooth and sexy. He sat facing me, his black eyes filled with concern.

"How'd you get here so fast?"

"I was in the neighborhood when you called. One of my guys had trouble on a job and I stopped by to help him. He was working in that new condo building on Chestnut and the apartment owner… let's just say he went a little too far."

Luke owned a wildly successful house cleaning business and we'd been friends for what seemed like forever. Even better, we were friends with benefits and, though Luke occasionally flirted with settling down, he was holding out for the right man and the right time.

"One of those days, huh?" I smiled remembering some of the odd problems he'd encountered. Running the business meant running interference for his guys who sometimes dealt with some overly frisky clients.

"The client claimed he ordered a nude cleaning session. He didn't. I took the call myself and that's not what he asked for. I'm almost sorry we offer nude cleaning."

"That's what got you where you are today." I said placing my flash drive on the desk.

"It's the part of the business that brings the most problems." He resettled himself in the soft chair.

"Too bad," I said. "I was going to order a week's worth of nude housecleaning."

"Yeah, and I was going to ask Uncle Han if he'd clean your placed dressed only in a thong." Luke winked and leered.

"He's not exactly what I had in mind. Still hard to believe you and your uncle are related."

"I made a list of Brad's friends I know about in case you need that," Luke said, waving a sheet of paper. "You probably have all the names already."

"Never hurts to have another list to check against. I found more at Brad's place. We'll combine the lists and go from there."

"How did you get…?"

"Believe it or not, Giuliani let me help one of her detectives break the news to Emily. I stayed after the newbie detective left. Emily's a wreck. She needed someone familiar with her and she asked me to investigate. I wasn't about to say no."

"Seems it's always been just Brad and Em. They didn't have other family, did they?"

"No. Now it's just Em. Which is why I wanted to be there for her."

"I'm sure she was glad. I've got to call her."

"She insisted I investigate. Something about not trusting the police. You know what that's about?"

"Nope. Brad worked for me part-time a while back. Never heard anything about police problems."

"There must've been something. Anyway, she let me go through Brad's stuff which is how I found all this." I held up the flash drive. "It's a start. I'll have to do a lot more digging before this is finished."

"Wow. You downloaded everything?" Luke's face lit up.

"There wasn't much." I paused. "Emily said a name I'd never heard Brad mention."

"A boyfriend?"

"A stalker. That's what she thought."

"Somebody was stalking Brad? A client? Or someone else? He never mentioned that to me."

"Emily didn't know who it was. She only had a first name. Johnny. That's all we've got to go on. Maybe we'll catch a break and he'll appear on Brad's client list."

"Just tell me what to do."

"First thing is getting through the names. Clients, friends, all of them. That's priority one. We'll divide them up and call them all. I'll take a close look at his schedule, too. He could've left a notation or something that might give us a lead."

"You think three of us is enough to get through the stuff?"

"You two are the only ones I trust completely. But we *could* use more eyes."

"When's the Hungarian hunk getting here?"

The sound of soft, low laughter floated into the room and we both looked up to see Anton and Jean-Claude moving through the reception area toward my office. There was something cozy about the way they walked, shoulders bumping softly now and again. Anton listened, head bent toward Jean-Claude, as if they shared some secret. Jean-Claude laughed looking over at Anton with a shyness that never appeared when he stripped onstage.

For some reason, I was rattled at the sight of them together. I felt a pinprick way back at the edge of consciousness when I noticed how comfortable they appeared with each other. Had I been so oblivious that I never saw this coming? I'd been taking Anton for granted. Letting my work come before almost everything else. I'd been an absentee friend. I observed the two of them, feeling as if I'd misplaced something and had no idea where to search or even how.

"Hey. I brought reinforcements." Anton said and flopped into the club chair next to Luke. Jean-Claude hung back near the door.

"Who's this?" Luke sized up Jean-Claude.

"Jean-Claude is one of my dancers," I said and frowned at Anton. I hadn't asked him to bring anyone along. "Anton. Can we have a word?" I stood at my desk and indicated with my chin that he move back into the reception area.

Taken aback, Anton studied my face, then stood and walked out of the office.

I closed the door behind me and stood face to face with Anton. His eyes, golden and clear, betrayed his confusion. I couldn't be angry if I tried.

"What's going on?" Anton said, all innocence.

"What's *he* doing here?" I whispered.

"He's… helping. I thought you said you could use all the eyes you could get on this."

"I can but… Jean-Claude? Since when…"

"Isn't finding Brad's killer more important than your feelings about Jean-Claude not being up to the job?"

"Of course, it's impor… what are you talking about? I have no feelings about Jean-Claude's competence." Or, did I? Of course, maybe I had other reasons.

"Then why not let him help? Do you feel threatened by him?" Anton teased.

"Threatened…? You're kidding, right?" Good question, though. Was I feeling threatened? By what? The comfortable way they interacted or by the idea Jean-Claude wanted to horn in on my business when he became a private investigator? I'd go with the P.I. threat. The other possibility could only lead to no good. "I don't feel threatened. It's… Jean-Claude doesn't have much experience."

"Excuses. This is the kind of work he wants to do, he's perfect for it. Besides, Jean-Claude idolizes you. Or didn't you notice that, either?"

"He'll get over it. I can't have an inexperienced kid possibly missing something important."

"Then let him work with me. I'll help him gain some of that precious experience you think he needs."

"Keep an eye on him. A lot depends on this."

"You're a real beast today." Anton leaned in to peck me on the cheek. "Brad was important to me, too. I want to find whoever did this." He mussed my hair and drew one hand down the side of my face sending an electric tingle through me.

Back in the office, I took out a sheaf of papers.

"So this is where you do it." Jean-Claude whistled, his eyes wide.

"Do… it?" I felt the edge to my tone. "What do you think goes on in here?" I laughed but I know it didn't sound genuine.

"You know what I mean, Mr. Fontana. This is…"

"Didn't I warn you about that?" I feigned mild anger. Actually I didn't have to do much feigning. I *was* mildly angry and didn't want to think about why.

"What?! Did I do something?" Jean-Claude looked worried.

"You keep calling me Mr. Fontana. Every time someone says that I think my father walked into the room."

"Oh… oh, *oui*, yes. *Désolé*. I forgot." The color returned to Jean-Claude's face. His broad chest expanded and contracted rapidly as his breathing returned to normal. Poor kid.

"What do you need us to do, Marco?" Anton looked at me. It wasn't exactly a sweet glance.

I fumbled with the papers on my desk. "We've got a list of names. Friends, clients, who knows? We need to see if any of them has any idea what might've happened. Or, if Brad had any trouble they were aware of."

"How do we do this?" Jean-Claude asked.

"I'll divide up the list. You all have your cell phones?"

Everyone nodded.

I divided the papers I had. "Okay, I'll take the first third. Luke you take the next group. Anton and Jean-Claude can share the rest." I distributed the lists. "Some guys are Brad's clients. They're not gonna be happy about being called."

"So be discreet, right? I know the drill." Anton said.

"I don't know what Brad's arrangements were with different clients, if you know what I mean. Assume this is not something the client wants widely known."

"Anything else," Jean-Claude asked, already scanning the lists.

"There's one thing. Look out for the name 'Johnny' whether it's on a client sheet or any other list."

"Johnny? Just Johnny?" Anton asked, glancing at the papers in his hand. "We have a last name to go with that or is he one of those one-name people?"

"He might've been stalking Brad. We don't know his last name. Any Johnny on your list will have to be considered. Just bring me the information. I'll handle the Johnnys."

Luke chuckled as he looked over his list.

"What's funny?"

"One of the names on this list, Ricky Sorba, the radio talk show host. A big-mouth bigot and a homophobe. Kinda nice to see his name here. Can't wait until I get him on the phone."

"Not today. Save it for another time. Today we do what we can for Brad."

"Gotcha." Luke said, his smile dissolving.

"Look at this," Anton commented. "Brad must have been one hell of a masseur."

"He was." I said.

"There are a couple of names on this list… like Hank Musto. Isn't he a state senator?"

"Was a senator. Resigned last year. Took bribes or something. My company used to clean his place." Luke commented.

"Here's another name that sounds familiar. Denny Shuster."

"He's the campaign manager for Pat Kelley, the State Rep who wants to be a Senator." Luke said. "Another piece of work."

"Brad was good at his job," I said. "And he was discreet. I'm not surprised he had high profile clients. Word gets around."

"Last night you told me Brad was good. He must've been *really* good to get these clients," Anton said.

"No idea what Brad did or didn't do with his other clients. With me he was always legit."

"For you, *oui*. For others, he could offer the extra services, no?" Jean-Claude said. "I have friends who do the massage here and back home. They do more than you may think, eh?"

"All the more reason to be discreet," I said. "They might have information and we don't want to scare them off."

We talked about how they should approach clients. I told them to keep it nonthreatening. Ask if they saw or heard anything unusual during a session. Ask if they remembered anything out of the ordinary. The important thing was keeping them from feeling threatened, from worrying about exposure. That was a problem in an investigation like this.

"Whatever you do, take notes. Especially if someone sounds suspicious or evasive. We'll split up so we won't hear each other talk. Luke you take the outer office. Anton, why don't you and Jean-Claude use the conference room at the back?"

"Whatever you say, boss." Anton winked at me.

"Try to get to everyone. Especially any big names like Sorba."

"You suspect him?" Anton asked.

"Not yet. I want the big players to understand what we know about them. You never know what'll fall out of the tree when you shake it."

Anton looked at me then, with Jean-Claude, walked into the conference room and shut the door.

Once everyone was settled, I called the first person on my list. Voicemail. I left a message for Jack Adams and moved to the next name.

"Selig." The nasal voice was abrupt.

"Mr. Selig. My name is Fontana. I'm a private investigator."

"What?"

"A private investigator. I'm calling about Brad Lopes."

"Don't know him," Selig said.

"Maybe you didn't hear me, Mr. Selig. I said Brad Lopes of the DreamSpa."

"Nope, sorry."

"You were a client there. I've got your…" His name was on the client list.

"You've got me confused with someone else."

Next thing I heard was dialtone. I made a notation. If I had to, I'd visit Mr. Selig in person and see what he had to say then.

A Mr. Toricelli was next.

"Hallo. What can I do ya for?" he said. His voice spoke of a happy go lucky guy.

"Mr. Toricelli?"

"You got him. Whaddaya wanna do with him?"

"Marco Fontana. I'm a private investigator."

"You're shittin' me, right?"

"I was hoping you could help with an investigation."

"Now you *are* shittin' me," he laughed. "Help with an investigation. Who put you up to this? My brother-in-law?"

"Unfortunately, no, Mr. Toricelli. I'm investigating the death of Brad Lopes. I believe you knew him?"

"Sure I know him. He can't be dead. I just spoke to him a couple days ago. Made an appointment. He's a great guy."

"You saw him in April, right? April twenty-fifth."

"If you say so. I know it was April. I go once a month and good ol' Brad helps readjust my back, if you know what I mean." I imagined him winking theatrically at me.

I was all too sure I knew what he meant.

"You recently made another appointment?"

"Yeah, sure… once a month. Like clockwork," he said then paused. "You say he's… dead? That… can't be." His voice lost some of the joy and life it held a moment before.

"I'm sorry, Mr. Toricelli. It's true. He was killed last night."

"He can't be… I don't know where I'm gonna find a guy nice as he was. Y'know? We… we were… he was…" He trailed off and became silent.

"Was there anything different you noticed when you spoke with him about your appointment?"

"Nah, Brad was always Brad. Nice, caring guy. Made the appointment and that was that. One of the things I liked about Brad. No fuss."

"Nothing out of the ordinary when you saw him in April?"

"Same great massage as always. Nothing strange, just good."

I crossed Toricelli off the list and did the same song and dance with the next seven clients. Like slogging through mud. No one knew anything. At least the ones who admitted they'd been clients. A few of them were saddened by the news and one choked up when he spoke about Brad.

None of them were his actual friends but some were long-time clients according to Brad's notes so they could have known him well. His habits, subtleties of his behavior. Massage, even legitimate massage, is an intimate act. You get to know one another after a long association. I hoped one of his clients might have detected something out of character with Brad. Something that may not have made sense to them but might help me. So far, it hadn't panned out.

Luke ambled into the office, list in hand, disappointment on his face.

"Nothing," he said. "I have exactly nothing from any of them."

"Not even Shuster or Ricky Sorba?"

"Great reactions from both of them, even funny if this wasn't so serious," Luke said. "Shuster had some words for you when I told him I called on your behalf."

"You mean he called me Fontana the Sweetie Pie?"

"He said you were a rotten, nosey son of a bitch."

"And Dead Snake? What'd he have to say?"

"After I'd explained why I called, he said, 'Fuck you, faggot.' and hung up."

"Nice man. I'll make sure to look into him personally," I said.

"The rest of the guys on my list didn't remember a thing. So they said."

"Pretty much the same story for me. A lot of people were out. I still have calls to make."

"Give me half your list," Luke put out his hand.

"You sure? I mean…"

"I'm sure. I want to get the bastard who did this."

I handed him a couple of sheets. "Any luck finding Johnny on your list?"

"No. Not one Johnny."

Jean-Claude rushed into the office waving a paper.

"Got something. Mr.... uh... Marco. This is something," he said, eyes bright, a serious look on his face.

"Slow down Jean-Claude. Let's see what you have."

Luke gazed at Jean-Claude but said nothing.

"What've you got?" I smiled. He seemed so boyishly innocent it was difficult to be angry with him. Which was not a quality I liked in myself but I couldn't help it.

"I think I have what do you call it? The clue?" He read from the page he had. "A Mr. Fillmore says maybe he saw someone bothering Brad, eh?"

"Bothering Brad? What'd he say? Exactly."

"The day he has the appointment with Brad, he says some guy tries to get into the room. This is... he says this creeps... how does he say this?" Jean-Claude paused. "Yes, he says this thing 'creeps him out'? This is an expression, no?"

I nodded.

"He says Brad tells the man to leave but the man bangs harder the door, until Brad says he will call the police. Then the man leaves, eh?"

"Did you get Fillmore's address? I need to talk to this guy."

"Of course." Jean-Claude handed me a page with the guy's name and address.

"Good work, Jean-Claude. Ready for more?"

He looked as if he couldn't believe I trusted him with more work.

"Here's another page." I gave Jean-Claude the remainder of my list. "You and Anton can finish up. I've gotta see what Fillmore has to say."

On the way out, I tossed the spare office keys to Luke. "If I'm not back in an hour, lock up for me, will you, cutie?"

"Will do, boss," Luke said, smirking. Even a smirk looked cute on his face.

Chapter 6

I raced to the parking garage in my condo building and didn't wait for the valet workers to get my old BMW.

Figuring I'd call Bart Fillmore as I drove, I activated the new GPS system for directions to his place in Manayunk. I didn't need a GPS device, but an old client gave it to me as a gift and I thought I should use it. The directions had me driving through center city and up the Parkway.

I'd punched Fillmore's number into my phone before I left the office so I could drive and talk without fuss. He answered almost as if he expected my call.

"Mr. Fillmore? This is Marco Fontana."

"Your assistant said you'd call."

"I'm headed out your way, Mr. Fillmore. If you have a few moments, I thought we could talk before my next appointment." I wanted him to think it'd be a quick conversation. Less likely for him to refuse.

"If you don't mind talking while I work. I'm getting ready to open a business and we're already behind schedule."

"As long as you can work and talk at the same time, I can listen." I wasn't about to let my most promising lead get away. "What's the address?"

"Near the corner of Main and Levering. You'll see a shop with a bright red awning. That's me."

I disconnected and followed the robotic female voice of the GPS device.

Manayunk is a unique part of Philly. Not far from the downtown, it has the feel of a small town. It's a cozy part of Philly I hardly ever get to but when I'm there, I soak up the amiable atmosphere. Hilly streets and steep inclines, twists and turns, give it a compact character worlds apart from the rest of the city.

The directions had me pulling onto Main Street in short order and Levering Street came up quickly. For a small fortune, I left my car at a parking lot on Levering. They know when they've got you by the short and curlies.

You couldn't miss the red awning with "Bart's" in white cursive. I stepped into the shop and spotted a jolly, overweight guy in denim overalls directing several young workers. I figured the supervisor had to be Fillmore.

The noise of hammers and electric saws filled the place giving me a flashback to a childhood memory of my father's lumber mill. I smiled with the memory and inhaled the sweet smell of fresh lumber. Wooden curlicues skittered away as I approached the guy in overalls.

"Hey, there," the roundish man called out to me. "You must be Fontana. No mistaking your Italian looks." When he said "Eye-talian" I knew he wasn't originally from Philadelphia.

"Right the first time," I said, extending my hand. "Thanks for taking the time to talk, Mr. Fillmore."

"Call me Bart. Let's go outside." He moved quickly out the door. When we got to the sidewalk, he said, "No need for everybody to know my business." He winked. His large, apple pie face was comforting. He smiled and I got the feeling he was somebody everyone felt they could trust. Which made him dangerous.

"I know you're busy, Bart, so I'll make this quick."

"Yeah, no problem. Your assistant told me Brad was dead? Murdered? How's that possible? I mean, the guy was so likeable."

"We don't know anything for certain yet. That's what makes you so important." Never hurts to flatter but in this case, as my only lead, Fillmore *was* important.

"Well, anything I can do, y'know. Brad was a friend."

"You knew him a while, then?"

"Several years. I was one of his first clients. Nice guy. Never made an issue of my weight. Some masseurs won't touch a fat guy."

"When's the last time you had an appointment with him?"

"Back in April. I know because I couldn't get my usual appointment for a coupl'a weeks. Brad said he was on jury duty and his schedule was backed up and would I mind scheduling two weeks later than my usual. So I drove in for an early evening session." He paused, smiled, and appeared to be reliving a pleasant memory.

"You had your session and…?" I tried moving him along.

"But… Brad was kinda nervous. Like I said, he'd been on jury duty. The trial was over but he complained about all the time he'd missed. I felt for the guy, y'know. I understand business."

"I gather something happened during the massage?"

Fillmore placed a hand to his chin and closed his eyes. He exhaled then looked at me. "Well, I wouldn't call it *something*, it was something but nothing big."

"Was this when you first got there?"

"No, not right away. Everything was normal. I let myself in and sat in reception like always, only this was at night so everything looked different. Felt a little strange. Know what I mean?"

I nodded. I knew exactly what he meant.

"Brad came and took me to the large massage room. He left and I got undressed and hopped onto the table. Well, not hopped exactly. Guys my size don't hop, 'cause when we do, things happen. I was on the table when he came back in. Sometimes I think he's got a peephole 'cause he comes in right after I get onto the table. Every time. He just knows when I'm ready."

"What happened then?"

"Brad started that relaxing music he plays in the background, made sure the air was scented with something nice and began the massage. But it was all wasted."

"Wasted?"

"As soon as he started, someone came pounding at the door. Ruined everything." Bart's expressive face registered annoyance. "I was half asleep, y'know? The atmosphere made me drowsy and I was falling asleep. That pounding woke me up and I looked up at Brad. He seemed frightened.

At least that's what it looked like to me. I guess he could'a just looked surprised. Fine line there, y'know? He was probably surprised. Anyway, he was disturbed."

"What'd he do?"

"He just stood there for a minute. The guy kept banging on the door. Lucky he always locks the door."

"How'd you know it was a guy?"

"Because Brad called out and told him to go away. And the guy yelled back. It was a guy's voice, so that's how I know it was a man. He said he wasn't going anywhere."

"Did Brad open the door? Did Brad ever say the guy's name?"

"Brad never opened the door. Told the guy he was going to call 911 and the guy pounded again." Bart paused, seemed to be trying to remember. "Yeah, then Brad went over to the door. I remember because he was standin' there and flinched when the guy started pounding again."

"You're sure Brad didn't open the door? You never saw who was out there?"

"The way that guy was pounding on the door, even a hunk like you wouldn't open it and let him in. Brad kept that door locked."

"Then the guy just goes away…?"

"He didn't. Not right away. Brad stayed near the door and mumbled something."

"A name? Something you remember?"

"He was talkin' kind of low. It was hard to hear. I think Brad called him something like Matt or Max. Sometimes it sounded like Mattsz. Like I said, he was mumbling against the door. Couldn't hear clearly. It started with an M, that much I remember. M-something… coulda been Matt, coulda been something else but it started with M. Who could hear straight anyway? I was tense… hell, I was scared. There I was naked on a table and this crazy man is pounding at the door. I don't know what I heard. I wasn't hearin' right is all I know. I was afraid the guy would break down the door. Then what would I do, naked as a jaybird?"

"Matt or Max? That's what Brad said?"

"Could've been Mazz or Mattsz. There was some kind of z-sound sometimes when he said it. Brad's voice was shaky and he was up against that door mumbling. He was on edge. Like I was. Maybe worse. Nah, I think I felt worse, after all I was the one naked on the table. At least Brad had his clothes on." Bart chuckled.

"You sure Brad didn't say the name Johnny?" It was worth asking.

"Johnny?" Fillmore seemed to swirl the name around in his mouth trying to remember. "No. Nope. Not even close. I'd've remembered because my niece just had a baby. Named him Johnny. No that wasn't it."

"The guy never entered the room?" Sometimes you ask the same question and you get a different answer.

"Nooo. No siree. Gawd, that *woulda* been awkward. Brad never opened the door. He yelled again about calling the police and the pounding stopped."

"The guy say anything after that?"

"Yeah, kinda scary. He said whatever it was, it wasn't over. That Brad was going to pay for what he did. Sounds scary crazy to me, don't it to you?"

"How'd Brad react to that?"

"He was shaken up. Asked me if I minded waiting a few moments for him to calm down." Bart laughed. "Shit, I needed to calm down myself so I *knew* he had to be rattled."

After talking a bit more, I left Bart to his work. He'd begun looking like he wanted to get back to his shop and I needed to move on the information he'd given me.

The drive back to center city felt a lot longer than the ride up. Probably because I wanted to get to work finding this guy Max or Matt or Mazz or whatever his name was. Sounded like the thug might know a lot.

I needed to get back to my office in a hurry. So this time, I allowed my building's parking valets to take my car and said a silent prayer I wouldn't find a new dent or ding when I picked it up the next time.

I had the vague feeling something was wrong or off-kilter but I couldn't figure out what. When I reached the corner and saw the sleek black Ford parked, illegally I noted, outside the building. I knew what that odd feeling had meant.

I had unexpected guests.

Chapter 7

The car's tinted windows kept its secrets well. I'd find out who was in there soon enough. Strolling by the car and into the tiny lobby of the office building, I figured my uninvited guest would be at my back before the elevator arrived.

I was wrong. The elevator arrived at the same time as Denny Shuster tapped me on the shoulder. He was agitated. I saw his puffy, haggard face in the mirror next to the elevator. I guess staying up late working on campaigns while worrying people will discover you're gay takes a toll.

"What's up?" I said without turning around. Shuster's reputation for being a major shit to a lot of good people didn't make me feel the need to be courteous. I knew what was up. He wasn't happy about having been called earlier.

"What's up is my dander." Short and stubby, with one too many chins framing his baby face, Shuster could barely contain the fury in his voice. "We need to talk, Mister."

"Sure thing. Just call my secretary on Monday and make an appointment. In case you hadn't noticed, today is Saturday and I'm not here." I stepped into the elevator and turned to hit the button for my floor.

Shuster made as if to enter.

"Uh-unh, bucko. Private office. Step out or I might not stay so polite."

The chubby little politico quivered with rage but didn't make another move.

"You listen to me, Fontana. Stay out of my business. And if *any of this*, any of this at all, gets to the wrong ears, you'll wish you'd been born on another continent." Shuster turned and stomped out, a gesture that, for his size and weight, was comical.

The elevator door closed and I was zipped up to my office. Luke and the others were gone but they'd left notes on my desk. Seeing the paperwork reminded me about Anton and Jean-Claude. Had they gone home together? Was there something brewing between them? I stopped those thoughts dead. I had no business wondering anything about them. I hadn't earned that right and yet I felt a sense of loss.

I needed to forget. I needed to concentrate on the case and on finding Matt or Max or Matz, whoever he was.

After scanning the client list, I found no Max and no name even close to Matz but there were three named Matt. The notations Anton and Luke had left next to the names indicated these clients were fans of Brad. Of course, even fans do crazy things. So I couldn't ignore them.

Picking up the phone, I tapped in the number of the first Matt. Next to his name, Anton had written "A real sweetheart. Wants to contribute money for flowers for Brad." The Sweetheart's phone rang several times before he answered. His voice had that scratchy vague kind of hoarseness that some people acquire with age.

I explained why I called, and he was eager to talk. The more we spoke, the more convinced I was this wasn't the man who'd terrorized the spa. He was an old time client, enamored of Brad. It also didn't sound like he had the strength to pound on anything or make much of a racket.

For the next Matt, Anton's note said, "Odd but harmless." I wondered how Anton could tell. He was great at reading people in person, but over the phone?

When Matt the Odd answered the phone, I realized immediately why Anton's perception was correct. This Matt had a Marilyn Monroe voice that threw me for a minute. I asked if Matt was available, and the voice at the other end claimed to *be* Matt. Although he didn't sound like the type to go battering down doors, you never knew.

The third Matt was equally harmless. Luke had left a note saying he was "A laugh riot." When I got him on the phone, I saw Luke was right. The man didn't let an opportunity for a joke pass him by. I didn't have time for laughs, so I cut that call short. He wasn't playing with a full deck, but I didn't get the feeling he was dangerous.

I wouldn't cross these guys off yet. I'd seen too many people who had vastly different personalities under varying circumstances. The three Matts would stay way at the bottom of my list, but they'd definitely stay.

Whoever had been pounding on the spa door wasn't on Brad's client list. Nothing close to Max or Mazz or Matz appeared. I pulled up the rest of Brad's files and ran searches on variations of the name. Struck out every time.

There were a few possibilities. Considering it was a high stress situation and Fillmore was frightened, maybe he hadn't heard correctly. Or, Fillmore missed some detail because Brad was "mumbling" as Fillmore had described it. A more disturbing possibility was that Brad didn't want any record of the guy to be found and never placed his name in any file.

From Fillmore's report, this couldn't have been Brad's first encounter with this guy Mazz or Max or whatever. So I considered the possibility that he'd told somebody about the man. The first person he'd tell should have been Emily. If he had, then why hadn't she mentioned the name earlier?

I picked up the phone and keyed in her number.

"You found something?" Her voice was a mix of hope and fear.

"Not yet. Someone gave me a name but no one in Brad's files matches."

"What name? Who told you?"

"A client. Claimed there was someone who harassed Brad."

"I told you that was going on. Someone bothered Brad. Was it Johnny? Did the client say it was him?"

"Are you aware of anyone with a name like Matt or Mazz in Brad's life?"

"No… no. There was a boyfriend once a long time ago. Brad's first boyfriend was named Marty. But he… well, he died."

"You know how?"

"Drugs," Emily sighed. "Years ago Brad and Marty were part of a fast crowd. Parties, bars, crazy stuff. They went to some circuit party and Marty tried crystal… something."

"Crystal meth?"

"That sounds right. Seems like so long ago. After that, Marty was different. Drugs became his life. Eventually…" Emily was silent.

"And Brad?"

"Brad? No. He tried things, sure. But he never went overboard. He was destroyed by Marty's death. Felt responsible. His whole world collapsed.

"So there was no one named…"

"Not by those names, not Matt or…

"The witness thought the name could also have been Max or something like that."

"Max…? It can't be. He's gone… We thought… he was…"

"Who? Tell me what you're thinking, Em."

"Max. You're sure it was… Max?"

"It could have been Max. Did Brad know someone named Max?"

"Y-yes." Emily paused, took a breath. "Max. We tried forgetting him. We needed to move on. But… maybe…"

"Who is he? What did he have to do with Brad?"

"Max was an ugly man. I don't mean his looks. Max had an ugly soul. Mean and small and vicious."

"How did Brad know this creep?"

"They were involved for a while. Well before Brad started the spa."

"How long were they together?"

"Long enough for Max to give Brad a black eye a couple of times. Long enough for Brad to get injured in what he claimed was a simple accident at home. I knew it was Max. It had to be."

"Brad never went to the police?" I knew the answer as soon as the words left my lips.

"They don't often take women seriously when it comes to domestic violence. You think the police would believe a gay man?"

"No. They wouldn't." I knew the statistics on domestic violence in the gay community were the same as for straight couples. Except gay men who get abused aren't taken seriously. A cold chunk of ice settled in the pit of my stomach. I'd seen this kind of abuse before. "Having a complaint on record is something that can be used later on, even if they don't believe you. It's too bad."

"Brad wasn't thinking right at the time. How could he? He was too frightened." She paused again. "Do you think Max did this?"

"I don't know, Em."

"We never knew what happened to Max.… We thought… hoped… he went away…" Her voice trailed away. It became a small sound and sad.

"How did things end with them? How long ago was it?" Funny that Brad never told me about Max. It was probably something he didn't want to remember. Or, it could have been shame. So many men in that situation don't want to admit they've been abused. At least Brad made it out alive. I wondered how he'd gotten Max off his back.

"It was years ago. Brad was just out of college."

"Was this before or after Marty?"

"Max came along right after Marty died. Brad was vulnerable and wasn't being careful. He could never see what people were actually like anyway. Max was strong on the surface and offered Brad stability. I never trusted him, and I told Brad."

Strong on the surface. That's what bullies are like. They take advantage of anyone who can't see beneath the tough surface to the soft, pathetic creep inside. I knew the type.

"How long before Max began hurting Brad?"

"He didn't start out hurting him. Not physically. Things happened a little at a time. First he kept Brad away from his friends. They'd been his only support other than me. Max prevented Brad from going out or meeting anyone new. Eventually Brad was never allowed out unless it was with Max."

"Brad just let it happen?"

"He didn't see what was going on. Not at first. He so wanted to forget what had happened to Marty that he accepted anything Max demanded. He went along with anything Max said." She paused. I heard her struggling to speak.

"And then…" I coaxed.

"Max got physical. When they argued, he'd hit Brad. Of course, Brad made excuses for him. Don't they always?"

"That's the pattern." I'd seen it happen in gay and lesbian relationships more often than people imagined.

"I saw Brad with black eyes, bruises, cut lips… I told him he had to do something." Emily's voice was stronger now.

"He was too afraid, right?"

"Max told Brad he'd regret it if he tried to leave. Max could be very intimidating."

"Bastard."

"I couldn't convince Brad he had to leave. Until…" Her voice softened.

"Until what?"

"Brad fell down the stairs. A whole flight of steps in their home. It was bad."

"Mygod," I said. "I never knew."

"Brad never wanted anyone to know."

"How badly was he hurt?"

"A broken arm. A broken leg. Broken ribs. Cuts and bruises. Sprains. Stress fractures…." She was silent so long, I thought she'd hung up.

"Em? You okay?"

"He was unconscious when they brought him to the hospital."

"How did they know to call you? I mean, how'd Max allow that?"

"Brad has… had… me as his emergency contact of record with his doctor. The hospital must've had access to those records. Anyway, I thank God that they called me."

"That's when Brad decided to leave?"

"Yes, but he never admitted Max pushed him down those stairs. He said Max had had a rough life and couldn't help himself. Brad didn't want to make things worse."

"That was the end of it?"

"Not exactly. Max tried to get back together. Brad finally got a restraining order against Max."

"Did it help?"

"Max made a few more attempts. Then all of a sudden he disappeared."

"Like out of town disappeared? Or…"

"We never knew. At the time I thought he was out of sight because he was doing the same thing to some other poor guy. I still think so."

"He came back recently?"

"Brad never said that exactly. I suppose he didn't want me to worry. I overheard him talking on the phone one night. Sounded like Brad was trying to get someone to stop calling. He brushed it off when I asked and said that someone was being a nuisance. I tried getting him to talk about it but he said he could take care of it. That it was nothing..." Before ending the call, she said, "If your witness heard his name, then it has to be Max."

Chapter 8

Max, Brad's abusive boyfriend, and the mysterious Johnny, were two of the better leads I had. Actually, they were my only leads.

Knowing Brad as I did, I couldn't believe he'd been involved with a creep like Max. It was a long time ago and he'd obviously changed. The Brad I knew would never allow that to happen again.

Now Max was at the top of my list. I wanted to see him up close, not just because he was a suspect, but I wanted to look the scumbag in the eye and tell him what a loser he was. All I had to do was find him.

Emily told me his name was Gibson which gave me a place to start. I pulled up a browser and after a bit of searching came up with a list of Max Gibsons. Some sites give you a person's gender, an approximate age, and other useful tidbits. That information helped narrow my list to a few who lived in Philly. There was no guarantee Gibson had stayed in the city but I had to start somewhere.

I made some calls. The first two Gibsons weren't home. None of the others owned up to being the Max Gibson I was searching for. Not that I entirely believed them. I'd get Olga to do a deeper search in better databases.

One of the Max Gibsons was evasive, couldn't answer a question head on, which raised red flags all over the place. As I peppered him with more questions, I heard a woman's voice in the background. "Honey, what're you doin' on the phone so long?" He moaned, telling me to get the hell off his back and that one nag was enough for any man. I took him off the list. A jerk, maybe, but not the jerk I was looking for.

The Max Gibson I needed didn't seem to be among the names the Internet had spit out. Meaning, the guy was a dead end until I could dig up more information. I silently wished Emily had known more about him.

I was about to call some of Brad's clients that I'd missed on the first go round, when I remembered the crime scene pictures I'd taken with my cell phone. In all the rush and after dealing with Emily, I'd almost forgotten the photos.

Not often cooperative about giving up its contents, my way-too-clever smart phone decided not to give me a problem and immediately coughed up the pictures. Two photos interested me more than the others: the appointment book and the dead client.

I scrutinized the picture of the appointment book on the reception counter and jotted down sets of initials Brad had penciled in on the day he'd been killed. "SW" and "PV" were listed without notes indicating who they were.

The fact that they were missing any notation was a bit strange considering Brad's usual practice. On past visits to his spa, I always glanced at his appointment book. It's what I do, you never know what information might come in handy. He usually had full names listed. Sometimes last name and first initial but never just initials. To make sure that was what he always did, I checked the computerized version of his appointments. No plain sets of initials there. That confirmed it was not something he ever did.

Listing only initials was a departure from the norm and could either be an innocent lapse or something more meaningful, even sinister. I'd have to puzzle it out. As I tried squeezing more juice out of that orange, the phone rang.

"Fontana."

"How you holding up?" Anton's voice was throaty and wrapped me like a warm blanket.

"I could use some company."

"Meet me at The Village Brew in five. I'm leaving the gym."

I pictured Anton, undoubtedly standing in the gym's lobby, clad in sweats and an old Rehoboth tee-shirt from a trip we'd taken a while back. He was probably attracting all sorts of attention. As a part-time trainer, his body was his best advertising tool. But though Anton was fully aware of the effect his looks had on men, he never exploited that power, never took advantage of others because of it. That was one of the things I liked most about him.

"I'll be there. One more thing to do." I was right around the corner from the café so I could finish up and be there with time to spare.

I synched my phone to the computer and transferred the pictures I'd taken at the spa. I didn't want to chance losing them. When the dead client's picture hit the screen, I stared at his face a moment. He was a handsome, distinguished-looking, older man. I wondered again who he was and if Giuliani or Shim would tell me when they knew.

Closing the files, I stared at the monitor and winced when the muscle cramp in my left leg returned, reminding me that Brad wouldn't be working his magic on it ever again. I ignored the pain, I'd deal with it when this was over and Brad's killer was caught.

The chair squeaked when I stood. The tiny sound brought the larger silence into focus. Weekends in this office provided noiseless distance from the world outside. Only rarely did small sounds crack the hush. The lack of distractions should have made it easier to think, but the lack of noise was itself a distraction. Real silence was pocked with random sounds. The creaking of stairs, wind rattling windows, a stray voiced word. Things that reminded you of the deeper silence all around.

My thoughts were tense, unfocused. I needed to get out to think clearly.

People laughing and talking, strolled the crowded sidewalks. The perfect Spring weather made people feel alive. But I felt numb, something I couldn't afford. Emily was counting on me and I couldn't let my feelings throw me. There'd be time to reflect later. Once before I allowed something like this to get to me. The results had been disastrous.

"Hey handsome." Sean, the barista at The Village Brew, stood against the wall just outside the café, taking a last puff on his cigarette before tossing it away. His "Caffeine Works for Me" tee-shirt revealed everything about his gym-sculpted chest.

"Shouldn't you be putting cream in somebody's coffee?"

"You have a dirty mind, Fontana." Sean winked. "I like that."

"Right now I need caffeine. Plenty of it," I said as I neared the entrance.

"I know just what you need and it isn't caffeine." Sean held the door open for me but didn't move. My arm slid up against his perfect pecs as I entered the café. He leaned in to kiss me on the cheek and whispered, "I'd like another round with you. How about it, my own private eye?"

"You know where I live."

"Couldn't forget if I tried." Sean winked and strolled through the café to the counter, lightly touching patrons he knew as he moved.

I took a table near the wide front window and watched the neighborhood boys walk past the café until everything blurred into a muzzy Spring haze. Next thing I knew Anton was sitting across from me and Sean approached with a cup of coffee.

"Back from your trip?" Anton asked. He looked concerned and stretched out a hand to touch my face. "I've been sitting here a few minutes and so was your body. But…"

"My mind's a thousand miles away. Rough day. Still trying to figure it all out."

"I knew Brad a long time. This all seems impossible." Anton placed his hand over mine, the warmth of his touch pleasant and comforting. "A lot of people are going to miss him."

"All the more reason I need to get the bastard who did this."

"With you and the police working, you'll find him," Anton stared into my eyes. "You seem… I mean, this seems more personal with you somehow."

"Damned right," I snapped. More harsh than I'd intended. "I'm sorry, Anton."

"Forget it. I understand."

"No, you're right. This is more personal. Brad was a friend. You go out of your way for friends, right?"

"Yes… but…"

"I know, I know. Letting personal feelings overwhelm me will screw things up"

"It's understandable. It's all still fresh. It was only this morning. You haven't had a chance to let it settle."

"I've got to get some distance."

"It's your hot Italian temper. Which sometimes I like. Give it time. You'll find whoever did this. The bastard is as good as caught."

I took Anton's hand in mine and squeezed. "Thanks."

"What about the other man... the one you...?"

"The other...? Oh, the other victim." I pulled up the man's picture on my phone and turned it toward Anton. "Recognize him?"

"No." Anton stared at the picture with an expression something between fear and pity. "Poor man. Has... had a nice face even if this picture is kind of grizzly."

"At first it looks like he was just somebody in the wrong place at the wrong time. Except I'm not sure he was."

"How so?" Anton perked up. He likes a good mystery almost as much as I do.

"I kind of noticed there wasn't anyone listed by name in Brad's appointment book for last night or today... other than me."

"Kind of... you mean you snooped."

"My job. There were no names but there were initials listed for last night."

"Maybe this guy," Anton indicated the picture, "needed anonymity."

"Could be. Brad usually listed full names but he *was* known for his discretion." I began to wonder if there were others Brad left off his lists.

"The guy might've been a walk in or a last minute and Brad didn't have time to note a full name," Anton offered.

"Brad could have expected this guy for a reason he didn't note. Or didn't want to note. Of course, the initials could belong to other people entirely."

"True. You didn't find anything else at the spa?"

"There were two sets of initials in the appointment book."

"Two? But..."

"Maybe one set is the dead guy. The other set must be someone else Brad expected. Could'a been a no-show or maybe he did show and he's the one."

"The one what?" Anton scrunched up his nose giving his square-jawed face a boyish, confused look.

"The one who did it. The killer."

"How do you figure?"

"Brad might've expected two people. Let's say they both show up. Later, Brad and one of them is dead. The other one is gone."

"That could mean a lot of things." Anton said.

"Right. One possibility is that the second set of initials belongs to the killer. Things went sour on Friday night. He kills Brad and the other guy," I said.

"Or the second person got lucky and arrived after the murders, or left before the killing took place. Either way, he missed getting killed." Anton enjoyed spinning theories.

"Of course, the possibly missing guy might've known the killer and helped set it all up," I said. "There are a lot of possibilities. The identity of the dead client might help, especially if one set of initials belongs to him."

"How're you going to do that? The police won't be helpful."

"I may have an inside source." I wiggled my eyebrows suggestively. "Giuliani put a new detective on the case. Really new. Young, and like they say, wet behind the ears."

"You're too transparent, Marco. You want more than police work out of the new detective. Your tone's a dead giveaway."

"Me? How can you say that?" I smiled. "I need to get this newbie on my side. He can help big time. He seems nice, even if he's playing tough and distant. He'll let some information fall my way if I play my cards right. Even if he believes what Giuliani tells him about me."

"You have other contacts on the force, don't you?"

"Sure, but this guy, Shim, is the lead detective on Brad's case. It's gold. Like I said, I think he'll play ball."

"Yeah. I know the kind of ball you intend to play," Anton smirked but there was a note of disappointment in his voice.

"I noticed you were pretty cozy with a certain dancer we both know."

Anton didn't answer. He blushed and shook his head slowly.

"Jean-Claude has been coming on to me and I'm not sure how to handle it. I don't wanna alienate him. He's sweet and kind of lost. Y'know?"

"Seems to know his way around pretty well," I said a bit too hastily.

"He doesn't," Anton countered. "Not really. This is a new town and he'll be starting school... He's not as confident as he looks. I sort of like helping him and... I don't know... he kind of needs me. I like that."

"Anton…" I was at a loss. I'd never pushed Anton away. In fact we'd been cozy together, if you don't count the no-sex-allowed thing. Truthfully, though, I'd never given Anton much reason to believe I'd ever settle down. I suppose I never made him feel like I needed him either. Yet… I felt I was about to lose something important. Someone I truly did need. Except, I didn't know what to say or do. Didn't even think I had a right to say anything.

"We've both got a lot on our plates," Anton said after clearing his throat. "We can talk about this some other time."

I said nothing and let the moment pass. I knew I'd missed an opportunity to tell Anton how much he meant to me. But I felt relieved putting off "the talk." Maybe because I didn't know what I wanted to say. Still, I couldn't give up on Anton.

"We could have dinner, just the two of us and forget everything else for a while. As if the world doesn't exist." I felt like an adolescent, feeling my way for the right thing to do.

"Not tonight, Marco. It's Amateur finals and I've got a lot to do. I'll understand if you don't feel like being there…"

"I'll be there. I won't let you down."

* * *

I left Anton sitting at the café. He wanted time to himself before setting things up at Bubbles. Anton was the best and I was lucky he was so committed to StripGuyz. But I'd dropped the ball on a personal level and I wouldn't stop kicking myself over that.

Glancing back at the café from a short distance away, I watched him sitting alone. The warm, yellow café lighting washed over Anton and held him in a golden bubble. Tough and strong as he looked, there was something sad about the way he picked up his coffee cup and brought it to his lips. He sipped and stared into space, seeming lost and forlorn. A wave of longing hit me unexpectedly. I almost turned back and swept him up and out of the place. Almost. Something stopped me and I didn't fight it. Instead I walked away and felt as if I were turning a corner against my will.

Twelfth Street led me to Walnut where I walked west nearly without thinking about it. Up ahead I spied lights and movement. Even before reaching the building, I saw the huge "Kelley for Senate" sign. Bright lights spilled over the frontage and filled the interior. People carrying signs, folders, and leaflets streamed in and out. The buzz of activity on a Saturday was a sure sign the primary was close. Kelley's campaign was in high gear. It made sense to campaign heavily in Philly. Pull in enough votes here and in the burbs and you had the best chance of winning almost any statewide election.

Shuster's earlier tantrum came to mind. I wondered if he'd be hanging out in the headquarters. I wanted him to know I wasn't through with him. Sometimes I can be a pain in the ass but only when it's necessary to get at the truth. Besides, Shuster's attitude rubbed me the wrong way. I decided to annoy him into talking with me.

I pushed open the plate glass door and entered a world of throw-away desks, phone banks, tables piled high with flyers, and committed workers intensely engaged in firing up the base. A humongous poster of the dweebish Kelley hung suspended from the ceiling.

"May I help you?" said a short, balding man wearing a plaid vest sweater and huge owl-eyed glasses.

"Looking for Mr. Shuster. He around?"

"Mr. Shuster's not here. He and Mr. Kelley are at a townhall meeting somewhere in the suburbs. I can give him a message for you." The little man glanced here and there presumably looking for paper and a pen.

"Yeah, why don't you? Let me write him a note."

He found some paper, then reluctantly took a silver pen from his shirt pocket and handed it to me as if he'd never see it again.

I wrote Shuster a note and told him I'd be at Bubbles later, if he wanted to talk. I was sure he would.

Chapter 9

I t wasn't yet dusk when I returned to my building, puffy clouds lit by the setting sun looked unreal. As I entered the lobby, I realized I'd been on the run since I'd left that morning for my massage. At the thought, everything tumbled back into consciousness. Tremors of shock rippled through me with each memory.

Brad was gone. We were left with a bunch of questions. He'd obviously gotten mixed up in something none of us knew anything about. Something way over his head.

"Hey! Mr. Fontana! How ya doin'? You look like ten days rain." Clem, the shortest and most energetic of the front desk security always noted my comings and goings because he loved hearing about cases. Some days, it was a good way for me to decompress. But not today.

"Tough day, Clem. You know how it is sometimes." I gave him a shrug and a wave and kept moving toward the elevators. He was probably disappointed.

Thankfully the elevator was empty and I got to ride in silence to my digs near the top of the building.

Once in my apartment, I stepped onto the balcony to watch the city wink into twilight life far below. The slowly darkening sky painted the landscape with an interesting mix of light and shadow. I stood and stared. It was always a breathtaking sight and usually soothing, but two fewer people walked those streets now and I wanted to know why.

There was no use checking my landline voicemail. It'd be filled with messages from friends asking about Brad. The voicemail would be there after I got back from Bubbles.

I needed time to myself, to clear my head so I could do what needed to be done. I needed a shower. For me, relaxing meant a hot shower. Stripping off my clothes, I padded into the bathroom. The shower stall was a sleek, glass-tiled refuge. I turned the valve. The water bucked and hissed, then rained down full force. When the room steamed up, I slid open the glass door and stepped inside. Hot water cascaded over my body. Tension melted. Problems got lost in the steam. The heat reached deep into my muscles and the ping of the water spray tingled on my skin.

When I stepped out, all I wanted was a beer and a movie. But I had no intention of disappointing Anton. I'd done more than enough of that. Wrapped in a towel I walked to the kitchen to get some food.

After nuking a plate of leftover pasta, I grabbed a Molson's and sat on the couch. Flipping on the TV, I channel surfed to some innocuous wildlife show. Of course, as soon as I'd placed a forkful of linguine and clams to my mouth, the phone rang.

"Fontana," I said around a mouthful of pasta.

"Mr. Fontana. Detective Shim." His voice was softer over the phone. "Got a minute?"

"Sure, Detective. What can I do for you?"

"I'm gonna have to search Brad's home. I was wondering if you'd like to tag along?"

"You're not afraid of Emily are you? She won't bite. She's actually pretty sweet."

He probably figured I could smooth the way for him, considering Emily's attitude. Of course, I wouldn't mind a second crack at what I might've missed at Brad's place, so it was win-win.

"Yeah. It was sweet the way she said she didn't trust cops. That look she gave me… Could'a split logs." Shim chuckled. "I'm keeping you in the loop. Like you asked. I thought this would be a good opportunity to talk about the case."

We arranged to meet Monday morning. Shim would notify Emily.

No sooner had I placed the receiver in its cradle than the phone rang again.

"Fontana." I looked wistfully at the shivering linguine.

"Boss is not taking nap with cats? I am expecting voicemail, not real boss," Olga said. "I am having informations for you."

"You found something on Gibson?" I'd given her Gibson's name, the dates he and Brad lived together, and their old address. Which is all Emily remembered.

"Searching is finished on Gibson and others."

"The others can wait. What've you got on Gibson?"

"Is what I am not having." She sounded cryptic but also disappointed.

"Maybe I didn't hear you right, Olga. Do you have something on Gibson?"

"*Ničevó.* I am having nothing," she said. "Gibson is… what you are calling people who no one is seeing?"

"A ghost?"

"*Da.* Gibson is ghost. One minute is here, next minute poof! He is ghost."

"So you've got nothing?"

"No more than boss already is knowing."

"Email me whatever you've got. You never know."

"I am e-mailing now. Olga is pressing button and you are having the informations."

"Thank you, gorgeous. Remind me to buy you lunch."

"I am not needing lunch," she said. "You are wanting details on other names you order me to search?"

"Order you…? Olga… I'm your boss not the Czar."

"Boss. Czar. Is same thing. Both give orders. Both want things yesterday. So, are you wanting…?"

"Sure, email all of it to me." Maybe she had better luck locating a couple of Brad's more elusive clients.

"Is done," Olga said and hung up the phone.

Still in my towel, I walked to the computer. Olga's e-mails popped up. She'd managed to narrow the search to one Max Gibson who'd lived in Philadelphia and worked for the City during the time he and Brad were supposed to have been together. The Gibson Olga had uncovered fell off the face of the planet around the time Emily said he and Brad had broken up. Maybe he'd changed his name or started living off the grid.

Olga had gone as far as she could with it. Now I'd have to depend on what I liked to call my Geek of Last Resort: Nina a successful programmer and web designer. She also, and only for a select clientele, namely me, did some hacking. I counted on her and paid her well. I'd pay her a visit in the morning. For now, Anton was depending on me to help with Amateur Night.

* * *

Heading over to Bubbles, I felt a small rush of excitement. People bustled along the sidewalk, laughter floated on the air, and problems seemed miles away. The city looked particularly good. Could've been the new lights splashing the façades of Broad Street's buildings. Could've been the great weather. Or, maybe I was just glad to be thinking about something other than murder even if it was only for a few hours.

The closer I got to the bar, the more faces I recognized. Regular patrons, wannabe strippers, hangers on. A gaggle of street kids acted out their latest weird antics, yowling and shouting rude comments loud enough to be heard a block over. Smokers huddled together outside each bar practicing their vice, managing to look defiant and guilty at the same time.

Bubbles was packed, as usual on Amateur Night. Nothing like seeing new flesh on display for the first time. I was jostled a few times as I wedged my way through the crowd. The music pounded and thumped and my eardrums vibrated. Guaranteed to quash any serious thoughts lurking in my mind.

"Marco! A lotta new hotties tonight?" Someone shouted from within a tight knot of men off to the side.

"You'll see," I called back. "You realize… I keep the best ones for myself, right?"

I made it to the stairs mostly intact and unfazed. I started up and the music faded out behind me to a dull buzz. A few guys stood in silhouette against the second floor lights. Lithe dancers with perfect forms and graceful poses, nervously shuffling like high strung thoroughbreds waiting for a race to begin.

"Hey, Marco," Jamir said. His nut brown body glistened with a light sheen of sweat. "Got a lot of hopefuls waitin' for you."

"Thanks, Jamir. How come you're sweating? You haven't even started dancing."

"Who says I ain't been dancin'?" He gave me a come hither look.

"You've got fans waiting downstairs. It's gonna be a long night, Jamir." I smiled. "Did you see Anton anywhere?"

"He's everywhere," said Cal coming up from behind us. "You know how Anton is. Gorgeous and in charge. I wish I looked even a little like him."

"Cal, you're gorgeous all on your own," I said, tossing him the compliment he'd been fishing for. "You always attract a crowd. The show wouldn't be the same without you." Fluffing egos was part of the job and these boys had plenty of ego to work with.

I figured Anton would be in the office, and when I opened the door, he was hunched over a dancer whose face I couldn't see. Whoever it was sat in my chair as Anton apparently worked on his face.

"What's going on?"

Anton looked up quickly. "Marco. Just taking care of something. Hold on."

"I see that. What're you…"

Anton stepped aside and I saw Ty, slender and pale, with curly golden blond hair, and a ripening black eye marring his delicately beautiful face.

"What the hell happened to you?" I said. In the same instant I knew. Ty's boyfriend occasionally used him as a punching bag. "Don't tell me. I already know." I moved to his side and saw that his eye was swollen shut. "Why do you put up with this, Ty? We can keep you safe. Your boyfriend's name is what…Eddie? We can handle the slimeball for you. You don't have to go through this."

"N-no. Eddie called and said he was sorry. He's gonna meet me after the show tonight."

"Ty, sweetie. You believed him? You actually believe he was sorry?" Anton said, his voice gentle and sad. "He's made promises before and he's never kept them. Right?"

"This time'll be different. He promised. I'll let you talk to him if he… I'll let you talk to him, Marco. Okay? Just not this time."

I'd never met Eddie and wasn't sure I wanted to because if I did, I might make him swallow his teeth or worse. In fact, I decided, that might not be such a bad idea.

"Yeah, next time. Make that a promise," I said. "Listen, Ty, are you hurt anywhere else? I could take you to the hospital." I looked at the poor kid and winced at the pain he must've felt.

"No. Just my eye. It isn't that bad. Just… I'll be all right. Can I stay in here tonight? In the office…?"

"Sure. Take a break. You can't go onstage tonight, Ty. You probably don't feel like dancing anyway."

"I kinda need the money, though." His lower lip trembled and he looked forlorn.

"Don't worry about money, Ty. I'll pay you," I said. "I'll even throw in some extra for the tips you'll miss. But you gotta promise me something…"

"Like what?" Ty looked at me with distrust. Why should he trust *any* man? I understood that.

"Like you won't let this goon hit you ever again. And you'll let me have a talk with him *this* time not next time." I'd make sure the guy not only got the message but also got a one way ticket out of town.

"S-sure, Marco," Ty said and lay his head back against the chair, drained of his ability to resist.

I almost felt guilty, as if I'd beaten him into submission with the promise of money. But if I didn't give Eddie a talking-to, Ty wouldn't stand up to him and he'd get another black eye, or worse.

"Let him rest here, Marco. We need to go over some details for tonight anyway." Anton gently nudged me out of the office and into the hall where some of the other dancers stood chatting and primping.

"What's up, Anton?"

"I'm glad you pressed him on Eddie. You've gotta have that talk with Eddie soon. Or I will. The bastard can't keep hitting this kid." Anton's eyes darkened, his face clouded with anger. When it came to something like this, Anton's temper equaled mine. "You can't let it happen again. Next time it'll be worse."

"I'm on it, kiddo." I stroked his cheek with the back of my hand. "Don't scrunch your face up like that. I'll take care of it. These are my guys just as much as Brad's case is my case."

"Make sure Eddie won't... or, I swear, I'll..."

"Believe me. Eddie won't be hitting Ty again after I find him."

"You want me with you, I'm there." Anton said. His hands balled into fists at his sides. The muscles of his arms flexed, and I could only imagine what Eddie's face would look like if Anton had a "talk" with him.

"No need, Anton. I've got just the enforcer in mind..."

Before I could say more, my cell phone started ringing.

"Fontana."

"I got your note." Shuster's voice brimmed with rage.

"Ready to talk?" I winked at Anton and signaled that it was business. He turned to enter the dressing room.

"Let's get this over with," Shuster hissed. "Now."

"I'm at Bubbles. You know where to find me."

"I'll only meet somewhere neutral. It's one thing to walk into that bar on a political pub crawl, it's another to be seen there as if I'm a regular."

"I do see you here, bucko. Don't go getting all coy on me."

"You're a bastard, Fontana."

"Sometimes. Right now I feel generous. Where do you want to meet?" Wouldn't hurt to give the guy a break, especially if I might get information out of him.

"The Cocoa Café in ten minutes. I haven't got all night." He disconnected without another word.

The Café was around the corner from Bubbles and picked up the overflow from Bubbles' own café, but it was straight enough for a closet case like Shuster to feel comfortable.

I ducked into the dressing room to let Anton know where I'd be and was surrounded by a sea of naked amateur contestants pulling on g-strings, thongs, or micro-underwear. Even in the bright lights of the dressing room most of them looked fantastic. And they knew it: As they posed and practiced dance moves, their thongs or underwear strained and bulged. The room barely had space for everyone. I squeezed through, sliding past sculpted bodies and breathing in the heady aroma of men. It was surreal. All that flesh, all that beauty. It never gets old.

Anton stood at the back, ticking names off a list. I sidled up next to him and told him where I'd be, and a sad frown passed across his face.

"I suppose I can get someone to MC for you." He sounded world weary.

"I won't be long. It's a lead on Brad's case. I'll be back in time. I said I wouldn't let you down and I won't."

* * *

The Cocoa Café did a booming late-night business. Customers rolled in at all hours for the sweet confections and desserts. Exterior flood lights swept the walls of the converted bank which housed the café and several eateries. Inside, the Café buzzed with conversation and background music.

Denny Shuster sat at a table toward the back next to a wall of windows facing Juniper Street. I made my way to him and sat down.

"Okay, Fontana. You got me here. What could you want from me?"

"One of my guys tried asking you something on the phone today but you hung up on him? Kinda rude. He asked about you being a client of Brad Lopes. Remember?"

"So you say. I'm not affirming anything."

"Don't have to confirm it. Brad did that for you. He's got you in his database."

Shuster stayed mum. One of his chins quivered a little. I took that as a good sign.

"What I want to know, Shuster, is if you saw or heard anything unusual during your sessions with Brad in the past month or so. Anything out of the ordinary."

When the pudgy campaign manager shifted in his seat, I noticed something in the tiny street outside the plate glass windows. Standing a few yards away, staring intently at Shuster and me, was a tall man with blond hair and a face like a brick wall.

I shifted back to Shuster, pretending not to notice the stranger.

"So, Shuster? Got anything for me?" I stared at him but slowly lifted my gaze to take in both Shuster and the man watching us.

"You're assuming I had appointments with him."

"Not assuming anything," I said, leaning in as if he were about to tell me something good. I caught a glimpse of the stranger inclining toward the window as if he wished he could hear what we said. "Brad had you scheduled for several appointments. Must be nice having a massage anytime you want it."

Shuster squirmed. He knew I had him and glared at me before finally giving in.

"They were just massages. Running campaigns for prima donna politicians is tough work. I need to relax. If you think anything else went on with Brad…"

"Listen, pal. I don't care if you two played hide the salami, did a jig between the sheets, or just played canasta. I just wanna know if anything odd happened at the spa when you were with Brad. Any disturbance or something that broke the routine."

The stranger edged closer to the café window but kept to the other side of the street. He looked like he wanted to jump through the glass to hear our conversation.

"As far as I remember nothing unusual happened. Nothing."

"No strangers turned up? Nobody came looking for Brad?"

"Nothing. Nothing but a massage. Just a massage. Satisfied?"

"Not really. Don't think you're off the hook, pal."

Shuster snorted contemptuously.

"Listen up," I snapped. "On my signal, we leave this place together, understand?"

"Who do you think you are?" Shuster looked startled, indignant.

"Somebody's been watching us. Not sure if he's got his eye on you or me."

Shuster twisted his head this way and that.

"Stop moving. You'll spook the guy. Just do what I tell you."

"W-who is it? Are you sure…?" Shuster's face darkened. "You're trying to scare me. You think you're so…"

"Shut up and listen, Shuster. When I say so, get up from your seat. Casually. Straighten your clothes and tie. Stay casual. As you're doing that, glance out the window nonchalantly. Don't make it obvious. The guy's standing against the wall across the street. Light hair, tall, unshaven. Take a brief look, then head out. I'll be right behind you."

Shuster nodded tentatively.

"Okay, let's both stand. Be nonchalant."

Shuster stood clumsily. I supposed that looked natural enough.

"Straighten your tie. Nice, by the way. What'd that tie set you back, like two-fifty?"

Shuster glared at me and, as they say, if looks could kill…

"Don't forget to glance outside… that's right. Good boy." I spoke while smoothing my shirt and brushing off my pants. "Make your way to the door. I'll follow."

On the sidewalk, Shuster looked shaken and confused.

"D'you know the guy?"

"W-What guy?" Shuster said. His voice quivered and his hands shook. "That man s-standing by the window? I don't recognize him. No."

"You look shaken up, Shuster. You sure you don't know the guy?"

"I'm shaken up because you've shaken me up," Shuster gulped some air. "I don't know the man. Besides, he's looking at you, not me."

The oddball could have been staring at me. But Shuster was shaken. Of course, he was already upset at being caught on Brad's client list and now I'd let him think someone was spying on him.

"Who else knew you were meeting me here?" I asked.

"No one. You seriously think I want people to know why you're badgering me?" He fiddled with his tie and buttoned his jacket. "Look, Fontana. I've had it. First you bother me with nonsense, now you try to scare me half out of my mind. All I did was have a…" He stopped himself, lowered his voice so no one passing could hear. "All I did was have a massage. Okay?" he said whispered. "There. Now you have it. I'm guilty. Of being pampered, not of committing murder or anything remotely close. Satisfied?"

"Doesn't take much to rattle you, does it? I mean, all I did was call your attention to somebody spying on us."

"I'm in the middle of a tough campaign. My face is all over the news almost every day. Now you tell me someone is spying on us…"

"He was staring at you and me with a lot of interest. Why'd that rattle you?"

"The sonofabitch could be a tracker. Know what that is?"

"Sure. So you think he's from Terrabito's campaign doing oppo research?"

"Trying to catch the candidate or someone close to him in something that'll make headlines and sink the campaign. So, sure, I'm flustered. Maybe he reads lips, maybe a lot of things. He connects me to a dead masseur and Kelley's campaign will stumble over that for days. Did you notice if he used a cell phone or a camera?"

"Didn't see one but he might've had one. Too bad, Shuster. Things do come back to bite you in the ass, don't they?"

"With your help, they do. You're a bastard… This makes the news, it's all your fault, Fontana."

"Just doin' my job."

"Your job. Give me a break." Shuster looked past me at something. "Well maybe you gave me new white hairs for nothing. That 'spy' is just meeting his girlfriend or something. See? They're together. Doesn't mean he's not a tracker, but…"

Sure enough the guy did look like he was meeting someone, but the woman in question didn't seem all that comfortable. Maybe she didn't really know him.

"See what you wanna see, Shuster. The guy had you in his sights."

"Are you finished? I have a campaign to run." Shuster drew himself up, expensive suit making him look more important than he could ever look without it.

"I'll be seein' you, Shuster. I'll probably have more questions." I turned to walk back to Bubbles and realized Shuster was right behind me.

"Goin' my way?" I said and let him catch up. "How's the campaign going? Your boy Kelley going to win?"

"Do you really care, Fontana, or are you just trying to get me to trust you? Because it won't work."

96

"Oh, I care. Politics is kind of a hobby with me. I sorta like knowing all about the people trying to screw us over while they make money hand over fist."

"Kelley's not like that. He's a rarity. An honest politician."

"Nice talking point, but I don't believe it." I glanced over at the crowd in Starbucks as we walked by. Kinda sad. Seemed like they wanted something else out of life but didn't know where to look.

"You've got a choice," Shuster said. "Terrabito won't do a thing if he wins. If you think he's a good guy, you're deluded. Terrabito's been on the take from day one."

"I guess there's 'on the take' and there's 'on the take.' I don't like any of the candidates. Can't we start over with a new bunch?"

"Kelley is as good as you'll get this time around. I should know."

"I get off at this stop," I said when we rounded the corner and Bubbles came into view. Sure you won't have a drink?"

"Be serious, Fontana."

"In that case, I'll see you around."

I ducked into Bubbles and headed upstairs, taking the steps two at a time. When I got to the landing, Anton stood there, clipboard in hand.

"Just in time, tiger. Curtain's up in ten minutes." Anton smiled.

"Here I thought I was in for another lecture about being late."

"You said you'd be here and here you are." Anton smiled again. "I never doubted you... much."

I took the clipboard from him and our hands touched. I grabbed Anton around the waist and pulled him close.

"I told you I wouldn't let you down." I brushed my lips against his and felt his breath on my face. The warmth and the closeness felt good. I didn't want to let go.

"You've got a job to do," Anton said, gently pulling back. "And I've got dancers to herd."

He seemed uncomfortable, ill at ease. I felt rebuffed.

"Are we still on for dinner? Just the two of us?" I tested the waters.

"You haven't said when or where yet," Anton said.

"Tomorrow. Let someone else handle scheduling. You have some back-up who can do it?"

"I'll see what I can do. Nothing special on tap here tomorrow anyway," he paused. "Now get down there to meet the finalists and start the show."

I zipped down to the backstage area where the contestants waited nervously. Some paced back and forth, others jogged in place, others waited motionless as stones.

"Okay, guys. We're about ready to start. Everybody fill out a form?"

Heads nodded with nervous speed. One very cute amateur, looking as if he'd just fallen off a school bus, peered up at me as if he'd done something wrong.

"I... uh... I didn't have proper ID. Is that okay? I can go home and get..."

I asked him to step aside for a talk after I got everyone set up. He moved to a dimly lit corner of the backstage area as if he'd been scolded. I hadn't wanted to scare him but I run a legitimate business and having a kid dance, especially one who looked like he'd just stopped wearing diapers, was a no-no without proper ID. I didn't understand how he'd gotten through the door. Someone had slipped up.

After I'd instructed the others, I turned to the kid. The look in his platter-sized green eyes nearly melted my resolve. Except getting Bubbles closed down and being put behind bars were not on my list of things to do. I explained the consequences for the bar and for me if we used an under-age dancer. I told him to run home and fetch his ID or just run home and come back when he was twenty-one. Eyes glassy with guilt and regret, he appeared defeated. He nodded and headed slowly back to the dressing room.

Before long I walked out from behind the curtain of glittering tinsel and faced the rowdy crowd. A sea of young and old, drawn to strippers like bees to flowers.

"Welcome to the Amateur finals. Who's ready to take part in choosing new dancers for StripGuyz? Let's hear it if you are..."

Cheers and whistles. Clapping. Hoots and howls.

"Then, let's get warmed up with Bruno and Pete! Everybody's favorite soldier boys! Remember, when they come around, tips go into the side of the g-string only! Put your hands together... Heeeeeeres Bruno and Peeeete!"

The duo's music started as they snaked their way on stage in camouflage fatigues. The evening was finally underway. Both dancers sported buzz cuts.

They danced together, writhing against one another, generating heat between them. Bit by bit, starting with their green camo tank tops, they removed their clothes. Just before hopping onto the bar top, they ripped the pants from each other and stood, g-strings bulging, hips gyrating forcing patrons to moan in unison. Connecting with their eyes and sometimes with a touch, Bruno and Pete knew what to do. Their oiled skin glistened in the focused beams of the baby spots and the audience went wild. Hands reached out beckoning the dancers with dollar bills, like a field of grass in the wind. Bruno and Pete each worked his part of the bar, pulling in bushels of cash.

Standing with the patrons, I surveyed the room for potential trouble spots. With two dancers on the bar and more to follow, it wouldn't be easy keeping track of errant hands or people trying to get more than a peek.

I did my best to keep problems to a minimum. Kent still worked overseeing things. He'd been here part time for quite a while and had proven good at his job, so I'd put him in charge of training new House Eyes, as he liked to call them. Even with all the help, on overly crowded nights, it never hurt for me to join in scanning for trouble before it developed into something major.

Moving around the floor greeting regulars and newcomers, I caught sight of the man who'd been spying on me and Shuster. He didn't seem interested in Bruno or Pete. When his eyes locked onto me, he'd obviously found his mark. Maybe Shuster was right and he'd been after me all along.

I don't like making a scene, but I really hate guys who think they can intimidate with a stare. The would-be spy kept his eyes trained on me with a cold, vicious gaze. Takes a lot more than a set of steely eyes to make me quake. So, I sauntered toward him.

At first he seemed confused. Like I'd caught him with his hands down his pants. I drew closer and he glowered as if to say, 'Back off.' Yeah, like that was gonna happen, and on my own turf. The stranger had another think coming.

"What can I do for you, pal?" When I stood next to him, I realized I was at least half a foot taller.

He remained stolid. Then turned to stare at the stage.

"If you're here to look, house rules say you need to buy a drink now and then." Not that we ever paid attention to that rule unless we needed to hassle somebody. "If you're not gonna play by the rules, then I'm gonna have to…"

"Hey! Stop! Stop that guy!" Kent's voice sounded over the music and the crowd noise.

"Stop that fucker!" Bruno yelled, and I saw him jump down from the bar, just as the bartender threw Pete a towel to cover himself.

I spotted a dark-haired young man, Pete's iridescent green g-string held aloft in his hand. He pushed roughly through the crowd, shoving customers aside and spilling drinks as he ran for the door.

Taking off after him, I managed to pin him against the wall until the bouncer arrived to take him upstairs where we'd decide how to handle the situation.

When I turned back, the stranger was gone.

Chapter 10

I slipped out of bed and walked to the window. Nina still hadn't called.

"I guess this means I have to get up, too." Luke yawned, still wrapped in the sheets.

"No, I'm waiting for Nina to call. Can't sleep."

"You don't have to sleep. Just get back in and…" Luke wiggled his eyebrows. He'd met me at Bubbles before it closed and decided to spend the night.

I moved back into the bed and cuddled with Luke.

"I can feel the tension," he said. "You're like a rubber band stretched to the limit."

"It's the case. And…"

"I understand. I liked Brad, too." Luke sat up. "Maybe I should make some tea. Sitting around worrying won't make Nina call any faster."

"You're right." I was impatient. Though Nina had said finding Gibson wouldn't be easy, I knew it was geek inflation talk. Nobody was Nina's equal at ferreting out information on the Internet. "Tea sounds good."

I watched Luke stand and stretch by the side of the bed. He was sleek and his light-tan skin was smooth and supple.

"Be back in a flash." Luke said.

I heard him working in the kitchen as I threw on a pair of shorts and a tee-shirt and walked out onto the balcony. The air felt clean and cool. The city was still not fully awake, and I enjoyed the quiet.

"This'll help." Luke, dressed now, carried a tray with pot and cups out onto the balcony. Placing it on a table, he sat and looked up at me.

"Gibson is the best lead I have. Can't count Johnny. He's just a name. No trail."

"Gibson was Brad's old boyfriend?"

"According to Emily. They were together way before any of us knew Brad."

"Is he the one who ki… did this?"

"He's at the top of my list. He's practically the only one on the damned list."

"Hard to believe anybody can be so obsessed with someone," Luke said as he poured the tea.

"I'm not even sure about Gibson. All I have is an ear-witness who wasn't certain about the name he heard."

"Not a lot to go on," Luke said.

"I've gotta check it out though. If I don't and Gibson gets away…"

"Not gonna happen, right? If he's the one, you'll get him. I know you."

"That's the plan." I sat across from Luke and took one of the cups.

"What about the guy last night? At Bubbles? Could he be Gibson?"

"The thought crossed my mind. I made calls yesterday to all the Gibsons in the book. None of them admitted knowing Brad, but people lie. One of them could have been the real Max Gibson. Would've been easy for him to find me at Bubbles."

"So, it *could've* been him last night?"

"I don't know what Gibson looks like, never saw a picture, and Emily's description was so vague it fit the guy last night and a shitload of others."

"There's no one else on your list?" Luke refilled our cups.

"Unless you count this Johnny ghost, I've got zip else," I said. "That's the frustrating thing. No witnesses yet. The police most likely canvassed the neighborhood. I've gotta call the detective and see what I can get out of him. I'll do my own canvass, if I have to."

"I can't believe Giuliani will tell you anything."

"No. Of course she won't. But the detective she put in charge of the case might."

"She's not handling Brad's case?"

"Giuliani will take credit when it's solved, depend on it. For now, the new guy's in charge. She'll be pulling his strings, but she'll give him some leeway."

"What makes you think *he'll* cooperate, if she's still running the show?"

"Just a feeling I got when I went with the detective to Emily's place yesterday. He played tough but something about the case moved him. Besides, Detective Shim as much as said he wouldn't mind having my help. Giuliani wouldn't be caught dead uttering those words."

"Shim. Sounds Korean. A friend in college had the same name. He was a hottie."

"Shim is kind of cute. More than cute. Not what you'd expect in a police detective. He's not flashy, but he's not drab either. Sort of trendy fashionable. He's tall and slender. Thick black hair and deep eyes. Got a face that makes him look like he left the Academy yesterday, except he was just promoted to detective, and that takes a few years."

"Doesn't the fact that he's Giuliani's man deter you at all?"

"Deter me? From what? What makes you think…"

"There's this look in your eyes. And I've heard that tone of voice. I know you, remember? Poor guy. Maybe I should call and warn him."

"Think you know me that well."

"I do. Doesn't mean you can't surprise me now and then. Just not this time."

"Whatever happens, happens. As long as Shim sends some information my way. I want them to solve this case."

Luke nodded.

I sipped the tea and the bitter taste it left matched my mood. Brad was dead and I was nibbling around bits of information that so far led nowhere.

"Like the tea?" Luke asked as if his self esteem depended on it.

"It's great. I'm edgy. I'd rather be down on the streets finding answers." I peered out over the city which, from this height, was splayed out like a map.

"It all feels even worse because Brad was a friend."

Before I could say anything, my cell phone rang.

"Nina. You find anything?"

"An address. Wasn't easy. Had to hack my way into some tight spots. If this is the guy you're looking for, then this is his address."

"You're amazing!"

I jotted down the information and stared at it. He lived on Parrish Street in a tough, troubled area of the city called Brewerytown.

"She found him?"

"That's what I'm gonna find out right now."

"I'd tag along, but I promised I'd meet my cousin Chunxue at her place. She wants me to meet somebody. Business or something."

"I can handle this. Anyway, if Gibson is as bad a boy as he thinks he is, it could get dicey, and I don't want you hurt." I pulled Luke in and gave him a hug. "You mean too much to me."

Luke nuzzled my neck then lifted his face to mine and kissed me. "That's for luck. Come back in one piece."

Chapter 11

If you wanted to lose yourself and make sure no one knew you existed, taking up residence in some parts of North Philly was one way to do it. You could live off the grid and stay hidden for a while. It was easy, but it wasn't safe. Brewerytown was a poor neighborhood and one the city didn't pay much attention to. Developers and young couples, though, had decided certain areas of North Philly needed gentrifying and they'd begun the long slog toward making headway into some neighborhoods. They had a lengthy fight ahead, and Brewerytown wouldn't be easy. It was a rambling neighborhood and parts had a seedy, dangerous quality. Just the kind of place where a guy could be anonymous, even invisible.

If this was where he lived, Gibson liked flying under the radar.

I drove up, parked my car a block away, and approached the property on foot. Parrish Street jumbled together the shabby and the neat in a messy way. Red brick houses, mostly ramshackle affairs, looked tired. In fact, the whole neighborhood had a drowsy feel. As if this end of Brewerytown had nothing to do and nowhere to go. Evidence of gentrification was scant. Maybe neighborhood newbies didn't want to draw too much attention and the crime that comes with it.

Gibson lived in one of the red brick, two stories that looked in need of a lot of work. "Rundown" didn't even begin to describe it. I stepped onto the dirty marble stoop and pressed a buzzer. Just in case that wasn't working, I banged on the front door rattling its dried out frame.

There wasn't a sound in the air. No kids playing on the street, no cars, the neighborhood was as dead as it was dreary. I listened for some sign of life or noise coming from within the house but heard nothing.

I thumped the wooden door again. Faded paint chips flaked off, floated down. A few stuck to my fist.

Just as I was about to abandon the place and head back to my car, I heard a shuffling inside the house. Then the door edged inward, and I saw an ineffectual chain bolt stretched across the dark slit of the opening. Slowly, from the shadows within, a face, or what I could see of a face, appeared through the narrow opening. One eye stared out at me.

"Sorry for bothering you," I said, unable to see if I was talking to a man or woman. "I'm trying to contact Max Gibson. He live here?"

I saw the slightest shock wave pass through the eye peering at me from that shadowy face. It was momentary but real. I knew I had to be gentle, nonthreatening, and soothing. I softened my expression.

"Sorry for the bother. I could really use your help." I smiled. I'd been expecting resistance and instead met fear.

The person said nothing. Didn't slam the door in my face either. That was a good sign. Whoever it was seemed to be struggling with a decision: Was I good or bad, was I was trying to pull something over or being sincere? Probably most importantly, did I look like the type to use force if I didn't get what I needed?

I felt pity for the person behind that door.

"I didn't mean to bother you. I'll be on my way." I pulled out a card with my name and number and slowly, in a nonthreatening way, held it up for the person to see. No hand came out to take the card. I very gently placed it on the top step, squatting down so I could keep an eye on whoever it was behind the door. Can't be too careful.

"W-wait," his voice was hoarse, as if he hadn't spoken for a while. "D-don't have… have to leave it there."

The door jiggled as the man behind it moved around. Then a hand, or the fingers of a hand in a white cast, appeared and he wiggled them. Signaling I should place the card between his fingers.

I stood slowly then gently gave him the card. He withdrew his hand. The door remained open but still chained. After a moment, during which a musty odor wafted from within the house, I heard him clear his throat.

"M-Max is… is away. He's away for a while."

"Do you know where or when he'll be back?"

"H-He'll wanna know… why you wanna see h-him. Why? W-what do I t-tell him?"

"I'm working a case. I'm a private detective, and I could use his help. Could you tell him that?"

"H-he won't like that."

"Okay… then how about…"

"I-I gotta go, Mister. I s-said too much. N-not supposed… I g-gotta go."

The door shut. He didn't slam it but I heard him turning locks. Door like that, a kid could kick it in, locks or no locks.

All the way back to my car, my imagination was on overdrive. All I could think was that this was another poor soul who Max Gibson had beaten and intimidated into thinking this was what a relationship was all about. The poor guy thought so little of himself that he bought Gibson's version of reality.

It was hard for me to swallow the idea that a guy would allow another guy to do this. I realized, if *I* was having a difficult time believing this could happen, you could bet your ass the police would never believe domestic violence existed in a same sex relationship.

Of course, my suspicious nature led me to think Max Gibson was still in that house. The guy at the door was fearful because Gibson was probably not far behind, seeing and hearing everything.

Either way, if he was out of town or hiding in the house, that didn't make him look innocent. Didn't mean he was guilty, either. I was determined to find out though.

* * *

Intending to buy lunch before I returned to the office, I detoured down Locust Street to a new salad bar. You get what you want and pay by the pound. The kind of place where it didn't pay to have eyes bigger than your stomach.

I filled my Styrofoam box with steamed veggies and noodles and I noticed a customer across from me gingerly picking pieces of broccoli and cauliflower out of a pan. His face was blocked, but the expensive suit and svelte shape were familiar. Never one to pass up the sights, I toted my lunch around to get a better look.

Josh Nolan, finished with the broccoli, was deciding between spicy chicken or Singapore noodles.

"The chicken is great if you like things hot," I said.

Nolan spun around as if he'd been goosed. I couldn't suppress a laugh.

"You... you're... I'm sorry... I remember meeting you but..."

"Sounds like you use that line a lot." I stuck out my hand. "Marco Fontana. We met at Bubbles." I watched for his reaction.

"Bubb... you're mistak... oh, wait..." His face drained of color.

"Coming back to you now? Lots of Long Island Iced Tea, lots of men, and some politicians."

"Right. Right!" Nolan looked relieved.

"Have some time to talk?" There were still questions I had for Terrabito, and maybe Nolan could help.

"T-talk? You mean now?"

"Yeah. I'm not hitting on you. I'm investigating a murder. Got some questions for your boss and you."

"Murder? What are you talking about?"

"You probably haven't heard about it." I wasn't so sure he hadn't. "A friend of mine was murdered. Double murder in center city, actually. One of his clients was also killed." I waited for a reaction. Nothing.

"A client? What did your friend do?"

"He was a masseur. Owned the DreamSpa," I said. I imagined Nolan was conjuring up happy ending scenarios. "He ran a legitimate operation."

"Of course," he said almost too quickly.

"I'm running down a few leads."

"What's this have to do with Senator Terrabito... or me?" He drew into himself protectively.

"Not sure, exactly," I said wanting to knock him off kilter. "You and your boss were at Bubbles on Friday."

"Yes," he said, drawing the word out. Caution signs popping up.

"That's when the murder occurred. Friday night."

"Well, as you just said, we were at Bubbles."

"Right. You there sopping up the booze."

"So I guess that proves…"

"Nothing much. You were there, but not your boss. Terrabito came running in late looking all rumpled."

"Look… Who sent you? The Kelley campaign? You're working for them, right?"

"I'm investigating a…"

"You were pretty cozy with the StonewallVotes woman. They hire you to smear the Senator?"

"My client couldn't care less about Kelley or Terrabito. She wants her brother's killer caught."

Nolan was edgy. "You… you can understand if I'm suspicious."

"Yeah, campaigns can be dirty."

"The Senator's a good man. Kelley is trying to dig up anything he can."

"That's not me. I'm trying to find out who killed my friend."

"It wasn't the Senator. He's… you don't know the man. He couldn't do anything like that."

"I need to talk with him."

"The campaign's not going well. He's got a 24/7 schedule."

"It could help him, y'know? If I clear him. Nobody can touch him."

"Maybe. I don't want to see him lose. He's a good man. I'd do anything to see him win…" He looked embarrassed, as if he knew just how that'd sounded.

"Get him to talk to me. I'm not trying to scuttle his campaign."

Nolan didn't respond.

We finished lunch and I watched Nolan walk back to his campaign offices. He reminded me of a ranch hand. An expensively dressed ranch hand but with the same confidently masculine stride, the same set of the shoulders ready for anything.

* * *

I didn't have to show up at Bubbles but I went anyway. Something about that poor guy behind the door had sucked all the joy out of me and sitting alone at home was not an option. Nobody'd be in the bar either. The show was hours off and I'd still be sitting alone. So I opted to sit at Café Bubbles and cheer myself up with dessert.

Moving through a gossipy group of smokers outside, I stepped into the café and looked for a place to sit.

"Marco! Hey Marco!"

I recognized the accent and turned to see Jean-Claude waving me over to his table. As I moved closer, I saw an embarrassed-looking Anton sitting across from Jean-Claude. Interesting. Of course, they could always be discussing business. Who was I kidding?

"Marco, we were just talking about you," Jean-Claude said.

"Oh? What's the verdict?"

"On what?" Anton said, his face flushing.

"Me."

"We were just trying…" Anton started but he stopped as if suddenly shy and reticent.

"We were wondering how you were doing. And how the case is going." Jean-Claude said. "You know I can help if you need."

"I know, Jean-Claude." His constant requests to help were beginning to work. I decided to put him on something to keep him busy. "I've been giving it some thought, and I can use you." Except I didn't know for what yet.

"Oh, *fantastique*! This is so cool!" Jean-Claude laughed. I also noted the way he patted Anton's hand. How Anton didn't move that hand. More and more interesting.

"We'll talk tomorrow. Right now I need coffee."

"Why don't you sit with us?" Anton offered. It was sincere. I've known him long enough to know that. I also took it as a sign that maybe I was wrong about what was going on between them.

"Hey, I don't want to interfere. You two looked like you were discussing things and…"

"Don't be silly, Marco," Anton said. "I'd like you to join us."

"You're sure?"

"We were just having coffee before the show," Jean-Claude said innocently.

"Tell you the truth I could use the company."

I told them about Brad and Max and my encounter with the guy in Brewerytown. Jean-Claude listened with an intensity that surprised me. Maybe he *would* be a big help. Anton, though, was all compassion and wondered what kind of life the poor guy at the house was living.

After a while, they both had to start prepping for the show. I decided I needed an early night.

As we walked out, something on the TV above the café's counter caught my attention. I stopped and stared.

"...police have not released the name of the victim, pending notification of next of kin. The Police Department spokesman said the body dredged from the Schuylkill River early Sunday morning was that of a Caucasian male in his late twenties or early thirties. Police were notified by a passerby who called 911 to report the body floating in the river. According to police this is the third body found in the river this year."

"If this city doesn't get a grip on things, people will start calling it Killadelphia again," Anton said. "Great publicity."

"I've got a strange feeling about this one, though, Anton," I said as we left.

Chapter 12

Olga opened my office door, looked in at me, and grinned.

"Young detective waits in outer office for boss. I am letting him in or you are not wanting him?"

"Sure, Olga, let him in."

I quickly spread folders and papers on my desk so it'd look like I was swamped. Never hurts.

The door opened and Olga waved the Detective into the room. Shim entered as if he'd been in my office a zillion times before. Comfortable in his own skin, he wasn't tentative in his movements, making him even more attractive.

"Have a seat, Detective."

Shim gave a curt nod and sat in the leather club chair, my one office extravagance. I got a more thorough look at the man as he sat waiting. Neat, well-cut, charcoal-gray suit, white shirt, red tie, and shoes polished to a high gloss. He looked younger than his years. If I had to guess I'd put him around twenty-nine or thirty. His face was angular with a strong jaw and no nonsense eyes. Slender but muscular, he sat ramrod straight and stared directly at me. There wasn't a hint of innocence or vulnerability about him, but I knew there had to be soft spots.

"Thanks for meeting me before we go to Emily's," I said.

"No problem. She insisted you be there. She probably told you that."

"And more. She doesn't trust you guys."

"Why is that, Fontana? It's not just that stalker thing she mentioned. I can tell."

"You're unfortunately right. Seems the police didn't help her brother a long time ago when Brad needed protection from an abusive boyfriend. She's never forgiven them."

"She'd better start trusting someone because we've got nothing so far."

"CSU didn't come up with anything?"

"The spa was a motherlode of fingerprints and DNA. It'll take weeks to sort it all out. It's a spa. There's bound to be all sorts of trace there. It's like walking into a bar and trying to catalog all the prints and every bit of DNA you can find."

"Nothing helps narrow it down?"

"No weapon, if that's what you mean. No blood other than the victims."

"Any clue about who the other guy was and why he was there?"

"Got a name. Well known businessman and developer. He wasn't the shooter, that's about all I can say. Probably just a client."

"Who was he?" This might be nothing but I could check it against Brad's lists, not that I would tell Shim I already had those lists.

"Hold on," Shim flipped through his notebook and nodded his head. "Guy's name is… was Wheeler. Smithson Wheeler. Recognize it?"

"Should I?"

"Well, he was…"

"Oh I get it. You think he was a client. And I was a client. All us clients know each other, right? We get together to choose Mr. Gay Masseur every year in Vegas."

"Not what I meant, smartass. I see what Giuliani means now…" Shim let that comment float on the air. Then, "I thought maybe he was someone you've heard of for some reason."

"No, never heard of the guy."

"Figures. That's the way everything's been going. Can't catch a break."

"Giuliani on your back about the case?"

"On my back, in my ears, and slowly getting into my head. She wanted it solved last night."

"Good old Gina."

Shim took out his cell phone and checked something.

"Guess we'd better go. You ready, Fontana?"

"I can't keep calling you Detective and you can't keep calling me Fontana," I said as I stood. "The name's Marco."

"You can call me Detective." Shim laughed. "Kidding. Just kidding. You can call me Dae. My name's Jung Dae but my friends call me Dae." He flashed a rare smile.

That smile cracked the hard contours of his face revealing a boyish, mischievous quality. Something about his manner had the needle on my gaydar dial vibrating.

"So, Gina's really on your ass?"

"In a manner of speaking. She's a demanding boss."

"If I can give you any pointers, lemme know. Gina and I go way back."

"So I've heard. Like I said Saturday, she doesn't exactly like you."

"Nahhh, it's all an act. She loves me."

Dae looked confused.

"It's not me she has a problem with. It's my brother."

"Then why…?"

"My brother and I look alike. We share the same genes. I must give off a pheromone that annoys her."

Dae laughed. "She never says anything bad about your investigative skills, if that means anything. She sends plenty of other signals about you. None of them good. She warned me not to get too cozy."

"Yeah, I'd watch out if I were you. Wouldn't wanna make Gina angry. But what she doesn't know won't hurt either of us." I wondered about her warning to Shim. What did she mean by "cozy"? What did that mean about Shim? Curiouser and curiouser.

"See, now that's just the kind of thing she said you'd say."

"Busted." I laughed and Shim chimed in.

We walked in silence for a while, Shim periodically checking his notebook and cell phone.

"You guys canvass the neighborhood for witnesses?"

"Sure, whaddayou take us for, some kind of rube hick deputies? We blanketed the whole area."

"And? You gonna make me beg for it?"

"Good thing I'm a nice guy, Marco. You don't have to beg. We got nothing out of anyone. No one heard a shot. No one heard yelling or arguing. No one heard anything." He turned to look at me. "Remember all those people on the street when we left the building Saturday morning?"

I nodded.

"How is it they didn't hear gunshots, didn't notice a damned thing during the night?" He shook his head. "They want police protection. But we're supposed to pull answers outta the air."

"Witnesses are never reliable anyway, especially in cases like this."

"Woulda been nice to have *something*, you know?"

"What're you hoping to find at Emily's?" I asked, hoping to change his mood.

"Nothing of hers."

"I figured that, wiseass. They teach smartass responses at the Academy now?"

"Maybe there's something in Brad's stuff that'll help make sense out of this."

"Nothing about the murder makes sense."

"You know... knew him well?"

"Brad and I became good friends over the past few years. He's not the kind of guy who makes enemies."

"A guy with no enemies. That's good. Even my father has enemies and he's a popular realtor in the Korean community."

"I didn't say there were no bad people in Brad's life, just that he wasn't the kind of guy who made enemies."

"Sounds like you know something."

"Brad had a boyfriend way before I knew him. The guy abused Brad mentally and physically." Since I'd already mentioned the ex-boyfriend I had to tell Shim the rest.

"You think this old boyfriend might..."

"Don't know. His name is Max Gibson." I watched Shim jot that down in his notebook. Now he owed me one.

"This pans out, I owe you, Marco."

Bingo, I thought.

We were still a few blocks from Emily's place and had some time to talk. Shim puzzled me and I wanted to know more. Nothing about him said "police" except that he was so serious most of the time. That demeanor could have developed when he decided to move up in the ranks. Want to be a bigger shot, you need to look like you're serious about the job. Even better if you actually *are* serious about the job.

"So why'd you join the force?"

"The usual reasons," Shim answered.

"Didn't know there were 'usual' reasons," I said. "I joined because I thought I could do some good."

"Giuliani said you almost made it but you washed out after the Academy. What happened?"

Nice deflection. Now he wanted to know all about me. That'd come after I got answers from him.

"Long story and one I keep tryin' to forget. So why did *you* join up? Gonna save the world?"

"Family."

"Your family wanted you to join the force? Don't hear that much."

"No, my family was opposed. My cousin was murdered when we were both in high school. The police never solved the case, and she never got justice. Not as far as I'm concerned."

"And you...?"

"I don't want that happening to anyone else, if I can help it. She and I were close and when she was killed..."

"I understand. Believe me. I understand."

"That's why I joined. Hei was family. She never got her day in court."

"Ever think about opening the case again?" I already knew he must think about that every time he stepped into the office, or the evidence lock up, or the case file room. Maybe Shim had an agenda: Work on the force, advance to detective, maybe higher. At some point he'd have enough juice to get the case reopened. It wasn't ambition that drove him. It was justice. That could be more dangerous than ambition.

"Been a lotta years, Marco. The case is too cold." His voice was filled with a sad, even hopeless tone.

"No case is too cold. You ever decide you wanna reopen the case and you need a private eye to do some legwork, say the word." I meant it. Maybe it made me think about Galen and finding him. That case was cold, too. Colder, since Galen left nothing for anyone to go on. Except for a note, which didn't help. At least I had hope he was still alive. Shim's cousin was dead. That didn't leave room for hope.

"I hate having to bother Emily like this," he said changing the subject. "If we're going to find…"

"No one wants this solved more than she does. Besides, I'd like a crack at some of the information, too."

"You can look, Marco. But Giuliani said that you weren't to get any help from the department. She made sure I'd tell you, too. She's not happy about you conducting your own investigation."

"She'll be happy if I find the shooter and give you guys the collar. Right?"

"She's not a very happy lady in general. Maybe you noticed?" Shim said. Maybe he wasn't as new at reading people as I figured.

Shim took the lead once we got to Emily's home and, though she glanced my way a few times, she didn't give him any trouble.

* * *

"Can't say there was much to go on. Brad didn't leave much of a trail. Appointment book, client list, address book," Shim complained as we walked back to my office. "This case is going nowhere fast. Giuliani is gonna put my nuts in a vise."

"She's not that bad. She's probably got the brass pressuring her, so she shifts some of it your way. A double murder in center city is bound to make the mayor blow a fuse. Then he makes the Department unhappy and they lean on Giuliani. Wait'll you get to where she is."

"I know the whole pressure-from-the-top thing. Doesn't help when you're the one down below catching all the grief," Shim said.

"Been there. Got over it. You will, too."

"Yeah."

"At least you've got some leads even if they're weak. Like the dead client."

"The other db? Smithson Wheeler?" Shim took out his notebook again. "Sure, he's on the list but he doesn't come with much. No family. Lived alone in town. A developer with community ties. Had offices in center city. We're working on it."

"Maybe there's a different link between him and Brad. Something other than being a client." I knew I'd be hunting down a connection as soon as I got back to the office.

"We're one step ahead of you on that. There's no connection we can find. We're short-handed, so it all falls to me and one other guy who's even newer than I am."

"If I hear anything, I'll give you a call."

"I was going to…" Shim hesitated then went silent

We continued walking down Fifteenth Street toward Walnut. I wondered what he'd been about to say and whether or not to try and pry it out of him. I was feeling my way with him and wanted to make sure he stayed on my side, if he actually *was* on my side. If he wasn't there yet, I didn't want to push him further away. Having someone on the inside during an investigation was better than gold. Even more, I wanted Shim to pull me into the investigation with tacit permission to help. Of course, there was another, unspoken reason: he was attractive and I wanted a chance to see if my gaydar was still working at 110%.

I decided to pry.

"What were you about to ask, Dae?"

"Hmmm?" He clutched his notebook and stared ahead as if he were trying to make up his mind.

I could see he wasn't ready to talk. "You've got a lot on your plate. When you remember, let me know."

Before he could say anything, his cell phone rang. A no nonsense, plain as concrete ringtone.

"Detective Shim." He listened for a moment. Then, "Mmm-hmm. Yep. That's right…. Got what I could… No… Wasn't much… Well, yeah, the new detective could help. I was planning on… What's that? Oh. We caught that one, too? No… no, not surprised. Be back at the station soon." He shoved the phone into his jacket pocket, swiped a hand over his face, and shut his eyes for a moment.

"What'd they dump on you now?" The new guys catch a lot of work. If they come through in one piece, they climb the ladder faster.

"Shit! Dammit!" Shim glanced at me, blushing. "Sorry about that."

I said nothing. Looked sympathetic.

"That was Giuliani. We caught another case and she piled it on me. Like I don't have enough with this case already."

"What's the new one?"

"The guy they dredged from the Schuylkill yesterday."

"Heard about that."

"Turns out he's a journalist named Vega. Worked for a hot shot website called AllNewsAllNow.com. Giuliani's making it a higher priority than Brad's case."

"Shit!" Now it was my turn. Not that I'd have dropped my investigation anyway, but now… there was no reason for me to play nice. I'd investigate and let Giuliani bust a gut trying to stop me.

"Don't worry, Marco. I'm not giving up on this case. But… it could…" He wavered again.

"What?"

"I hesitate to ask but now we've got the Vega case, I could use some help."

"You askin' me in, Detective?"

"I'm asking you to help but stay under the radar. See what you can find out. If Giuliani catches wind of it, I never said a thing to you. We never had this conversation. Got it?"

"Gotcha, Dae."

"Keep me in the loop, Marco. That's essential. I'll be busy with the new case but I won't give up on this one."

"You said his name was Vega? The dead journalist?"

"Yep, Peter Vega. Did a lot of muckraking stories for the site. Heard he was good."

When we arrived at my office building, Shim took off for district headquarters and I headed into the lobby.

The journalist's name kept clanging in my head for some reason. Peter Vega. There was something about the name, but I'd never heard of him before he became a floater.

Chapter 13

Olga pounded away on her keyboard while squinting at her computer monitor when I arrived at the office.

"That keyboard do something to deserve a beating?"

"Yes. Keys are sticking. Board makes Olga crazy."

"I have more reasons for you to bruise your keyboard."

"You are having file?"

"No. Just two names. I want as much as you can get on both of them."

I gave her a slip of paper with the names Smithson Wheeler and Peter Vega. She'd know what to do. When she was given a project, Olga usually went into silent search mode and wouldn't look up unless some kind of nuclear device went off under her desk.

She'd made coffee for me and on my desk sat a plate with a slice of almond cake and a few Russian tea cakes. Olga had obviously spent the weekend baking and was determined to make me fat. The almond cake was worth a few extra miles on the treadmill.

Peter Vega. The journalist's name rolled over and over in my mind as I poured coffee into a mug. I couldn't figure what there was about the name that bothered me. It wasn't familiar. I'd heard of AllNewsAllNow.com, everyone had. It wasn't exactly a scandal sheet but its reporters loved digging for dirt. Peter Vega's work for the site was totally unfamiliar to me, though.

Despite the fact I didn't know Vega, I couldn't shake the feeling his name gave me. There was nothing connecting him to Brad's murder. Except that Vega's murder pushed Brad's case off the table. I tried forgetting about Vega for a moment.

Papers, folders, bills, and the pastry stared up at me from my desk. I picked up the plate, closed my eyes, and breathed in the sweet aroma of almond cake. Placing it back on the desk I pushed it to the side. That would be a reward for actually getting some work done.

I couldn't ignore those names. I took out a sheet of paper and wrote: Smithson Wheeler and Peter Vega. I hoped staring at them would focus my mind. It didn't. They meant nothing to me in and of themselves. Except they were both dead. But they weren't dead in the same place or at the same time.

Wheeler had been in the spa and might've been there as a client, even if he wasn't listed as one on the night of the murders. That was the logical place to start for Wheeler. The journalist was another case entirely. His body was found miles away from the spa, on a different day. Nothing made him useful to Brad's case as far as I could see.

Olga would undoubtedly come up with information. Even with my office door closed, I could hear her keyboard squealing under her meaty fingers. She'd find something or that keyboard would collapse under her efforts.

I needed to work Brad's files to see if Wheeler appeared anywhere in them. I started with the client list and searched on Wheeler. Sure enough, Wheeler appeared in the client list. Had regular appointments, too. He was also listed in Brad's address book, but only with a number and the notation: "private cell phone" next to it. Maybe Brad and Wheeler had some dealings outside the massage room. Few clients had listings in both the client database and the address book.

As a regular client, it was odd that Wheeler hadn't been listed in the appointment book for that Friday evening. If he'd been a last minute walk-in, it was the unluckiest choice the guy'd ever made.

If he wasn't there unexpectedly, then what was he doing at the spa? A romantic interest? From what I knew of Brad and his taste, Wheeler wasn't his type. There had to have been some other connection. I recalled Brad talking about looking for investors when I'd asked how he was managing the mortgage and renovation expenses. Maybe Wheeler was a financial backer.

It was odd Brad had no investor files. On the other hand, Wheeler might have been his only investor or could have wanted it kept secret. I'd have to run that down.

Wheeler's name teased me from the screen. Smithson Wheeler. A classy name and, from the photo I'd taken, it appeared as if, in life, he'd probably been a classy looking man. You could almost see that in the picture, if you didn't count the being-dead thing.

But there were still questions. Who was he to Brad, and what was he doing at the spa that night?

I tooled around in Brad's files a while longer and saw again that he left notes with the names of most clients and contacts. Sometimes a few words but often a few sentences describing the type of massage the client liked, what kind of pressure, what oils or lotions they preferred. He'd noted client health considerations like asthma, diabetes, heart or other conditions. Brad also left notes about frequency of visits, whether or not the guy was a good tipper, or if he was a decent person and not a weirdo.

Two or three names had either no notes or only a sketchy phrase without detail. A person named Carney popped up several times. His name, a time and date, along with the notation: "showed up again." Carney never had an appointment, and didn't have an address or phone listed. J. Hoyer and R. Blitzer, appeared in a contacts file. Brad noted that Hoyer had "potential as a backer" and Blitzer was an "annoying salesperson."

One possibility was that Brad had told Charlie, his substitute, something about these guys.

Since the phantom Charlie hadn't returned my calls, I assumed he hadn't yet returned. I decided to leave another message anyway. Dialing his number, I realized he might not know about Brad's death, and I'd have to break the news to the poor guy.

Placing the receiver back in its cradle, I continued puzzling over the names Wheeler and Vega. They still buzzed around the edges of my mind, the answer just out of reach.

Olga buzzed the intercom.

"Is Detective on line for you," she said and put the call through without waiting.

From the serious tone of Olga's voice, I knew I'd hear Giuliani's voice and I wasn't wrong.

"Just giving you a heads up," she said. No greeting. Straight to the point.

"Good afternoon, to you, too."

"Not in the mood to spar, Fontana. Since Brad Lopes was your friend, I wanted to let you know what's been happening."

I was suspicious. The old Gina would make a call like this. Once upon a time, when we were friendly. The new Gina was about to let me know, without saying it directly, that Brad's case was being assigned a lower priority. She obviously didn't know I was already aware of what was going on.

"Not much is happening, I gather from Detective Shim. Or was he just being close-mouthed?" I thought it would be good to hint that her guy wasn't giving away secrets without her say so. That way, she'd pat him on the back and he'd keep doling out information to me.

"We've got a name on the dead guy you found in the spa. Other than that, we've got nothing. The lab is still processing trace evidence. That'll take a while. I don't have a lot of hope they'll find much."

"Why's that?"

"It was a spa. Everybody and his grandfather was in and out of the place. It's like processing a hotel lobby. We have too much trace and it'll give us a lot of nothing. The bodies will tell their own story. I'm waiting to hear from the coroner."

"So… what're you saying, Gina?" I knew but I wanted her say it. Not that she would.

"I'm saying we've got nothing. It'll be slow going. We've got our hands full and not enough people to do the work." Her voice was tense and she hadn't corrected me for using her first name. That meant something, too.

"In other words, you're putting Brad's case on a back burner."

"Not my words, Fontana. We're still investigating. Just wanted to let you know where we were. It's not an easy case. There's too much we don't know yet."

There was no use pushing her. I knew the deal and I knew how to handle things. Gina's a smart woman. She had to know I wasn't going to let this case go. I was hoping somewhere deep down she wanted me to jump into the investigation. Nah, that'd be too much to ask.

"What was the dead guy's name?" I asked pretending I didn't already know. I like to play the game.

"The… why're you asking?"

"You know me, Gina. I like knowing things."

"Yeah, well, this is one thing you don't have to know yet. Keep your shirt on and I'll get back to you. Like I said, we're overloaded."

"Just don't forget I'm here, or that Brad was a friend, Gina."

She hung up without saying good-bye or that she'd keep me in the loop. Didn't matter. I was making my own loop.

I glanced at the computer monitor. Before Gina called, I'd been thinking about Wheeler and Vega and trying to figure out why those names kept doing backflips in my head. Wheeler was a client, maybe even a backer. He was relevant to the case. But Vega wasn't connected to the whole mess. So why did his name keep rolling around in my thoughts? I couldn't shake the feeling that Vega had some significance, and that got some wheels turning.

Brad had always left a note of some sort, even if it were only a name, in his appointment book. He'd been a little compulsive in that, but it also served as a business record and a bare bones diary. Which meant he'd have left some note of Wheeler's visit the night of the murders. Even if he was a last minute walk-in, there'd have been some notation. That's when I remembered the only note Brad had left about visitors he'd had on Friday night.

I turned to my computer, opened the folder with my pics from the crime scene and found the photo of Brad's day book showing two sets of initials: "SW" and "PV"

Bingo!

Chapter 14

The initials in Brad's daybook matched the initials of the two dead men, Smithson Wheeler an Peter Vega. There was no way those initials meant anything else. Not even coincidence, which I never buy, could account for that.

Olga was still tracking information on Wheeler. In the meantime, I couldn't ignore the possibility that Vega had been in Brad's spa. I'd bet my grandmother's silver that Vega was there following a story and not getting a massage. Another possible lead. Things were looking up.

Tapping a few keys, I pulled up AllNewsAllNow.com, Vega's online employer. The page flashed onto the screen with a screaming, huge headline: "Peter Vega Murdered" I skimmed the story just in case they had information I could use but they were as clueless as everyone else about the details. They didn't even seem to know what story Vega was working when he was murdered.

All News All Now's contact page gave phone numbers, e-mail addresses and a street address. I decided to skip calling and drop in on Laura Leahy, the Editor-in-Chief. I like starting at the top.

I sailed through the office. Olga, still engaged in slapping her keyboard around, hardly noticed me until I neared the door.

"Boss comes back soon?" She tilted her head and looked in my direction, her eyes having that, bleary, been-staring-at-the-computer-too-long look.

"Later on." I glanced at the wall clock. "You need me for something or…?"

"I am maybe having report on businessman. Some are calling him king of pins. Many sites are saying he is big in cheeses. So far, I am finding no cheese or pins. But Olga keeps looking."

I smiled. "Take it easy, precious. You're the only secretary I've got."

"Is true."

I winked at her and left the office.

All News All Now had an office in an old commercial building on Walnut near Sixteenth. The city was littered with aging office buildings housing tiny business ventures. With the success of All News All Now, I'd have thought they could afford classier digs. Internet fame doesn't often translate into big bucks.

Claustrophobically small, the threadbare lobby had probably never looked good. A speck of a guard's desk with no guard faced the front door, next to it a battered directory with letters knocked askew or missing, and two rickety-looking elevators. I hit the call button.

When the elevator arrived, a woman dressed in what looked like a tattered blanket sauntered out. She wore a bicycle helmet from which her frizzy hair was trying to escape and carried a leather briefcase.

The odor of something pungent suffused the elevator and stayed with me until the door slid open and I entered a corridor only marginally better than the lobby. The combination of cheap carpeting, peeling paint, and crackling fluorescents overhead made for an eerie downbeat atmosphere. It was hard to believe this was home for one of the Internet's brighter stars.

I moved down the hall scanning signs until I came to an old oak door with a cracked plastic sign: "AllNewsAllNow.com"

Knocking, I pushed open the door and was faced with a fair-sized office, a couple of desks, a long table on the right supporting three monitors, and windows looking South which lit up the room considerably. Odors of stale smoke and food filled the air.

Curls of cigarette smoke rose above one of the monitors which was strategically placed on a desk facing the door, preventing visitors from seeing who was behind it.

I cleared my throat. Loudly.

No response.

Cautiously I moved toward the coils of smoke rising with increasing frequency. When I was near enough to see the woman sitting behind the desk, I cleared my throat again.

A gasp. A cough.

Expelling clouds of smoke from nose and mouth, the woman half rose from her chair and turned her startled gaze on me.

"You oughta get a buzzer," I said. "Or one of those bells visitors slap so it rings when they're about to creep up on you."

"Who the hell are you?" she snapped, stubbing out her cigarette angrily in an ashtray piled with abandoned cigarette butts. "You another cop? Somethin' about you says cop."

"Close. Private Investigator. Marco Fontana." I stretched out a hand.

Her dark eyes flashed suspicion. She stood in a defensive posture. Dark hair against her pale complexion gave her a faded appearance. Sharp eyes and a generous mouth were set in a pleasant face. There wasn't a lot of trust in that face but I figured that went with the job. In her thirties she appeared older, probably because of the black circles under her eyes. Her bone-tired look probably due to the late hours she must keep making All News All Now successful.

"Laura Leahy." She squeezed my hand. "You sneak into offices a lot, Fontana?"

"Only when I have to. This place, I didn't have to, the door was open."

"Damn. I always forget that and I shouldn't. The guard at the desk is as useful as a toothless Yorkie." She snorted. "All News All Now makes enemies. I have to watch my back."

"Peter Vega seems to have made some enemies," I said.

"He had a knack, but…" She sat back down and indicated I should find a seat.

I half sat on the desk next to hers.

"You were saying…"

"I'm gonna miss Pete. He was one of my best. His work was miles better than what passes for journalism in the mainstream media. His stuff was red meat. Always took risks. Found details no one else could." She lit another cigarette, inhaled deeply, then blew the smoke away from me and over her shoulder. "And, yeah, he made enemies. When you expose the truth you make enemies."

"Any idea what story might've gotten him killed?"

"Who're you workin' for, Fontana?" She took a long drag on her cigarette and kept the smoke down a long time.

"I'm working another case. Trying to see if they're connected. Short answer is I'm not working for anybody connected to Vega."

"I see. You don't give much away, do you? I'll bet you want lots more than you give." Leahy stubbed out her half-finished smoke. "What can I tell you? I told the cops everything I know which is zilch."

"How's that possible? You're his editor. Wasn't he working assignments for you?"

"That's not the only way we do things here." She turned to survey her office. "You see anybody but me?"

"No."

"Most of my reporters work on their own terms. I make sure they know what's important to cover. I give assignments to a few. My best, they work their own beats. They'll give me a heads up on stories they're following. I make sure there's no overlap. Even if they stumble onto the same story, they always have different angles. I usually iron everything out. It works."

"Vega? What was his beat?"

"Vega was special. He'd proven himself to me. I gave him latitude to do whatever he wanted. Besides..." She brushed ashes from her blouse.

"What?"

"Vega had sources. Sources he never talked about. He got stories no one else could or did. So I gave him plenty of room. No one complained."

"Must work, you guys are a success."

"Tell that to my bank account."

"So you don't know what Vega was following when he was murdered?"

"Like I said, most of my reporters tell me what they're working on. Vega... Vega was different."

"More secretive?"

"More paranoid." She looked at me as if she'd said the wrong thing. "Don't get me wrong. He was smart. An ace. He knew what he was doing. He just didn't like anybody else knowing until he was ready."

"Why was that?"

"Hey, if I knew things like that, I could make a fortune in another career." She pulled another cigarette from her pack. "Could be he had leads stolen in the past. Could be he was just eccentric. The Internet is a funny place. Hard to keep secrets. But Vega never got scooped."

"Any of his other stories ever result in physical violence."

"Police asked the same thing and I'll give you the same answer. No. Not that I was aware of. Threatening calls. Nothing recent."

"E-mail threats?"

"He said he'd gotten some on past stories. After the fact e-mails. You know, like, 'You'll be sorry.' Stuff like that. We never got any real threats here that I remember. Run of the mill stuff. Most people like to shoot off their mouths and that's the end of it."

"Who'd know what he was working on? Even if he was paranoid, he'd have to have a confidante, right?"

"Wasn't me, if that's what you're thinking." She puffed away on her cigarette which seemed more like a pacifier than an addiction. "We got along fine but he never told me diddly about stories until he turned them in."

"He didn't have a place here in the office?"

"Does this look like the city desk at the Times? Nobody's got a place here but me. Sometimes when I need tech assistance, I clear out space for her and her gang. Otherwise I'm the only one tied to this desk." Leahy eyed her dwindling pack of cigarettes.

"Gotcha."

"Vega had a laptop, of course. It was like his best friend and mistress at the same time. Never went anywhere without it. Shame they didn't find it when they found him."

"I'm guessing it's at the bottom of the Schuylkill," I said.

"That's just what the cops said. They'd searched his place before they came here looking for the same stuff you're looking for. They came up empty and they weren't too happy when they left here either."

"Did he ever work with anyone? Another reporter?"

"You kidding?"

"You're sure there's no one…"

"There *was* someone he'd take along sometimes when he was finishing up a story. I guess by then Vega was sure no one else could get a handle on the piece if word got out. Far as I know he never told the guy much of anything."

"Then why'd he take him along?"

"Guy's a photographer. Vega needed pictures. If he could get them. Some of his stories… let's just say not everybody wanted pictures. Sometimes he took the photographer along just in case."

"Worth a shot. The photographer might know something."

"If you can find him."

"You had to pay him, right? Yo've gotta have records. A name, an address."

"He didn't work for All News All Now. He worked for Vega, and Vega paid him cash."

"You had to credit the guy, right? Who'd you attribute the pictures to?"

Shaking her head, Leahy brought up a file on her computer.

"Take a look," she said leaning back in her chair.

The file was a mostly empty contact sheet. It had a name, Barton Studios, and a list of photos published.

"His name's Barton? That all you've got? Too much to ask if that's a first or last name?"

"That's how we credit his pictures. I'm not sure it's even a real name. The photographer knew how volatile Vega's stories could be. He liked being paid but he didn't want Vega's subjects knowing how to find him."

"That's it, huh?"

"As far at the photographer is concerned. I never met him. Did see him with Vega once, outside the building. Young guy. Cute, if you like the nerdy, curly-haired type. Big camera around his neck. Had one of those camera vests with a lot of pockets."

That was a fair description of the guy I'd noticed standing outside Brad's spa Saturday morning as Shim and I started out for Emily's place. Curly hair, big camera, multi-pocket vest. If I saw him again, I'd know him.

"No one else in Vega's life?"

"An ex-wife. They're happily divorced. She lives in Colorado. She did call about his insurance, though."

* * *

Leahy lit up another cigarette as I left her office. Second hand smoke clouding my lungs, I headed for the pavement and the relatively clean air outside.

The streets looked shabby. Maybe it was my mood. I hadn't gotten enough information from Leahy, which didn't brighten my day. It was better than nothing, and I headed back to my office to try finding Barton Studios.

Olga was still tapping keys when I opened the door.

"Still at it, sugarplum?"

"What is sugarplum exactly?" She hardly glanced up when she spoke.

"A term of affection."

"Candy is better," Olga said.

"Any calls?"

"Messages on desk. Luke is calling with no informations. I am searching."

"Keep it up, sugarplum." I went into my office and shut the door behind me. Pouring what was left of the coffee into a mug, I eased into my desk chair and stared at my monitor. The sea life screensaver dissolved when I touched the mouse.

I googled Barton Studios. There were web design offices in Montana, Nebraska, California, and Texas, but nothing in Philly. Several more searches led me absolutely nowhere. I toyed with the idea of letting Nina use the photographs themselves to reveal the photographer. I'd read that all digital pics have embedded codes. I decided to call her in the morning to see if what I was thinking was even possible.

Picking up the phone, I made another call to Charlie that went straight to voicemail and I added another message to the pile I'd already created. I wondered how Brad had used him as a sub if he disappeared so much.

I sipped my now cold coffee as I reviewed the progress I'd made. So far, I hadn't gotten an inch closer to a solution. I'd collected a lot of missing persons though: Charlie the sub, Johnny the stalker, Max the abusive ex, Matz the other possible intruder at the spa, and now the photographer.

Even if I found those guys, there was no guarantee they were connected to the killings. A lead's a lead, I'd track down every one. Including Shuster and Sorba the shock jock both of whom feared exposure. I'd also have to look into whatever jury Brad had served on. That could lead somewhere. There were other possibilities, like the contractors who'd worked on the renovations at the spa.

I glanced at the time and decided dinner and some company might do me good. Then I'd head over to Bubbles to make sure things were on track for the show. Mondays were slow. Slower than slow sometimes. Anton usually scheduled the Best Buns contests for Mondays, which always packed the house.

Anton. Despite the frustration of the case, Anton was on my mind. Lots. I speed dialed his number and he picked up immediately.

"Marco! Funny you called right now." Anton sounded guilty and happy. "We were just talking about you."

"Oh? I was just thinking about *you*. Still at home?"

"Don't worry I'll be at Bubbles soon. I haven't forgotten," Anton sounded miffed.

"You've got it all wrong. I was *hoping* you'd be home. I want us to have dinner."

"Oh. *Oh*, I thought…"

"See, I'm not that bad. Can we have dinner? Unless you're already occupied? You said 'we' a moment ago. If I'm interrupting…"

"Yes… No… I mean sure I want to have dinner. Jean-Claude is here. He came by to pick up stuff for the contest. I thought I'd let him do set up. I need the help."

"I was hoping dinner would be just the two of us."

"Where should I meet you?" Anton ignored the implications of what I'd said.

"How about Knock in twenty minutes or do you need more time to get ready?"

"Uh, let's see. I've got all my clothes on. The bed is made. I live right around the corner. So twenty minutes is excessive."

"All right, all right. I know when I've been chastised. I'll meet you there as soon as you can get there. I'm leaving now."

* * *

If Knock's elegant wood doors hinted you were entering a place with class, the interior made you certain. The bar, a golden-brown, polished wood island at the front of the house, was crowded. Men chatted, laughed, and drank. You felt the friendly vibes the minute you entered. As in any bar, people looked up to see who entered, then they retuned to their friends and their drinks.

Nick the manager, tall and sophisticated, waved me over.

"Marco! Been a while. How's my favorite Italian?" He smiled.

"Stumped, Nick. Stumped on a case. How're you? You're lookin' like a million bucks. As usual."

"Flattery will get you everywhere." Nick laughed. "Got a table for you in the back, if you want privacy and quiet. You alone tonight?"

"Anton will be here. In the meantime I'll have a drink at the bar."

"You got it, Marco."

I wandered over to the bar, found an empty seat and plunked myself down. For a moment I felt far away from everything and happy.

"What're you having, Marco?"

I looked up, and the bartender was staring at me. I should have remembered his name but I didn't. Young and cute, he had coppery red hair and striking blue eyes so light they were almost transparent. Then he smiled, and I was sunk.

"You still make that killer mojito?" At least I remembered that much about him.

"Comin' up." He pulled a few bottles, swung around, and began mixing the drink. His well-rounded glutes jiggled with his efforts.

I mouthed a hello to a few familiar faces stationed around the bar and before I could think another thought, the mojito was placed before me.

"Let me know if I'm still as good as I was," the bartender said seductively. "At making a mojito, I mean." He winked.

Before I could taste it and give him a report, Anton walked through the door. Again, heads turned. I heard one person next to me whisper "Who's that?" and I smiled. Anton's magnetism was undeniable. More than a few patrons cried the night Anton announced his retirement from dancing at Bubbles.

"Hi, boss." Anton pecked me on the cheek.

His pine forest aftershave made me want to hold him closer. I placed a hand around his waist and pulled him to me. "Glad you're here," I said.

Anton smiled and gently moved back so I could stand.

Sweeping up the mojito from the bar, I glanced at the bartender who looked disappointed. I gave him a wink, and turned toward Anton.

"You have a glow tonight." I said to Anton as Nick escorted us to our table and placed menus in our hands.

"Probably the apricot scrub." Anton smiled, then peered at his menu.

The back room was quiet. Nick had given us a table in the corner and it felt like we had the room to ourselves. I was happy we could spend time concentrating on one another.

"So..." Anton started.

A slender waiter in tight black pants and a white shirt sidled up to the table.

"Can I get you something to drink?"

"You're having your usual," Anton said to me. "I'll try something different." He looked up at the waiter. "How about a Tahitian Tea?"

The waiter raised his eyebrows. I was sure he had no idea what the drink was. But that was the extent of his reaction. He returned to his professional demeanor.

"Thank you, sir. I'll be back with your drink."

"I guess I threw him. I wanted something different, and I saw that drink mentioned somewhere."

"The bartender will know what to do."

"So, what's the occasion?"

"Does there have to be an occasion? Can't I have dinner with you just because I want to?"

"I suppose. Only... I know you Marco, and I know there's never just a simple dinner or a simple anything else. Is something wrong?"

"I'm at a dead end in the case. The police aren't pursuing it aggressively now that they have another high profile murder. Most of my leads are no better than phantoms. I needed some time away to let my mind work without me interfering. You know?"

"Oh." Anton sounded disappointed. "I think so."

"Really though, I wanted to see you. We haven't had dinner, just the two of us, at a nice place in a long time. I wanted some alone time with you."

"Oh," Anton said. His voice was low, almost sad. "You know I'm always here for you, don't you?"

"You've never let me down." I paused and stirred my mojito with the stick of sugar cane. "Which is more than I can say for myself. I know I've let you down lots."

Anton was silent. He was either choosing his words carefully or he agreed and didn't want to say it out loud.

"You deserve someone who can give you everything you want."

"You're saying what... exactly?" Anton looked at me.

"I'm saying that you need someone who'll be good to you and good for you."

"Why're you..."

The waiter placed Anton's drink in front of him.

"Ready to order?"

I looked over at Anton. He stared down at his menu.

"Give us another minute, okay?"

The waiter scuttled off.

"Why're you saying all this, Marco? Are you trying to tell me something?"

"I..."

"Because if you are, just spit it out. Don't play games with me."

"It's... lately I've seen you and Jean-Claude kind of hitting it off... you two look good together. He treats you like you should be treated. I don't want to... you know, I shouldn't..." I was tongue-tied.

Anton peered at me as if my head was about to topple off my shoulders.

"Marco... I'm not sure what you think... but there's nothing..."

My phone chose that minute to ring. I ignored it, determined to give my complete attention to Anton.

Then Anton's phone rang, and he looked startled.

"Something's going on," he said. "Can't be a coincidence."

"Go ahead answer it."

He flipped open his phone. "Anton." He listened a moment. "He's right here with me. No... why? What's wrong?..." He listened, his eyes widening. "Did you call 911?... Right. We'll be there in a minute."

Closing the phone he looked at me.

"We've got to go, Marco. It's Ty. He's been hurt."

Before he stood, he took my hand in his and squeezed.

* * *

Paramedics rushed out of the ambulance as Anton and I arrived at Bubbles. Pushing our way through a small knot of people near the entrance, we saw Ty lying on the floor, an EMT attending to him. Ty's slight form was crumpled like a tissue used and discarded. The paramedic attempted to make him comfortable.

Ty looked still and even more pale than usual. Blood smeared his face, hands, and even his golden, tangled, curls.

I knelt on one knee and looked into Ty's face, one eye still swollen shut from the other night. The paramedic tried to stanch the bleeding from a large gash over Ty's other eye. His jaw was bruised and his right arm was bent at an awkward angle. I could only imagine the bruises on his wispy body.

Ty squirmed and moaned as the paramedic stopped the bleeding and gently felt for broken bones before they would lift him onto a stretcher.

"Who did this, Ty?" I whispered. As if I didn't know. Eddie, his boyfriend, was responsible and this time I'd make sure he paid. "Ty, can you hear me?"

"We've got to get him to the hospital, sir. If you could…"

"He works for me. I need to know who did this," I was reluctant to touch the kid, fearing I'd only add to his pain. "Ty, tell me. I'll take care of it. Was it…"

Ty's mouth was swollen where he'd been punched. Red and painful-looking, I hated having to make him talk.

"Can you nod your head, Ty? I know it hurts… but… was it Eddie?"

He squirmed and squirmed as if trying to back away.

"Move," Anton said to me as he knelt to talk to Ty. "Let me do this." He was right, he and Ty were close. The kid always went to Anton first. He'd tell Anton before he'd tell me anything.

"Ty, who did this to you, sweetie?" Anton, who on the surface looked like a seasoned athlete, was gentle with the guys when he had to be. I could see why they all gravitated to him when they needed comfort or a hug or just a warm smile to know that someone cared about them.

Ty seemed more calm, his body relaxed. He turned his head toward Anton and I saw a small tear squeeze out from his good eye and spill over his cheekbone onto the floor.

"Who did this, Ty? Marco and I want to help. Tell me who did this."

Ty's lips quivered, it was painful watching him struggle. I heard a faint gurgling whisper.

Anton lowered his head to just above Ty's lips.

"Did you say... Eddie?"

Unable to muster the ability to speak again, Ty moved his head slowly, with great effort, in an affirmative nod.

"We'll take care of you, sweetie. Don't worry." Anton whispered.

"I'll fix it so Eddie won't hurt you again." I stood and felt a vicious anger thrum through me.

Anton stood and faced me. He wiped at one eye. Anger twisted his features.

"Son of a bitch!" I hissed. "I knew it would come to this. The kid is lucky to be alive."

"I'll go to the hospital with him," Anton said. "He doesn't have family in the city. I'll call them only if..."

"I'm gonna look for Eddie. You have Ty's address? I think he told me Eddie lived there, too."

"Be careful, Marco. He's dangerous. Take someone with you."

"Eddie only hits guys who are smaller than he is, weaker than he is. He lays a finger on me and it'll be his last act on earth."

"Take someone with you."

"Look after Ty. I'll find Kevin. That'll freak out the bastard."

The paramedics gently placed Ty onto a stretcher and got him into the ambulance. Anton slipped in behind them and they pulled the doors shut. Sirens blaring, they took off into the night.

"A shame," Jean-Claude said. He'd come to stand next to me.

"Did you see what happened?"

"No. It was outside. We heard noises. Someone shouting. There was a sound like something is shoved against the wall, you know? Then Ty, he

comes in and collapses. I called 911, then you and Anton. I ran out to see
if anyone was still there, but the street, it was empty. Was this right? Did I
do…"

"You did the right thing," I said. "Can you find Kevin for me? Tell him
I need him."

Jean-Claude moved off, and I spotted a familiar figure sitting at the bar,
staring at me. Same mean face, same cruel curiosity. The guy who'd spied on
me and Shuster. He was back, and I intended to find out who he was and
what he wanted.

Before I could move an inch Kevin stood blocking my view with his
enormous, gym-built figure.

"They said you needed me." Kevin's arms bulged, his chest a massive
muscular machine. He stared around at the house patrons ready to take their
heads off at the first sign of trouble.

"Yeah, Kev. I'm gonna need back up. Get someone else on the door and
meet me outside.

I looked over to where the guy had been but he was gone. He was quick,
I'd give him that. Sooner or later, he'd slip up and I'd catch him.

Right now I wanted to catch Eddie.

Chapter 15

Anton scribbled Ty's address on a paper which I stuffed into my pocket. I stalked out of the bar with Kevin in tow. There was no guarantee Eddie would be at home. I didn't even know what the guy looked like, but I had to make a try at stopping him from hurting Ty again.

First step was to put a scare into the bastard, then I'd work on making sure he didn't do this to Ty or anyone else ever again.

Ty lived on the other side of South Street in a slightly seedy section of the Bella Vista neighborhood. Still being gentrified, Bella Vista had a way to go. At least it was a relatively crime free area. Of course, with Kevin at my side, anywhere we went was bound to be safe.

My anger had propelled me, getting us to Eighth Street in record time. Kevin easily kept up but once or twice glanced at me as if I were on fire. I was. I wanted to find Eddie before he went to ground and we'd have a harder time catching the creep.

This part of town consisted of older housing with new development haphazardly thrown in here and there. Bella Vista is the first neighborhood settled by Italian immigrants. One of my grandfathers had lived somewhere in the area. That era had long ago faded to nearly nothing.

Some older homes had been redone by newcomers, a large segment of which were gay men who felt it was close enough to the center of town but not as expensive. Except as soon as they started moving in and upgrading, costs and taxes began rising. Parts of Bella Vista butted up against historic sections of the city and the closer you came to that, the better things looked and the more they cost.

Ty wasn't lucky enough to live in that part of the neighborhood. His apartment, near Seventh and Fitzwater, was in an old building, waiting for a fix up that might never happen.

"Got some friends who bought a house down here," Kevin said as we walked through Bella Vista. "Nice neighborhood but too far out of the way for me. I like being in the middle of town."

"Too close to family for me to feel comfortable," I said. "No way am I moving anywhere near South Philly. Too many memories." This neighborhood was so close to family territory, I felt it on my skin like a subtle change in the air's electrical charge.

"You think we'll find this guy?"

"If we don't find him tonight, I'll find him eventually. The longer it takes, the sorrier he'll be."

"What're you gonna do?" Kevin asked, and I could hear Kevin's alter ego speaking. Hugely muscled and tough, Kevin occasionally reveled in his drag identity as Germaine Shepherd. His transformation usually caused considerable dissonance but also gained him a lot of fans.

"I'd like to wring Eddie's neck until his eyes pop out. Even better, I'd like to make him feel the way Ty must've felt. Cornered, scared, helpless. I'll settle for making him squirm and getting him out of town until I can figure out how to decommission him." I felt my heart thump with anger.

"Wow, you really got it in for the dude."

I did have it in for him. I wondered whether it was having seen Ty, sylph-like and bloodied, being trundled away in an ambulance or whether I was thinking about the fact that someone like Eddie might've killed Brad. Or was it something in myself I was reacting to? Whatever it was, the feeling was real and strong. I needed to control it before I did something stupid.

We neared Seventh and Fitzwater while it was still daylight and I gazed around looking for Ty's apartment house. On one corner, a quirky old building sporting an odd clock tower reminded me of a very different time in South Philly and made me feel good whenever I passed by. Not this time. This time I had Eddie on my mind and all pleasant thoughts had fled.

New row homes squatted on one side of the street with a parking lot at one end. Halfway down the street towards Eighth, I spotted a familiar building. I'd dropped Ty off one night after work. I'd only seen the place from the outside.

"We're not gonna be able to get in easily. Whatever way we do it, we'll spook Eddie. Let's scope it out first." I pointed to the building.

"Got it," Kevin said. "What do you want me to do?"

"See if there's a back way out. An alley, a fire escape. Or some way he can evade us. I'll see how we might get in without a fuss."

Kevin loped away, his eyes trained on the building. His skills as a bouncer, with a good eye for trouble, came in handy.

The building's façade was marred by a hundred years of caked on dust and grime. The once-red brick was a muddy brown. The doorway, flanked by two oblong windows, was decrepit. No decorations, no sign of life.

"Wouldn't be easy for him to escape out the back," Kevin said returning to stand with me. "A long drop and no alleyway. He'd have to hop over roofs then jump down three stories."

"He wouldn't do that. He loves himself too much."

"Did you find a way in?"

"Not yet. I'm workin' on it." There wasn't much to work on. Only so many legal ways in.

"I'll stake out the corner in case the creep finds the balls to jump three stories. Should be easy catchin' him if he does." Kevin winked at me and took up a position leaning against the waist-high wall of the parking lot.

As I peered at the three story building wondering how I could finagle my way in, an old, very old, Italian-looking woman walked slowly toward me from the direction of Seventh Street. Small and thin, her back ramrod straight, she moved with an unhurried, steady gait. The no nonsense look on her face told me she was tougher than steel.

Her flower print dress blew about her, as she neared eyeing me with suspicion. Her natural Italian defenses against strangers had gone up and locked themselves into place.

"Whaddayou lookin' at?" she said in a commanding voice loud enough for neighbors to hear. "You gott'a business in this building?"

"Good afternoon, ma'am," I said smiling.

"Whaddayou smilin' about? I didn't say nothin' funny. I don't like people who smile wit' no reason."

"My name's Marco. Marco Fontana." I extended a hand which she ignored. She reminded me of my Great Aunt Gemma and her world-hardened dignity. I'd have to tread lightly if I wanted to get anywhere with this woman.

She said nothing. Kept moving forward.

"I'm a private investigator and I could use your help, Miss...? I didn't get your name."

"I don't give my name to strangers." More and more she was looking like Aunt Gemma who could make grown men weep with fear.

"There's a young man who lives in this building. Right now, he's in the hospital and maybe you could help me catch the one who did this to him. How about it?"

I looked over at the building again. Shook my head.

The woman paused. I took that as a sign of something. Good or bad, I wasn't sure.

"Do you know anyone who lives here?" I asked.

The struggle she went through with herself was visible on her face but just barely. Her stubborn strength had obviously kept her going all these years. She didn't let down her guard easily.

"Yeah, *I* live here. Lived here a long time. Before you was born, I bet."

"You rent out some space to a couple of young men?"

"It's not illegal. Besides, it's an apartment, not just *some space*. A full apartment that my husband, rest in peace, built with his own hands."

"My father does stuff like that, too. He's an all around kind of guy, y'know?"

"Whaddayou wanna know about my tenants?"

All business, she plowed on.

"Okay, how well do you know the guys?"

"Lemme tell you, at first it was just the one kid. Cute, sweet. Looks like an angel with that curly yellow hair. But he's skinny. Him I know. Or, I thought I knew 'im."

"Why do you say that?"

"The other guy. That's why. One day he brings home this *cafone*. Big deal kinda guy. Thinks his shit don't stink."

"Name's Eddie, right?"

"Eddie. Yeah. Noisy guy. Ty, the angel, he never made no noise. But now with this other one... They argue a lot. I heard things fallin' and the little angel is screamin' and the big *cafone* is like an animal."

"Is he..."

"I want him out. But I keep my mouth shut for the little angel. He's got no place else and nobody else. You gonna get this Eddie out for me?"

"Ma'am, I intend to get him way out. He's the one who put Ty in the hospital."

"*Che stronzo*! Get 'im outta my house."

"He's there now?" I asked hoping she knew his habits.

"He's alla time there. Don't work. Not that I can see. How's my little angel?"

"He was beaten pretty bad."

"*Poverello*. You tell 'im I'm prayin' for him."

"Can my friend and I get in to talk to Eddie?"

"Talk? 'Ats all you gonna do? Talk? If I was your age, I'd make sausage outta him."

"Don't worry. He's gonna be tied in knots when we get through."

The old woman quickly climbed the three steps to the door, looked back at me, then brandished a key.

"There's no back way out, is there?" I asked.

"Not unless he wants'a break his neck. I pray to God he does." She looked skyward.

I motioned Kevin over and the woman nodded approvingly.

"You bringin' in the big guns now, huh? Good. And I don't care if you make noise. Just make him pay for what he done to my poor angel."

Unlocking the door, she held it open for me and Kevin.

"Third floor apartment. He was there when I left." She stayed outside. A wise move since she had no idea what would happen. My mother, on the other hand, would've insisted on coming up with me to get Eddie, or she'd have taken command of the kitchen to make some sauce for after.

Kevin and I slipped into the house without a sound. With few windows, the downstairs was dimly lit. Things looked comfortable, neat, and fresh. The pleasant fragrance of something cooked in olive oil lingered in the air as we moved to the stairs.

At the foot of the stairs, I pulled my gun and moved ahead of Kevin. As I climbed, I turned and signaled him to be quiet. He nodded.

I stopped mid-climb and listened. Not a sound.

The next step I took resulted in a squeak from the old wood. I froze and listened. If Eddie was up there he wasn't bothered by house noises.

On the second landing, I halted and Kevin nearly bumped me into the wall. I could tell he was nervous. I knew he wasn't afraid because I'd seen him take rowdy customers and fold them like cheap umbrellas. Hunting around in a strange house, not knowing where your target was likely to be would unnerve most people.

I placed a hand on his shoulder and nodded signaling we should move.

The second flight of stairs was a tighter climb. I heard Kevin huffing as he squeezed himself up the narrow stairs.

On the third floor landing, we faced an old wood door. Not a solid piece of construction. I stood to one side of the door and indicated Kevin should take the other. He moved swiftly and flattened himself as best he could against the wall.

Gun in one hand, I pounded at the door with my other hand. The old boards rattled and dust motes flew in all directions.

"Eddie! We need to talk." I stopped and listened. I heard a faint sound. "Eddie!"

There was shuffling. I heard him latch the door and scuttle back. "If you're not the police then get the fuck out," he shouted.

"Open the door or you're gonna wish I *was* the police."

"Who the hell…?"

"I'm Ty's boss, Marco Fontana. You and I have some talking to do."

"Get the fuck out." He was silent a moment. "Ty sent you, didn't he? The little fag. What a pussy. You his daddy now?"

"Open the door, we can talk nice and civil. Whaddaya say, Eddie?"

I signaled Kevin that I was going to break in the door and he should be ready to catch Eddie if he attempted to run.

"Get the fuck away or I'll call the police."

I moved as I spoke. "Yeah, you do that, Eddie."

In front of the door now, I breathed a silent prayer that Eddie was unarmed.

"Go ahead and call."

Before he could respond, I shoved my right foot against the lock midway up the door. The old boards splintered and the door collapsed like it was too tired to take any more.

I held the gun steady and moved in on a wide-eyed, gawky Eddie. He was tall, slender, and had a face which I knew a lot of guys would find attractive. Kind of cruel and sweet at the same time. Except I knew what was under that face and it didn't look so hot to me.

"What the fuck! You got a gun?" Eddie gasped. When he looked over my shoulder and saw Kevin, he wet his pants.

"Help!" Eddie yelled but by this time his voice was small in his throat. "You got no right comin' in here. Somebody help! He's got a gun!"

"Landlady let us in. Her property. You're not on the lease."

"Stay away from me!" He backed away, fumbling over his own feet.

"We wanna talk. About Ty." I waved the gun airily as if it was just some gadget I happened to have with me. Eddie's eyes bugged out.

"I got nothing to say. Ty's my boyfriend. I got nothing…"

"I think you got plenty to tell me. If not, I got plenty to tell you." I advanced on him.

Tripping as he shuffled backward, Eddie eventually came to the bedroom doorway where he fell on his ass into the room. He looked up startled, like a baby who'd fallen for the first time.

"Why don't you leave me and Ty alone? We're happy together."

"Yeah. I saw how happy Ty was a minute ago. He's so happy they had to rush him to the hospital."

Eddie's face crunched up into an ugly version of his usual and he started to cry. "I didn't mean to hurt him. I didn't. He was always doing things to make me angry. I told him… I told him."

"Big man we got here, boss." Kevin said, and with his size thirteen foot tapped one of Eddie's feet. Eddie pulled back as if he'd been zapped with a cattle prod.

"Yep, Eddie's a big man, Kev. Think you can handle him?"

Kevin bent down and pulled Eddie up by his shirt sleeves. He held him at arm's length, avoiding Eddie's piss-soiled pants.

"No problem boss." Kevin stood Eddie against a wall. "What should I do with this piece of shit?"

"You could flush him down the toilet. But what a waste of water."

I walked over to Eddie and took his jaw in my hand. The look of fear in his eyes almost made me feel a little something for him. Then I remembered the blood on Ty's blond hair and I squeezed Eddie's jaw. Hard. Just to get his attention. Then briefly relaxed my grip.

"You know what I don't understand? I don't understand what Ty sees in a guy like you. Maybe he's nicer than I am and he can see good where there isn't any. Maybe he's too trusting and you led him on. Whatever it is, you gave him a raw deal."

"I didn't wanna hurt him. He made me…"

"What was that?" I squeezed again. I wanted to crush his jaw in my hand but that wouldn't have been playing nice. "He *made* you beat him to a pulp? He *made* you break his arm?"

Eddie could barely move his head but he tried to nod.

I leaned my weight onto him pressing the breath out of him.

"You mean, like you're makin' *me* mad right now? And you're makin' me hurt you. Is that how you mean it? Ty bothered you like that?"

Eddie couldn't breathe let alone say a word.

"I'm tryin' here, Eddie, really but I can't see your point… *You* see his point, Kev?"

"Naw, can't say I do, boss."

I let Eddie breathe again but held onto his jaw. He sucked air as best he could.

"Got any relatives, you leech? Or did you get belched out of a sewer?"

Eddie strained to nod his head. His voice made a small squeaking sound as he attempted to say something.

"What was that?" I asked looking into his terrified brown eyes. "Did you say something?"

I relaxed my grip on his jaw.

"I-I g-got… fam-family…"

"Where?"

"H-Harrisburg… near… near H-Harrisburg."

"You're gonna visit them."

"I-I can't… got no…"

"That wasn't a question, smart guy. I said you're *gonna* visit them. Today."

"I can't afford…"

"I'm buyin' you a ticket. You're stayin' there until I decide what to do with you." I squeezed his jaw again. "Got it?"

"T-they…"

I squeezed.

"I… I got it."

"Now, Kev is gonna help you pack. Show him what's yours and go clean yourself up. Try anything and you'll be leavin' in a box."

Kevin let Eddie show him where his clothes and possessions were, and Kevin threw things into a large duffle bag he'd pulled from a closet. I heard the shower turned on in the bathroom.

I flipped out my phone and called Anton.

"How's Ty?"

"He's going to be all right eventually. The doctors said it'll take time, but he'll be all right."

"That's a relief."

"Did you find Eddie?"

"We're at Eddie's place right now. How're you holding up?"

"Better than I thought," Anton said, and I could hear the relief in his voice. "The doctors said Ty had a broken arm, broken ribs, a slight concussion, and some other injuries but everything will heal. In time."

"Everything except his emotional state."

"He's going to stay with me until he can do for himself," Anton said.

* * *

Philly's Greyhound bus station near Filbert Street is not my favorite place in town. The only word to describe the area is drab. It's not run down, it just has no character, nothing to distinguish it, not a speck of pretty about it. Drab, dull, and worth missing.

Gypsy cab drivers scrambled over to us seemingly out of nowhere. They might've just been poor slobs hustling up work but their sleazy, under-the-table air didn't make you want to hop into their banged up vehicles. One hard look from Kevin warded them off.

We walked Eddie into the station crammed between us. Kevin had a firm hold around his waist so there was no chance he'd escape. Not that he'd want to after I'd told him what would happen if he even thought about it.

We bought his ticket and waited with him for the bus.

"This everything? No other contact numbers?" I asked waving a paper on which he'd scribbled his mother's address and phone number.

"N-no, you got it. Her and my sister. That's all the family I got."

"You call me when you get in," I said and checked my watch. "…which should be in about three hours if the bus arrives on time."

"Calls to Philly are expensive. My mom don't have money."

"Call collect. I want you to check in with me every day."

"Why? Who're you? You ain't the police."

"No, I *ain't*. I'm worse. I don't let go once I get my hooks in. Miss a call and Kev here will be on the next train to Harrisburg with two buddies who look just like him."

"How long I gotta stay there? I hate it out there… there's nothin' to do."

"I'll tell you when you're comin' back." If I could get Ty to press charges and if I could get Giuliani to help put the slimeball away for a while, I'd escort him back to the city myself.

* * *

I told Kevin he could take the night off. Couldn't ask him to work more than he had although he said he'd enjoyed himself. As he was turning the corner at Spruce, he puckered up and blew a Germaine-sized kiss at me and smiled broadly.

My cell phone rang a moment later.

"Fontana."

"Listen, Fontana. Something weird is going on and I'm wondering if you know anything about it." Shuster didn't bother to announce himself, just assumed I'd know his whiny voice.

"Shuster, listen. First you have to tell me what this something is before I take the blame."

"You remember that creep who was watching us at that café?"

"Yep," I answered, not wanting to tell him I'd seen the guy again.

"He cornered me. He actually cornered me outside my office. Around the corner in an alleyway. Threatened me. Told me to keep my mouth shut."

"Here I thought he was after *me*," I said, feigning disappointment. "You get all the hotties, Shuster."

"You're a big help, Fontana. This is a dangerous guy and you make jokes."

"Any idea who he is? 'Cause at the café you said you never saw him before."

"That was the truth. I thought he was connected to one of your cases and he was after you. I didn't know him. I'll bet he saw us together and assumed I was helping you with whatever you're doing. Now he's after me because he thinks I'm helping you."

"You report this to the police?"

"Are you crazy? How would this look in the middle of a campaign? People would think who knows what? It could hurt Kelley in the primary. He'd kill me and I'd be finished in the business. So, no, I did not report it to them. That's why I'm calling you."

"Okay, calm down, Shuster. Got time to come into my office tomorrow?"

"I'll be there first thing."

* * *

They didn't need me at Bubbles and I was happy for the opportunity to get home early. Of course, the best laid plans… As I strolled past The Village Brew, Sean was leaving and spotted me.

"Hey, Marco. Funny bumping into you. This card reader who comes in and trades readings for coffee, told me I'd meet the man of my dreams tonight. And here you are."

"Funny man, Sean." I looked at him. For some reason, Sean, always a sex bomb, was even hotter just then. Maybe it was his skin tight shirt or his curly mop of hair or his Botticelli face. Whatever it was, he stopped me in my tracks.

"Not funny, she's real. Come in some night and I'll prove it. Wanna have that drink you promised me the last time?"

"I'd love to. But truthfully I was headed home. Been a long couple of days."

"We can drink at your place," Sean said, slipped up next to me, and took my arm in his.

"If you don't mind a mess. My maids and butlers all quit a few days ago."

"Well, I can swing a mean dustmop, if you need a live in houseboy…" Sean looked at me suggestively.

"That's a thought. First let's see how good you are at mixing drinks… and other things."

Chapter 16

Slugging down the powerful coffee Olga left for me in the coffeemaker, I let the caffeine kick in. After a pleasantly lively night with Sean and not much sleep, the coffee would keep me going. I felt refreshed. Having a night without thinking about the case or anything else, had helped. I'd been too wound up and wasn't thinking clearly. Sean managed to distract me completely.

Now I had to get back into the short list of leads that went nowhere. I didn't like it. I was no closer to Brad's killer than I had been the morning they'd found him.

I couldn't drop the feeling I was missing something right in front of me.

About to pick up the phone to see if the phantom Charlie had gotten back to town, I heard voices and laughter in the outer office. My door opened and Luke walked in followed by a slightly taller, elegantly dressed, Asian man whose chiseled features reminded me of a movie poster I'd seen somewhere. I hoped Luke wasn't bringing me a new client. If so, he'd have to get in line.

"Luke!" I stood and walked over to hug Luke. He felt warm and familiar, his scent intoxicating. I closed my eyes remembering the day before.

"Marco," Luke said, pulling out of the hug, "I want you to meet someone." He looked from me to the stranger and smiled. "This is Xinhan. And this…" Luke waved a hand in my direction, "is Marco."

Xinhan extended his hand. His jeans and expensive-looking silk shirt didn't hide the slender muscularity of his figure. The handshake was firm but he obviously didn't feel the need to prove anything with it. He exuded a magnetic air of calm self control.

"Nice to meet you, Xinhan," I said, replicating Luke's pronunciation which sounded like, *Shinhan*. I indicated they should take seats.

"Nice to meet you, as well, Marco. After everything Luke said, it's a pleasure."

"I may not live up to Luke's PR."

"Don't let the humble act fool you, Xinhan." Luke wiggled his eyebrows and smiled.

I shrugged.

"Any news?" Luke asked.

"A few nibbles. Nothing solid. You?"

"I made more calls like you asked. Just a bunch of guys either sorry to hear about Brad or who claimed not to know him. Nothing suspicious far as I can tell. I don't have that Italian ability to see a suspect behind every face. Here's the list." He pulled a paper out of his messenger bag.

Placing the list on my desk, I glanced at Xinhan, then at Luke. He must've noticed the question in my look.

"Xinhan's tagging along. My cousin Chunxue introduced us and we've been trading stories from back home. Xinhan comes from the same town."

I noticed Xinhan staring at the corkboard I'd set up with pictures and notes from Brad's case. He tried joining the conversation but kept getting drawn back to the board.

"Something bothering you, Xinhan?"

"Yes. That man. The older gentleman..."

"One of the murder victims in this case. Smithson..."

"Wheeler." Xinhan said finishing my sentence. "Yes, I thought that was him." The air of peace surrounding Xinhan wavered for a moment but he regained composure seamlessly. "Smithson was a business friend. A supporter of Chinatown initiatives and development. How did this happen?"

"That's what we're trying to figure out, Xinhan. Maybe you can help with a little background. Right now I don't know all that much about Wheeler."

"He was an exceptional man, an astute businessman. Smithson was the definition of honor. He was a friend to Chinatown and to me personally. Other than that…"

"What was your connection to Wheeler?"

"I own a business in Chinatown."

"He's being modest, Marco. Xinhan is one of Chinatown's business leaders. He owns the Green Dragon kung fu school and two restaurants. Not shabby at all."

"Chinatown depends quite a lot on friends like Smithson. He will be missed for many reasons," Xinhan said, a touch of mystery in his remark.

"How exactly did he help you?" I asked. Xinhan's expression tightened with reluctance. My question was intrusive, too personal. I figured he'd react this way but I needed information. "I don't mean to pry, Xinhan. Anything I can find out about him may help catch the people who killed him."

"Yes." He nodded. "Yes. I understand." His smooth, deep voice was shaded with sadness.

"What was Wheeler's involvement in the community? Did he help you in particular or…?"

"He did many things for a lot of people. Many years ago, his father had some sort of business in China. Smithson spent a large part of his childhood there and in Hong Kong. He spoke Mandarin well. Loved everything about China and the Chinese."

"Okay," I said taking notes.

"He was instrumental in obtaining financing for a number of businesses including mine, at a time when things were difficult. Not everyone is as enlightened as Smithson was. Not everyone is as free from… let's say, their own feelings about others as Smithson was. He did what he could."

I looked up at him.

"It was all open and above board," Xinhan added. "Everything went through the banks. Smithson had influence with banking firms. He saw to it that banks cooperated and we were given fair deals."

"That was probably a big help."

"He had a genuine interest in the Asian community in this city. His childhood experiences affected him deeply, from what I understand. Smithson wanted our community to thrive. He wanted us to be a bigger force in the city. He told me once that the surest way to more lasting power was to get involved politically."

"He was right," I said. "You can't depend on other people to have your interests at heart."

"The Chinese community here is learning. Smithson knew a lot of politicians and exerted influence on our behalf."

"He obviously enjoyed taking a hand in things for Chinatown."

"Please don't think he had a patronizing, colonial mentality. He wasn't like that. No one I know ever felt that way about him."

"I'll take your word for it. Sounds like he was pretty generous with the connections he had." I paused and looked at him. "I'm grateful for the information, Xinhan.

"I thought you had Wheeler figured for an innocent bystander at the spa," Luke said.

"Still do. It never hurts to know a victim's background. Sometimes things aren't what they seem."

"We've got to go. Clean Living doesn't run itself and Xinhan promised me he could get my housecleaners into several new condos and businesses. So, we have some talking to do." Luke stood up and Xinhan followed suit.

"I may have a few more questions depending on what else I uncover. That okay with you, Xinhan?" I asked and stood to see them out.

"Luke knows how to get hold of me," he said and smiled.

I nodded. I caught the double meaning.

"I'll call you later. Some things I need to tell you," Luke said.

That meant he was bursting with juicy news or gossip. I guessed it had to do with the elegant Xinhan.

I watched them leave, wondering how much Xinhan really knew about Wheeler. Like why he was at the spa that night? Was he one of Brad's investors? Was he gay? Or, both? Or did Wheeler play a more integral role in the case? Xinhan wouldn't know all the answers but he might know something. Even if it was a detail meaning nothing to him, it could make a difference and give me a lead.

After they left the office, I sat back in my chair and the aroma of coffee tickled my nose. Before filling my cup, I decided to call a few of Brad's clients. If I got anything, the day wouldn't be wasted.

Half an hour later, I'd made twenty calls only five of which connected. Of course, none of them recalled anything unusual during their sessions.

About to put the list aside and get some coffee, I noticed Ricky Sorba's name heading up the next page and Anton's notation next to Sorba's name: "Extremely rude"

I figured I should give the right-wing nut a call myself. I dialed the number Brad listed.

"Sorba."

"Marco Fontana. I'd…"

"How'd you get this number, pal?" His grating voice crackled with annoyance.

"Got it from Brad Lopes. You're on his client list."

"Don't know the guy. Who'd you say you are?"

"I'm investigating the murder of Mr. Lopes. You were a client of his."

"I deal with a lotta people, pal. What's this murder got to do with me?" His voice lost some of its bravado.

"Mr. Lopes was a masseur. You were a client. I'm questioning as many…"

"Listen up , pal. I don't deal with fags. Not queer masseurs or queer anything. I was never a client of this faggot. Got it?"

"Never said he was gay. Looks like you know more than…"

Next thing I heard was a click and some dialtone.

I needed coffee. As soon as I stood to fill my cup, Olga buzzed me.

"Is man waiting to be seeing you."

"Who is it?"

"Is waiting here Mr. Shooter… Shoeser…"

Had to be Shuster. Just as I had the thought, his angry voice hissed through the intercom, "It's Shuster! Shoo—ssster!"

"Send him in, Olga."

Shuster attempted making a grand entrance. Except his stubby little form wasn't made for grand entrances.

I glanced at the clock on my desk. It was past eleven.

"You call this first thing in the morning, Shuster? Maybe I should get into politics. I'd get more sleep."

"Always a wiseass. You think having my life threatened is a joke."

"Hey, I get threats on a regular basis. Its no big deal. Depending on who's making the threats."

"I don't know the thug who made this threat. He was the creep who spied on us at the café. I can't have this sort of..."

I interrupted him. "Just tell me what happened."

"Right before I called you last night, he threatened me. He's a psychopath. The look in his eyes was enough to make me vomit. There was nothing behind those eyes. He was just there to hurt me and enjoy it."

"Did he? Hurt you, I mean?"

"Well... n-no. No... not physically... No. That's not the point, Fontana."

"Like I asked, tell me exactly what happened and what he said."

"I'd left the office, headed for a late meeting at Kelley's headquarters. I thought something was odd, like someone was following me. I passed it off as caffeine jitters. I knew I should have turned on Broad, but I walked over on Juniper. It's shorter. All of a sudden this lunatic jumps me from behind and pulls me into some filthy alcove." Shuster paused. His breathing got heavier as he relived the event. He was scared of something.

"Want some water? Coffee?"

"W-water. Thanks."

I went to the mini-fridge and pulled a bottle of water for him. He took it and the act of opening the bottle and taking a drink calmed him.

"What'd the guy do then?"

"H-he pushed me against the wall and pressed his arm against my throat. I could hardly breathe. I couldn't squeeze out a sound." He swallowed more water. "I can still smell his breath. Smoke and... ugh... something, I don't know...something rotten...I don't know what it was."

"What did he say?"

"At first nothing. He just looked at me as if he was making sure I was the one he wanted. Then he stared into my eyes. Just stared. He's got strange eyes. Cold. Deadly."

"He eventually say something? Threaten you?"

"Yeah, but I don't know why," Shuster's voice shook, as if he were trying to forget something or hide something or make it all go away.

"What exactly did he say?"

"He told me to keep my mouth shut. Told me if I said anything…" He shuddered.

"What were his exact words, Shuster."

"I… I don't remember. He said I should keep my mouth shut. Or he'd…" Shuster paused. "Or… he'd… he pulled a knife then, with his other hand and held it up to my face. He still had his other arm on my throat. I couldn't make a sound. But he made sure I saw the knife and knew what he'd do. I… I don't know what he wanted. It had to be…"

"What?"

"It had to be connected to you. Something you're doing. One of your cases."

"Why pick on you then? What've you got to do with anything?"

"He saw me talking to you that night. He probably thinks you told me something. That's got to be it…" He took another swig from the water bottle.

Did I buy this crock? Maybe Shuster was assaulted. He seemed genuinely shaken. Something happened. He'd been threatened, that much I could believe. But I wasn't buying the details he put out. Was it the guy he claimed? Or, was it someone else? Like maybe a trick gone bad? Shuster was a big time political closet case.

Maybe he was telling the truth. Nah, I couldn't swallow that. He was telling a piece of the truth. That much I could buy.

"Look, Shuster, I'm not saying I don't believe you…"

"How can you not believe me? This is all your fault. If it wasn't for you…"

"Listen, prick, you came here asking for help. Now you're blaming me for your problems. Which do you want? Help or a boot out the door? 'Cause I don't have time for games."

"H-help. I need your help, Fontana. Even if it…"

"I need more, Shuster."

"More? What? Like money? What're you…"

"More convincing. Gimmie something I can go on. How do I know it was the same guy we saw that night? Could be somebody you're screwing in an alley and he turns on you. Could be you just want a scapegoat if some sex video turns up on somebody's radar. Like your boss. He gets wind of your hanky panky, and you're out on your ass. Am I right?"

"No! You're all wrong, Fontana. This was the guy who followed us that night. I swear."

"Say I believe you. What do you want me to do?"

"Stop him. He's dangerous. Keep him away from me."

"Tell you what, Shuster. This guy comes around again, tell him to see me. Tell him I'll take care of his problem."

"Like *that's* gonna happen. He'll cut my throat next time."

"Not if you do what he says and keep your trap shut."

"I don't know anything."

"Then you're home free. You can't talk about something you don't know anything about."

"You think so?" He relaxed into the chair and drank the rest of the water.

"Not really, Shuster. I don't think so at all." I watched his eyes grow wide. "I think it was dumb for you to come to my office. If that guy is actually keeping tabs on you, then he'll know you were here. He thinks you're reporting to me and he *will* slit your throat."

Shuster stood, a panicked look on his face.

"You... you're right. What was I thinking?" He pivoted left then right as if looking for a secret way out. "I... I've got to get out of here. Is there a way out that...?"

"If he saw you come in, it doesn't matter. If he didn't... There's the service area and loading bay at the back. The elevator gets you there. Lotta garbage, though. You won't smell so pretty when you get back to work. But, hey, you work in politics. Nothing smells good anyway."

He flew out of the office and down the hall to the elevator.

"Again boss frightens clients?" Olga asked after Shuster left. "You are not needing business to pay for new offices?"

I was still laughing when my cell phone rang.

"Fontana."

"Mr. Fontana, my name is Charlie Porter. You've been trying to reach me?"

Chapter 17

Charlie Porter agreed to meet at More Than Just Ice Cream. Said he wouldn't be comfortable meeting in the office which was just as well since it was lunchtime.

I arrived early and took a seat against the back wall, so we'd have some privacy. I felt a wave of anticipation that perhaps now some questions would be answered.

The waiter was new. Bouncy, my old favorite, wasn't on duty so I'd have to do without his permanent smile, sunny disposition, and skintight jeans. The new guy looked like an undernourished mouse with his mop of dull brown hair and glasses three sizes too large for his face. Cute in his own skinny-nerdy way, but he was no Bouncy.

"Can I get you something while you wait?" the Mouse asked.

"Just some coffee." I smiled up at him trying to remember the word my Great Aunt Gemma had for guys who looked like this.

He nodded and scurried over to the service area.

The sun poured in through the wall of windows, lifting my mood. I hoped Charlie could fill in some of the blanks Emily hadn't been able to. Emily assumed Brad told her everything but sometimes you want to protect the people you care about from some of the seamier things that happen. I suspected Brad hadn't told Emily the whole truth about everything.

Charlie was a different story. Brad might have confided in him. They worked the same beat, so to speak. They knew the trouble a masseur could get into, the risks and dangers of the work. It seemed Brad had trusted Charlie, giving him the keys to the spa, allowing him to work as a sub with long time clients. Yep, I was betting heavily that Charlie knew a lot Emily didn't.

The Mouse brought my coffee and carefully set it down. He stood back looking at me as if waiting for something. I grabbed some sugar packets, tore them open, and spilled their contents into the coffee. The Mouse continued to stare.

"Thanks for the coffee," I said, thinking that's what he wanted. He nodded and continued staring. The lunch crowd hadn't arrived and the other tables had already been served. The Mouse had time on his hands.

"I'll be back when your friend gets here," he squeaked finally. "If you need anything…"

I smiled and looked down at the newspaper I'd picked up on the way in. The little Mouse edged away.

People began entering in twos and threes but no Charlie. He said he'd be wearing something blue. Okay, he said "baby blue" to be specific. Blue's blue to me. So far, no one who entered wore anything remotely close to blue.

I went back to the newspaper. As I read, I heard the door whoosh open and shut a few times. Then I heard a voice.

"Hiii, sweetie. I haven't seen you in ages."

Looking up, I watched someone from the kitchen embrace a man wearing a blue, maybe even baby blue, tank top. When they broke the embrace, the kitchen man went back to his station and I got a clear look at the guy who had to be Charlie Porter.

Not what I expected.

Medium height, thirties, slender almost skinny, with a head of frizzy, unmanageable red hair, Charlie peered around the place as if looking for someone. His gaze settled on me and I waved him over. As he approached, I realized he was younger than I'd suspected. His lack of weight and scruffy facial hair contributed to the impression that he'd been around the track a few more times than he actually had.

"Marco," I said taking his smooth hand in mine.

"Charlie," he said. "Nice to meet the man behind the voice on all those messages."

"You're a hard man to pin down, Charlie."

"I kinda like it that way." He took my cue to sit.

"Makes things difficult for a guy in your business, doesn't it?"

"I do all right." He placed his canvas bag over the back of his chair.

The Mouse appeared at the table as if out of thin air. "Can I get you anything to drink before you order? Or... uh... are you guys ready? To order, I mean."

"Bring me some iced tea," Charlie said. "I'll be ready when you get back." He picked up a menu. "Got any favorites?"

Charlie looked at me and I saw he had gray eyes. Expressively sad gray eyes. Made me wonder if he knew what had happened to Brad. I'd never left any details in my messages.

"Everything's pretty much good." I waited for him to look over the menu then I cleared my throat.

"You ready?" he asked.

"I... yeah... I'm ready." I had little choice since the Mouse was setting the iced tea on the table.

"What can I get you guys?" He drew out an order pad and waited, pencil poised.

We ordered, the little Mouse scuttled off, and I decided to take the plunge and find out what Charlie knew.

"Charlie, I've got to ask you something..."

"Like do I know what's going on with Brad?"

"Do you know what's happened? Have you heard anything in the past few days?"

"I left town maybe three weeks ago. Could be longer. I've been helping take care of my father. He's totally incapacitated. When I'm there, I concentrate on him. I don't take calls. I don't do anything but help out with caregiving."

"Then I've got to tell you..."

"Something's happened to Brad." He sighed as if I'd added one more weight to his slender shoulders. "I kind of guessed as much from all the messages you left. You never said what happened, though. I suppose that means it's bad. Right?" He looked at me with sad expectation.

"Brad... I'm really sorry to have to tell you, Charlie, but Brad was murdered." I watched his eyes widen and become even sadder.

"Murdered? Mygod. I thought you were going to say he'd been beaten up, he's in the hospital. You know, he's never careful about where he goes on outcalls. Always keeps that spa open late and the door's usually unlocked. I thought maybe he'd been hurt. But... not... How? Why?" His hand shook as he reached for his water.

Charlie stared into my eyes as if searching for hope or a reason I was wrong.

"I'm sorry. Sorry to tell you like this."

"You're sure? He was... was murdered? How? Who did it?"

"The police are stumped and Emily asked me to investigate. She mentioned your name and gave me your number but I gather she didn't know you."

"No... no... she didn't... not really," Porter said. His voice became slow and dreamy. He faded out like an old radio.

"Charlie. Listen to me. Charlie?"

"Oh... I was... just remembering the last time I spoke to Brad. He was... all right. I never thought to call while I was away. I never call anyone when I'm with my family. It's just the way it is. I should've called Brad."

"There's nothing you could've done, Charlie. Not then. But now..."

"What can I do? I don't even know what happened."

"We're trying to narrow down possible leads. Emily mentioned a couple of things but she didn't know details."

"Poor kid. She must be feeling so alone right now. Brad and she only had each other."

"That's one reason I'm thinking maybe he spared her some details of his work."

"How so? He told her just about everything. That's what he said."

"Emily mentioned a guy named Johnny. That ring any bells for you?" I watched his face.

"Johnny?... Hmm... Johnny... well..." A small smile crossed Porter's face. "You probably mean Johnny Carney."

"Could be. Tell me about him." If this was the right Johnny, I now had a last name to track him with.

"Johnny Carney was Brad's client. Once, maybe twice. Then Brad asked me to take Johnny off his hands, so to speak. That's when Johnny started in on how much he loved Brad. Couldn't ever deal with anyone else. You know the deal."

"Emily thinks he stalked Brad."

"Johnny was harmless." Porter absently scratched at what passed for his facial hair.

"Nobody's harmless, Charlie. Nobody."

"Oh, Johnny is. He's like a little kid. I think the guy is kind of slow, if you know what I mean."

"How serious was the stalking?"

"I guess you could call it stalking." Porter smiled as if remembering. "He came around two, three times a week according to Brad. Sat in reception which is all he ever did. I saw him a few times when I was there. He's a peanut of a guy. Below average height. Big head. Forties and paunchy. He whines a lot but never does much of anything. He'd sit in reception for a while, then he'd leave."

"You ever take Johnny as a client, like Brad asked?"

"I would'a, but he only wanted Brad. Like I said, he claimed he was in love. Love. Whatever that is." Charlie sighed a deep, sad sigh.

"Did Brad ever say Johnny maybe carried a weapon?"

"Nah, Brad wanted to filed a complaint about the stalking. I've gotta laugh at that word, though. There was never a weapon and never any danger. Brad didn't want Johnny scaring away other clients is all. Which would'a been the basis for his complaint. Brad never followed through on it."

Balancing dishes, the Mouse brought our food and gingerly set everything down.

"Can I get you guys anything else?" He lingered, swaying like seaweed as he stood there.

"We're good, thanks." I smiled up at him. He blushed and moved off to another table.

"That it?" Porter asked. "You just wanted to know about Johnny?"

"You telling me there's something else I should know?" I already figured there were other things.

"I'm not sure. Y'know? There were things…"

"Like…?"

"Like Brad *was* worried about something or someone. It wasn't Johnny but he never told me about it. Just said he was afraid something would get out of hand."

"What?"

"He never said. Just said he was sorry he got involved and wished he had better sense. Whatever that meant."

"Did he mention a former boyfriend?"

"He mentioned he had one. An ex, I mean. Not a current boyfriend. He said the ex was a shit."

"That what he was worried about?"

"Could be. Coulda been something else."

"Why do you say that?"

"If you ask me… You are askin' me, aren't you?" Porter looked me in the eye and smiled. "Brad wasn't worried like boyfriend-worried, if you know what I mean. He was more worried than that."

"His ex was violent. Out of control. He tell you that? He tell you the boyfriend had put him in the hospital at least once?"

"N-no… mygod… no, Brad never told me any of that." Porter looked horrified. "Why? I mean, why'd he stay with that kind of man? I guess that puts everything in a new light."

"How so?"

"Brad coulda been upset over *that* kind of guy. I did get the sense there was some kind of physical threat involved. That's just my intuition. Brad never said that."

"He ever say a name? Like who might've threatened him? The ex's name maybe?"

"Well… not exactly…" Porter glanced from side to side as if he felt guilty about something.

"You remembering something, Charlie?" I could tell Porter was the kind of guy who knows lots more than he lets on. Probably because he had ways of learning things that might be considered unconventional at best. Sneakily intrusive is more likely the way he operated.

"I might be…" He looked as if he wanted to say more but was ashamed. "I kinda heard something once…"

"Wanna share, Charlie?" Easy to see he needed reassurance, or maybe absolution, for his methods. "Listen, Charlie, nobody's gonna blame you for overhearing something. Can't be helped sometimes." Overhearing, I was being nice. Porter was not the kind of guy who found things out accidentally. I saw that now.

"I did overhear something but…"

"Nobody has to know the information came from you. Understand? This is between us." Never hurts to say things like that even if you can't actually promise.

"It was just a conversation, y'know? Didn't make any sense. At least not until you told me about the violent boyfriend."

"What'd you hear?"

"I was cleaning up after a client left and I heard Brad talking on his phone. His voice was raised. Sounded kind of excited. Maybe frightened, now I think about it."

"Okay. Did you hear what he said?"

"Bits and pieces." Porter paused. "He said something about not expecting to be put on the spot. He also said he didn't like being forced to do anything against his will."

"Any names come up in this conversation?"

"Not that… well… I'm not sure it was a name. Sounded like a name. Like I said I could only hear so much."

"Try to remember what it was, Charlie."

"I thought I heard him say Nat or Natas. Or it coulda been Matz. Of course he coulda been talking about bath mats for all I know."

* * *

I made sure Charlie knew how do get in touch if he thought of anything else. He hadn't lied but he hadn't told me everything either.

My cell phone rang as I walked back to the office and Shim's name appeared on caller ID.

"What's up, Detective? Any progress?"

"No wonder you and Giuliani don't see eye to eye," Shim said. "You both have only one thing on your mind."

"And that would be... sex?"

"Now I see the other reason you and Giuliani don't get along," Shim laughed.

"Tell me you've got a lead that's gonna break the case."

"I was going to ask if you had time for a drink. I could bring you up to speed. But don't get your hopes up," Shim said.

"You mean about you asking me out for a drink, or..."

Shim was silent. I'd obviously crossed a line he wasn't ready to have me cross.

"We can do this over the phone, I guess," Shim said. "You have some time now?"

That was disappointing and encouraging at the same time. Maybe he was interested but couldn't deal with it except in his own way and time. Maybe I rowed out a little farther on that lake than he expected right then. Whatever it was, we were back at square one.

"Call me back in ten minutes, if you can. I'll be back in my office."

"In ten. Will do." Shim hung up without a good-bye. Must'a been a real a sore spot I'd hit.

I wondered if he'd ever try again or if I'd scared the pants off him. Too bad because I'd have liked scaring the pants off him. Okay, maybe not *scaring* them off.

As I walked, lost in thoughts about Shim and missed opportunities, I realized someone walked alongside on my right. I turned to see Sorba, the radio loud mouth, matching my stride, his shoulder touching mine in a too-close-for-comfort way.

"Sorba, what a pleasant surprise," I said.

He didn't respond. As I was about to speak again, I felt a large presence to my left. Same shoulder to shoulder maneuver, except this guy was built like a refrigerator. An industrial model.

"Great afternoon for a stroll, fellas." I kept my attention on Sorba.

"Yeah," Sorba said. "Nice day, Fontana. You wanna keep it that way?"

The two of them moved in and the squeeze was on. They obviously didn't want me slipping through their meaty fingers.

"I'm on my way back to the office. What about you guys? Goin' to an all-you-can-eat raw meat buffet? I hear there's a good…"

"Shut it, Fontana," Sorba said. "I'm thinkin' we'll go to your office with you. I got a little somethin' to say and my friend here… Oh, excuse my manners. This is my good buddy Hatch. Short for Hatchet. Don't let the name fool you, Hatch is a cruel sonofabitch. He'd just as soon rip off your face as look at you."

"Hatch! You remind me of a guy I used to know named Moose. Big chump in the fight game. Mind if I call you Moose?"

"Funny man, Fontana. Maybe, some morning, assuming you get to see another morning, the business *you're* in. Some morning, I'll have you on my show," Sorba said. "You can crack wise there all day. My audience loves a wiseass."

"Then I guess your ratings are up? What can I do for you?"

"It'll keep till we get to your office."

The walk was stiff, trapped as I was between two slabs of beef. We did a kind of prison shuffle as we moved through the gayborhood. The sidewalks were crowded and we got some pretty odd looks. I can only imagine the ideas people got when they saw us. For my part, I tried to figure out how to get rid of the goons. Probably the best course was to get them to the office, hear them out, then kick them out.

"We're here, boys. Let's go up and you can tell me all your secrets."

Chapter 18

The "boys" squeezed into the elevator with me. Not that there wasn't plenty of room for all of us. They just didn't want *me* to have much. I was able to breathe again once we got to my floor.

When we walked through the outer office, Olga glanced up. I placed a finger to my lips signaling her to keep calm. She glared at the two men, her eyes beady with suspicion.

"Boss is needing coffee for guests?" This was Olga's way of asking if I needed her to call for help.

"Nah, sugarplum. Not worth the effort. Besides these jokers won't be here long."

I opened the door to my office and walked in, keeping my back to them. The two nubby goons were right on my heels. Sorba, a loud-mouthed, right-wing fanatic, and a cretin on issues I cared about, was undoubtedly living out his tough-guy fantasy. His every move was probably copied from things he'd seen on television. It was comic.

"So, what can I do for you, Sorba?" I flopped into my chair, eased back, and stared at him. I had a gun in the top drawer. Easy to reach.

Sorba, eyes fixed on me, walked to the front of my desk, leaned in and stared. His knuckle-dragging goon, with what I suspected was a gun in his jacket pocket, stood to one side taking everything in.

"You and one of your butt boys keep callin' about some dead fag masseur," he said, then sat in a chair facing my desk.

"You know why that is, right?" I stared into his eyes.

Silence. Of course, he knew.

"C'mon. No idea why you'd get these calls? How about you Moose?" I looked at the goon. "Any idea why your boss gets calls about a gay masseur?"

Moose looked confused. Like he thought he had to supply an answer but had no idea what the answer could possibly be.

I looked at Sorba again. "Comin' back to you now, bucko?"

Sorba looked like a pot aching to boil over. His eyes narrowed.

"I have no fucking idea, you goddamned idiot. That's why I'll break your fucking neck if I get bothered again." His pasty face went raw meat red in under five seconds.

"I'll try to worry about your threats when I have time," I said. "For now, let me give you a clue. Personally, I think you have this clue tucked away already, but you don't like people knowing. You got called because you're on a list. You're on the gay masseur's client list."

"I'm not on a fucking list. Somebody's…"

"You're on Brad's list of clients. A long time regular. Big tipper. You were his client even before he opened the spa. He's got cute little notes about what you like and where you like it. The kind of massage oil you like and…" I turned to the goon. "Hey, Moose. I should maybe show you the notes… your boss is gonna need a new pair of hands takin' care of him. Maybe you…"

"Shut the fuck up!" Sorba stood and shoved my desk against me. "You got no idea what you're getting' yourself into. Try to ruin me, and you'll find out what you're up against. Just like that…" Sorba stopped abruptly.

"Just like Brad. You telling me that…"

"I'm tellin' you nothing, Fontana. I don't know the fag." Sorba rushed around the desk to confront me.

I towered over him and was in much better shape. He pushed forward anyway, getting right into my face.

"You made the appointments, bucko. Not me. You asked for the special services." I placed a hand on his chest and shoved him back so hard he nearly toppled over, but Moose came to his rescue.

"You got no idea what I can do to you." Sorba swiped a hand across my desk scattering the papers, my mug, and everything onto the floor.

"You can make it all go away, Sorba. Tell me you have an alibi for Friday night. Then I forget all about you. See?"

"I don't have to tell you a fucking thing." He poked me in the chest. "Not one goddamned fucking thing."

"Nope, you're right. You don't hafta tell me a thing. After all who am I?"

"Goddamned right. Who the fuck are you?"

"When the police ask, I'll tell them you're kinda excitable. That you have a reputation you'll do anything to protect. You'd hate anybody finding out you're a… what did you call Brad… oh yeah, a fag. You're a fag who likes kinky massages with a hot guy. And you'll do anything to protect your reputation. Think the cops will get the picture?"

I watched him approach the boiling point again.

"Tell you what *I'm* thinking," I continued. "You feared Brad would tell your secrets. You didn't hit the big time until after you'd been seeing Brad for a few years, right? So, he was excited having a big-time radio personality naked on his table. Maybe you thought you needed to shut him up. Or maybe you wanted to scare him. Then it all went wrong. Cops are gonna get the same idea? Especially if I give 'em that idea."

"That *never* happened." He got into my face again. His breath was stale. Spittle flecked his lips. "That's not me you're talking' about. I *hate* fags. I *hate* you people. You're all sick."

"That's motivation. You hated him. You hate all of us. What I think? You hate yourself, too, enough to kill somebody else."

"You're a crazy motherfucker, Fontana." He turned away. "People say you're crazy. Now I see. My audience will love this shit. You'll be real popular. All your fuckin' fag secrets, everything you do. I'll talk it up every day."

"Gonna tell your audience why you're targeting me? You could tell 'em about the way you like having a guy stick…"

"Fuck you!"

"You have no alibi for the night Brad was murdered." I picked my coffee mug off the floor, the handle was broken. Coffee had splattered the paperwork. "If the press gets wind of things, y'know? I mean, look at that singer who… all he did was…"

Sorba swung his arm, knocked over a chair, and motioned Moose to his side. There was an odd look in Moose's eye. He'd just gotten a dose of Too Much Information. He moved to Sorba's side but occasionally glanced over at Sorba as if he didn't know him anymore.

"Tell these lies to anybody, Fontana, and I'll make sure you meet up with people who are experts at things you don't even wanna think about."

Before I could say anything, Olga buzzed me. I hit the button on the intercom, ignoring Sorba.

"Is Police Detective on line. You can be speaking now?"

"Put him through, sugarplum." After a moment I heard Shim's voice.

"Mr. Fontana, you got a minute? I wanted to catch you up…"

"Hey, detective," I said. "I've got a couple of clients here but you can come right up. They'll be going…" I slid a glance up at Sorba and smiled.

"Well… I hadn't intended….," Shim hesitated. Naturally, he had no idea what was going on and must've thought I'd lost my mind.

"It's no problem at all."

"What the hell. I'll be there. I'm not far."

"See you in a few, Detective." I hung up and smiled at Sorba.

"This must be your lucky day, Sorba. The police will be here. You can tell him all about hating fags. And you can tell him where you were Friday night."

Sorba glared at me.

"One word, Fontana. One word gets out, you won't know what hit you."

I stared at him as if I knew more about him than he did about himself and watched as a thousand emotions played across his face.

He growled in frustration, then placed both hands on my desk and leaned in to face me. "I'm not like you. I never was like you, and I never will be." His voice shook. He'd lost his confidence.

I glanced at the clock. "Hang around. The detective will be here soon."

"I have friends in the Department. High up the food chain. They won't let you pull me down. I give the word and you sink, not me."

With his eyes, Sorba signaled Moose. The lumbering piece of flesh looked around the room. Moving forward he elbowed a picture of me shaking hands with the former Mayor shattering it. Trapped behind my desk, I watched as he stomped toward me. Before I could move, Moose lashed out one meaty hand and grabbed my throat. He was quick for a slab of ham.

I began seeing those proverbial stars but I didn't budge. When I refused to give them the reaction they wanted, Moose's hand squeezed tighter. I felt my eyes bulge and knew I had to move before I passed out. I brought my knee up forcefully and sent a message to Moose through his balls. His eyes crossed and his grip loosened. I shoved him away and gulped air.

Moose stumbled backward, crashed into a wall destroying another picture of me standing with some pop star. Startled and still holding his breath, Moose wobbled until he came to a stop beside Sorba.

"You were lucky today, Fontana. A lot worse can happen." Sorba warned. "Like permanently worse."

He and Moose moved toward the door. Sorba nonchalantly, Moose as if he still felt my knee in his groin.

"Lemme know when you want me to appear on your show, Sorba. Got a lot to tell your audience." My voice hoarse. I rubbed my throat sure Moose's handprint was permanently etched there.

* * *

It took Shim more than a few minutes to get to the office, giving me time to clean up. Olga had poked her head in wanting to help, but things were under control.

Sorba was violently worried about his reputation. I guess a right wing audience wouldn't be happy if their idol turned out to be gay and loved male masseurs who gave happy endings.

I swept up the glass and thought about Sorba as a possible suspect. Especially if Brad had threatened to out Sorba for some reason. But why? Maybe Sorba tried to pressure Brad into something Brad didn't want to do? He never revealed client secrets. If he'd threatened to do that to Sorba, there'd have been a serious reason.

There was a sinister explanation. Something I didn't want to believe. Feelings aside, though, I had to entertain the probability that Brad threatened to blackmail Sorba for money. Brad was driven to make the spa successful. All he needed was money.

Maybe Brad thought threatening someone like Sorba, a homophobe and a bigot, was justified. I couldn't see Brad doing that, but I'd seen people do far worse over money.

Only Brad and Sorba knew the answers. Brad was dead and Sorba was effectively dead inside. He'd never be honest with himself let alone anyone else.

Olga walked into the office, surveyed things, and gave me an enigmatic look.

"I am having new file," she said as she waved a manila folder. "If I am putting folder on desk, maybe is getting lost."

"It'll be fine, gorgeous. Just put it on top of everything."

Olga looked from the desk to the floor, back at the desk, then at me.

"Desk is empty. Floor is full. I am putting file on top of everything on floor or on empty desk?"

I laughed in spite of her implied criticism. "Put it on the desk. I promise not to lose it."

"*Da*. Olga believes when Olga is seeing." She plopped the folder onto the desktop with a satisfying slap, then turned to leave.

Before she shut the door behind her, I was at the desk paging through the folder. She'd found the basics on Wheeler as well as a bundle of news items on the man. He was a quietly wealthy businessman with his fingers in several concerns including a development firm but he seemed to spend most of his time fostering new entrepreneurs, helping start-ups, and generally helping keep Philadelphia businesses thriving.

His firm had offices on Delancey, a swank address in town. I put it on my list of places to visit.

A soft knock at the door made me look up as Shim entered the room. I guessed he'd told Olga he was expected, maybe even flashed his badge, since she hadn't announced him.

"Dae. Welcome back. Have a seat," I said.

Shim sat across from me with a serious look on his face which I attributed to his earnest attitude toward police work. That and the fact he was new at it, so he took everything with a big dose of serious.

"You said you had some news..." My voice was still hoarse.

"You have a cold or something?" Shim didn't miss much. He looked at me and as his gaze swept over my face he obviously saw the red marks on my neck. "What happened to you?"

"Bad day," I said, not wanting to go into details just then. "Being a private eye has it's down side."

Shim stared, a look of concern softening his features.

"Tell you all about it another time. You said you had news…"

"That's an optimistic interpretation of what I said, Marco." A quirky half smile crinkled his face. "I said I wanted to catch you up on what was going on."

"You probably hoped I might add something useful to your notebook. Right?"

"Like they say… one good turn…" He took his notebook from his inside jacket pocket and flipped it open.

"I'm all about good turns, Dae. Lemme hear what you've got."

"That's just it, Marco. We don't have a hell of a lot. As far as your friend's case, I'm waiting on the autopsy and ballistics. Like I told you, the murder of the journalist takes precedence. The Mayor wants it fast tracked."

"Figures. Got anything interesting on that case?" I wondered if they'd made any connection to Brad's case. Though I had my suspicions, I didn't have a solid link or I'd mention it. All I had was a hunch and they don't buy you much when you're trading favors.

"Ballistics are in and so is the autopsy report on Vega. Poor bastard wasn't dead when they tossed him in the river. Shot him enough times. Must've been strong."

"Gruesome way to go. Any ideas why he was murdered?"

"Lots of them. Take a look at the stories he worked. Sketchy deals, corruption, criminal organizations. A reporter who smokes out dangerous people is asking to be sliced and diced. Not many journalists would touch the stuff he wrote about. You ever take a look at AllNewsAllNow.com? They specialize in edgy and controversial. The list of people Vega exposed? He's lucky he wasn't shredded a lot sooner."

"So, nothing solid?"

"Nope. The crazy editor at All News All Now claims she doesn't know much. Said Vega worked alone, left no notes, and was kind of paranoid. Only guy he'd work with was a photographer."

"You find him?"

"She gave me a description. Curly-headed, scruffy, and young was all she'd say." Shim shook his head.

"Sounds like a kid I spotted the day I discovered the body. Outside the spa. He was watching everything."

"You think he…"

"Had something to do with all this? Odds are he's some kinda paparazzi wannabe. Probably wanders around looking for photo opportunities he can turn into cash. All the action at the spa caught his attention."

"Could be…," Shim was being thorough. He'd grasp at any possibility same as I would. This case must've had him banging his head against a wall. "Think you can remember what he looked like? Enough to describe him to a department artist?"

"Maybe," I said. "Probably." Not before I tried finding him to see what I could get out of him. "I'll give you a call."

"Do that. Soon." Shim became all official again.

"Anything else you can give me? Giuliani won't say much when I talk to her except she didn't object when I said I'd be looking into things on my own."

Shim's face hardly betrayed his surprise at this news. I'd hate playing poker with him.

"I'd say that's something. She's usually a hard case. But the bodies keep piling up. Even she's treading water," Shim said.

"She might be in over her head, but I'm not sitting around and waiting. Keep me in the loop, will ya? Especially now you know she's given me tacit approval."

"I'll expect the same. Like you coming in to work with the artist."

"I hate to end this gabfest, but I've gotta get ready for tonight."

"Been a long day for me. You working another case tonight?"

"It's my other job. My assistant over at Bubbles is off tonight so I've gotta be there. You know the place?"

"In passing." Shim said not giving anything away.

"You oughta come have a drink with me one night. On the house, of course."

Shim said nothing. Instead, he intently scribbled something in his notebook.

"Tonight's the Best Buns contest. That's always fun. Maybe you'd like to…" I teased.

"We'll talk another time," he said, all business. He stuffed his notebook back into his jacket pocket.

* * *

"Be seein' you, Olga." I opened the door to leave. Shim had gone a while before and I was feeling frustrated with the case. Dinner and a hot shower would help.

"Is nice man?"

"Who… Detective Shim? He's a cop. I'm trying to get him to share information. "

"Olga has eyes. Maybe nice detective is needing warning?"

"Warning? About what?"

"About boss. Yes? Boss has look in eyes. Boss is wanting more than informations from nice Detective. Olga is seeing this. But I am only secretary. What must I know?"

"Olga, what would I do without you?"

"Sit in middle of mess and cry."

I laughed all the way to the elevator. Because it was true. Olga organized my office and a big part of my life. Before she came on board I'd gone through ten others who'd been unable to cope. Not Olga. She took command the minute she entered the office, even before I hired her. She knew what was needed and how to get things done. Maybe that's why she lasted through four marriages and was still standing.

Walking up Walnut on the way back to my condo, I had to pass the Pat Kelley campaign offices and decided to check in on Shuster. The place bustled with activity. As the primary drew closer, staffers grew more frantic. My brother Nick had been involved in someone's failed campaign for mayor a few years back and I'd seen firsthand just how crazy things got.

A block away, I saw Josh Nolan leaving Kelley's HQ. He looked agitated. Now that was unusual. The Chief of Staff for Terrabito, Kelley's rival, seen exiting Kelley's command center? Interesting in the extreme.

By the time I reached the door, Nolan was long gone. I walked in and hardly anyone noticed. People worked the phones, stuffed envelopes, engaged in mini-conferences, and generally attended to the necessities of a campaign. One more guy bouncing through the office was invisible. I had free passage through the chaos.

Shuster's office was at the back, from what he'd told me. There was a half open door at the rear of the room. I knocked and the door opened wider revealing Shuster and Kelley in the midst of a heated altercation.

Shuster turned toward the door, his face showing the strain of the campaign and the argument. I wondered if they'd been arguing about Nolan.

"What? What is it?" When Shuster saw me, his eyes widened.

"Checking in. Wanted to give you an…"

"This isn't a good time, Mr. Fontana."

"Go ahead. See what the man wants," Kelley snapped. "You and I aren't getting anywhere."

"Nice to see you again," I lied. The little gray man, angry and sour, was unpleasant.

"Sure. Where was it we met?"

"A couple'a times. Anyway, I'll just take a minute of your man's time."

"Don't rush on my account. He's not listening to reason." Kelley riffled through some papers then pulled out a cell phone and tapped in a number.

Shuster pushed me gently out the door and followed, shutting Kelley out.

"What're you doing here?" he hissed. First Nolan barges in, now you."

"What did the hot Mr. Nolan want?"

"Not that it's any of your business but his boss was steamed about something and demanded a meeting with Kelley. Personally delivered the invite. Kelley made Nolan feel like a worthless slug."

"That why he was so agitated?"

"That and another matter."

"Not gonna tell me, are you?"

"What exactly are you doing here anyway?"

"Just checkin' in. You see that character again?"

"I haven't. No thanks to you." Shuster looked wild-eyed. "What am I gonna tell Kelley? He'll want to know why you were here. He's a fucking micromanager. He'll want every detail."

"Tell him it's none of his business."

"You don't tell a man like Kelley things are not his business. He thinks the world revolves around him. Takes a shit and expects the press to ask what color it was."

"Let me handle it." I pushed past Shuster and into to the office.

"No! No. What are you…" Shuster wasn't quick enough to stop me and his voice trailed off as I entered the office.

"Well?" Kelley asked imperiously. "You finished? We have a campaign to run."

"Wanted to thank you for his time. I needed some information about the campaign event the other night. I'm working a case."

"Yes, well, and you're… what? You're investigating a case? Is Shuster invol… Shuster are you involved in something I should know about?" Kelley stood abruptly, the tufts of hair standing out from the sides of his grayish-pink dome made him comical.

"A murder. Not that your boy had anything to do with it. Not as far as we can see…" I don't know why I said that. Watching the two of them waltz around the idea was entertaining.

"No! Sir, I had nothing to do with anything. Fontana here needed some…"

"If the primary wasn't around the corner, I'd fire your ass and find someone competent."

"But… I'm…" Shuster looked puzzled and confused.

"I'll let you two work things out," I said, "Don't go too hard on him. The campaign's almost over."

I turned and left. Shuster slammed the door and the yelling started. I could hear them argue as I pushed my way out of the bustling headquarters.

The crowds and noise at Bubbles would be a pleasure after this.

Chapter 19

"Hey, Marco! You entering the buns competition? I really wanna see 'em."

I turned to see one of the old regulars planted on a barstool, laughing suggestively. He lifted his glass in salute then gulped down its contents.

"Not tonight, Dale. How about you signing up?"

"Couple more a'these, I might just take my pants down. It'd be more fun to see *your* tush."

"Don't drop your drawers yet, Dale. Sign up and get on stage first."

I climbed the stairs to my office allowing the rest of the day to peel away with each step I took. Anton had requested the night off to help Ty who was recuperating physically but having a difficult time emotionally. I told Anton to take a few days if it'd help. I had plenty of guys who could work the contest and keep things rolling. Jean-Claude, Bruno, and Kent would lend a hand with the Best Buns crowd.

I entered the office and tucked myself behind my desk. Jean-Claude had made photocopies of entry forms. Bruno would get the stage ready and put the Best Buns "screen" in place. Jean-Claude and Kent would keep track of contestants. All I had to do was schmooze with customers while waiting for showtime. Then I'd MC the show and keep my fingers crossed that nothing went too far off script. You never knew what would happen when men take off their clothes for an audience. Always had to think a few steps ahead.

I was about to look for Bruno when Jean-Claude sauntered into the office.

"Jean-Claude," I said, with a little more frost than I intended.

"Marco. Did you get the copies?"

"Right here. You're gonna be in charge of collecting forms and making sure the IDs are legitimate. You ever do this?"

"I have watched Anton do this many times."

I'll bet you've watched him, I thought. Instead, I said, "I'll hang with you for the first few signups. Most important thing is to check IDs."

"I did a good job, no?" Jean-Claude's eyes twinkled reflecting the office lights.

"With the forms? Sure."

"No, at your office. I told you I would work well for you, no? And...?"

"You did. You were a big help," I said. I felt annoyed with him and was afraid it would show. Whatever I thought was going on between Jean-Claude and Anton clouded my judgment. The kid had been a big help and I'd never complimented him. "Yeah, Jean-Claude, you did a great job. Never did thank you for that."

"This means I will be able to help again? Yes? Maybe on this case?"

"Let's see what..."

"But I have already made the proof, no? I did a good job?"

"Right now the case is stalled. When something comes up I'll let you know."

"It's a deal." Jean-Claude smiled and put out his hand.

I shook hands reluctantly, unable to shed my feelings. Jean-Claude was sweet and actually a good worker. Maybe I assumed too much about him and Anton. Maybe I'd read things into situations that weren't actually there. Whatever it was, though, it felt real to me, and I couldn't put it aside. At the same time, I wondered why I felt I had any right to intrude into Anton's life. We'd made no commitments, and that was my doing.

"You see Anton today?" I had to ask.

"No. He says he will be helping Ty which will be difficult. Then he wants what he calls the 'alone time.' So I have not bothered him."

"You and Anton seem to get along well…"

"Oh, Anton and I are like the two peas in a pot." He smiled, and it was one of those lopsided, masculine, spine tingling smiles.

"You mean pod. Yeah, sure seems like…"

Before I could dig a deeper hole, Bruno walked in.

"Boss man. How's tricks?" His gruff voice rumbled through the room. Topless, his bronzed skin and perfect pecs dazzled the eye. He carried himself with a macho grace and swagger, his compact muscular body conveying power and energy.

"You sure you're ready for tonight? You've never handled contestants before."

"Got my whip, what else do I need to keep them in line?"

"Funny man."

"Who's bein' funny? I seen guys when they enter this contest, they're all outta control. They need a whip to make 'em behave." Bruno produced a coiled bullwhip from behind his back.

"You weren't kidding," I said.

"I never kid, Marco. You know that."

"Tonight how about we simply use persuasion. Keep the beatings to a minimum. Is everything ready?"

"We need to check out the screen. Comin'?" Bruno asked.

"Yep." I turned to Jean-Claude. "See me tomorrow, we'll see if anything turns up." I didn't know what that'd be but I'd think of something. "Right now you should set up backstage."

He nodded, took the forms, and left.

* * *

We made sure the "buns" screen was intact. The large wall-like structure on wheels had five rounded holes for contestants to show their cheeks to an eager audience. Then, I took a spin around the bar to scope out potential trouble in the crowd.

The contest wasn't for another hour or so and already the place was packed. Stan would be happy with the cash receipts and he had me to thank for that. Since we'd struck a deal to let me use Bubbles as the base for

StripGuyz, he's hardly ever had a bad night. The only off times came when the Pennsylvania Liquor Control Board found violations where there weren't any. Even the smallest thing can shut you down quicker than a politician can lie.

This is why I needed eyes on the crowd.

Kent stood toward the back and nodded when I approached. He usually spotted trouble before the customer thought about it. He'd be graduating soon and looking for a "real" job.

"How's it looking?"

"We've got it covered," he said, all official.

"I'll announce last call for contestants, but we've got quite a few already." I laughed.

"Shout if you need me," Kent said.

My "last call" announcement cut through the happy chatter and I watched people make last minute decisions to bare their asses. The convivial party atmosphere, not to mention free flowing liquor, often made people jump into the contests we held. The results were always fun.

Scanning the crowd, I noticed a face I recognized. He wasn't wearing his photographer's vest with its gazillion pockets. He looked uncomfortable. Could be his first time in a gay bar. Could also be he had a purpose and was anxious. Realizing how paranoid he was to be known as Vega's photographer, I understood why he might be nervous. What ever the reason, I didn't want to spook him before I could talk to him. I decided on a different approach.

I signaled Kent. He quickly moved to my side.

"See that guy? Curly hair, scraggly beard?" I nodded in the direction of the photographer.

Kent peered at him. "Yep. Is he trouble?"

"He might have some useful information on the case I'm working. I need to get to him without him running off.

"I'll approach him from the other direction and engage him in conversation."

"My thought exactly. I'll come up behind him and he'll have nowhere to go."

"It'll take a minute to circle around. Soon as you see me talk to him, move in, " Kent said. The sparkle in his eyes told me he enjoyed this.

"Go," I said, and Kent moved quickly but without urgency.

Keeping my eye on the photographer, I edged over a little at a time so I could reach him as soon as Kent showed up.

The photographer seemed to be sizing things up, as if figuring out good camera angles. Still jittery, he hadn't turned in my direction. Seeing me heading toward him might make him bolt.Unless he'd come here knowing I'd be here.

Kent's head bobbed through the crowd of men who gazed at him longingly. Kent broke through just short of where the photographer stood. I watched as he paused to collect himself then sauntered over to the photographer. Standing next to the guy, he asked a question.

That was my cue. I moved in and stood next to the photographer in seconds.

"I've been looking for you, man. Funny you should turn up here," I said.

The photographer glanced up at me then at Kent. I stood close enough to feel his body tense. But there was no indication he'd run. If he tried, Kent was blocking his way.

"I… I was…"

"You were looking for me. Am I right?" I said.

"You were outside that spa." He paused. "I wanted to talk."

"You know something? Something that can help?"

"I know what I saw and what Pete told me. But… it's not much. I don't even know if it means anything. All I do is take pictures. That's it. I don't get involved…"

"This is no place to talk."

"Wh-why not? It's public… I like…" He glanced around nervously.

"Best reason it's not a good place to talk. Too many ears."

"Where then?" He looked apprehensive.

"My office upstairs."

"O-okay." He waited for me to lead the way.

"Kent." I clapped him on the shoulder. "Thanks for your help. I've gotta talk to Mr.…." I looked over at the photographer.

"Tell you later," he said.

"I've gotta talk with Mr. Tell-You-Later. I'll need someone to coordinate the contest, if I don't get down in time. Somebody's got to MC and keep things moving."

"Okay, who?"

"I was thinking *you*, Kent. You've seen a hundred of these. You can handle it."

"I hate speaking in front of people." Kent's voice a shaky whisper.

"Believe me, they won't care what you say. They probably won't even *hear* what you say. They'll be glued to the asses on display and won't notice anything else. I guarantee."

"B-but you'll get back down before I have to go on, right?"

"There's plenty of time before it starts. I'll be here."

I left Kent wondering what he'd do if I wasn't back in time and led the photographer to my office. The hall was relatively empty since fewer dancers worked on contest nights. Four or five guys in g-strings stood waiting to go onstage. Laughter filtered through the door of the dressing room where the rest of the dancers gathered.

The photographer peered around at the setting and the dancers as if discovering new subjects for his photo work. His wide-eyed expression was almost comical.

"Never even thought about male strippers as subjects, have you?"

"It never occurred to me. Really didn't know about this whole world. I mean I know about gay life and all. I'm not... y'know... not gay. But I know about it. Not this though..."

Opening the door, I allowed him to enter first, then shut the door behind me and locked it.

"Why'd you lock the door?" Edging away from me he backed into a wall. Not hard to do since the office was a sardine can.

"So we won't be interrupted. Don't worry, you're safe. I've had my man quota for the day." I grinned, hoping he'd relax.

He didn't.

I motioned for him to sit at my desk. He looked at it as if wondering where the restraints were hidden. Satisfied there was nothing untoward, he sat and looked up at me expectantly.

"Okay, then…You sought me out, so you've obviously got things to tell me. Am I right?" I half sat on the desk.

"I can't say I know much."

"Why'd you come looking for me?"

"I saw you there… that day. When they found the guy at the spa. I saw you there, man. So…"

"That led you here tonight, why?"

"People talk, y'know? They say you're nowhere on this case."

"Word gets around." I wondered who this guy knew. "You're right. I got nothing. Nothing that amounts to much."

"What I hear, you hit a total dead end."

"Maybe you don't hear so good. Doesn't matter anyway. I'm not goin' away."

"Can't say I'm gonna be much help."

"Think you know something that'll crack the case?"

"Anything's possible…"

"Cut the paranoid act. Let's start with your name."

Hesitating, his eyes searched my face for reassurance. I didn't give him any.

"You can't be honest about your name, what good is anything you say?"

"J-Jenks…"

"That's better," I said.

"I… Not sure why I came here… "

"You worked with Peter Vega." I decided on another tack.

"On and off. It wasn't like a regular thing. When he needed something, he'd call."

"Now he's dead, and you believe it's connected to his work. Right?"

"Hadda be, man. The dude got into real bad shit sometimes. Made enemies. That's why I took pictures, collected my money, and never asked for credit. I don't need crazy fucks on my back. Not like it was Pulitzer work anyway."

"Was Vega at the spa the night Brad was killed?"

"He… Pete was supposed to be there. Told me to meet him. Said he needed pictures… y'know… of the people."

This wasn't exactly proof the deaths were connected. It was closer than I'd gotten so far, but only if he knew Vega had actually been at the spa.

"Did he show up? What happened that night?"

"I waited across the street. That's how we do it. I never go in ahead of Pete. I'm in and out in a hurry. I don't want people rememberin' my face. I won't go into the fucked-up places he picks unless he's there to cover me…" Jenks paused, looked lost in thought. "Pete was a good guy, y'know. One of those crusader types. Enjoyed helping people, liked uncovering rotten stuff and making it right. I admired him even if I was too chicken shit to put my name to anything. I admired the guy."

"I've seen some of his work online. I know what he was capable of."

"That kind of work makes enemies. He exposed hypocrites. Especially the high and mighty ones. That really stirs up the shit."

"Vega knew the risks."

"Yeah. I guess."

"Did you see him at all that night?"

"He always called me once he got to a site. He knew I wouldn't budge unless he was there. That night he never called. I waited. Waited a long time. He never called and I never saw him go in or out of the place."

"What'd you do?"

"What was I gonna do, man? I went home. I had other gigs. It happened with Pete sometimes. His subjects don't show, or they get camera shy."

"You know what he was working on that night? What photos he wanted?"

"Oh man, Pete was secretive. Like me times a hundred. He only told me the basics. The dude was paranoid. Never told me much and honestly, man, I never wanted to know too much. I took the shots and got out."

"He told you at least something, right? He didn't keep you totally in the dark."

"He… sometimes… yeah."

"What'd he tell you this time? Anything about the story he was working or the people?"

"Coulda been a couple of things from what I remember. Of course, coulda been something else, too. That's the way Pete worked."

"What were the possibilities?" I coaxed.

"Pete was workin' two maybe three pieces. One was domestic abuse. How the police still don't take it seriously. Especially with the gays." He paused, looked up at me apologetically. "Pete made a few enemies on the force doin' those interviews. I heard about a couple of crazy gay guys who wanted to punch out his lights."

"And the other story?"

"Had to do with some trial. Eastern European dude up for murder... no... kidnapping, maybe... or somethin' else. Kon... Branich... Dubich... Odak... who knows?... I try to forget names. Less trouble."

"What about the trial? Why was he investigating it?"

"Think he mentioned somethin' about jury tampering or... maybe a dirty lawyer... some trial thing... I don't know. It's always serious shit with Pete. That's how he rolled. He had a sense for that stuff."

"You said there might've been a third piece?"

"Could'a been. He mentioned contracts and lawyers or maybe it was politicians. He was really vague on that one. But it sounded like it could be hot."

"What kind of contracts? Any..."

"Pete would never tell me that kinda thing."

"Why go to the spa? What did that have to..."

"Good question, man. Sometimes he met people in odd places. Just in case... He liked throwing people off the scent, that's what he said. He loved hidin' one story inside a different one. A fake out. It was, like, part of his paranoid thing."

"You think that's why he used the spa?"

"The spa is kinda out of the way. But the spa could'a been involved. Depends on the story he was workin' which he never told me much about and I didn't care but maybe this time I should'a. I told him things would come back to bite him in the ass. Pete was a weird dude. I loved him but he was weird."

"Did he say anything about who he was meeting or who he wanted you to photograph?"

"All he said was 'somebody who knows a lot' and 'somebody on the inside' and that's all. No... he... he said the dude was scared, and I could

only take shots in silhouette. Could'a been about domestic abuse. Somebody
he got to tell his story. About the abuse... y'know."

"That's all he said?" I felt as if I'd come so close and then nothing.

"Don't ask for more details 'cause I don't have any. That's all I know."

Even if he knew more, he wouldn't crack, yet.

"You see anybody else go in or out of the spa that night?"

"N-no... I don't think... No... Guess I wasn't watchin' the door that
close. Y'know? I wait for a call from Pete. I don't hafta watch."

"You didn't hear anything... gunshots... anything like that?"

"Naw. I wasn't that close to the place."

"Where can I reach you, Jenks? The listed address of your studio is an
empty lot."

"I... I don't wanna get involved. This was it for me. I gave you what I
know. That's it."

"Not good enough, Jenks. I may need..."

"No, man!" He stood and the desk chair spun into the wall with a thud
and a crack. He moved to the door, jiggled the knob. "Unlock the door. I
told you everything I know." The fear in his eyes was painful to see.

"Vega was mutilated pretty bad you know." I moved slowly to the door.
"Couldn't even tell it was him until they did some tests."

"That's what I'm talking about, man. Whoever did this, they don't fool
around. Cops are lucky they found Pete at all."

"That's all you owe Vega? You tell me a couple of nothings and that's it?
He's rotting on a slab in the morgue and you run home to your little hole in
the wall, like some rat."

"It's not like that. You see what they did to him, man. I don't want that
to happen to me."

"It's not gonna happen to you. Help me, and we put whoever did this
away. He's not gonna touch you or anybody else."

"I..."

"Not even certain I'll be calling you. Just in case I need you... How
about it?"

Jenks jiggled the doorknob, without much force this time.

"Pete was a good guy, y'know," he said, his voice thick with fear or
sadness. "This shouldn't'a happened to him."

"Then stand up for him, Jenks. Pete wasn't afraid. He went after tough stories because he knew it hadda be done. Something like this happened to you, he wouldn't stop till he found your killers. You know I'm right."

"Yeah… yeah, you are…" Jenks drew a shuddering breath. He went back to the desk. "Got a pencil?"

"On the desk. Paper's there, too."

Jenks wrote out a series of numbers.

"This isn't my number but it's how you get me. It's how Pete reached me." He paused. "You can't tell anybody. Not even the cops. Especially not them."

* * *

I watched Jenks leave Bubbles, and sensed he had more to tell. It'd take time and trust.

To Kent's great relief, the contest hadn't started by the time I got backstage.

"He's back," Bruno called out to Kent. "Now you can stop quivering like a little *puta* her first night on the streets."

Kent laughed nervously. "I don't care what you say, Bruno, as long as I don't have to get up in front of those screaming queens, I'm happy."

"How many contestants?" I asked.

Bruno shuffled some papers.

"We got…" He flipped pages. "Twenty-eight but don't count on all of them goin' through with it when it comes time to show their ass. Some'a them looked scared."

"Where are they all?"

"In the back room," said Jean-Claude appearing from behind a curtained-off area. "This is right, no? Anton says they must be kept together or we lose them." Jean-Claude laughed. "They are like the kittens wandering all around."

"Good job, guys!" I smiled at them and picked up the registration forms. "Guess it's showtime!"

Everybody went to their stations and I headed out on stage. I was distracted. After talking with Jenks, my mind raced over my next steps. If

Jenks was right about Vega's work, I'd have to make another attempt to find Max, Brad's ex. I'd also need to look into the trial where Brad had been a juror. Jenks had mentioned a possible third story but had no details.

Then there was Wheeler's office. I'd be making a trip there, too. Someone might know why he was at Brad's. They might not want to talk about Wheeler and a gay masseur, but what they wanted and I what I needed were two different things.

I had my work cut out for me. Things felt more solid.

I forced my thoughts back to the stage just as the baby spot washed over me with a golden glow.

"All right guys, it's time for Philly's Best Buns…," I shouted over the applause and hooting. The night was off and running.

Chapter 20

I woke with a start to the muffled sound of my cell phone. Jumping out of bed I scrambled to figure out where I'd left it when I got back from the Best Buns Contest the night before. Then I remembered it was still in my pants pocket. My jeans lay in a heap on the floor where I'd stepped out of them. "Fontana." I headed back to the bed and sat down. It was still warm and inviting.

"Marco, sounds like I woke you up." Detective Shim sounded all too alert and raring to go. Gave me a headache.

"You did. Late night." I yawned. My bedside clock read 7 AM which meant I'd gotten four hours sleep. No surprise I felt woozy. Of course, Shim was perky, he was so straight-laced he'd probably gotten eight hours sleep. I decided to try and disrupt his schedule one of these nights.

"The business you're in, I can imagine." Shim laughed. "Must be tough."

"Yeah, looking at bare male asses all night can get pretty rough. But…"

"Oh… uh… I was just…" Shim stumbled over his words, obviously thrown off by the mention of bare asses.

"You think it's easy scrutinizing men's asses all night?"

"Uh…" He cleared his throat. "I… uh… wanted to uh… I have the autopsy reports," he said, effectively cutting off talk of the buns contest. "You can look at them if you want. There's nothing you don't already know."

"I'd like to take a look anyway," I answered. "Not that I don't trust you, Dae. I'm a hands on kinda guy. I like seeing things for myself."

"Be my guest. Call when you want to set it up. I should—"

"Got a question for you. Maybe you can save me some work."

"How's that?"

"I'm following every lead I can think of on Brad's case. You know, the one you guys placed on a back burner?"

"Hey, listen. We did no such—"

"Let's not argue the point. Maybe you can help."

"Shoot. If it's one of those 'no go' areas, don't expect much."

"You remember Emily told us Brad had been on a jury recently?"

"She said he was upset about it interfering with his work."

"Right. Any hints on the easiest way to get my hands on trial information, like transcripts? Assuming I can guess which trial." I had my own contacts, but I wanted to see how helpful Shim was willing to be. Besides, he might know some shortcuts.

"For criminal proceedings you go to the Criminal Justice Center. They've got some stuff on the web, but don't expect much."

"Been there. I'd have to know exactly what I was looking for on that site and I don't. Got any contacts at Criminal Justice?"

"Can't think of any… haven't had that much time on the force and haven't bumped up against the court system much yet. Haven't had time to develop contacts."

"Nose around a little… you never know what you'll come up with," I said. "I guess I'll just have to do it the old fashioned way. Bribes and threats."

He didn't respond but I could hear his breathing quicken. Shim took me too seriously. I'd have to remember that. Hard to believe he was so innocent, or maybe it was just that he believed Giuliani's assessment of me. "Just kidding," I said. "You knew that, right?"

"According to Giuliani, I should take seriously whatever you say. But I think I know when you're kidding and when you're not… right?"

I didn't answer.

"Right?" Shim said again.

I laughed. "Don't believe even half of what Giuliani says about me."

"I'll try to remember that."

"Thanks again for offering the autopsy reports, Dae. I owe you a drink."

"We'll see," he said noncommittally.

"Right." At least he didn't say 'No' flat out. That was progress. I'd make sure to keep my promise on this one just to see if he'd go through with it. He was tough but I wasn't about to give up. There'd be plenty of time after the case was closed.

"Did you make that appointment with the Department artist yet? Remember?"

"I'll do it today… maybe tomorrow. Promise." I felt a little guilty for not telling him about Jenks. But Jenks hadn't given me much and he'd made me promise not to tell the police. I was skirting around obstruction and I knew it. If the case went south, I might find myself wearing orange for a while.

We ended the conversation and I slipped back under the sheets, placed my head on the pillow and tried imagining I was on a beach in a hammock between two palms. It was no use. My mind raced over details, schedules, and lists. Four hours sleep or not, I was wide awake.

* * *

No city offices would ever be open at seven in the morning, so I took some extra time getting myself going. Even wide awake, I felt the downward drag of too little sleep. A shower, some oatmeal, tons of coffee, a glance at the morning news, and I was as ready as I'd ever be. Still feeling as if I were walking in sand, I left the apartment.

Carlos was on the front desk. The early shift was his domain. Dark haired, with eyes black as coal, he surveyed things from his perch behind the gleaming mahogany counter. As I walked past, he gave me one of his sultry smiles. This morning he threw in a wink. I waved and smiled as I breezed through the automatic doors and onto the street.

Cool May air wrapped itself around me and finished the job of waking me up. A trip to City Hall was at the top of my agenda. The patronage bees who worked in that hive wouldn't be on duty for a couple of hours. Working the jury angle would have to wait until there was someone available to unlock the secrets.

I'd have to call Nina to see what she'd discovered about Max. Vega was working a story on same-sex domestic abuse, so Max was back at the top of my list.

The photographer implied the domestic abuse story had ticked off the police, putting Vega in their sights. But that made no sense. Angry police officers committing a triple murder over bad press? Couldn't buy that. That line of inquiry wasn't worth pursuing.

Talking to the photographer convinced me to explore whether or not Vega's death was connected to Brad's and Wheeler's. Except there was no solid way to link the three murders. What Jenks had told me wasn't enough.

The initials in Brad's appointment book nagged me. They could mean Brad expected Wheeler and Vega. But why? Was Vega just using the spa as an unlikely meeting place away from prying eyes? Or, was Vega meeting with both Brad and Wheeler? Or was there some other explanation? Then Vega gets murdered before he gets to the spa for his meeting. He's blown away by some random thug for an entirely different reason? Too coincidental, too convenient. Someone didn't want Vega getting to that meeting.

A horn blared as I stepped off a curb and shook me. I'd been so lost in thought, I'd nearly walked into traffic. The muffled voice of the driver shouting some obscenity seeped through his window as he sped past.

The city woke up around me as I continued down Broad Street to Spruce. Blue-jeaned attendants splashed water over sidewalks. Workers gave plants a morning dousing. Window washers ran their squeegees over plate glass storefronts.

People hurried up and down the sidewalk in front of the Kimmel Center. A flock of art students on their way to the University of the Arts, straggled past laughing and squealing. Dressed in oddly ragged clothing, the college girls huddled together at the front of the pack accompanied by a few flamboyantly gay boys. The rest of the boys followed dragging their feet. As a rule college boys are cute and these guys were no exception. But they were by far the skinniest group of guys I'd ever seen. I like sizing up guys as potential members for StripGuyz. Cute as these boys were, it'd be like a collection of bones dancing on stage. Not what most patrons want to see.

Joseph R. G. DeMarco

I turned onto Spruce and headed for my office. I passed the Community Center, doors still shut, a few people clustered together on the steps waiting to get inside.

I was surprised to see Olga working at her computer when I arrived. "You're early, sugarplum." I stopped and pecked her on the cheek.

"Dark circles under eyes making boss look charming." When she said "charming" it came out "charmink." The tone of her voice was affectionate and she looked at me with concern. "You are needing kidnap."

I had to think for a moment. "No time for a catnap right now."

"Always work, work, work. Remember dark circles." She went back to her keyboard.

My office was quiet. Olga had made coffee as if she'd expected me to roll in early. Sometimes I wondered just how connected she was to my rhythms. I filled a mug then planted myself in my chair. Leaning back I closed my eyes and reviewed what I'd have to do for the day. The trial was a good place to start.

I opened Brad's computer files to find the exact dates of the trial which I'd need to get anywhere researching court records. When Brad's calendar popped onto the screen, a sad, guilty feeling slipped over me for going through his personal files. I still felt the need to protect his privacy and dignity.

I found the trial dates and closed the file. That should narrow the field. "Sorry Brad," I whispered to the screen. "I'll get to the bottom of this."

Gulping my coffee, I placed a notebook in my pocket. Next stop, City Hall. It wasn't far so I took a long way around since it was still early. I walked to Thirteenth Street. The block between Spruce and Locust was seedier than it should have been, the hotel for transients on the corner setting the tone for most of the block. A down and out, subtly criminal atmosphere struggled with the gayborhood surrounding it. I glance up cautiously, never having forgotten the urban legends about what folks in the hotel tended to toss out the windows. Never knew anyone who'd actually been hit by anything, and hadn't ever been conked myself. I always looked up, though.

Ambling past the gay bar on the corner of Thirteenth and Locust and on down the street past Woody's, the atmosphere changed entirely. The area was experiencing a renaissance with new restaurants and shops lining both sides of the street. The lone holdouts from the old days, a porn shop and an all-male theater, did their best to fit in and stay put.

When I got to Market Street I turned left and looked up. City Hall, one of the city's gems, had been given a cleaning which took years and I, for one, wasn't happy about it. Sure, everyone wants clean buildings but now City Hall looked as if it came in three colors, a medium gray, then a light gray tower, with a darker gray topper to the tower. Four colors if you count the dark patina on the statue of Billy Penn who gazed off toward the Northeast as if searching for a way out of town until the building got dirty enough to look one color again.

The best thing about the clean building was that scores of knockout sculptures studding City Hall's façade were easier to see.

I entered through one of the building's massive arches and reached one of the many doors leading into the maze of hallways. Navigating City Hall's corridors to find an office is almost as difficult as understanding some of the legislation City Council devises. No matter how many times I've walked those halls, I've seldom been able to find an office on the first try.

This time I accidentally entered the door to the hall leading right to Mort Zucker's office. Must've been some strange synergy or something. The dreary threadbare, linoleum-lined hall, had a monotony occasionally broken by old oak doors looking majestic but sad. Shingles hanging on the wall outside the doors announced what you might find inside. Mort kept an ancient caricature of himself taped to his door. "Doc Zucker, the Fixer" it said, and in it he was young and dapper, even if it emphasized his less than pretty features. The boardwalk artist in Ocean City had captured his essence.

Zucker's usual answer to requests was, "No problem. I can fix you up." Mort could hook you up with all sorts of information or people who could get you anything from a scrap of information to a job. Mort never charged a cent. Of course, he didn't have to charge. The taxpayers footed the bills while Mort sat in his City Hall digs and twiddled his thumbs. Still, Old Mort was known to take cash slipped to him to grease the wheels a little faster. Mort was nobody's fool.

I turned the brass knob and pulled open the door. If the halls were dreary, the offices were even more dismal. With the exception of City Council offices which had just gotten an expensive overhaul while the Council debated raising taxes.

True to form, Mort sat facing the door. His portly body planted firmly in a comfortable, padded swivel chair. Head resting on the chair's back, eyes closed, a gentle snore escaping every couple of seconds, he appeared blissfully asleep. I stepped to the counter and quietly leaned forward on my elbows. Mort continued working on his pension with a few more snores.

Clearing my throat softly, I stared, willing him to wake up. No dice. I repeated the action, this time louder, which only caused Mort to issue a rip roaring snort that rattled papers and fluttered his jowls but didn't wake him up. Slapping my hand on the counter's surface finally startled Mort to wakefulness. His feet dropped from their perch on his desk, his eyes widened, and his mouth hung open.

"Son of a bitch!" A bit of drool slurred his words. " What the fu… hell do ya think you…?" Mort focused and saw me. "Marco! That wuz you?"

"Me? Me who? What's up, Mort?"

"You woke me up. That's what's up." Mort laughed, a phlegmy sound. "Son of a bitch, disturbin' a workin' man."

"How's tricks, Mort?"

"Nothin's what it used to be. Goddamn mayor is tryin'a pile more work on all us poor slobs. Imagine? We work like slaves and he cracks the whip even more."

"Yeah, I kinda wondered why things seemed so busy here."

"So? What can I do for ya?" Mort snorted and snuffled as he gathered himself together. "I ain't under no illusion that you come in here for a social call. Right? Got no flowers and no candy. That means you want something."

"I'd'a known you wanted flowers I'd have brought 'em. I never figured you for a flower guy."

"Wiseass. All'a you wops are wiseasses."

"You mean wiseguys, right?"

"I said wiseass and I meant wiseass. If you was a wiseguy, I'd be sittin here talkin' to you with my throat cut by now."

I laughed.

"So? What can I do for you, Marco? I don't see you in a dog's year, I know you want somethin' now. But, hey, I don't care. As long as you still remember Morty."

"You're right, Mort. I'm sorry I haven't been in for a while…"

"A few days is a while. A month is a while. But I ain't seen you in six months, a year, maybe."

"Hasn't been that long, Mort. A day doesn't go by I don't think of you."

"Yeah. Cut the bullshit. Nobody thinks about this old man except when they need something."

"A friend of mine was killed, Mort. Murdered."

His expression melted into one of pity. He'd seen his share of trouble. One of his brothers had been murdered and he'd never gotten over that. "Whaddaya need? Just tell me. You got it."

"Turns out my friend, Brad, was on a jury not long before he was killed…"

"And you're thinkn' it's connected? This is serious, Marco. You gotta go to the cops, not that they'll do much good but you gotta protect yourself."

"Thing is, the cops are already on the case but they have other murders with higher priorities than a dead gay masseur."

"Yeah." He sighed with the new burden then sat forward in his seat, and swiped one hand over his balding head. "So what can a guy like me do?"

"I've gotta know for sure if there was some connection between the trial and Brad's murder. That means I need information. Names of lawyers, other jurors, maybe even a trial transcript."

"They got all this at the Criminal Justice Center."

"But not yet and maybe not for a long while. I need it yesterday. So, I thought maybe you had some…"

"Shortcuts?"

I nodded encouragingly.

"Marco, you ever know me *not* to have a contact someplace?" The phlegmy laugh again, which went on longer and transisted into a cough.

"You cut down on the smoking yet, Mort?"

"Ahhh." He waved away the question and I knew he was still two packs a day. "Listen, I got contacts at Criminal Justice but it's gonna take more than a minute."

"As long as I get it yesterday, Mort."

I gave him the dates I'd gotten from Brad's files along with Brad's name, so the mysterious contact could zero in on the right trial.

"Lemme call you after lunch. I'll fix you up."

* * *

Back out in the vast and empty City Hall courtyard, I took out my cell phone and called Luke. I wasn't far from Chinatown and I needed more information on Wheeler before I visited his offices. So I decided to set up a lunch meeting.

"Clean Living," Luke said sounding all business.

"Got any nude house cleaners who know how to treat a guy right?" I half-joked, knowing how Luke felt about his nude housecleaning division. That division survived because it made money and because Luke was afraid someone else would capitalize on the idea if he dropped it.

"Wh...? Marco? You're a crazy man. No naked house cleaners for you." Luke laughed. "What's up?"

"I'm down here at City Hall and you know what's close by."

"Um... The mayor? No... wait... you're not a fan of the mayor so it can't be him. Give me a minute... is it the cute chauffeur who works for the President of City Council?"

"The answer is Chinatown. I wanted to know if you had plans for lunch."

"I kinda do, Marco."

"No problem." I'd hoped to coax Luke to invite Xinhan so I could get more information from him about Wheeler. "Business or something hot?"

"I'm having lunch with Xinhan."

"That's a coincidence."

"You don't believe in coincidences. How many times have you told me that?"

"In murder investigations, no. In things like this... Okay, call it synergy or something. I was gonna ask you if you could set up a meeting for me with Xinhan. Like maybe all three of us having lunch."

"Oh." Luke said and was silent.

"I don't want to horn in if you have plans. Xinhan's a hottie, if I were you, I'd have plans."

"As a matter of fact…" Luke laughed.

"Knew it. I won't interfere. Tell Xinhan to call me. I need some inside information on Wheeler. Tell him the sooner the better."

"You know what?" Luke said. "You're not interfering. Lunch is just the prelude anyway."

"Nah, you two have lunch, I can…" I didn't want to watch them mooning over one another anyway.

"No. It's settled. You're coming to lunch. What happens after… you know what they say, 'two's company, three's a crowd.' You'll hear all about it later."

"Countin' on it."

"We're meeting at the *Five Mountains* on Tenth Street near the arch. It's one of his restaurants."

"I've heard good things about it. He owns that, huh? He's a keeper then."

"Oh, get real, Marco. We're having lunch. And now you'll be chaperoning. Meet me at eleven-thirty."

"Will do," I said and disconnected. I could tell Luke and Xinhan had a lot more in common than their home town. Despite Luke's protests, I knew he was excited about the possibilities. I was happy for him. So why did I feel so strange?

* * *

"Nice" would not have been the word I'd have chosen for the Five Mountains. Maybe "elegant" or "serenely beautiful" or "exquisite" would begin to describe it. Once through the exotic golden pillars at the entrance, I found myself in a vestibule with delicate bamboo plantings. A copy of a terracotta soldier from the tomb of the First Emperor guarded the doorway. The fresh flowery fragrance wafting through the air and subtle lighting created a peaceful transition from the sunlight and urban noise outside. The interior was a knockout. A rectangular pool of water ran along the entire length of one side of the restaurant with pink lotus blossoms set in deep green leaves floating on the gently moving water. The walls were faced with green stone that appeared both modern and ancient. Gentle lighting suffused the restaurant with an air of tranquility.

After City Hall's pedestrian, tired-looking interior, I felt as if I'd been transported to another planet. As I gazed at a wall hanging with the most elegant golden dragon I'd ever seen, I realized Xinhan was standing next to me. He fit right in. Cultured, serene, and handsome. "Mr. Fontana. I didn't expect the pleasure of your company again so soon. Welcome to *Five Mountains*." Carefully chosen words. He was too much of a diplomat to say I'd intruded on what he'd hoped would be a private lunch. He offered a subtle bow and I returned the favor.

"I'm impressed. This is fantastic."

"I'm glad you approve, Mr. Fontana. Luke tells me you have good taste."

"Call me Marco." I smiled. "Where's Luke?"

"He's already here. I've taken a table for us in another room. I hope you don't mind but I've ordered some of our specialties."

"Not at all. I hope you don't mind me horning in, but the case is stalled without more information on Smithson Wheeler and you graciously offered to help." I could at least be diplomatic while intruding.

"Then you haven't made any progress?"

"Not as much as I'd hoped. I'm getting closer. If you can fill in some details, I'd appreciate it."

Walking to the back of the restaurant, we turned left into a huge room with a ceiling that was fifty-percent skylight. Tropical plants grew everywhere and music flowed like a river through the space. Two areas at the back were set off by waterfalls contained between sheets of glass, providing privacy and soothing sounds. The bubbly flowing water allowed observers to see people in the room only as blurred silhouettes.

Rounding one of the water walls, I spotted Luke sipping tea from a delicate cup.

"Marco! Beautiful place, isn't it? Very classy. Just my style."

"You kinda understated that a bit, don't you think? This is beyond nice. We're in Palace of Versailles territory here."

Xinhan smiled and took a seat next to Luke. The only other chair was across the table from them.

I sat and reached for the teapot but Xinhan beat me to it and poured a cup for me. Sitting back he nodded at a waiter who'd been standing by. The young man moved off quickly.

"How long has this place been here?"

"We've been open about a year," Xinhan answered. "It wasn't easy putting all this together."

"We've been to Xinhan's other place a hundred times," Luke said.

"We have?"

"*The Golden Phoenix* is on Race Street. They have killer dim sum every weekend. Coming back to you now?" Luke smiled.

"That's your place, too? Luke's right. Been there a lot. Never noticed you there, though."

"My businesses keep me running."

Before we could say more, a female server arrived with a large bowl. She nodded as she set it down, then retreated.

"Chengdu chicken," Luke said, his eyes gleaming with approval. "My favorite."

My lips had been numb for a week after the first time I ate that dish some years before. It had enough spicy heat to warm the East Coast. Chengdu chicken eventually become a favorite of mine. The sight of the food suddenly brought back a memory of Galen: a few years ago, Galen had come to dinner with me, Luke, and others and told us how he'd fallen in love with Chengdu chicken when he'd traveled through China working for the mysterious outfit he never named. His face was so clear in my mind, smiling as he savored the spicy chicken. I wondered where Galen was now and if he ever got to eat Chengdu chicken.

"Marco?" Luke said. He stared at me. "You all right?"

Still caught in the memory, I hesitated and before I could speak, a waiter brought bowls of brown rice for each of us. "I'm good. Just remembered something I hadn't thought about in a long time."

Luke nodded solemnly, and I knew he understood what I meant. He and I were always on the same wavelength.

A third waiter, sultry and seductive, placed two large platters before us. One I recognized to be specially prepared kidney. Yet another spicy dish. The other was an eel dish with a purple leaf spice.

"Please," Xinhan said, indicating with a wave of his hand that we should start.

After we'd been eating and chatting for a while, Xinhan looked at me. "You have some questions I can help you with, Marco?"

"I hope you can help. I'm trying to pull together the few elements I've got so far..."

"If I can assist, please..."

"You said you knew Wheeler pretty well, right?"

"Smithson was a private person. I only knew so much but I learned to read him well enough over the years. I could often tell what he was thinking and how he might respond."

"I'm going to his offices later. I'd like to know whatever I can before I get there."

"So you can tell if they're being honest with you." Xinhan stated.

"Marco's good at seeing through a liar but advance information never hurts," Luke said.

"The more I know, the more I can find out. Knowing the right person to approach would help. Who'd be the most knowledgeable? Who was closest to Wheeler?"

"That would have to be Phil Caragan, his personal assistant. He's worked for Smithson a long time."

"An honest guy?"

"If Smithson was ever out of town or otherwise involved, I could always count on Phil."

"Anyone else there I should talk to?"

"No one else has Phil's knowledge or access. Smithson gave Phil the keys to the kingdom, so to speak. He knows almost everything Smithson knew."

"This is a big help, Xinhan. I owe you."

"Luke said you were good at what you do and for Smithson's sake, I'm glad."

"Mind a few more questions?" I looked him in the eye and noticed just the merest sign of annoyance but his sense of noblesse oblige was strong.

"He's relentless once he gets started," Luke said. "I warned you." He laughed and Xinhan smiled.

"Please ask. If this will get you closer to Smithson's killer..." His voice wavered a moment but he quickly controlled whatever feelings rushed through him. "I want to help."

I sipped some tea thinking about how to proceed. I wanted to ask questions Xinhan might not like. "Was he worried about anything before... that night? Did he seem preoccupied or upset?"

"Before... let me think." Xinhan closed his eyes for a moment. "I seem to remember him being concerned about money."

"His own financials?"

"Not his own money. Smithson was quite wealthy. It was something else. I entered his office for a meeting as he was quietly finishing up a phone call. I heard him say that things were out of control and that nothing was going as expected."

"Did you ask him about that?"

"Of course not." Xinhan was miffed. "This was obviously private business. It was not my place to intrude."

"Right. I understand," I said. "Did you know Brad Lopes?"

"The other man who was killed? The masseur? Not exactly."

"Was there any indication that Mr. Wheeler saw Brad on any sort of a regular basis? You have any idea if they were involved?"

"Again, Mr. Fontana," Xinhan said, slipping into formality which meant I'd hit a sensitive area. "This was Smithson's private life. What he did and with whom was his business. He didn't often share that with me."

"I'm not trying to smear the man's reputation, Xinhan. That gets me nothing. I'm trying to connect things so it all makes sense. Maybe it'll help solve the case. You want that, too. You said as much."

"Certainly. Smithson meant a lot to me."

"Stands to reason you'd want to protect his reputation. None of what you tell me has to get out unless it has to. Even then we'll try our best to control it."

Xinhan nodded, looked at me pensively.

Luke glanced from me to him, torn about what he should do. "Xinhan," Luke said gently. I knew that tone of voice. Had heard it many times. "Marco's right. He's a good man, the best I know. He won't reveal anything that doesn't have to be out there. Believe me. I trust him with my life. Already had my life saved by Marco more than once."

Xinhan looked across the table at me as if peering into my soul, and taking my measure. "It feels strange, having another man's reputation in your hands. Smithson wasn't a person who sat back and did nothing. I should follow his example."

I said nothing. It wouldn't have helped anyway.

Xinhan exhaled then leaned on the table. "Smithson was gay though he never broadcast that fact. Not that he was ashamed. As I said, he was a private person. Not showy, not flamboyant. Through and through, he was a good man."

"Did you know Brad?"

"Not exactly. As I said. I knew *about* him. Smithson was very fond of him."

"They were…?"

"No. That would've made Smithson very happy, though. They were good friends and Smithson helped with some financing for Brad's spa."

"Did he back it personally?"

"Smithson was an investor. Usually very astute. This time I'm afraid his heart did the thinking. Still, he believed Brad's business was sound. Smithson enjoyed supporting gay business ventures. He had enough money to indulge his heart and his whims."

"Do you know if there were other backers?"

"I don't know. Smithson did say Brad would need much more money to realize his plans. Something about that worried Smithson."

"Worried? You mean, he was concerned Brad wouldn't raise the money?"

"That, of course. But it seemed more than that. He was troubled about Brad and money in general. The scale of Brad's plans surprised him. "

Xinhan paused and Luke poured us each more tea, then set the teapot aside with the lid ajar signaling the waiter we needed more.

"Mr. Wheeler never gave many details about Brad and money issues?"

"Nothing concrete. I'm sorry. All I know is that Smithson worried Brad was digging himself too big a hole and might get desperate."

"Do you remember anything else?"

"Smithson was surprised that Brad scheduled pricey renovations on the spa. He wondered how the money had been secured."

"Did Wheeler ever tell you anything further concerning his worries about Brad?"

"Smithson was a complicated man. He may have known more but Brad was a favorite and he'd never sully Brad's reputation. Smithson was the kind of man who took care of things for himself."

"Got it," I said. This is why Xinhan's help was valuable. No outsider would know these things. The money issue Xinhan hinted at was too vague. Nothing to hang a theory on. Maybe Phil Caragan knew more.

"Brad wasn't his only worry, Marco. Smithson wasn't a love struck fool. He was a prominent businessman and had other things on his mind. Don't place undue emphasis on his connection to Brad."

"What else bothered him?"

"The usual. Fellow developers always sought his attention or cooperation and politicians constantly badgered him for money. He did his best to steer clear but if you know developers and politicians, well, pit bulls are distracted more easily."

"Was there anything unusually bothersome lately?"

"I surmised as much from things Smithson said but I believe he was trying to protect me from whatever it was or whatever the fallout from it might be. I have nothing concrete to base that on, however."

"Smithson sounded like a good friend to have. You must miss him, " Luke said. He looked at Xinhan and I saw a lot in that look. Luke wasn't often taken with someone but it appeared that Xinhan had made an impression.

* * *

We finished lunch, said our goodbyes, and I left them sitting there. I turned back to look at them through the curtain of bubbling water and I saw their silhouettes as they leaned in toward one another. I turned away, suddenly feeling the need to get outside into the sunlight and the bustle on the sidewalk. Chinatown was always busy, and I could lose myself in the crowd.

As I moved through the peaceful bamboo vestibule, my cell phone rang and I imagined the terracotta soldier's fierce expression was aimed at me for disturbing him. I answered the call outside.

"Fontana."

"Get yer pencil out, I'm gonna fix you up with information."

For some reason I was overly happy to hear Mort's voice.

Chapter 21

Mort gave me his contact's name and a trial title. So I headed for the Criminal Justice Center to meet Sam Paspatis and see what he'd found. Mort's old pals owed him plenty. What he'd done to gain those favors, I didn't think I'd want to know.

The Criminal Justice Center is newer than City Hall by almost a hundred years. In all that time, you'd think the city could find an architectural firm with the imagination to come up with something even a little inspired. Impressive design isn't high on the city's list. Years before, a skyscraping disaster known as the Municipal Services Building, north of City Hall, was built and made cereal boxes look good. The fact that the Criminal Justice Center is just another cardboard box with windows, is no surprise. It's what they know best.

The problem with getting into the Criminal Justice Center is you've just about got to strip down for them to prove you aren't a threat. Easy to understand. When you've got every kind of criminal and their lawyers trudging in and out all day, being careful is a way of life. I was fine with the meticulous security procedures until it came to my gun. I have a thing about leaving my gun with strangers. Never makes me happy.

After squeezing through security, I searched for Mort's contact. The halls were crawling with lawyers, police, and assorted others. On the surface it looked like the well oiled machinery of justice. That was on the surface.

Finding Paspatis wasn't difficult. With a moniker like that, almost everyone knows where you're located. I was directed to the office by a bored security guard. Paspatis was headquartered on a busy floor flush with lawyers and clerks. I found my way through and pushed open the door.

A tiny, dark woman, sat at a desk situated behind a low counter. Of indeterminate age, her leathery flesh suggested she'd had one too many tanning sessions. Head down, concentrating, she didn't appear to hear me enter. The office had a stale, acrid, old food and coffee odor.

"Good morning," I said.

No reaction.

"I'm here to see Sam Paspatis. This is his office, right?"

That got her attention. Her head snapped up and she gave me a death-ray stare. Her light brown eyes, surrounded by the heavy tan and dark hair, were startling. "This is my office. Who're you?" She casually fingered her necklace of green beads the size of walnuts.

"Marco Fontana. Mort Zucker sent me to talk to Sam Paspatis." It dawned on me that I *was* talking to Sam.

"You're the private dick Mort told me about." She paused to look me over, her eyes had a tough and hardened quality that gave her an intimidating edge. "Said you were one'a the good guys. Didn't say you were so cute." The way she said it didn't sound like a compliment.

"Makes us even. He didn't tell me you were a woman."

She laughed then stared at me again. "So, you want a transcript."

"Right. The Branko trial? That's what Mort said the defendant's name is."

"Court reporter just gave us the uncorrected draft. You're gettin' something nobody's seen yet. You tell Morty he owes me big on this one."

"Will do."

She smirked.

"Mort said that includes the names of lawyers, jurors, and witnesses?"

"It does. It's got everything you want," she said and laughed. "All right, maybe not *everything*." Her look sent a feeling down my spine I didn't want to experience again.

"Sounds good," I said.

"Boy is Morty gonna owe me." She winked. "*You're* gonna owe me, too. Got that? I got a big family and you never know..." Whatever she meant by that, she let her words hang in the air a moment before holding up a sheaf of papers. "The transcript."

I stretched out my hand but she didn't move. I looked questions at her.

"I didn't hear you promise," she snapped.

"What?"

"You forgot already? You owe me for this. You and Morty both."

"Sure. I promise," I said and held out my hand again.

She placed the papers in an accordion file and handed it over. "You don't know where you got this... understand?"

I nodded.

* * *

Getting out of the Center was lots easier than getting in. I had a sweet reunion with my gun when they returned it. They didn't appear happy about giving it back but they couldn't argue with my permit.

Outside the Center, I briefly watched the parade of people in and out of the place. Even if you paid attention to the news, you could never get a clear idea of how much crime there was and how many people passed through the system because of it. I almost felt sympathy for Giuliani and Shim and the load of cases they dealt with. Still didn't make me feel better about them putting Brad's case on a back burner.

At least they'd given me room to maneuver on my own. That was something.

With the trial information, my list of leads had suddenly expanded. Since Brad's ex, Max, was still in the wind, I figured I'd concentrate on the trial and see if that led anywhere. I skimmed the top sheets of the transcript which summarized everything.

No use trying to talk to Branko. With his shiny new guilty verdict, he'd be locked snugly away and unavailable for a sit down. According to Mort, Branko was a second rate mobster from "over there" which, in Mort-speak, meant somewhere in Europe. With a name like Branko, the guy could have come from any one of several places. Russia, Serbia, Slovakia, you name it. What mattered was that after he crawled out from under his rock, he ended up in Philly and did his dirty work here. I'd never heard of the guy but that just meant he was a behind-the-scenes type. Not one of organized crime's show horses.

With Branko locked up, his lawyers were next on my list. Messina and Jarrette, headed up one of the city's sleazier law firms. I may not have heard of Branko, but I knew Messina and Jarrette all too well. They'd long been lawyers for a variety of mob figures. One of the firm's associates was rumored to have been a consigliere to a local don who'd eventually been blown to bits. It was only a matter of time before the law firm started branching out to the Russians and other Eastern European organized crime families. An equal opportunity criminal law firm.

Lucky me, I got to go face to face with them for a little info. Sometimes this job is nothing but fun. First I'd have to do my homework. Reading the transcript would give me what I'd need when I questioned them.

* * *

I arrived at the office and found Olga bent over her keyboard and Jean-Claude sitting on the couch reading a magazine. He popped up his head when I entered the room.

"Marco!"

"What's up, Jean-Claude? What're you doing here?" I was unintentionally sharp and he appeared surprised.

"You asked me to see you. About work? You don't remember? You said that maybe there would be something to do. For this case you are on."

I vaguely remembered telling him that I might have some work for him. Since he'd planted himself here I decided to show him how boring investigative work could be. "You're here at the right time," I said. "Come on in and we'll get started."

Jean-Claude jumped up and was at my side like an eager puppy. Just as cute and cuddly, too.

"Olga, I'm gonna have some work for you, too."

"Is why I am living." She looked up at me, smiling insincerely.

"Thank you, sugarplum."

"Messages are on desk," she said over her shoulder as I moved into my office followed by my new best friend. I caught a whiff of brewing coffee and was instantly energized.

Jean-Claude shut the door behind him and took a seat. I went around to my chair, placed the transcript on my desk, and sat down.

"This is exciting, eh?" He was ready for a scene out of *Magnum, P.I.* what he'd be getting would be more like *Magnum, The Librarian.*

I was almost sorry to disappoint him.

"Detective work is not all guns and chases, Jean-Claude. Once you start school, you'll find that out. There's a lot of legwork, desk work, and things most people would find boring."

"Nothing a detective does is boring. This is what I was born to do! And to learn from you... it is... an..."

"Okay. Okay. Don't say I didn't warn you." I took two yellow highlighters from my desk and handed one to him. Then I slipped the transcript from the folder, took a large part for myself and gave him a good chunk. The rest went back into the folder. "Sometimes you've got to slog through a lot of crap to find leads. The papers are part of a trial transcript which might contain information we can use."

"What should I do?" Jean-Claude looked from the transcript to me, no sign of disappointment.

"Look through the pages, highlight any names you come across in testimony or in the questions the lawyers ask. We'll make a list to check against other lists I have."

"*Oui, je compr...* I mean... I understand, Marco." He stared at me and said, "Then... we...?"

"Get going. We've gotta get this done today." I chuckled. For a guy who stripped to pay his way through school, Jean-Claude seemed innocent and naïve in so many ways. Maybe that's what Anton found so charming.

"Sure, Marco." Jean-Claude sat back, crossed one leg over the other making a surface for the papers, and began reading, highlighter at the ready.

I watched him for a few moments. He was handsome, more than handsome. His features made him appear strong, even fierce, but also had a vulnerable quality. I knew from observing him at the club that he was gentle and caring. It was easy to see a lot of guys swooning over him. Anton was obviously falling for him. And I wasn't doing much to change that.

I shook off my feelings and got down to reading the transcript. There was a long witness list. The prosecution and defense had lined up quite a few people. I ran a finger down the names, looking at each, to see if there was anyone I recognized. At the end of the prosecution list Smithson Wheeler's name was crossed out. As if they'd intended to call him but did not. Of course, it'd be easy enough to check. The rest of the names on both lists were unknown to me.

Forty-five minutes later, we'd both finished the shares of the transcript we'd taken. After a break, we tackled the rest and created a list of names mentioned in testimony. By checking our list against the witnesses, we were able to pare down the number of names we'd collected. With that I'd search for any connections to Brad and the murders. The other jurors would be on my list, too.

"Bored, Jean-Claude?" I asked as I massaged my temples. My eyes were bugging out after skimming the transcript. I needed more coffee.

"Disappointed? *Pas du tout.* Not at all, Marco."

"Not as exciting as a gun battle. But a lot safer."

"The man on trial sounds dangerous. So maybe this will not prove to be so safe, this case, eh? It is like we are going through his laundry."

I laughed.

"This man... the man on trial... he is in prison, yes?"

"He's away for a long time. Nothin' to worry about. Besides, you wanna be in this business, you gotta be able to handle guys like him."

"Yes. I don't fear this man."

"We've only seen him on paper. I'm sure in real life he's even more scary." I laughed when Jean-Claude's eyes widened. "Just a joke, Jean-Claude. Now I've gotta deal with this maniac's lawyers. That oughta be a lot of fun."

"Be careful, Marco. Anton will worry when I tell him where you are going."

There it was. *He'd* be telling Anton where I was going. When did I stop doing that?

Chapter 22

Messina and Jarrette occupied offices in a distinguished three-story building on Lombard Street in Old City. The cream colored shutters on the windows of the red brick structure lent it a classy appearance. Small electric candles burned in every window.

They tried offsetting their huge sleaze factor with a fashionable location. Except no amount of sophistication in a neighborhood could wash away the stain they carried.

I hadn't called, I'm not inclined to warn people I'll be on their front step wanting an interview. I like surprises. For other people. There's always a chance your target might not be at home, but catching them off guard is always sweet. In this instance, if I found only one of them in the office that'd be even better. They wouldn't be able to coordinate their answers.

I pushed open the door and was faced with a sleek, high-tech operation. A glass wall separated the vestibule from the receptionist and offices beyond. The door in that wall sported the names Messina and Jarrette etched in the glass and layered in gold leaf. A few other names in much smaller lettering trailed beneath the big guns, as if they were an afterthought.

Opening the door, I stepped up to the receptionist's desk and cleared my throat.

"May I help you?" She looked up at me, and I was sure any straight man would have fallen desperately in love then and there. Her eyes were a liquid brown that spoke of dreams not yet achieved and a wish for something better.

It was wasted on me, but I didn't think it was a conscious effort on her part anyway. She reminded me of a guy I knew who had the same eyes, that same look, and the identical hypnotic effect on men. Getting involved with him had been a mistake.

"Marco Fontana to see Messina or Jarrette. Or both, if you've got 'em."

"Are you expected?" She trained her eyes on me, and I noticed a quiver of uncertainty. Maybe because I didn't melt when she spoke.

"No. I have business regarding Konstantin Branko. He was a client of theirs. That's what I was told." I stared at her.

Involuntarily she started looking over her shoulder, as if seeking out one of the big kahunas for advice. She stopped herself in mid-turn, snapped back to look at me. "You'd have to talk with one of them."

A man in a dark, expensive-looking suit emerged from one of the doors in the hall behind the receptionist. Jarrette. I'd seen his picture in the papers often enough to know who he was. Small and thin, like an insect, he moved forward. Seeing me, a broad smile stretched his leathery features. The bright white teeth looked unreal in his swarthy face. He probably assumed I was a potential client. As he drew closer, I saw his sharp gray eyes more clearly and they said more about him than his practiced smile. He was cunning, sly, and dangerous. His eyes held it all.

"Ah, Terry, does this gentleman need some help?" He stood behind her, his smile frozen, guarded.

"He... uh, this is... Mr...?" She looked to me having already forgotten my name.

"Marco Fontana," I said and stretched out my hand over the desk toward Jarrette.

"Bin Jarrette," he said, reaching out to me.

His hand was cold and dry. He quickly withdrew it and straightened his mint-green tie.

"Nice to meet you, Mr. Jarrette."

"What can I do for you, Mr. uh... Fontana, did you say? Any relation to the Fontanas in Bay Ridge?"

"Anything's possible. I come from a big family. Some of 'em live in Brooklyn." I watched his face. He was obviously trying to see if I was "connected" in any way and I didn't want him getting the idea that I wasn't. Even if I wasn't and never wanted to be. Okay, maybe on really bad days I wished I had the kind of connections that could get things done in a hurry but that was all fantasy. That kind of help came with a price tag I couldn't afford.

"I see. You're in need of legal help? Terry can set up an appointment and we'll discuss your case."

"I'm kind of in a hurry, Mr. Jarrette. I need information on the Konstantin Branko trial. Kinda need it yesterday, if you know what I mean."

"I don't know what I can tell you that isn't public knowledge. The trial is over. The man's been convicted."

"There are a few things I know that maybe the public doesn't know."

He chuckled. "There isn't anything of the sort. You're bluffing, Mr. Fontana. You and I both know it."

"From what I hear the police have opened up another investigation," I said. All right, maybe they hadn't. But they might. "Are you aware of that?"

"If there were a new investigation, I'd have heard about it. So, either lay out your case or hit the bricks." He paused and the smile returned, this time a little less broad and a lot more phony.

"My case is just this, I'm investigating a murder and there've been some indications that a connection exists between Branko and the case I'm on," I said. At least that was one theory I was working on. "I've got some questions about Branko's trial, maybe you can set me straight."

"Mr. Branko is a legitimate businessman. He's a respected man. He was brought in on trumped up charges, most of which were dropped. The state couldn't prove much. He was convicted of one count of extortion. Bad enough, true. We'll be appealing the guilty verdict. There isn't much more to sa—"

Jarrette wouldn't add more if he didn't have to. Couldn't keep me from asking, though. "What about the allegations of jury tampering?"

"The alleg—?" Jarrette's face went all squinty.

"One of the jurors from Branko's trial was murdered recently. Maybe Branko didn't like the way things turned out. Seems like more than a coincidence to a guy like me. But then…"

"Terry…" Jarrette said, placing a weathered hand on her shoulder, about to direct her to do something. Maybe call the police. Nah. That wouldn't be smart. Maybe he had goons at his disposal. One call from the sad-eyed secretary and they'd be here.

I tried looking bored while he decided what to do.

"… hold my calls," he said to her, then glanced up at me. "Follow me, Mr. Fontana."

He strode back to his office, a slight wobble replacing the straight-backed confidence he'd displayed earlier. He'd been dealing with thugs his entire career, you'd think he'd at least know how to act like one. Maybe he was more civilized than I gave him credit for being. Or, maybe he was just a wimpy rat.

The short walk to his office was enlightening. Expensive paintings adorned the walls and antiques lined the hall. The fragrance of honeysuckle hung in the air accompanied by a stream of classical music. Defending thugs and mobsters obviously paid well. So Jarrette could surround himself with enough beauty to help him forget the muck he wallowed in every day.

His personal office was over the top. The baroque, overly gilded ambience gave me a hint of the man's mind as well as his taste. Walls dripped with gold, gilt sconces in the shape of bunches of grapes held candles that were never lit. The ruddy-colored curtains and ochre carpeting were beyond plush. He must've had minions scouring antiques fairs to find every possible piece of gold-leafed furniture. I felt tired staring at it all.

"Shut the door," he said as he sat in a gilded chair off to one side of the room. "Take a seat."

I walked over and sat in an equally ornate stuffed chair.

"Now, let's get something straight, Mr. Fontana. No matter what you've heard about this firm, no matter who our clients are, and certainly no matter what they've been accused of doing, we are a respectable firm. Our clients go beyond the famous names you may have heard. We have a healthy pro bono schedule and do more than our share. There are people who would be in jail, innocent people, if we had not intervened."

"Sounds nice, Mr. Jarrette. No doubt, all true. But that halo over your head doesn't mean you don't sport a pair of horns now and then."

"Why don't you tell me what it is you *think* you know? You mentioned jury tampering…"

"My sources tell me there's an investigation. Preliminary, of course, but an investigation into possible jury tampering."

"If that were true, Mr. Fontana, why is my client behind bars? Isn't the objective of jury tampering to have a client found not guilty?"

"Good question. Fact remains someone claims there was an attempt at tampering with the jury. One member of which is now dead."

"Coincidence." Jarrette looked edgy, like he wanted to be anywhere but sitting with me.

"Maybe," I said, not believing that for a minute. I decided to move on. "Your list of character witnesses was pretty impressive. Remy Berwick, Charles Ransome, and other heavy hitters in the development arena."

"As I said, Mr. Branko is a respected businessman. All of those witnesses were longtime associates. Mr. Ransome, Mr. Berwick, and others testified gladly."

"What kind of business did he have with the witnesses?"

"It's all a matter of public record. Land deals, housing and shopping developments. All above board ventures."

"And the extortion charge?"

"I'm sure you've read about it in the papers."

"Yeah I have. Sounded like a pretty good case. Which is why he's behind bars, I guess."

"There was little real evidence. Mr. Branko never hurt anyone, never touched a hair on the head of that man or his family."

"Never threatened them or got anyone else to threaten them?" I asked, knowing full well that the evidence was there and so were the witnesses.

"We'll be restating our case when we appeal the conviction. Maybe you'd like to drop in and hear what we have to say then?" He made as if to stand.

"One more question, Mr. Jarrette…"

He sat back down. "Go on," he said as if he were suffering the peasants their pittance.

"Why was a Mr. Wheeler dropped from the witness list?"

"You tell me, Mr. Fontana. He was a prosecution witness. *They* dropped him. Maybe they'd found out he wasn't credible, or he might've been lying to get even with Mr. Branko for some difficulty they'd had in the past. You'd have to ask the prosecutors."

"Right." I thought he might have something juicy on Wheeler. He *did* mention a past disagreement. That was juicy enough.

"If that's all...?" Jarrette stood and blinked "I've given you more than enough time."

I hoped I'd given him something to worry about with the tampering suggestion. Maybe he'd slip up or maybe Branko would do something stupid reaching out from his cell.

* * *

Back in my office, I realized what a visual overload Jarrette's place had been. My Spartan, no frills surroundings felt about right for me. Spartan if you didn't count a couple of comfortable chairs, coffee maker, refrigerator, and a few other essentials. Nothing had gold leaf anywhere.

I paged through the trial transcript and found the name of the prosecutor who'd handled the case and placed a call hoping I'd catch him.

The receptionist said the man I was looking for had taken a job in D.C. with the Department of Justice. She was nice enough to give me his number without any questions. When I asked if there'd been anyone who'd assisted on the Branko case, she referred me to a person who she said was on vacation for the next two weeks.

I tried the D.C. number and got so tangled in DOJ voicemail, I had to call back... twice. On the third try I reached the guy's voicemail. He sounded seriously nerdy and officious. I left an ambiguous message and hung up.

The next number I dialed was Shim's.

"Detective Shim."

"Dae, it's Marco. Got a minute."

"Tell me you've found something and I've got all the time you need," he said sounding sexy and a little desperate for leads on the case.

"I wish I had something so I could take you up on that. Unfortunately, I've got hunches and theories and I need a favor."

"Can't promise anything, but…."

"I've been doing some digging on Wheeler."

"I figured you would. We've already been over that ground and haven't found much. The guy was a respected businessman. For some people he was a real saint."

The police must have talked to some of the same people, but Shim didn't seem concerned about Wheeler's aborted part in the Branko trial.

"I did come across something that you probably already know about. But…"

"Like the Branko trial and the fact that Wheeler was scheduled to testify?"

"You *have* covered a lot of ground," I said. Of course, they'd know about that being right in the middle of everything and able to get that information at the push of a button. "There's something that bothers me about that business."

"Okay," Shim said, a wary tone coloring his voice. "If you're thinking there was a connection, I wouldn't be too sure. Wheeler was cut from the witness list."

"Yeah. That's what got me wondering."

"How so?"

"Why was he dropped? What was that all about? Doesn't that raise any flags?"

"There were a lot of changes to the witness list. Wheeler wasn't the only one cut."

"True." I'd seen the list and he was right. But Wheeler was the only one on that list who turned up dead a couple of weeks later. "Any other witnesses who were dropped get themselves murdered?"

"What's the favor you need?"

I realized that this was Shim's way of either shutting me up or conceding I had a point. Whatever it meant, he was obviously considering hearing me out.

"Not asking much, actually."

"Let me be the judge of that."

"The prosecutor on the case…"

"Works in D.C. now. Apparently took the express train out of here as soon as he could. Ambitious guy according to Giuliani. She wasn't surprised he took off and wasn't sorry to see him go."

"I tried reaching him. Even in D.C. but no luck so far."

"You're thinking maybe I could get to him for you."

"I like the way you think." I knew he'd be a good contact to develop inside the Department.

"Since you asked so nice... I'll give him a buzz."

"And not because it might help you, right?"

"Of course not!"

I could almost see the smile on his face.

* * *

On the way home, I called Anton to see if it'd be all right to talk with Ty. He didn't see any reason not to, so I found myself in the lobby of Anton's building.

"How ya doin' Mr. Fontana?" Tib, the man on the desk had held that job about a million years. He knew everyone and everyone knew him. He might've been getting up in years, but he was sharper than most people. Unless he knew you and knew you well, you practically had to show a passport to get into "his" building which is how he liked to think of it.

"Not bad, Tib. You?"

"Same ol' same ol' you know how it is."

"That I do," I nodded as I went past to the elevators.

Everything about the building, halls, elevators, art on the walls, reminded me of Anton and some part of me felt a strong emotional pull. Was he growing distant? Or was I just feeling guilty at not paying him enough attention?

I exited on the fifth floor and walked down the long, carpeted hall to Anton's apartment. As if he sensed me coming down the hall, Anton opened the door as I reached it. I walked into the vestibule.

"Hi, stranger." He looked me in the eye as if he hadn't seen me in months.

I wrapped him in my arms and squeezed. "You feel good."

Anton held on without saying a word, pressing me close. We stayed that way for a while clinging to one another.

"You're so warm, you're always so warm," Anton murmured and moved back so that I was able to take his face in my hands and pull him to me for a kiss. A kiss that lasted a long time.

"I've missed kissing you," I said when we finally, reluctantly pulled apart. Anton placed a finger lightly against my lips. "Shhh. Don't spoil the moment." Then he kissed me lightly on the lips and pulled back again.

I stood there staring at him. His beauty always startled me. The strong lines of his face, the high cheekbones and finely shaped nose gave him a masculine yet sensitive appearance. His eyes, though, were what drew me in every time.

"Ty is watching TV. Go on in, and I'll bring you... what? A beer or some coffee?"

"I've gotta get to Bubbles later, and I haven't had dinner yet. So make it coffee?"

"Right." He moved off toward the kitchen.

"Hey," I called softly to him. "Think you can leave the kid watching television and you and I can get some dinner?"

"If you're a good boy. I have homework to do so let's make it a quick one." He winked at me.

I felt myself flush as I turned to find Ty. He'd commandeered the sofa and was watching something intently. As I got closer I realized he was engrossed in one of those real life crime shows.

"Ty," I said.

He didn't budge.

"Ty." I raised my voice a little and he turned, a frightened look in his eyes. "It's me. Marco."

"Oh... M-Marco. Yeah, Anton said you were coming over."

"How're you feeling?"

"Lots better. Anton is wonderful. I feel like I don't have to do anything. He takes care of everything. I don't deserve it. Really."

"Yes. You do, Ty. You deserve that and better." I sat on a chair next to the sofa. "That's kinda what I wanted to talk to you about."

"Y-you're not… you're not firing me, are you? I mean, I love dancing. And—"

"Firing you? Where'd you get that idea?"

"You said… I deserved better… and you wanted to—"

"I meant you deserved better treatment. Better than Eddie."

"Eddie, is he… did you see him?"

"He's packed his things and is out of town. He won't bother you again."

"But he… he's really not that bad. You know? He's got problems. Like everybody. He's a nice guy. He loves me."

"That kind of love you don't need, Ty."

"But…"

"I guess you probably won't want to press charges? Against Eddie?"

"Press charges? Why would I—"

"Because he beat you to a pulp. He broke a couple of bones and put you in a hospital. That kind of thing happens, people usually press charges."

"I know. I mean, I do know. I understand."

"If you press charges then we can take Eddie to court."

"Then what? He goes to jail? That isn't gonna help him. I know Eddie and he needs help not jail."

Anton walked in carrying a tray loaded with coffee, cookies, and snacks. "Break time," he announced. "Would you help me get something?" He looked at me, jerking his head in the direction of the kitchen.

"Sure." As I stood, I turned toward Ty. "Think about what I said, Ty. We can talk more another time."

I walked to the kitchen where Anton was waiting, leaning against the counter.

"Don't press him!" Anton said. "He's had enough trouble. He still thinks he loves Eddie, so you keep on him and he's just going to feel abused all over again."

"Somebody's gotta do something."

"It won't be Ty. Not this time."

"Next time he could be dead."

* * *

"Diner okay with you?" I asked Anton as we exited his building.

"It's the quickest alternative. I've got a lot of work left to do."

"Not easy babysitting and all the other stuff you've got is it?"

"Ty's no trouble and I kind of like having him around. Like having a kid without all the messy years. It's homey and I like taking care of him. You know me, if it's domestic, I like it."

"Yeah." I knew it's what Anton wanted more than anything else. I just wasn't sure it was what I wanted.

"I hear Jean-Claude is doing a good job in my place," Anton said.

"He's doing all right. Does he report to you about work?"

"We talk every day. A few times a day sometimes. He's always so worried about getting things right."

"Oh," was all I could say. He and Jean-Claude spoke every day and I hardly ever called Anton anymore.

"He's a sweet guy. Attentive. And he worships you," Anton said.

"Yeah, well, he'll get over it."

"No. He won't. He looks up to you. Wants to be just like you. Really wants to get into private investigation."

"Uh huh," I mumbled. Yeah, I was sure he wanted to be just like me. Would like to be in my shoes vis-à-vis Anton, too.

"He appreciates you letting him work with you—"

"Can we talk about something other than work?" I snapped and immediately regretted it. "I'm sorry."

Anton said nothing.

"It's the case. There are a lot of threads, and I'm having a tough time. The police are even further behind."

"You sure it isn't Jean-Claude? I mean you never seem enthusiastic when I mention him."

"I'd rather talk about you. We haven't talked much lately."

"Not my…" Anton started to say something then stopped. "I know. So let's make up for it now."

We reached the diner and found a table way at the back where we could talk and not be disturbed.

* * *

Dinner with Anton was like a tentative dance around the big topic we
both wanted to avoid. Afterward, I'd walked him back to his place where we
shared a long embrace at his front door. I could feel his tentativeness, though
but I held onto him and nuzzled his neck trying to get him to laugh like he
used to.

Eventually, we pulled apart. Not that anything would've happened
anyway. I always had to content myself with a kiss.

All the way home and for the rest of the night, my thoughts were a
jumbled mess. It wasn't only the case scrambling my thinking. I looked
forward to working at Bubbles. The noise and the crowd would drown out
everything else for a while.

Chapter 23

The pounding headache I had when I woke up became sustained pressure over my eyes. I wanted to blame it on the weather, but it was more likely Brad's case. Either way, it felt like my head was a Thanksgiving Day parade balloon.

I had little choice but to keep moving. Olga knew I wouldn't be in until after I'd been to Wheeler's firm. I hoped I'd get something solid but I wasn't banking on much. This investigation led me into from one dead end to another. It was no wonder my head felt like it contained an off-key brass band gone wild. But I'd keep slogging.

Speaking with Jarrette hadn't been enlightening except for the part about a possible disagreement between Branko and Wheeler. I still hadn't gotten an answer on why Wheeler had been struck from the witness list but if my impressions about Shim were correct, he'd call if he found anything.

I headed out after my morning routine. Maybe Phil Caragan would make my headache disappear. Maybe I'd win the lottery.

Wheeler's offices were located in a four-story townhouse on Delancey Place near Eighteenth Street. The location spoke of wealth, influence, and status, the understated variety. The elite location was solid, stable, weighty. Which meant Wheeler was well aware of the power he wielded and what that power could do. He'd had no need to be ostentatious. The old and elegant townhouse showed its years but did it with style. Everything about it was clean and shiny but not new. If you came from old money you'd be comfortable here. If you were a brash, wealthy newcomer or a developer on the make you might be fooled into thinking Wheeler was wealthy but not up to the brave new world. I'd learned that more than a few people tried conning Wheeler into deals and schemes they'd dreamed up, only to find themselves on the short, dirty end of the stick.

Wheeler had been no fool. Which made his involvement with Brad's spa more interesting, even curious.

Armed with information I'd gleaned through Olga, Xinhan, and other sources, maybe Phil Caragan wouldn't be able to duck the truth. If he was as close to Wheeler as Xinhan suggested, Caragan should know a lot. Then maybe I'd be a step or two closer to a solution.

The red sidewalk pavers echoed the red brick of the townhouse façade and gave the area an earthy, ancient feel. Somber black bunting draped the entrance. I climbed the white marble steps to the door and pressed the buzzer for Wheeler Enterprises. It didn't take long for the responding buzz which let me in.

The interior was subdued and filled with antiques, comfortable but expensive-looking furniture, and walls hung with paintings, some of which I recognized. In a reception area to the left stood a mahogany desk buffed to a high gloss. Propped on the desk, facing out, a black-framed picture of Smithson Wheeler.

Prim and proper, a middle-aged woman sat at the desk, her attention focused on me as I approached. Faded blonde hair, no make-up, and a sweet, sad smile gave her a comforting, motherly appearance. "May I help you?" Her voice was raspy.

"I'd like to see Mr. Caragan," I said.

"I'm afraid he's quite busy. Shall I make an appointment for you?"

"Couldn't you squeeze me in?" I gave her my sincerest forlorn puppy look. Who can resist a puppy?

"We've suffered a terrible loss and Mr. Caragan is... well, with Mr. Wheeler gone... He's awfully busy." She folded her hands over her daybook and stared at me pleasantly, if her watchdog gaze could be called pleasant. Obviously puppies meant nothing to her.

"This isn't something that can wait."

"Oh?" She raised her eyebrows and gave me a look I could interpret easily.

"I'm sorry. I should have identified myself." I stuck out my hand. "Marco Fontana, private investigator. I'm looking into the deaths of Mr. Wheeler and Mr. Lopes. And—"

"The police were already here." She obviously thought that should settle things.

"I'm not the police," I said.

"My point exactly." Her comforting, motherly appearance froze into a hard defensive shell.

"If it helps any, I'm working with the police. Mr. Caragan might be interested in cooperating."

"He's not available," she said, bulldog stubborn.

"Why don't you let *him* tell me he's too busy to help solve Wheeler's murder? While you're asking Mr. Caragan about his availability, tell him the police are a bit curious about his alibi for Friday night." Okay, so I told another lie. If it opens a door and solves a case, what's one little lie? Most it'd cost Caragan was a few white hairs.

"The police…? They never said anything like that." She eyed me as if she suspected I was lying but didn't trust her own senses.

"Listen, lady, the police aren't gonna tell you exactly what they know or what they suspect. They don't like it when people are uncooperative. They have the crazy idea that being uncooperative isn't the way innocent people act." Of course, that wasn't entirely true either, but most people believe it.

Comforting and Motherly picked up her phone and buzzed someone. She turned around to whisper into the phone, then turned back to glare at me.

"You can go in." She looked decidedly unhappy. "The oak door at the end of the hall."

"Thanks a bunch."

The hall was short, painted a restful green, and lined with gilt framed landscapes. The oak door was ajar. I knocked and waited.

"Enter," came a reedy voice.

Sitting behind an expansive oak desk was Phil Caragan, combination nerd and businessman. Limp brown hair and goggle-sized glasses contrasted with his fashionable dark silk suit and high-design tie. He removed his glasses and stood to greet me.

"Mr. Fontana is it?" He extended a hand.

"Right." We shook and he waved me to a seat. Neither of the barrelback chairs looked comfortable. I took the one allowing me to look directly at Caragan.

"What can I do for you? Maggie said you mentioned Smithson and the murder case? I've already talked to the police." He took a pencil from the desk and fiddled with it in what he must've considered a casual gesture.

"The police are tied up with a number of other cases. I'm helping investigate the murder of Brad Lopes. I understand he and Mr. Wheeler were good friends. Maybe…" I wanted to test the waters and see what he'd admit to.

Caragan again tried looking nonchalant, but it just wasn't in him. He picked up his glasses, placed them back on his face, took them off again and held them down on the desk as if they'd try escaping. Nerdy as he was, Caragan had a quirky but attractive face. Small turned up nose, sensuous mouth, strong chin. He was thin as a wafer, and that undercut his looks.

"T-they were friends, yes. Mr. Wheeler also had a financial interest in the spa Mr. Lopes was renovating. Apart from that…"

"Nothing else went on between them?"

"Of course not. Mr. Wheeler was above reproach."

"Sources tell me Wheeler was upset about something lately. I'm told Brad was the cause."

"Mr. Wheeler wasn't the kind of man you could apply the word 'upset' to very easily. He was calm and reasoned in everything he did."

"Yet, he's found dead in the midst of a very sordid scene."

"Mr. Fontana." Caragan stood abruptly. So thin he was lost in his clothes. "I've told the police everything I know. Surely they—"

"Did you happen to tell them why Wheeler was scheduled as a witness at the Branko trial and was struck from the witness list at the last moment?"

"I… The police never asked… not about the trial. Why is that even relevant?"

"I understand that Wheeler was not merely upset at Brad but outraged. Tell that to the police?"

"As far as B-Brad… Mr. Lopes is concerned, Smithso… Mr. Wheeler was not outraged. Not in the least." Caragan sat down again, dejected.

There was something in his voice when he spoke Brad's name, but I couldn't quite figure out what it meant. Longing, disappointment?

"Did you know Brad?"

"I… I'd met him. You couldn't exactly say I knew Brad… uh… Mr. Lopes." There it was again, his voice signaling something. This time it sounded more like sadness. A missed opportunity? Unrequited feelings?

"How'd you and Brad meet?"

"Mr. Wheeler was one of Brad's backers, as I said. Mr. Lopes came to the office to sign some papers," Caragan peered down at the vast desk in front of him as if remembering Brad and the papers and that day. "I handled those things all the time. I met many clients but never got to know any of them."

I decided to try a softer aproach. "You were Mr. Wheeler's right hand man, from what I understand."

"Yes. Yes, I was. Still am, really. There's no one else. No family, no business partners…" Suddenly he looked lost, as if he'd just arrived at the realization he'd have to handle every detail until things got sorted out.

"Mr. Wheeler must have trusted you a great deal."

"I was the only one who knew everything. Everyone here knows something but no one knows how everything works together." He paused. "Except… except me, of course."

"So, then you'd know all about his dealings with Branko?"

Caragan squinted at me as if he hoped I was some kind of illusion. He fiddled with his glasses still on his desk. A painful expression crossed his face and he appeared caught between annoyed, frightened, and distracted. "What?"

"Konstantin Branko, big time mobster. Small time developer. Sound familiar?"

"Mr. Wheeler had no dealings with Branko."

"You're sure?"

"I told you Mr. Wheeler had me handle everything, told me everything."

"Sounds to me like Wheeler had something to do with the Branko case considering he was set to testify at the trial. He must've encountered Branko. But you're tellin' me he didn't know the mobster?"

"He had nothing to do with the man. That much I know." He paused. "You said it yourself, Mr. Wheeler was struck from the witness list. That should tell you he didn't know Branko."

Okay, maybe the nerd was telling a shaded variety of the truth but he wasn't about to tell me much more. Not here anyway. Wheeler had some connection to Branko. Whatever it was, Caragan knew enough to tell me a half truth and make it sound close to the real thing. Except, I don't trust a word most people say and I can spot a liar. Caragan skated around the truth. Not lying but not being honest. "That's too bad."

"How's that? How is the fact that Mr. Wheeler never had anything to do with some criminal a bad thing?"

"Newspapers, bloggers, and websites are gonna shout all about it tomorrow. They'll say Wheeler must have had something to hide. His office won't talk about his connections to Branko in light of the trial." I said. "That's just for starters. Then there's Branko's defense team. They're gonna implicate Wheeler somehow when they appeal the conviction. They seem to know about some altercation between Branko and Wheeler a while back. Maybe they'll run with that to get Branko out of jail. Y'know, Wheeler is on again, off again as a witness, maybe the prosecution found some nasty connection to Branko that made Wheeler useless to them."

Caragan stared at me, a growing look of horror creeping across his soft features.

"Have I got it right, you think? You deal with the press all the time. You know how they'll play this, am I right?"

"They… they can't…" He stared in my direction but I was sure he wasn't seeing me. His expression changed from horror to sorrow, his eyes turned glassy.

"They can and they will. As long as you don't get out in front of this, the press will spin it whatever way gets them the most readers. They don't give a damn whether something is true or half true or even a lie. If it sells, they print it."

"What about Smithson's reputation? His friends, the communities he helped..."

"Yeah, I understand," I said with exaggerated concern. "Those people who knew him well will know the truth. Won't matter what the press says, right? His reputation..."

"Will be destroyed. All the good work he's done..."

"Not much you can do, I guess..." I made as if to stand.

"Wait. Don't go yet..." He stood as if to stop me.

"Listen, you don't wanna talk, that's cool with me. I've got to run down some other leads." I slipped one of my cards from my pocket and handed it to Caragan. "You think of anything else you wanna tell me, call. That's my cell number. You can always reach me there."

"Wait. Please..." Caragan crumpled back into his too-large chair. "I can't let that happen. I can't let them do that to him."

"Then...?"

"Can we talk somewhere else?" Caragan stood. He seemed nervous now, no longer defensive.

"Sure. Got somewhere in mind?"

"There's a café not far from here. *La Poule.* You know it?"

"Been there a time or two," I said. Been there and hadn't felt comfortable. Pretentious was the word of the day at *La Poule.* Poseurs of every stripe occupied tables nursing micro-sized cups of coffee while they sullenly read a book, or drearily tapped away at a laptop, or engaged in a heated conversation. A faux anger hung in the air at the café, like stale cigarette smoke, souring everything.

Caragan walked around his desk, his skinny body ethereal and light. He waved me ahead, closed the door behind him, and walked the short hall with me.

"I'll be back, Maggie," he said to the secretary who looked none too happy.

"The... accountants... the lawyers... how am I... when... when...?" she sputtered.

"Everything will wait, Maggie. I've got things under control. No one is due until late in the day," he said with a soothing, kindness in his voice.

Out on the sidewalk, he looked around at the dazzling sunny day and took a deep breath. He blossomed in the fresh air. No longer confined by the dour office, Caragan looked less the nerd now.

"Shall we?" He gestured me forward and we walked together toward Twentieth Street.

Caragan almost had a spring in his step. Was he just feeling let loose from the confinement of the office, or was he about to unburden himself of things he couldn't stand keeping secret? I was betting on the latter. He obviously carried the weight of having to protect Wheeler's reputation.

"How long have you worked for Wheeler?"

"Since I graduated from college. That's longer ago than you might imagine. Smithson took me in as a favor to my uncle, his associate."

"Seems to have paid off…"

"I considered it a stepping stone. A way-station on the road to something better. Something exciting."

"Like? A career in what?"

"That was the problem. I didn't know. Lots of kids seem to know exactly what they want, where they want to go, and just how to get there. Not me."

"You've got that wrong. Most kids don't know much about what they want. They go to college then just float into something or luck into something and whammo a career is born."

"Some of the people I went to school with had definite ideas about where they wanted to be. I was one of those that lucked into something, like you said."

"Paid off. You're running the business now."

"That isn't what I want. I was satisfied behind the scenes. Didn't have a lot of responsibility… I had responsibilities, but I wasn't running the show. You know what I mean?"

"Now…?"

"Even if I wanted to run the business, Smithson had other ideas. He outlined his plans for me and spelled everything out in his will. There won't be a Wheeler Enterprises anymore." He resumed walking again.

"What happens to you?"

He stopped to scrutinize me. "Is *that* what this is all about? You want to know if I had something to do with Smithson's murder?"

"The thought had occurred but—"

"Did it ever occur to you that his death might put me out on the streets?"

"Does it? You going to be destitute now?"

"Smithson always said he'd take care of me. He told me he'd already provided for me in his long range plans, even in the event he sold the business."

"And now…?"

"I assume the same conditions apply but I don't know details yet. There wasn't a grand rush to find his will. So, it's not like I killed him for money."

"How about for love? Did you have a thing for Brad? Maybe Smithson—"

"Don't be absurd, Mr. Fontana." Caragan deflected my questions. That wouldn't stop me from asking again.

By this time we'd arrived at the café and took a corner table near a window. I always found the strangely mottled walls disconcerting. Weird slashes of muted colors all around, nothing coherent or soothing. I faced the window instead.

I left Caragan at the table and went to the counter. As I'd hoped, the cute-in-the-extreme, curly-headed guy was still serving his house blends. I asked what his favorite was. I already knew it was the Moroccan blend. I just wanted to hear him rhapsodize about it in his killer French accent, as he filled two cups and placed them before me. He was the best thing about the place and the only reason I ever stopped in. I brought the coffee back to the table, the French guy's voice still tickling my erogenous zones.

"So, you wanted to tell me something about Wheeler and Branko but not at the office. That's why we're here, right?"

"I… I didn't want—"

"Didn't want the secretary to hear what you had to say? I thought *you* were in charge."

"Maggie's efficient. Professional. But she doesn't like me and she's close with other developers. Men who'd love to swallow the business whole."

"Not if Wheeler has his plans in place."

"Maggie's clever, Mr. Fontana. She has access to things and I'm afraid she could do some dirty work. So, I don't want her to hear any of this. Not a word. Clear?"

"As a dewdrop," I said. "Shoot. What's Branko's connection?"

"You're sure this won't..." He looked at me and there was pain in his eyes. Clearly conflicted about whatever it was he knew or thought he knew, Caragan must have felt a great loyalty to Wheeler.

"I can't make many promises, Mr. Caragan. I can tell you that I'm not here to ruin anyone's reputation. But this is a murder investigation. Sometimes people get involved in things they never might have if it weren't for some pretty strong reasons."

"I... I understand... it's just that Smithson... he was kind and generous. I have a hard time believing anything bad about him. But—"

"Just tell me what you know. I promise I'll do what I can."

"Honestly, I don't know every detail but I know, from what I've overheard, that there was some kind of connection."

"Overheard?"

"Smithson told me everything about the business. But there were some things I never knew about. They weren't business related, like this... this... whatever it was I overheard."

He paused, put precisely three packets of sugar in his coffee, shook them until not even sugar dust was left, then stirred. As his spoon clinked against the cup, I watched his face. He appeared younger than the late thirties or early forties he must have been. Younger but tired and grieving.

"I overheard several phone conversations. The walls aren't thick, and Smithson raised his voice when he spoke. He was excited and his voice was loud enough to hear through the wall."

That didn't jibe with the unflappable Wheeler image Caragan tried to paint earlier.

"Excited how? Upset, angry, frightened?"

"All three actually."

"What kinds of things did he say?"

"What I heard was disjointed. Occasionally a whole sentence, but mostly phrases or words. Branko was one of the words..."

"How many of these calls were there?"

"I heard a few. There were probably others I didn't hear. I'm not in the office all the time."

"Might as well start from the beginning and go from there. Tell me what you remember as best you can…" I took out a notebook and a pen.

"Five, six months ago… something like that, is the first time I overheard him." He sipped some coffee and shut his eyes. "It's kind of like a dream now. Smithson said, 'Branko? Who is that? Are you sure about him?' Then he was silent, probably listening, after which he said, 'He'll take care of things? What exactly…?' Then he began whispering. I didn't have my ear against the wall. The only reason I paid attention was that he raised his voice. He'd never done that. Never."

"Must've been important for him to get worked up. Was that all he said?"

"He mentioned payments and how much something would cost, I don't know what. And who was going to handle things."

"When did the other calls occur?"

"What I'm telling you is only what I overheard. There may have been other calls."

"I understand. For the calls you did hear, when did they occur?"

"They were spaced out. One was a few weeks later. Another a few days after that. And the next…" He looked stricken.

"What about that next call?"

"It's just… You have to understand I wasn't listening closely. It wouldn't have been right. That would have been like spying on him. I only heard whatever came through the walls." He was weighed down with guilt.

"Why don't you continue from the second call, maybe as you work through it things will be clear."

"O-okay, I guess so. During the second call Smithson didn't mention Branko. He spoke about associates who were making contributions of some kind. He said the name Remy."

"You know who Remy is?"

"It has to be Remy Berwick. Another developer, one of Smithson's oldest associates. Very rich, very powerful. Sometimes they'd clash, sometimes they'd work together."

"Wheeler say anything else while he was talking to Berwick?"

"Smithson said the contributors Remy mentioned had high expectations. Remy must have been particularly pushy because Smithson shouted 'That's asking a lot.' Then he was silent a moment before he said, 'You're sure things will work out?' Something like that. I can't be sure."

"Contributions? Any idea what he was referring to?"

"No idea. He could have been talking about political contributions. Smithson and other developers often gave money to candidates. The cost of doing business. Smithson told me many times it's the only way things get done."

"Yeah, I know the drill. Is that all the second call was about?"

"Pretty much. Now that I think about it, Smithson used the same phrase in this call as in the first. He asked, 'He'll take care of things?' That's all I heard."

"The third call?"

"That was almost a week later. Mr. Wheeler was agitated that whole day. I heard him raising his voice again and he said '… realize the implications?' Then he was silent."

"That was it?"

"He stayed quiet for a while but then I heard him mention Branko and say that Branko's arrest meant trouble. He said '… serious for all of… Remy.' That's pretty much… oh!, right. The last thing he said was 'Will he talk?' Then he was quiet."

"Nothing else?"

"He spoke again but it was standard building and construction business. I don't think Smithson liked what he heard. I thought I heard him say 'code violations.' But there was no context."

"You said there was another call and something about it upset you?"

Caragan was quiet and I let him have time to think and remember. I finished my Moroccan blend and looked at Caragan who appeared uncomfortable.

"It's just that… I remembered something else…"

"About that phone call?"

"Yes. I keep thinking I'd overheard a total of four calls. But the fourth time I heard anything, there were actually two calls, one right after the other. That was the day Smithson was murdered." He stared at the empty cup in front of him.

"I'll get us more coffee," I said, keeping my voice low.

Caragan nodded. I figured he could use a few minutes to collect himself. I went back to the counter but the French heartthrob must've been on break. I took two more Moroccan blends and brought them back to the table.

"Feeling better?"

"I'm feeling numb," Caragan said, placing his hands around the cup as if for warmth.

"Wanna talk about the other calls?" I coaxed.

Caragan again took three packets of sugar and dumped them into his cup. "It seems so impossible. There I was in the office along with Smithson and later that night he'd be dead. Murdered. Neither of us gave a thought to anything that day except business. We went about our routine…" His voice faded to nothing as he stared down at his coffee.

"Neither of you could have known anything."

"Smithson might have known things were not good. He might've…"

"Why do you say that?"

"He seemed distracted and worried that morning. Later in the day when I heard the calls, he was not at all happy. He raised his voice again but these calls were different."

"Different how?"

"In the first call, it seemed he spoke with someone he'd never talked to before. It was like this person asked questions allowing Smithson to give only brief answers. It didn't sound like a conversation. Not like the other calls."

"More like an interview?" I suspected maybe Vega had made that call to Wheeler.

"Could be. All I know is what it sounded like through a wall. Smithson's answers were clipped. He did a lot of listening."

"Was Branko mentioned?"

Caragan nodded. "That's when Smithson said the most but it wasn't much. Smithson said the name Branko and the word 'conviction.' At one point, he shouted, 'They tried what?' then he was silent. I assumed he was listening to the other person. After a few moments, he said, 'I trusted him.' And—"

"Any idea who he meant?"

"Not at first. Smithson said, 'I'll be there.' Then he hung up. After a few moments he began speaking again. Just as loud."

"He'd made the call?"

"Must have. I didn't hear the phone ring. This time Smithson sounded furious."

"What'd he say?" I asked.

"It was brief. Muffled, at first, as if he'd walked to the other side of the room. I only heard him say 'betrayal of trust.' His voice became clear again and he said, 'I'll handle this myself.' He mentioned meeting someone and 'fixing' things or 'putting an end' to something. That's when I thought I heard him say the word 'spa' or something very much like it. If that's what he said, then I assume he was discussing Brad. I don't know what was going on. It was confusing. Smithson cared about Brad, so did... I mean it couldn't be him..."

I didn't want to press him. His lower lip quivered and he could barely grip his cup.

Chapter 24

Caragan wanted to stay a while longer at the café to sort out his thoughts. I imagined he needed time away from the office. Grieving wasn't possible there, and he needed to mourn. It wasn't just Wheeler he'd lost, but a way of life and a sense of himself that was all tied up with Wheeler Enterprises.

He'd given me a lot to go on, including Remy Berwick. According to Caragan, though, the guy was hardly ever in town, preferring to do business from ever-changing locations in other countries. I'd find him if I had to.

Unfortunately Caragan also gave me what sounded like evidence that Wheeler wasn't as saintly as Xinhan and others believed. It was circumstantial at best. Wheeler could have meant a lot of things by what he'd said on the phone. Caragan had only heard one side of the conversation. Still, it didn't sound good.

After calling Nina, I headed down to her place, which I like to call the Fortress of Geekiness. Geek is what Nina does, not what she is. She's more of a sultry computer genius who hides her figure under baggy clothes, and disguises the beauty in her swarthy face with oversized glasses and a chaotic hairdo. She also sports an unusual tattoo of a double-headed ancient Aztec serpent. One head nips at her left elbow while the rest slinks up her arm and onto her neck where the other head stares greedily at her throat.

Better than being a looker, Nina is smart. Computer smart as well as worldly. She can hack her way into places few others dare and never sweats the details of a job. If anyone could find the information I needed it was Nina and her crew.

As I walked to her place, I decided to give Shim a heads up about my research. Enough to let him feel I was keeping him in the loop. Enough to remind him he needed to do the same for me. We both knew we were holding out on each other. That's the game. He answered on the first ring. That was interesting.

"Just wanted to catch you up on where I am on the case."

"I hope you've got more than we do." He sounded frustrated and tense.

"Nothing on the journalist, yet? I was hoping you could help with some details."

"All we know is who he is. The former wife doesn't know a thing and hasn't seen him in a few years."

"No way to track what he was working on?" I asked wondering if they'd come across the photographer yet. I'd have to give up his name sooner or later.

"Nope. We've got nothing except the mayor nipping at our asses. Needs some good publicity."

"Nothing ever changes."

"What've you come up with, Fontana? And don't tell me nothing. I know you're holding back. I'm learning about you fast."

"Giuliani's a good teacher, no doubt," I said and laughed.

"She tosses me bits and pieces now and then. If you're anything like other P.I.s I've worked with, you know a hell of a lot more than you're saying."

Couldn't fault him there and I couldn't hold everything back. "I did come across a few things like Wheeler and that trial, maybe you should know about. Some of it is supposition… but—"

"Supposition is better than what I've got. Tell me when and where. I'll be there."

We arranged to meet at the Village Brew later that afternoon and I continued down to the Old City neighborhood and The Fortress.

* * *

Nina's townhouse was huge and secure. Deena and Hallie, Nina's partners in her company, InfoMonkeys, were protective of Nina. Way protective. I knew what to expect when I pressed the buzzer. An electrical whirr alerted me to the fact I was being scrutinized by security cameras. I waved and smiled just to annoy Hallie who probably hadn't smiled since she was an infant.

The metallic sound of locks pulling back was followed by the door whooshing open. I entered the vestibule and, for all I know, was hit with some kind of disinfectant laser beam. Eventually I was permitted entry into the sanctuary and saw Nina fussing with images that seemed to float in the air.

"*Jefe*, long time. How are you?"

"Gettin' by, Nina."

"I'm sorry about your friend." Nina's pretty face was drawn down into a sad expression. "You got the other information, right? On the creepy ex?"

"Yep, but he's still a ghost. Not making much headway and I need your help."

"You got it. Lemme get rid of this stuff." She flashed her hands over the images and they dissolved into thin air. "You wanna finish that up, Deena?"

Deena nodded and left the room. Hallie observed from the doorway, her eyes trained on me. Not a whole lot makes me shiver, but Hallie came close.

"Whatcha got, *jefe*?"

I explained about Brad, Wheeler, and Vega. I told her about Branko and the trial and about Berwick. Just about everything I knew so far.

"You got a lotta dots and no connections."

"That's why I'm here. I'm counting on you."

"How do you wanna start this ball rollin'?" She smiled so sweetly, you'd never know she was the best hacker this side of Moscow.

"I need anything you can get me on Branko and his local connections. That's easy for you."

"You don't need me for that. Olga is just as good when it comes to…"

"Yeah, you're right. She'll do that."

"So what's the real deal? I know you want more than that."

"What I need is financial records on a few people. Can you do it?"

"Question is not can I do it. Question is can you afford a lawyer to keep me outta jail?" She stared at me with a deadpan serious expression as if I'd just asked the dangerously impossible.

I knew she was kidding. She'd been doing this kind of thing for all sorts of people and had never gotten caught. Hadn't ever been close to getting caught. I knew for a fact she was a legend among hackers. "Like you'd need a lawyer. You'd have to get caught first and that's not happening." I laughed.

She smiled again. Two in a row. I'd hit a soft spot. "So, tell me what you need," she said.

I asked her for every financial record she could find tied to Brad. The money to redo the spa had to come from somewhere. Nina would know how to trace it to its source. I also needed financials on Wheeler, Branko, and Berwick which would be trickier, but I'd seen her tackle more complex stuff.

Of course there was the list of names I'd gleaned from the trial transcript. I needed information on as many of them as I could get. Olga would be overwhelmed but Nina had her partners and they could make quick work of the list. I showed Nina the names and watched her eyes widen. "I'm looking for political donations made by the three I mentioned and the businessmen and developers on this list." I pointed to the names on the list. "We marked each name with identifiers."

"You're not asking much, are you *papi?*" She patted my face then gave me a gentle slap.

"I'll double your going rate. I need this."

"I'm hurt, Marco."

"Why? What'd I do?"

"How can you imagine I would take money for this? This is for your friend Brad, right? To solve his murder?"

"Yeah, sure, but this is work, a lot of work… and it's dicey, too."

"This I'm not chargin' for. No way."

"Some of it could be dangerous…"

"Keeps me on my toes, Marco. Besides, I haven't hacked into banks for a long while. Gonna be like old times."

* * *

There was just enough time to hustle over to The Village Brew to meet Shim. When I arrived I found him sitting at a table near the huge front window engrossed in reading something. Shim glanced up as I sat in the chair across from him. He looked mildly uncomfortable surrounded as he was by tables of gay men and lesbians. I figured this would be good for him which is why I suggested the place. Maybe it'd begin the long process of dragging him out of his closet. My gaydar wasn't singing "Glory, Glory Hallelujah" yet, but it was sending out little pings of recognition. I'd give it time.

"Glad you could make it," Shim said looking at his watch as if I were late. When you're ill at ease time passes more slowly.

"Right on time, detective. Lemme get some coffee. Can I get you something?"

He shook his head, then stared down at his notepad.

Fortunately Sean wasn't working the counter or Shim would get the full treatment and that'd probably drive him further into the closet. I glanced over at Shim while I waited for my coffee and noticed that every once in a while he'd surreptitiously look around. I wondered whether it was out of interest in someone or just defensive reconnoitering of his surroundings. Several men stared longingly at Shim and whenever he accidentally caught their eyes, he hurriedly went back to reading his notes.

Coffee in hand, I sat down and faced him.

"You said you had things to tell me about the case?" Shim said. "I'm hoping you do. First time Giuliani gives me the lead on a case, it turns out to be a ball busting knot."

"I'll do what I can. If I break the case, you get the credit. It's your collar as far as I'm concerned. Finding Brad's killer is what's important."

"That's generous, Fontana. Not like some private eyes I know. I'll owe you big time if that's the way it turns out." The serious look in his coal-black eyes was disarming.

I smiled what I hoped was a sly, maybe even a little seductive, smile. I was sure he got my message from the way he squirmed in his seat.

"I did some digging on Wheeler, and I think he might've been one of Brad's backers." I only knew what Xinhan and Caragan had said. There was no paper proof yet. "How long would it take to get financial information proving that? I mean bank accounts and money transfers."

"Depends. In any event, I'd need a warrant. To get that, I need probable cause for wanting the warrant."

"So you're saying it'll take time."

"Don't these things always take time?"

"If you know where to look, it shouldn't take long. For instance, I managed to get some information on that trial I called you about."

"We've been concentrating on the Vega case and getting nowhere. I should have assigned somebody to look into the trial. But it's total chaos down there." Shim sipped some of his coffee, then massaged his temples. "This case is making me see double, you know?"

I nodded.

Shim looked at me then continued. "What've you got on the trial?"

"Wheeler was—"

"We already know Wheeler was struck from the witness list on some trial."

"It's not just *some* trial."

"Some thug named Branko was on the hot seat, right? That supposed to mean something?"

"I thought Konstantin Branko would be a big deal for you guys."

"Heard of him, of course. Wheeler was dropped from that trial. Case closed as far as that's concerned." Shim sounded tired.

"Not really." I crooked an eyebrow and nailed him with a look.

"Huh?"

"Remember Brad was on a jury, right?"

Shim nodded then it dawned on him. "He was on…?"

"Yep. Brad was on the Branko jury." I didn't think I needed to tell him I had the transcript. He had to do *some* work on his own.

"Okay. Interesting coincidence. So?"

"Add that to Wheeler being a witness, even if he was dropped, and it seems like something to me."

"Maybe."

"Then both Brad and Wheeler are killed. Any bells ringing?"

"Just one of those weird coincidences. It happens."

"No such thing, Dae. I'll give you this much, though. Maybe they were both connected to the trial as some sort of insane cosmic joke. Then Brad and Wheeler both turn up dead? That's taking coincidence to a whole new level. I'm not buying it. "

"I'm not convinced. Sure, it's weird, but I'm not seeing any sparks."

"It's something," I said. "Worth pursuing."

"I've heard people downtown talk about Branko. A lot of people want a piece of him but nobody's been able to get anything big to stick." Shim made a few notes in his little book. "I'll put someone on this. Giuliani wants me on the Vega case. She says it comes first. This will make her happy, though."

"Just doin' my part. You know, in the keep-me-in-the-loop game"

"I owe you, Marco. Thanks."

"Thanks? That's all I get? What about our deal?" I said.

"The deal… what…?"

"Coy doesn't fit you, Dae. Stop wearing it."

He looked me in the eye and smiled. I had to admit it was a dazzler of a lopsided smile, white teeth, pretty lips and all, but I wanted information and I wasn't about to let him distract me with a smile. No matter how appealing it was. Which made me wonder about just how conscious he was of his effect on another guy. Maybe he wasn't crammed as far into that closet as I assumed.

"Okay, okay. But we've got very little…"

"That's fine as long as it's something I can use. If you want me to keep feeding you facts, I need some quid pro quo."

He sighed. "You probably know more than we do, but I'll tell you what we've got."

After he'd told me what they'd turned up, I realized he was right. They didn't know half what I knew. I let him think he'd given me some primo information, anyway.

"Thanks, Dae." I drained my cup. The coffee had grown cold and I needed to get back to the office before I checked in at Bubbles.

"Anytime, Fontana." As he stood he took his cup and looked toward the counter.

"I've gotta work at Bubbles tonight," I said. "How about coming in for a drink. It'll be on me."

Shim stood there, cup in hand, as if he'd been short circuited, not knowing which way to turn or what to say. He glanced at me like I'd asked him to strip.

"No pressure, Dae. Just thought I'd ask since I've gotta hang at Bubbles for a few hours."

"Another time. Maybe... Or maybe—"

"Another place?" I smiled innocently.

* * *

As I entered the office, Olga was lugging a large stack of folders into my office. "Boss is arriving in time for big work."

"That a present for me, cupcake?"

"I am looking like cupcake? Dress makes Olga fat?"

"No, Olga. The dress looks good. Red is your color." I pecked her on the cheek as she set the folders on my desk. "You look delicious."

"Olga is too old for boss. And too... woman." She left the room shutting the door behind her.

Flipping through the files I saw she'd constructed dossiers for the names we'd culled from the trial transcript that she could locate in our databases. Businessmen, local thugs, and various other players. A long list. I decided to call Luke for help, since there were too many folders for me to cover quickly. If we could find connections between these people and Wheeler or Brad or even Vega that would be something solid.

Luke wasn't at the office which was unusual. Chip, one of Luke's original employees, answered the phone and said Luke had taken the afternoon off. It didn't take a private eye to figure out he was spending the afternoon with Xinhan.

I figured I'd better dig in and get started on my own. I filled my mug with coffee and opened the first file. Olga had done her usual more-than-thorough job.

By the time I'd finished six of the folders, it was easy to see that the businessmen were entangled with each other through corporate and social ties. It was also clear most of them liked playing the political game by making bipartisan campaign contributions.

I had no doubt they wanted something for their political gifts. Which is what got me thinking about just what they wanted and what they might do to get it. After all, here they were on witness lists or brought up in testimony at the trial of a vicious thug. That spoke for itself.

My head spun as I read through Olga's research. It was time to call it a day and get ready for my stint at Bubbles. The files would be there in the morning and I'd call in some help.

I needed a shower and a meal before I went to tame my guys at Bubbles.

* * *

Thursdays were usually an unofficial Audition Night with last minute sign-ups and audience judging. An easy night most of the time. When I walked in I spotted Kent and Jean-Claude taking names of would-be dancers.

"I guess you're in charge again tonight," I said to Jean-Claude.

"Anton told me he needed to study. He was surrounded by his books when I left," Jean-Claude said.

That sounded very domestic. While I'm out chasing leads that don't pan out, Anton and Ty get to be cozy and warm at home. It was beginning to sound appealing.

"You need me to MC or can I just hang?" I asked.

"Oh, no, I need you, Marco. I cannot be the MC," Jean-Claude said.

"Don't look at me," Kent said, his voice quavering.

"Good enough. Then Jean-Claude, you can open the show tonight. Light the house up and get everybody going. Got your g-string with you?" The way he danced he'd not only light things up, he set the place on fire.

"Sure. Always ready! I can use the extra cash." Jean-Claude handed the contestant list to Kent. "Textbooks, they will be expensive. The more I dance, the better for me." He took off up the stairs to the dressing rooms.

"Call me ten minutes before showtime, Kent. You'll handle the list?"

"Sure, as long as I don't have to read it to the audience." Kent laughed.

As I was about to head up to my office, I felt a hand on my shoulder. I turned slowly and there behind me was Shuster, short, stubby, and looking scared. He had that act down pat.

"I though you didn't get lowdown enough to come into places like this?" I shrugged off his hand.

"He assaulted me again."

"Who? Kelley? What's your beef? Isn't your job taking shit from him?"

"Not Kelley. The thug. The one who attacked me on the street. The one who spied on me when I was talking to you."

"I'm supposed to do what exactly?"

"Get him off my back. It's obvious he's coming after me because I talk to you."

"Then it was pretty smart to let him see you comin' in here. Maybe that'll make him think twice next time." I started up the stairs. "Don't you ever learn?"

"That's it?"

"What *can* I do, Shuster? I don't know the guy or how to find him. And I'm not your daddy."

Shuster glared at me. "I knew you wouldn't help."

"Then why're you here?"

"I hoped…"

"I have a question for you."

"Get stuffed, Fontana." Shuster turned to go.

"Something's been bothering me, Shuster."

"Like I should care?"

"Why'd Josh Nolan come to see you at Kelley's office?"

Shuster's face darkened and he opened his mouth to speak.

I interrupted. "Now don't give me the same bullshit you tried the other night."

"That was the truth. Nolan was—"

"Why was he really there?"

"I… he… Nolan was…"

"I've seen you two eyeing one another. Like at the pub crawl. I saw the looks crossing between you two that night."

"You're imagining things." Shuster's wall had gone back up.

"Just wonderin' is all." There was something going on between them.

"What about that thug? He might've followed me here."

"Call 911. The police take that kind of thing seriously.

"Funny when it's me he's after."

"Don't let the door smack your ass on the way out."

* * *

Stan's guys moved efficiently cleaning up and closing Bubbles for the night. Half of them would run over to an after hours club to party away what was left of the night. As for me, I wanted to clear my head and get to sleep. Working two jobs, even if one of them was watching strippers and managing their drama, wasn't easy. It'd take it's toll eventually. For now I could hack it.

Next door, Café Bubbles was bustling and would be for a few more hours. Late night strollers, refugees from the bars, tweakers from after-hours joints, all of them found their way to the café. Then there'd be a lull until the breakfast crowd came roaring in and the whole cycle would play itself out again. I took a pass on the café. I needed quiet. I decided to take a walk before going home. The cool night air would clear my mind.

I liked this time of night; between two and four in the morning, there was a silence that allowed you to think. Most other people out at that hour seemed to abide by an unwritten code allowing the peace of the night to take over. I strolled over to Spruce Street. Some of the old buildings there possessed a faded elegance that spoke of wonderful events more than a hundred years before. All secret now, all lost. These days, the old houses were home to apartment dwellers who enjoyed the ancient feel of the old buildings and medical students needing to live close to their hospitals.

After a while, I turned down Quince Street which held a lot of memories for me. Just the name "Quince" brought back a flood of thoughts about a certain someone who'd flashed into and out of my life in a few brief months. It was so quick, most people would've forgotten the whole episode. For me it represented something significant. The memory of the man at the heart of it had stayed with me.

A genteel street lined with trees and whoppingly expensive homes, Quince Street always gave me a sense of peace.

Not tonight. As I approached the darkened Mask and Wig Club, I felt rather than saw, someone tailing me. He was good because I hadn't noticed a thing earlier. I kept walking, not wanting to alert whoever it was that I was on to him. When I approached Cypress, an even smaller street, I slowed down and hugged the wall opposite. Whoever was following might have an accomplice waiting there.

I thought if I could reach Pine Street, I might be able to see who was following me or give him the slip. With a quarter of a block to go, I slowed my pace. I listened for anything that might betray the person tracking me.

Nothing. Not a sound. There wasn't even a breeze rustling the leaves. I slowly moved forward toward Pine. I knew the Kahn Place homes and the adjacent park would be on my left and Effie's Restaurant on my right. But Effie's would be long-closed and the Kahn complex would be dead asleep.

All I had to do was make it to Pine. There'd be traffic and light and maybe a way to lose the tail.

Nearly there, I stopped and listened again. Silence. Whoever was tailing me knew what he was doing. Wanted me to think he'd gone.

I could see the street lights on Pine. A few more steps and I'd break right and head for Twelfth Street and mix in with stragglers leaving the bars.

When I reached the corner of Quince and Pine, a black sedan pulled in front of me, quick and lethal. Long and dark with tinted windows, the car idled and a rear door swung open.

"Mr. Fontana…" A voice like dust and dried earth wafted from the interior of the backseat. "Get in."

I knew better than to take candy from strange men let alone get into their cars. Especially the car of some creep who sounded like he spoke from the grave. I briefly stared into the blackness of the sedan's interior. Before I could move, someone struck from behind, pushing me into the car. I tumbled onto the seat next to the dusty voice.

The thug who'd pushed me squeezed in next to me, slammed the door, and quickly pulled both my arms behind my back. He held my wrists together tightly with one huge hand. His crushing grip sent sharp stabs of pain through me.

A stale sweaty odor mixed with the smell of tobacco and sour food swirled in the darkness.

Tires squealed, peeling out on the street. I felt the forward thrust of the car as it rushed down Pine. All the while I scanned the coal black interior for a way to escape. There was none.

"You are a healthy man, *áno?*" said the heavily accented, dusty voice.

I stared into the darkness trying to see his face. The hat he wore added to the depths of the shadows engulfing him.

My wrists and hands lost feeling. Adrenaline pumped through me but I was in a vise.

"I am assuming you want to stay in good health? I am correct, *nie?*"

I twisted and writhed attempting to free myself from the iron grip of the man behind me. I turned my face away from the dusty voice.

"Mr. Fontana does not wish to speak, Matus. We must make him feel more welcome." The more he spoke the dustier he sounded.

The car bounced and bumped speeding over city streets. The driver made several turns which I felt as my body responded to the movement. I had no idea where they were taking me. I just knew I had to break free soon or end up a dead man.

There wasn't much chance to think because Matus, still gripping my wrists, slammed my head with his other meaty hand. I reeled forward then back, his hand connected again, bashing my head against the black glass partition dividing the front seat from the back. I felt blood trickle down my face.

"Matus! *Mravmi*, Matus, *mravmi*! Mr. Fontana cannot speak with injured mouth, *áno?*"

A hand, feeling as dry and frail as the voice sounded, grasped my chin. There was no strength in that hand but Matus had seen to it that my jaw felt any touch as pain.

"A pity. Such a face. You see, Matus?" He turned my head in the other direction, presumably so Matus could see. "Beautiful."

Matus grunted contemptuously behind me. "Pretty boy. No heart, no balls."

"Be gracious, Matus." The hand squeezed my jaw slightly so he could turn my face toward his again, which I still couldn't see in the murky blackness of the backseat. "Mr. Fontana comes from a noble line. Is that not so? I can see this in such a face."

Hey, as far as I knew the only throne my family owned was in the bathroom. If this guy thought I was a prince, he was nuts.

"Get your hand off me," I mumbled best I could between the squeeze and the pain. "What the fuck do you want? Who are you?" My words were garbled.

"A man of little importance," the dusty voice wheezed. "Except, perhaps, to you in this moment."

"Yeah, how so?"

"I carry a message. For you."

As if I couldn't guess what it might be. I'd ticked somebody off and this was the result. I also bet if I could see Matus, he'd be the guy that spied on me and Shuster that night at the café.

"Not impressed. You could'a picked up the phone."

"A sense of humor is a good thing," the voice said, fading into the darkness. "…but not for you. Not now…"

Matus cracked me again. He must've had a ring or keys or something sharp. I felt pain above my left eye and more blood trickled down my face."

"Do we have your attention now, Mr. Fontana?"

"Spit it out and tell your boy to lay off. I meet him in a fair fight and he'll see who's got balls and who doesn't."

"You are… *tvrdohlavý*… how do you say this in English?… pigheaded. Yes, you are pigheaded for such a pretty boy." He sighed and I caught another whiff of spiced tobacco. "I will spit it out, as you say," the man whispered.

"I'm listening."

"You have the talent for making people nervous."

"Only if they have a reason to be."

"Ah, but sometimes you are making the wrong people nervous, *nie?*"

"I never make the wrong people nervous… catch my drift?" I blinked away a drop of blood trying to slip into my eye.

"This time you have."

"That's too bad."

"Yes and no. Yes, it is too bad for you, if you keep going as you are…" He paused, coughed, cleared his throat. "And no, it will not be bad for you, if you go back to spying on little men who make life unpleasant for everyone with their petty desires."

"That your message?"

"Do you know what is *bieda?*... No, of course you do not. *Bieda* is misery. And we can make your world misery upon misery. For you and your friends. Until we choose to end your life. And it will be our choice, Mr. Fontana. Make not the mistake of arrogance."

"Yeah you got a lock on *bieda*. I get it."

"Good. You are not so dumb as it would appear."

"Now it's your turn..." I sat up as best I could with Matus keeping his death grip on my wrists. "You listen to *my* message. It's simple: Fuck off! I don't give up because some lackey in the shadows delivers a message of doom. Who owns you anyway?"

He chuckled. It was an ominous sound, filled with confidence and cruelty.

"You must'a really pissed someone off to be used as a messenger boy at your age."

"A pity." He turned his head to face front. I could only see his hat as he turned. There must've been a signal of some sort. He grunted something I didn't understand.

The car skidded to a stop. Matus swung open the door, backed himself out. Still gripping my wrists, he yanked me out with him. He shoved me to the ground and kicked me in the ribs a few times. He spat words that sounded like "*slaboch*" and "*buzerant*," as he kicked. At that point I wasn't sure what I heard.

He was about to continue when the dusty voice shouted his name, "Matus! *Prist!*" Tall and lanky, Matus slowly stood back, foot poised for another kick. He stood back and the light caught his face. It *was* the same guy who'd spied on me and Shuster.

The dry, raspy shout came again, "*Prist!*"

Matus stood over me and glared.

Once more the grating voice, "Matus!"

The rugged blond turned toward the car and stepped in.

His name echoed in my head "Matus." It sounded kinda familiar, too. My head pounded with pain and that was all I remembered thinking before I blacked out.

Chapter 25

When I came to, blurry lights and black sky crowded my vision. I spit out some blood mixed with dirt, lifted my head and spotted a few scraggly bushes. Or what looked like bushes in the semi darkness. Cars whizzed by somewhere and there were more blurry lights above. Street lights. The sedan was gone but a few other cars were stationed here and there. I realized they'd dumped me in an open parking lot. But where?

Slowly I sat up, my ribs were on fire but I didn't think anything was broken. My head ached and there was blood. Fresh blood oozed and dried blood covered my face and clothes. I remembered Matus knocking me around and felt a dark raging anger rise in me.

The pain in my head led the symphony of hurt I felt. I forced myself to think through all the pain throbbing through me with every move I made.

First things first, I told myself. I needed to know where they'd left me. Standing proved easier than I'd imagined until the tsunami of nausea and dizziness hit. I sank to my knees and upchucked whatever was in my stomach and then some. My ribs were like knives slashing my insides every time I retched.

After a moment, I inhaled a painful breath, swiped the back of my hand across my lips, and tried standing again. The nausea had subsided and I was able to get my bearings.

A short distance away was the Dockside residences, somebody's clever idea to make a condo building look like a cruise ship. I was in no condition to appreciate much but the slick architecture did provide a location. Turning around I faced the opposite direction which had to be North. Dusty Voice and friends had left me in an open lot near the I-95 ramp on Columbus Boulevard. With bushes and other parked cars giving them some cover, who'd have noticed what they were doing at three in the morning? They'd probably made a nice clean getaway onto I-95.

I had little choice but to hoof it over to Spruce Street a few blocks north, which was the nearest street connecting the center of town with the riverfront. My cell phone was intact and I checked the time. At near four in the morning there were few cars and fewer pedestrians. Just as well, looking bloody and beaten wouldn't make a good first impression.

As I trudged home, I thought about what had happened and who'd made it happen. That was the sticking point. Both Matus and the wheezing mystery man had accents. Accents that sounded awfully like Olga's, which meant they were probably Eastern European. That covers a lot of territory but not so coincidentally, it happened to be Branko's home turf. At least before he decided to come to the States and play mobster.

That made it easy to assume it was Branko who'd sent his minions to deliver the message. An assumption that was way too easy to make and I felt it was the wrong instinct to follow. Where was the percentage for Branko in stopping my investigation? Besides, even if I took him and his boys seriously and stopped, the cops were doing their own investigation and wouldn't stop. Unless Branko had some of them in his pocket which I found impossible to believe in Giuliani's case. She might hate me, but she was an honest cop.

Thoughts and suppositions ran circles in my head as I walked. The night was quiet and a chill had crept into the air which felt good. Once I reached the residential part of Spruce Street, my thoughts were so tangled I decided it'd be better to forget everything, get to sleep, and let my mind work on it overnight. I kept trudging.

Downtown Philly was quiet and empty at four in the morning. I liked walking through center city late at night. Liked it better without the lacerations, blood, and pain. In a little while people would start trekking to work but at that moment, everything was peace. Everything except my bones which were singing a hellish tune.

When I finally entered my condo building half an hour later, I passed Grace who was working the desk. Even tough-as-nails Grace winced when she saw me.

"Looks that bad, huh?" I hadn't thought about the caked blood on my face and shirt since I'd picked myself up off the ground.

"Who won the fight?"

"The fight?… Oh." I laughed. "You should see the other guy."

Grace chuckled as I headed for the elevator. I was whisked up to the forty-first floor and couldn't get to my door fast enough.

* * *

The next morning came painfully into focus as I lay in bed staring at the whirling ceiling fan. I remembered taking a hot shower before I'd fallen onto the bed and blinked out for what was left of the night. Next thing I knew, I was staring at the ceiling fan. The pain I'd ignored as I trekked home the night before roared through me now. Every rib had something to say, and the cuts on my lip and head added their own embellishments. I knew if I moved, I'd get a whole new perspective on what it meant to be a masochist.

There was no choice, though. I had work to do, and neither Matus nor his ancient amigo were going to stop me. I swung my legs over the edge of the bed and attempted to sit up without my head tumbling off my shoulders. That seemed to work. Big headache but my head stayed attached to the rest of me.

Stumbling over to the shower, I thought about the night before and the old man swathed in shadow. Mostly I remembered his enforcer Matus.

Matus. Tumblers began falling into place in my head. Matus. I remembered how familiar that name had seemed. The old guy made it sound more like Matuzz.

That's when it hit me. Matuzz or something very like it was the name Brad's client and Charlie remembered hearing. The Matus who'd kicked me around had to be the one who had pounded on Brad's door at the spa. If I was right, then Brad's abusive ex was off the hook. For now. Didn't mean

I wouldn't try finding Max Gibson some other time. He still had a lot to answer for.

Now I had a different avenue to explore. If the Matus who'd been after Brad, was actually the same guy working for Dusty Voice and his unknown boss, that opened a lot of new doors. Some unnamed boss had not only given orders for the little party they'd thrown for me in the car but had been involved in a lot more. Who was behind Matus and his friends and why? Was it Branko or was there someone on the outside working with Branko? Or, was it someone else with a different agenda?

Another hot shower pelted all the pain into a temporary numbness. After coffee and some oatmeal, I was on the way to my office feeling less foggy-headed. I paused when I stepped out of the building and looked into the clean blue sky. May was proving better every day. No rain, clear skies, and gentle breezes. Of course, nothing was perfect and with the primary a short couple of weeks away, campaigning politicians had negative effects on air quality. I took a deep breath anyway, winced from the pain in my ribs, and felt grateful the goons hadn't done worse damage. I was ready to dive back in despite the old guy's warning.

I noticed a gaggle of people on the corner of Broad and Locust directly in my path. As I drew closer, I saw Senator Bob Terrabito standing with a reporter in front of a KYW News van. Senator "Smiles" had drawn a crowd, but he looked annoyed. Without his signature smile it was as if he were naked, a thought I didn't need first thing in the morning.

I inched closer to hear what stole the Senator's smile.

"…saying it's a virtual dead heat between you and Kelley," said a reporter jamming a microphone into Terrabito's face.

"Polls are just that. Polls. A snapshot of the moment," Terrabito said. "The only poll that counts is the one on election day."

"Rumor has it you've lost ground because of the public's perception that you're in bed with the developers who want to significantly change the city's downtown. Any comment?"

"Then it's an awfully crowded bed. Everyone wants the city developed to its fullest potential. Every official I know has the best interests of the city and the Commonwealth at heart. If that means changing so that Philadelphia becomes a more competitive place where major corporations want to locate

their operations, then I'm guilty... of loving the city where I was born."
Terrabito's face showed the strain of a long campaign, but he knew how to
give as good as he got.

The reporter started to ask another question but Terrabito cut him off.
"I've got a meeting in the Doubletree. Sorry, boys and girls." He stalked
off, followed by his assistants who fended off reporters trailing behind.

I got the gist of what was happening and even why Senator Smiles wasn't
grinning today. I'd make sure Olga did another search on him.

I moved carefully past the political mob pushing its way into the
hotel, making sure my newly bruised ribs didn't get hit again. I marveled
at Terrabito's fortitude. There had to be something other than brass balls
allowing politicians to do what they did and take the endless crap they took.
Not that I admired any of them, because if it wasn't brass balls that kept them
going, it was something darker and much worse. I didn't think I'd like it if I
saw it exposed to the light.

My ribs ached when I arrived at my office, but I told myself it'd go away
soon.

"Boss!" Olga stood as if she'd been shot out of her seat and came around
to stand in front of me. "What has happened, *zaychik moy*? You are not
making shaving cuts."

"Can't get away with that, huh?"

"Olga is not being fooled." She stood on her tip toes to get a better look
at the cuts on my face and head. "Boss is all right?"

"Been better, but I'll be okay." I smiled and pecked her on the cheek,
though bending to do that made me wince.

"Boss is needing Olga's tea. And sitting." She opened my office door and
shooed me in. "Olga makes tea, Boss waits in soft chair." She shot me a stern
look and waddled out of the room.

My desk was still piled with Olga's folders. The beating had rattled me,
and I struggled to remember what I'd been doing with those folders. I finally
recalled I'd been sorting out entanglements between developers and others.
I'd made notes, luckily, and reading those would get me back on track.

After a few moments with my notes, I remembered I'd been thinking the
developers had some cozy money connections that I needed to explore. Since

I'd already asked Nina for financial records on these guys I felt I had things covered. Between her research and Olga's, something would pop.

I pulled the telephone around so I could sit in my softest chair and still do some work. I picked up the receiver and dialed.

"Infomonkeys." Deena had the sweetest mean voice. Monotone and a little psychotic. Very scary.

"This is Marco. Is Nina there? I need to talk to her."

"Marco who?" I tried detecting some sign of mischievous glee in her voice. There was nothing. Which was strange because I knew she took pleasure in breaking balls.

"Fontana. Marco Fontana. Remember me? Does staring into a computer monitor cause permanent memory loss?"

"Niiiiinaaaaaa," was her response.

After a moment, Nina picked up.

"It's Marco. And don't ask Marco Who? or I'll—"

"Deena's playing with you. You should see her face right now,"

"I'd rather see what info you've got for me." I winced from the pain in my ribs.

"Sure, *jefe*. You're all business today."

"After the night I had, Nina… You ever been drop kicked by a goon with sadistic tendencies?"

"No, can't say I have, *jefe*."

"I've got the fractures to prove it. It's painful to talk… so…"

"Sure, sure. I'm gonna shoot this to your computer right now. I'll call back in ten to go over it with you."

"Thanks, Nina. I owe you…"

"No. This is on the house, remember?"

I hung up after thanking her and leaned my head on the chair. It might not have been the best idea to get out of bed.

"Tea is coming," Olga said, mug clinking against the teapot on the tray she carried. I spotted some pastry she'd obviously spent a lot of time making, and felt my stomach growl.

"Smells delicious, Olga."

"Yesterday, I am making *kartoshka* and *pryaniki* and thinking Boss will like. But now cut on mouth is making difficult…" She placed the tray on my desk.

"It won't stop me from eating those goodies," I said. "Don't worry, sugarplum."

She poured me a cup of sparkling green liquid, which she'd made from her personal reserves of tea, and handed me the mug.

"Only tea today. Is better. Coffee is doing no good when Boss is looking like he loses fight with tractor."

Without another word, she left the room.

I stood and moved to my desk chair. It wasn't as comfortable as the soft one but it was the only way I could easily look at Nina's material. Pulling up the file she'd emailed, I saw it contained more pages than I expected. Nina had outdone herself.

Sipping tea, I paged through the material. Nina had apparently hacked through some high-security set ups to get this information. I'd've felt concerned except I knew she was beyond the reach of mere mortal authorities when it came to this stuff.

I noticed banking information with Brad's name heading it up. It appeared he had several accounts. Could be innocent but then again… Even if Brad was dizzy at times, this looked strange. There were also pages of financial information on Wheeler and Berwick and a host of their associates.

Before I reached the end of the file, Olga buzzed the intercom. "Boss is wanting to talk to Nina the Greek?"

"Put her through, Olga. And give yourself a raise, the *kartoshka* looks terrific!"

"Raise? Knock on head of Boss is more serious than I am thinking."

I picked up the receiver.

"Get a chance to look at the file?" Nina asked.

"Looking at it right now, *guapita*. You outdid yourself." I took a sip of tea. "I know you're good, but this is amazing."

"Why do I get the feeling you're gonna want more?"

"Because you're smart. Let's talk about what you have here."

Joseph R. G. DeMarco

"It's what you asked. I think Brad must have been a little *loco*, you know? I don't mean to say anything bad about your friend, but the man had maybe four bank accounts. Pull up the first few pages and you'll see."

"I wanted to ask about that. I thought I was seeing things," I said.

"Either he had a weird accounting system or there's something fishy."

"Brad wasn't the world's best businessman. Sometimes he was dizzy, but he wasn't stupid. Maybe a little naive." *Poor Brad*, I thought. He'd probably gotten himself in over his head with his dreams for the spa. I don't know what he thought when he opened the accounts. If he'd hoped to hide anything he should've known better.

"A lotta money passed through those accounts," Nina said.

"Can we find out where it came from?"

"There's always a way, unless he deposited cash. Then…"

"Think you can check it out?" I turned and bumped into the chair's armrest. I inhaled sharply against the pain.

"You all right, *papi*?" Nina asked.

"Yeah… I wasn't kidding about being drop kicked last night, though."

"You guys and rough sex. When you gonna learn?" Nina laughed. "Take a break. Let me check out the accounts. And next time go home with somebody nice."

She hung up, and I tried not to laugh. It'd hurt too much.

Nina's file gave me a lot to think about. Brad had made several large deposits some weeks earlier. There was an electronic transfer of some money as well. He'd also made sizeable withdrawals, which would explain the lavishly expensive changes I'd noticed at the spa.

In looking over Nina's findings on Wheeler Enterprises, I saw that some of Brad's money had come from Wheeler. This was recorded proof that Wheeler was an investor in Brad's business. The only problem was Brad's deposits amounted to a lot more than Wheeler's accounts showed.

The financials on Wheeler, Berwick, and other developers didn't appear out of the ordinary. If they *had* done anything irregular, they had ways of making it seem legit.

Both Nina and Olga had come up with the same information on the political contributions these men made. They all needed political connections to get things done, and money cemented the links.

I sat back and stared at Nina's work. Then I glanced at Olga's voluminous research. The solution to the case was in all those pages somewhere. I had to devise a way to mine the documents for what I needed. That would take time… and help.

The tea was still warm. I gulped it down and poured another cup. Olga was right, it did make me feel better. I even reached for the *kartoshka* and took a bite. Now *that* made me feel good, despite a small but fiery pain at the cut on my mouth. Except for the extra time I'd have to spend at the gym, eating that pastry was the best medicine.

I printed Nina's document so I could compare it with Olga's work and organize it in some way. Just having information didn't solve a case, it's the way you organized it. I had to avoid making the facts fit any theory I had. That was a recipe for disaster. Better to come up with a solid theory that fit the facts you had.

I took everything into the conference room where I lay papers and folders side by side to compare bits of information. The pain slowed me down and my head was still fogged up, but I sat and concentrated hard trying to hear what the information had to say. Something from that huge gob of facts would speak to me eventually.

"Hey! Need help?"

I looked up and Luke stood there smiling. When he saw my face, his smile disappeared and he moved quickly to my side. "What the hell happened to you?"

"Long story but the short of it is that I made somebody nervous with this investigation. You know how sensitive some people can be," I joked, wincing from the cut on my lip. I noticed Luke didn't find it amusing.

"Who? You know who did this?" He looked me over and when he touched my chest I grimaced. "You sure nothing's broken?"

"Pretty sure. They can't do much for broken ribs anyway…"

"When did this happen? Why didn't you call?"

"Let's see, I think you still have fifteen questions to go. Am I right?"

"Wise ass. I guess it isn't as bad as it looks." He smiled sympathetically.

"Oh it's bad," I said not wanting him to stop fussing over me. "I could use your help. Got some time?"

"That's why I'm here."

"How's Xinhan?"

"Busy as usual. He doesn't get to take a day off here and there like I do."

"You two seem to hit it off pretty well," I said, rearranging the papers on the table.

"On some levels. He's sexy, that's for sure, and that goes a long way. We have a lot of things in common. We come from similar backgrounds. I'm just not sure he's looking for the same things I'm interested in."

"Never know if you don't take time to find out," I said. I knew Luke would find what he was looking for when he was ready. Maybe it'd be Xinhan, maybe not. Luke and I had a good relationship with lots of benefits, but I didn't think I was "The One" either. "Xinhan seems like one of the good guys."

"He is. I think. A little on the demanding side but that may just be the businessman in him. We'll see…"

"Thank him for me, okay?"

"Why what did he do for you?" Luke almost seemed jealous.

"When we had lunch, he shared a certain contact in Wheeler's office."

"Oh, right! That was helpful?"

"If I can make sense of what the guy said and tie it into what I've got here."

"What *is* all this?" Luke waved a hand over the pages and folders.

"That's what I need help with." I paused. "Actually, you're perfect."

"Thank you. You're not so bad yourself. When you aren't all beaten up, I mean."

"*Now* who's the wiseass? What I meant was that you're perfect for this job because you're a detail man. I need to pull details from the documents and correlate them."

"Tell me what you want me to do." Luke took a seat at the table and looked over the papers. "Who did all this anyway?"

"Nina and Olga."

"Super Geeks to the rescue again."

"Shhh, don't let Olga hear you call her a geek. First, she doesn't exactly know what it means and second, she might get insulted and, bam! no more *kartoshka*."

"Okay, okay. Wouldn't want to cut off your karkrakoff supply."

"It's *kartoshka*. Don't knock it till you've tried it." I said. "Take a legal pad and I'll explain what we have to do."

What I wanted was a chart that showed each businessman and developer along with their political contributions, charitable giving, other large expenditures, contracts, and their development projects.

"Whew!" Luke said. "That'll take a while."

"After that it'll be important to make correlations. I want to know who was involved with whom and how they interconnect financially or contractually. I want to see which development projects they cooperated on and what contracts were involved."

"Sounds like we could use more help."

"I can call Anton. Maybe he's free."

"What about the French-Canadian hottie? What was his name? I wouldn't mind him hanging around for a while."

"If Xinhan finds out, you'll be one sorry guy."

"Hey." Luke held up his hands. "Do you see a ring on my finger? Xinhan gets to compete like everyone else." He winked at me seductively.

I picked up the phone and called Anton.

"Hello?" Ty answered so meekly tentative that I felt a wave of pity for the poor kid. Easy to see how Eddie had terrorized him.

"Ty. How're you feeling? Back on your feet?"

"I-I'm doing okay, I guess. I don't get dizzy so much any more. I'll be back to work…"

"Don't even think about work. Just get better. I'll take care of things until you do."

"Mr. F-Fontana… I… I don't…"

"Don't worry, Ty. Is Anton around? I need to talk with him."

"Anton?"

"Yeah, you remember, the guy who's taking care of you while you recuperate? Tall, blond, muscular. That Anton."

Ty was silent a moment. I heard him clear his throat. "He's out. He went out a little while ago. With… um… you know… that other guy."

"Okay." I had a feeling I knew who he was talking about. "Did he say when he'd be back?"

"He said he might not be back until after his shift at Bubbles."

I hung up and felt light headed. Maybe Matus had kicked me harder than I'd thought. Too much work, too soon, I figured. But this had to get done.

"It's just you and me, Luke."

"Like old times," he said. He softly rubbed my back then gave me a dazzling smile which warmed me all over. Like old times.

* * *

"Lunch break." I stood, a little wobbly, still wincing from my ribs. "I'm treating."

"Then we go fancy," He winked.

"How about Knock? The weather's perfect for sitting outside."

"You're on." Luke stood and stretched. His body had been steadily improving since he'd started working out.

"Keep working with your trainer and I'll hire you to dance with StripGuyz."

"No way! My nude-in-public days are over." Luke said referring to his earliest days as a nude housecleaner.

"Oh well… I hadda try," I said. "My stomach's growling. Let's move."

I told Olga where we'd be and she looked at me as if my limbs would fall off, followed by my head.

"Boss should be in bed," she said, a dour look on her chubby face. She turned to Luke, "And Luke should be getting Boss into bed."

Luke laughed suggestively as I walked out the door without saying a word.

The sun had warmed up the day considerably. Perfect sidewalk café weather. Luke nodded to one guy after another as we strolled toward Knock.

"Popular guy," I commented. So many men in the gayborhood used Luke's Clean Living that he knew more people than any five other guys combined.

"What can I say? They love me."

We took seats at the table nearest the corner and a slender, young waiter approached, gave us menus, and asked what we wanted to drink.

Once the waiter left, Luke turned to me with a serious look in his eyes.

"Tell me everything that happened last night. You made it seem as if it were nothing. But I can see what you look like. So give."

"I—"

"Don't try lying. I've picked up a lot of your Spidey-sense for catching out a liar."

"What's the difference what happened? It's all over. Last night was last night."

"They may try again. Anyway, you're my closest friend. Since when do you keep things like this a secret?"

I opened my mouth to reply, and he interrupted.

"Don't pull the 'you-just-want-to-protect-me' crap. I'm not buying. Spill it… all."

"Didn't you say Xinhan was too demanding? Maybe I see why that bothers you." I smiled. I tried for smug but the cut on my lip wouldn't let me.

"Stop evading…"

Just as I was about to speak, Detective Shim sauntered by. He looked over at our table and did a double take.

"Marco. I was just about to call you," he said then took a closer look. "What the hell happened to you?"

"That's my question," Luke said and put out his hand. "Luke Guan, friend of the great Fontana."

Shim shook Luke's hand and eyed an empty chair by way of asking permission to sit.

"Have a seat, Dae. Got time for lunch?"

"I can't stay but I wanted to check in with you." Shim sat across from us. "Now I see I should have checked in earlier. Who'd you tick off?"

"Truthfully? I'm not exactly sure."

"But you have a guess, right?" Shim said.

"Maybe *you* can pry it out of him," Luke said.

I not so gently nudged him under the table.

"Umpff…" Luke reacted to the hint and glanced at me to let me know he understood.

"I probably hit a nerve investigating Brad's death. It's anybody's guess who was behind what happened last night."

"You're holding something back, Marco."

I tried for an innocent grin. Swollen lips don't help.

"Sounds like you know Marco better than I'd have thought," Luke commented.

"With a little help from the ever-sweet Gina Giuliani, the detective has managed to learn a lot about me in a short time."

"Come on, come on. Whaddayou know that I don't know?" Shim asked.

"Now that's a loaded question…" I glanced at him and saw his normally placid expression slowly freezing into angry rigidity. I didn't want to push too far, I still needed the guy. "I'll level with you, Dae. I don't know a hell of a lot more than when we talked earlier.

"This case could get you killed, Marco. You've got to let us handle it," Shim said.

"I gave you what I found on Wheeler, right? He had connections in everything you can think of in the city."

"That's not news. And you already told me about the trial."

"You said the trial might open new leads for you. Don't I get credit for that?" I asked.

"Yeah, I thought the Branko information could help, but I'm not so sure anymore. My instincts tell me Wheeler was a poor slob in the wrong place at the wrong time."

"What makes you say that?"

"My guess? He was there for a massage," Shim said. "You know what I mean. He was friendly with Brad Lopes. He even invested in the business, like you said. Seems to me he went to the spa to collect on one of the perks of being an investor."

"That's nuts!" I said.

"To you, maybe. Not to me. I don't think the old guy was a target. More like collateral damage."

"It can look that way. If you want it to," I said. Perception is everything. If you wanted to see something a certain way, you would. Fitting the facts to your preconceived idea never leads in the right direction.

"Wheeler's a dead end, Fontana. Even Giuliani thinks so. Got anything I don't already know?" There wasn't a hint of sarcasm in his voice, just the frustration of a cop who couldn't make headway on a case.

"Like?"

"Like who mauled you last night and why?"

"I can tell you one thing about last night." I leaned in. Luke and Shim followed suit. "Whoever these guys were, they all had Eastern European accents."

Chapter 26

L uke presented me with a tidy pile of folders, each sporting a list tacked to the front cover.

"This is everything," Luke plopped them on the desk. "Beat you to it."

"Not by much." I stapled a list to the last folder in the pile.

"Now what?" he asked.

"Now we try and make connections.

"Like...?"

I pulled a large sheet of paper in front of us on the conference table. At the top I listed names: Terrabito, Kelley, Nussbaum, Clarke, McClintock, and others.

"Politicians." Luke said. "What've they got to do with anything?"

"I've got Nina and Olga working on that. Gimmie time."

I took out another sheet of paper and listed the names of five recent development projects. On another, I listed developers.

"I'm still not getting it." Luke frowned.

"Then let's put some things on these lists. Let's take a look at the first folder."

Luke pulled Remy Berwick's folder off the top of the pile.

"Now what?"

"Which politicians did Berwick make contributions to?"

"Nussbaum, Kelley, Terrabito, Clarke, and Murphy who isn't on your list."

"I'll put him there. You write Berwick and the amount he donated under each politician."

We went through every file that way and had a good, if incomplete, picture of all the politicians running in the primary and what donations they'd gotten from developers.

"Cool list," Luke said. "What's it got to do with anything?"

"Maybe nothing. Maybe everything. We're not looking hard enough yet. Let's see what the next list gets us."

We went through the folders agan, this time listing all the projects each developer was involved with in some way. Each project had two or three developers.

"Another pretty list but…" Luke started.

"One more piece of the puzzle. We have to keep pulling out pieces and eventually we'll see how they fit together."

"Sure we will," Luke said. "So far you've got developers and you've got politicians and you've got development projects. I don't see a connection yet."

"It's there, I know it."

"Anything else we can get from these folders?" Luke asked.

"We could see what other money changed hands. Other than political contributions. Investments in different projects. Preferably large sums," I said.

"What're you thinking?"

"Not sure. When I see it, I'll know." I picked up a folder and looked through.

Luke did the same. After a while we'd added lines to several of the developers. Nothing appeared significant.

"That's all the folders in my group. Looks like we narrowed the list again. Not everyone got new notations," Luke said.

"I'll study the lists, talk to a few people, and see what happens."

"You mean, like someone else coming around to smash your brains all over the sidewalk? Don't you think you should bring that detective in on this?"

"On what? What've I got here? Names, projects, and donations. What does it all amount to right now? I've gotta study it first. I show him now, he'll think I'm nuts. Maybe I am."

"When you put it that way…," Luke said. "Maybe the detective can help you figure it out."

"I could give him a call. Giuliani isn't going to like him spending department time on my theories, though. That's why she gave me tacit approval to investigate."

"I'd feel better if you got the detective involved."

"I will. Promise." I did my best Boy Scout honor sign and smiled.

Luke laughed.

"Remember I said that Wheeler's assistant, Phil Caragan, was sort of helpful?"

"Yeah, but you didn't know how to make sense of what he said."

"Caragan overheard Wheeler on the phone mentioning a certain name."

"One of these guys?" He gestured toward the folders.

"No. Branko. That's what the assistant thinks he heard."

"And… that's important because…?" Luke looked at me as if I'd lost my mind.

"Because Branko went on trial for extortion. Guess who was on the jury?"

"Wheeler?" Luke asked.

"No. It was—"

"Caragan? The assistant?"

"Brad. It was Brad. Emily said he'd been on a jury and hated it."

"Okay. Funny coincidence, right?"

"It gets better," I said. "Wheeler had been scheduled as a witness for the prosecution, then he gets cut from the list. No explanation."

"Even bigger coincidence, right?" Luke smiled weakly.

"You know me better than that, Luke."

"What's it all mean? How does it figure with the lists we made?"

"I haven't gotten there yet. I know it's connected somehow, but there are pieces missing. Important pieces."

"Looks that way."

"I'll just keep going. Something's bound to pop sooner or later."

"Don't be an idiot and get hurt again," Luke said and impulsively threw his arms around me in a tight hug which forced me to yelp and jump back.

"Ribs...ribs..." I panted. "Still... painful..."

"I just made it worse. Didn't I?" Luke stroked my face with his hand. "I'm sorry." He stepped back looking mortified.

"I'll be fine. It was the sudden pressure."

Luke pulled out his cell phone and looked at the screen. "I've gotta get going."

"Hot date?"

"Dinner with Xinhan and some instructors from his Kung Fu school. Wanna come along? I've seen some of these guys. Major hunks."

"Yeah?"

"Could be candidates for StripGuyz in the bunch," Luke said trying to entice me.

"Sure, they'd work out great as strippers. I can just see one of them accidentally kicking a patron and knocking his head across the bar. That'd be good for business." I laughed then sucked air from the pain it caused.

"If you change your mind, we'll be at the Golden Phoenix."

"I may surprise you," I said.

"I'd be happy if you did," Luke said moving close again. I stepped back defensively. "Not going to hurt you, big boy. I just want to give you a kiss."

"Lip's cut, remember?"

"I'll kiss where it isn't cut. Maybe I'll make it all better."

Luke moved in and placed a gentle kiss on the side of my mouth that wasn't cut and swollen. His lips were warm and soft. "Feels better, right? I knew it. Oldest remedy." Luke straightened his clothes, picked up his messenger bag and moved to the door. "Okay. Meet us at the restaurant. Xinhan would like that," Luke said and left.

* * *

The warmth of his kiss lingered and I felt oddly secure. Then a stray thought about Anton flashed through my mind and I wondered where he'd been all day and what he'd been doing. I'd talk with him at Bubbles later. I wasn't happy with the way things were between us. But I had no right feeling angry at anyone but myself.

It'd be hours before I had to be at Bubbles, and ribs or no ribs there was work to do. I pulled together the lists we'd made and took them back to my desk. One thing I needed to do was question the politicians on the list. Not that they'd ever admit to trading favors for contributions.

When Olga trooped into my office with another pot of tea, I asked her for a list of campaign headquarters for the list of politicians I handed her. Most were running for local offices, only Terrabito and Kelley had statewide races. With Philly and its burbs being the biggest prize in the state, both Kelley and Terrabito would probably be stuck in their Philly headquarters making last minute plans.

While I sipped tea and ate the second *pryaniki* Olga brought in with the tea, I realized there was one list we hadn't put together that might be relevant. I quickly flipped through the files and saw that the information I needed to make the list wasn't there.

I asked Olga to come in again.

"Boss is better? No. I am seeing Boss wilts like cabbage in soup." She looked at me and frowned. "Boss is tired. You must be going in bed but you…"

"I know, sugarplum, but who's gonna do this if I don't?"

"Dead people are not knowing how lucky they are being, having you around."

"Can you do a little more research for me?"

"Is why I live," Olga said. I knew there was sarcasm in there somewhere but her deadpan expression didn't betray her. "What informations you are needing?"

I showed her the lists of development projects Luke and I had compiled.

"Can you find the government contracts that go with these projects and which politicians are connected with those contracts"

"*Da.* Easy Peasy."

"Where'd you learn that phrase?"

"Television spy show. All English I am learning from TV. Is good, *da?*"

"*Da,*" I said. Television. Sr. Yolanda, my second grade teacher would be mortified.

Sitting around, pain or no pain, made me crazy. I needed to get out on the street and ruffle some feathers. I took my lists and made copies.

"I am having campaigning office list Boss needs." Olga waved a paper in the air.

Copies in hand, I took the list as I went back to my office to gather my things. Then I turned around and walked to the door.

"Gonna be out for a while, Olga. Hold the fort," I said passing her desk.

Staring at the monitor, eyes glazed, Olga didn't respond. She wouldn't come up for air until she'd found the information I'd asked for. She was as focused as a pit bull.

The day was slowly winding down. Luke and I had worked for hours, and I hadn't realized how late it was. Political campaigns didn't knock off at five o'clock like normal businesses. Campaigns are like zombies with even more voracious appetites.

I decided to start with Terrabito. I headed to Walnut Street. The Terrabito offices were west of Broad, I moved as quickly as I could, passing Kelley's headquarters buzzing with even more activity since the latest polls put him within striking distance.

On the corner of Fifteenth Street in a building that used to house a bank, huge "Terrabito for Senate" signs plastered the insides of the windows. As a state senator, he commanded big money and lots of help from the Party. For some reason, he wasn't getting enough traction with voters.

I walked through the doors expecting the usual flurry of activity but there wasn't much. Staffers sat at telephone banks, people fiddled with computers. With less than two weeks to go, however, there was no sense of excitement.

Moving to a desk that looked like it might be the center of the operation, I came face to face with a prim young guy who looked vaguely familiar. Then I remembered he'd been with Terrabito's entourage during the pub crawl.

"Excuse me," I said, rousing him from reading the newspaper. "Is the Senator here?"

"Do you have an appointment?"

"No, but—"

"Then the Senator isn't here." He went back to reading his newspaper.

"Weren't you with the Senator's party the night they visited Bubbles and the other bars? I thought I recognized you."

"Yeah, I was there. That still isn't going to get you in to see the Senator."

"Marco Fontana," I said stretching out my hand to him. I figured starting over might help.

He shook hands tentatively, eyeing me with a mix of interest and distrust. Thin as a post, he had blond hair and platter-sized eyes providing him with an innocent look. Which, I could tell, he was anything but.

"I'm investigating a murder and... you know how one thing leads to another," I said leaning in, trying to make him feel I was taking him into my confidence.

"Yeah?" He looked up as if I were about to tell him earth shattering secrets.

"I got a look at the victim's finances and the investors in his business..."

"Are you trying to say the Senator was one of—"

"No. Not at all," I reassured him. "No. Looks like the Senator might know one or more of the investors, though. You know how the press is, they'll try to link him with those investors and ultimately to the murder. Even if it's only a peripheral kind of link. Know what I mean?"

"Yes. This can be... wait one moment... I have... I need to talk with someone." He stood and, as he walked away, I thought he resembled a walking twig. A cute twig, but a twig.

After a moment he returned to the desk, his face flushed.

"The Senator actually isn't here but you can talk to his assistant. He'll give you whatever information you want. You want to talk with him?"

"Nolan? Josh Nolan?"

"Ye-yes, you know Mr. Nolan?"

"We've run into one another here and there."

He picked up the phone and told whoever it was that I was waiting. He listened then glanced up at me, his big eyes widening again.

"Go right on back, Mr. Fontana," he said. "Second door on the left."

I smiled at him and watched him blush. Then I walked down the hall to Nolan's office.

As I approached the door, it opened and Josh Nolan stood there, tall, handsome, and frazzled.

"Mr. Fontana, I keep bumping into you. Sorry I can't talk much, but we're stretched thin and—"

"It's your boss I need to talk with. Any chance you can set me up with a meeting?"

"Gonna be difficult. The Senator is scheduled up to his as... I mean ears."

"Like I told the receptionist, I'm investigating a murder. The killing took place the night you and all the others visited Bubbles. Things are moving on the investigation and your boss could get nipped by negative publicity."

"You mentioned that," he said as if he already had more than enough to worry about.

"After all the drinking you did that night, I was surprised to see you looking so lively the next morning."

"It's the adrenalin... cancels out alcohol, private lives, and a lot more."

"That night you did your best pretending to play sober when your boss ran in late. Politicians never get anywhere on time."

"Too many people make demands on his time. That's why he never shows up when he's supposed to." He swept his chestnut hair back with his hand and gazed at me. "I'll see if the Senator can squeeze in a meeting tomorrow. Next day at the latest."

"I'd appreciate it. Never know, the Senator might help solve the case. That wouldn't look bad on the news, would it?"

"Right now, with the dip in his polls, I'd take just about anything," Nolan said. "I can't understand how that weasel..." He stopped himself.

"One more thing..."

"Sure."

"I saw you storming out of Kelley's headquarters the other day."

"Campaign business. People don't realize it, but campaigns do communicate."

"Didn't look like you were communicating all that well."

"Looks can be deceiving."

"Yeah, I suppose. Matter of fact I noticed you and Shuster giving each other the eye, that night at Bubbles. Kinda looked like you two had something secret goin' on."

"If you're through... I'll try to arrange that meeting for you. I can't spare you more time right now."

I'd hit a soft spot. I handed him my card. "You can call me when you set up the meeting," I said, and left the room.

The receptionist had gone back to his newspaper. I called out a 'Thank you' to him as I moved past, and he blushed again.

Out on the street, people flew past on their way home from work or out to dinner. I considered my options. I needed to visit Kelley again or maybe even Nussbaum or Clarke. Sooner or later one of them would slip and say something truthful instead of giving me the runaround. There were still missing pieces. I'd just have to keep plugging.

Glancing down at Olga's campaign office list I decided who'd be next. I looked up in time to see a sidewalk bicyclist plough into an elderly woman who, lucky for her, crashed into me knocking me against the wall.

Fortunately the woman was uninjured, and I saw to it she was steady on her feet before I turned to look for the cyclist. Of course, the thug was nowhere. Having done his damage he'd disappeared into the fading light.

Every already bruised bone felt the shock of the crash and let me know it. The freshly renewed throbs of pain ordered me to forget the politicians and get home. I'd nurse myself with a beer and some food. I still had to make an appearance at Bubbles. My feet knew the way which was good because my head was still in the case.

* * *

Friday night at Bubbles usually brought in a decent crowd. There was an ebb and flow to bar life and we were entering the ebb season. Late Spring and Summer were slow times everywhere in the city. Which is why I scheduled events to bring in bigger crowds. My guys had fans and the fans had friends. Somehow, seeing men dance almost naked never gets old.

Customers stared at the empty stage waiting. Lit by pink and blue baby spots, the stage held the promise of men, nearly naked, creamy flesh available yet forbidden. The tinsel curtain upstage fluttered in a random breeze, teasing the patrons with the thought of dancers poised to emerge.

Music thumped and pumped, resonating in my chest, sending small shockwaves of pain through my ribs. I moved carefully through the crowd, back-slapping long time patrons, spending a few minutes with others. They all asked why I looked like a celebrity mug shot. I gave them the short, vague version before heading to my office.

Anton, seated at my desk, looked up when I entered the room. His eyes widened.

"What happened to you?" He jumped up and quickly moved to my side.

"Careful," I said, before he placed his arms around me. "Really sore ribs."

Anton gently stroked my face, drawing his fingers close to the cuts without touching them. His blue eyes darkened with concern.

"When were you going to tell me?" His tone was sad rather than accusatory.

"I… I didn't tell anyone… not really," I said. Normally he'd be the first one I'd tell about anything. When I'd called, though, he'd been out.

"You've been strange lately, Marco," he said. Then he moved as close as he dared, so as not to bump my ribcage. "I want to kiss you but…"

"Just be careful. Everything hurts."

Anton placed a gentle kiss on the side of my face, well away from any cuts or bruises.

"Feel better?" Anton managed a weak smile. "Tell me what happened."

I explained and smiled apologetically.

"Didn't tell anyone. Took myself home and nursed my wounds alone."

"Why? You could've called me. I'd have been there in an instant. You know that."

"It was four in the morning…" I paused. "Maybe… I wasn't happy these thugs took me by surprise. It's not supposed to happen," I said.

"Right, Not to you it isn't. You're immortal."

"I know how it sounds, and you're right. But I needed to be alone and get past those feelings. That kind of thing can ruin you for this work."

"You work one case after another and every one takes a little piece of you. Some of them take more. I've watched it happen, Marco," Anton said, frustration coloring his voice. "That'll never change, will it?"

I was silent for a moment. He was right.

"This work is all I know, Anton. It's all I've wanted to do," I said, tentatively reaching up a hand to cup his face. "Besides, most of the time, I like what I do."

"You *like* getting beaten to a pulp?" He stepped back beyond my reach.

"I didn't exactly get beaten to a pulp. Some cuts, kicks to the ribs, punches. I'm still in one painful piece" I smiled. "I can usually take care of myself. They just got the jump on me and... sometimes... shit happens, as they say."

"There's more to it than physical harm. You know that," Anton said. "Your work takes a toll on you in ways you can't see. Not like a broken rib. That's pain you can feel. What I'm talking about is deeper, more essential. You can still walk, still function. Until one day... you won't be you anymore. I don't know if I can stand to watch that happen." Anton paused. "It hurts watching what you go through every time. When you have feelings for someone... it hurts." He glanced down and moved back toward the desk.

"Is that why things have been so different lately?" I asked, my voice hoarse. "Everything's strained. Nothing is easy and comfortable the way it was."

"It's... you're right... I don't know what it is, but you're right. You've been distant. Maybe I have, too."

"I've been so involved with this case, but that's no excuse."

"It's not only this case, Marco. It's not your work."

"Then what? Why is everything different?" I had a pretty good idea of the reason. This was familiar and yet unfamiliar territory all at the same time.

"Truthfully, it's not just you." Anton stared at the floor, seemed to be carefully considering his next words. "A guy gets tired, you know? You want something for so long you just keep moving in the same direction even after there's nothing left to move you. You need a little something in return. A word... a touch... some sign to keep going..."

"I... what can I say, Anton?"

"If I need to tell you what to say, then what's the point?"

"I didn't mean—"

"I can wait just so long..."

"I know, Anton," I said. "I've seen how Jean-Claude looks at you. He adores you but he's too diplomatic to say anything to me. Or, maybe he's afraid."

"Let's not make this about him. He's a nice person. He's attentive and sweet."

"Whereas, I'm just…"

"No comparisons. That's not what I'm saying. Jean-Claude is a good guy…"

"Is he what you…"

"He likes me. He's actually interested in *me*. What I do, what I think."

"I can see the way he—"

"He's also been very considerate of you." Anton said.

"I can't fault him for being under your spell. You're—"

"I'm not casting spells, Marco. I'm just trying to make a life for myself. Is there any reason I shouldn't see where this goes with Jean-Claude?"

That was the opening I should have been waiting for. Should have been prepared for. Instead I felt immobile, unable to respond. What could I say to Anton? What difference would it have made anyway? No matter how I felt about Anton, I wasn't sure I could ever give him everything he wanted. I knew he wasn't interested in half measures.

I opened my mouth to say something but I couldn't find the words he wanted to hear. Anton looked at me expectantly. He stared into my eyes and I felt the warmth of what we'd had over the years envelope me, try to pull me close. But I couldn't speak.

"That's it then?" Anton asked.

I wanted to tell him he was wrong about me. That he should give me another chance. Something about that haunted me. I wondered if asking that was like Eddie and Max asking their victims for another chance. Given another chance, they always did what they always did. I couldn't ask for another chance unless I knew I could make an honest effort to give Anton what he needed. Making a commitment I wasn't sure I could keep wasn't the way to win back his trust.

Anton looked down at the floor and turned away. For a moment he stood there, back to me, silent. Waiting for something that even he knew wouldn't come. Then he left the room shutting the door behind him.

* * *

It proved to be a long night. I went through the motions, feeling emptier than I'd ever felt before. Anton avoided eye contact with me and made himself busy with something whenever I approached. He never entered my office when I was there and he left the bar without a word to me.

My chest felt as if my ribs were barbed wire but I decided to stay until the guys cleaned up the bar and closed the doors. I left and still didn't want the night to end, as if I'd find some way to change things if I could get the day to last longer. Out on the sidewalk, music and laughter floated through the air from Café Bubbles and snagged my attention. Instead of turning for home, I walked toward the café but when I reached the glass doors, the twinkling lights and tinny laughter were suddenly annoying. It brought up feelings I'd been trying to smother.

Turning around, I headed home. Every step of the way was punctuated by sharp pains in my ribs. With nothing else to distract me, the pain was more cutting. I stopped when I reached Broad. A familiar figure stood on the corner looking lost. As lost as I felt.

"Nolan," I called out and the handsome politico turned around.

"Fontana! I thought only political operatives and vampires crawled the streets at this hour. What're you doing here?"

"Just getting off my other job at the strip club," I said, purposely ambiguous. Nolan was as good as any other distraction to stop me feeling sorry for myself.

"You're a… you're… you do…," he stuttered and looked at me, eyes wide with disbelief. "No… nah… you're pulling my leg."

"I own a strip group," I said. "Why so shocked? Don't I look like I can take it off for an audience?"

"I… I'm no j-judge of these things…," he stammered. "I didn't mean to offend you, Fontana."

"Not offended. Just disappointed." I smiled.

"I didn't have a chance to set you up with the Senator yet," Nolan said, his expression serious now. "But I did want to talk to you."

"Okay, shoot."

"Not here." He looked around as if people could hear, though no one was within earshot.

"Let's see." I pulled out my cell phone and looked at the time. "It's after three. There are a couple of all night diners or you could come up to my place."

"Your... your place?"

"Don't worry. I won't jump your bones. Even if I wanted to, I couldn't. I'm not in any shape for bone jumping."

"O-okay." He peered at me. "Yeah, what the hell happened to you?"

"Never mind that now. Why do you need to talk in private?"

Chapter 27

G race, on the late shift as usual, watched with a strange look on her face, as I walked through the lobby with Nolan by my side. She reminded me of a very serious pug, given instructions to observe and make mental notes. Like all pugs, she couldn't help commenting on what she saw, with the set of her face or the flick of an eyebrow.

I tossed her a wink, and she nodded in return.

When we arrived at my door, I unlocked it, holding it open so Nolan could enter before me. He hesitated.

"Don't worry, I've disabled all the man-traps. Shame though, they do a nice job of capture and hold."

Nolan haltingly stepped over the threshold and into my condo.

One of the first things you see when you enter is the view from the balcony. It dominates the place and immediately catches the eye. It was no surprise when he stopped in the doorway and whistled his admiration for the cityscape.

"Wow! The only thing my Harrisburg apartment overlooks is the courtyard behind my building. I spend too much time away from Philly. I forget how nice it looks." He walked toward the glass sliding doors leading to the balcony.

"Yeah, the view always catches me, too." I followed him in and shut the door. "No matter how long I've lived here."

At the sound of the lock clicking he quickly turned to face me. He looked perplexed, like he had no idea what to expect.

"Want a beer?" I moved toward the kitchen.

"S-sure," he said.

"Go on out on the balcony. Have a seat. We can talk out there."

As I dipped into the fridge for the beers, I heard him fumble with the lock on the glass doors, then slide them open. The city sounds, even at this hour, came flooding in and it took a moment to let the noise become background static.

I stepped onto the darkened balcony. Light filtering up from the streets and surrounding buildings provided just enough illumination. I noticed he'd removed his jacket and loosened his tie.

"This is relaxing," he said as I plunked two beers on the table.

I sat and took a long drink from my bottle. He did the same looking as if he'd never stop. He drained the bottle and placed it on the table.

"There's more in the fridge. Help yourself," I said. "But there's a price…"

His body tensed and he looked at me as if to say he suspected as much.

"I didn't mean it that way." I laughed. "The price is, you tell me what you hinted at out on the street."

"Oh," he said. "Oh… right." He sounded relieved and I noticed his shoulders relax as he sat back into the chair. "Yeah. This view is so nice and sitting here is so peaceful, I almost forgot."

"This related to the case?"

The look of concern returned to his face, and I knew he had something big on his mind. "It's the Senator."

"What's the problem? Other than the fact he's sinking in the polls."

"The polls? No. It's something else. You reminded me of it earlier. Something I saw, something that happened that never happens. It's been bothering me ever since."

"You certainly have 'cryptic' down pat. What's this 'something' you're talking about? 'Cause right now, I'm kinda in the dark."

"It doesn't feel right, talking about him. It's probably all just coincidence."

"Lemme clue you in, Nolan. There's no such thing as coincidence. Santa Claus, maybe. Coincidence, no."

"I saw the reports on the murders and I recognized one of the victims."

"Who?"

"The older man, Smithson Wheeler."

"That's no surprise. He moved in a lot of circles. How'd you know him?"

"He's been a contributor a long time. Occasionally visits the Senator's office downtown. When Bob, the Senator I mean, is in Philadelphia, he works out of an office on Market Street."

"That where you saw Wheeler?"

"One morning I saw the Senator sitting in his office with Wheeler and a man named Berwick who's been a pain in the ass for us."

"How'd you see them all?"

"The Senator's office is a large corner room and the walls are totally glass. So, I can always see what's going on. If he needs something we've worked out signals."

"What's so unusual about meeting with people like Wheeler and Berwick? I assumed politicians always meet with business people. Especially if they want those contributions to keep rolling in."

"All true. This meeting seemed contentious, though. I couldn't hear anything but I saw them waving their arms and appearing to shout. They all appeared to be angry. After a while Wheeler stormed out. He didn't look happy."

"Your boss didn't follow him? Didn't try to make peace?"

"No, he continued talking with Berwick. Eventually he walked Berwick out. Both of them smiling."

That could all mean exactly nothing but it was interesting and I filed it away.

"Why'd that bother you so much?"

"I guess because I wasn't allowed into the meeting."

"That unusual?"

"Highly. I have access to everything. Always have. But the receptionist said the Senator left explicit instructions that no one was allowed in. Including me."

"So, me being a suspicious type," I said. "Maybe I'm thinking you're just dumping all this on me because you're a disgruntled staffer."

"No!" He sat straight up in his chair. "No. I'm just worried that—"

"That the Senator was involved in the murder somehow? That's kind of a stretch. Just because there was a meeting in his office. Even an angry meeting. Senators probably have more creative ways to take care of people they argue with than shooting them."

"I'm not worried about him being involved in the murder. That's crazy."

"He did come running in late that night at Bubbles. He might've had the opportunity to—"

"He was with me the whole night. I arrived at Bubbles a little before he did because he was talking with a big contributor at Knock, I think. That and he didn't want to be seen arriving at the same time as Kelley. They really don't like one another."

"I gathered. So what's got you worried?"

"Just the appearance of something incriminating. That's all they need, you know? A hint or a rumor. The press eats it up. Word gets out about him arguing with Wheeler on the same day the man is murdered and the fact that Wheeler stomped out… If the media finds out about it, we won't have a temporary dip in the polls. It'll be over."

"They haven't found out yet." I downed the rest of my beer.

"No. Not yet."

"You never did tell me what's with you and Shuster."

"It's personal. Nothing regarding this—"

"In a murder investigation, it's all personal."

We sat there a while longer soaking up the night and the view. Nolan hardly said another thing. It didn't matter, I enjoyed sitting with him in the semi-darkness. His presence made me feel settled, made all the static of the day melt away. He was strong but vulnerable and he obviously cared deeply about things. Gave me the impression he was a decent human being, too. It reminded me of evenings I'd spent with Anton sitting next to me, both of us connected in the silence, not having to say a thing. We enjoyed the friendship we had and the time we gave one another. I didn't want to lose that.

By the time Nolan left, it was nearly four-thirty in the morning. He'd given me things to think about. I knew for certain I had to quiz Terrabito. If he'd been meeting with Wheeler and Berwick, I needed to know what went on.

When I hit the bedroom, I was dragging. It'd been nice sitting on the balcony in the dark, talking with someone without all the sexual interplay and veiled possibilities. Nolan was a straight arrow, which was a real shame, but he was also an honest guy.

I knew there'd be nothing more than talk. Talk without the possibility of more than friendship. No sex, no disappointments, no hard feelings.

Saturday loomed ahead and with it another late night at Bubbles. There were a ton of people I needed to talk with before that, but I was so tired I couldn't think what had to be done. I drifted into an uneasy sleep.

* * *

Olga called and woke me.

"Boss is coming in to working?"

"Y-yeah, Olga? Are... are you at the office?" I floated up from somewhere far away. My mind slowly snapped back to the present moment.

"Is not where I am supposing to be?"

"It's Saturday, Olga."

"Boss is giving assignment. I am having results." Her uncharacteristically cheery tone was enough to get me out of bed.

"Give me a few to get ready." I sat up, a sharp pain in my ribs stopping me cold. Less than the day before but still thrumming.

"You can be taking time. Boss pays extra for Saturday working."

Ignoring the pain, I got myself showered, dressed, and fed in record time. Waiting for the elevator I thought about Nolan sitting with me on the balcony and how oddly secure it had made me feel. I'd never thought feeling secure or settled was that important.

I brushed off those feelings as I rode down in the elevator. The Cell Phone Sheriff entered the car next and I spent the rest of the ride watching her seethe just waiting for me to try and use my phone. Disappointed, she stalked off before me when we arrived.

The lobby buzzed with people. As I hustled through to the automatic doors I overheard Nosey Rosey saying, "...and they never found his wife. Now he lives here on the fourteenth floor with another woman."

Poor guy, I thought, *he'll be the talk of the lobby for weeks.*

The streets were relatively empty and the fresh air helped pull me back together again. Between the beating and the late nights, I needed more than just a good night's sleep. But that wasn't happening any time soon.

When I got to the office, Olga was seated at her desk her eyes focused on her monitor.

"Results are on desk. And treats for Boss who is looking like drugged cat," she said barely looking up.

"Like what the cat dragged in, you mean."

"If you are saying so."

Hot coffee waited in the electric maker and my desk was piled with more of Olga's confections. Getting beaten had its advantages. Pouring myself some coffee I sat and didn't even try resisting the pastry. The aroma filled my nostrils and I snatched one off the plate. As I munched on the *kartoshka*, I flipped through the newest file Olga had compiled.

She'd found lists of government contracts related to development projects in the Philadelphia region and the legislation supporting the contracts. More important than that, she'd listed the names of the politicians who'd sponsored the legislation and pushed to award contracts to the companies involved. It was a hop, skip, and a jump from that information to the owners of the companies that received contracts.

Reading through the names, I realized that all of the legislators and developers were as familiar as yesterday's news. Berwick and Wheeler were listed but but other well-known developers appeared on the list: The Chuffe Group, Dome Inc. and a few more. Nussbaum, Kelley, Clarke, and Terrabito headed up the political posse.

What I had before me was an intricate web connecting developers and legislators. Linked through contracts and the legislation awarding those contracts, they were also tied together through political contributions. It was a huge unethical orgy. But a connection to the murders wasn't leaping out at me.

After hitting dead ends on every lead so far, like Brad's ex, or the wannabe stalker, or even a closeted client like Sorba, the only thing left was the story Vega's photographer hinted at: the jury tampering piece.

Without Vega's notes, the trial transcript was the only thing to go on. There was no way to know how far he'd gotten on his investigation. The only thing I knew, because of Brad's appointment book, was that Vega was supposed to have been at the spa the night of the murders along with Wheeler and Brad.

It seemed like it should make sense. Wheeler and Brad were connected to Branko's trial. Vega was investigating that same trial for alleged jury tampering. Before Vega has a chance to go public, all three of them are murdered.

That's too much coincidence even for somebody who believes in coincidence. The trial and the jury tampering story had to be connected to the murders.

Seems plausible until you come to the Big Roadblock: Branko had been convicted. Usually you tamper with a jury so you don't get sent to jail. Not the other way around. Maybe the story was nothing. Just the lunatic fantasies of a paranoid journalist. Either that or something had gone wrong with the tampering plan.

Pieces were missing, pieces that would show Vega was on to something or was crazy. I felt I had some of those pieces in the documents I held. I couldn't yet make sense of them. I felt like I was at a crossroads with too many directions to choose from.

Staring at the names while eating more of Olga's pastry and swilling more caffeine, I scoured the contracts and the development projects, but I didn't see any connection between the legislation, the contracts, and the trial. Political corruption? Sure. Murder? Not so much.

The answer was in there laughing at me because I couldn't see it. Some fact that would make this file leap from corruption to murder was missing.

There was no apparent tie to Branko in the legislation or the contracts. Caragan said Wheeler mentioned the thug's name in his phone conversations. He didn't know why. There'd be no way to ask Branko. His lawyers would never permit it. Linking Branko and Wheeler would be a challenge.

The information in Olga's file gave me a headache. I had to take a break. Stacking things neatly, I walked to her desk.

"Olga, I'll be out for a while. Can you do me one more favor, sugarplum?"

"You are paying for favors, so I am doing favors," she said, peering at me sweetly.

"I have a hunch about these contracts." I handed her the file she'd given me. "See if you can locate any news stories about the land deals and the properties they cover. Anything."

"I am looking for anything? Boss looks for everything at same time?"

"Yes and no. I'll know it if I see it. Use those expensive databases, pumpkin. Might as well get what we pay for."

"If you are saying so." She took the file, opened it and I could see her formulating her search plans.

I left her happily hunting down information. Of everything her job called for, scouring the Internet made her happiest, no matter how she complained.

While I waited for the elevator, I made a call.

"Josh Nolan." His voice sounded nasal.

"Sounds like you got as much sleep as I did last night," I said.

"Probably less. The Senator called early this morning with some work."

"Did you happen to arrange that meeting for me?"

"I tried for today, but he promised he'd meet with you tomorrow. That okay?"

"Guess it has to be," I said as the elevator arrived. "Tell me when and where."

"Still up in the air. It'll definitely be tomorrow." Nolan sounded harried. "Uh oh, gotta go. Terrabito's wife just walked in. Talk to you later." Instead of disconnecting, he hesitated. I could hear him breathe. "T-thanks for the beer and the talk. I owe you one." He hung up without saying anything else.

* * *

Kelley's headquarters was on the way back to my office. The frantic activity at the campaign offices was significant. Kelley was moving ahead in the polls with less than two weeks to go. The momentum was in his favor at just the right time and his inner circle wanted to keep it going.

So it was no surprise Kelley stood on a desk trying to rev people up and propel them out the door with enthusiasm. I shook my head when I saw him. His lead in the polls and his towering position on the desk didn't change the fact that he was a gray little man who mumbled when he spoke and was about as inspiring as a sponge.

I stepped closer as he finished with, "...let's see if we can change some minds."

Hopping to the floor, Kelley came face to face with me. Shuster, Kelley's shadow, was nowhere to be seen. I knew this would be a good opportunity to corner the gray mumbler.

"Mr. Kelley. Or, should I say *Senator* Kelley?" Never hurts to slather on a little butter.

"Not yet, Fontana, not yet. But we're close," he said, unable to suppress a smile. "What brings you out so early on a Saturday morning? You're not running for office, too, are you?"

"Nah, couldn't do that. I still have my moral compass. Y'know, the one the Boy Scouts gave me. When they allowed my type in, once upon a time."

"Vitriolic as ever." Kelley turned and began a slow walk to his office, nodding to volunteers, patting some on the back, giving a thumbs up to others.

When we got to his door, he stopped and looked at me as if to say, 'This far and no further.' He didn't know me as well as he thought.

"Got some things I need to talk about," I said.

"What is it you need?"

"You sure you want to talk murder and corruption out here in front of the children?" I smiled innocently, nodding in the direction of the campaign workers.

"Whatever you've got to say, you can say it here," Kelley said, his hand on the doorknob but not turning it, an indication he was willing to negotiate if I bargained harder.

"Hey, maybe I'll talk to staffers first, see where they stand on the issue of corruption, of legislators who are bought and paid for. Legislators who act like paid servants, fetching contracts and seeing to it their masters get good deals."

Kelley threw me an "I-Don't-Care" stare then tried looking bored. Behind those eyes I saw a glimmer of concern.

"I'll bet your staff has strong opinions on legislators who sell their souls to big contributors. Not saying you're at all like that. But I wonder if your staff knows some of the things I know."

"My staff is made up of loyal supporters. Nothing you could say—"

"I could ask them about the CityWide development and the government contracts that wrapped it all up for a certain group of developers." I raised an eyebrow and tilted my head in his direction.

Kelley was mum.

"I could tell them who tied that package together. How he heroically got the state legislature to award contracts to a public-minded firm who'd contributed mightily to that legislator's campaigns, including one he's running now. For the U.S. Senate, I believe. You think they'll applaud that guy and think of him as an independent fighter for his constituents?"

Kelley turned the knob and opened the door to his office. "Get in. And be brief or so help me, I'll call the police."

"Hold on." I paused in the doorway. "I just had this little moment of terror thinking about the police coming to arrest me for nothing. Okay. It's gone now, nothing to worry about."

The look of disgust and contempt on Kelley's face made it worth getting up early. "Shut the door," he said.

"Don't want them to hear about your heroic efforts?"

"Get this over with and get out." He sat in his comfy well-padded desk chair and leaned back as if he had nothing to fear.

"I'm kinda curious about the contracts you helped secure for Berwick, The Chuffe Group, Wheeler, and others. They were big contributors to your campaigns."

"And to a lot of others." He looked smug because he was right. He wasn't the only pig at the trough.

"Turns out, all the politicians who received money from those people and their companies, eventually helped their contributors in lots of ways."

"Your point?"

294   Joseph R. G. DeMarco

"I have this strange feeling, that somewhere deep in the murky depths of the legislative process, all this deal-making and handshaking got some people murdered."

"Do you have any idea how?" he asked. "Or, do you enjoy barging into offices and making vague accusations."

"Yeah, yeah, I guess you have a point. There's one other name maybe you heard and maybe you can tell me something about."

"Another developer?"

"I think he's got that on his resume somewhere. He does a lot of other things, some of which the law doesn't like much."

"Everyone's got a dark side. Who are you tarring with your brush now?"

"Name's Branko. Konstantin Branko."

I watched for signs of recognition, fear, anything. Kelley came through. His face registered fear and he went pale, making his already ashy face look ghastly.

"You know the guy, right?"

"O-only by reputation…" Kelley said. "He's supposed to be a dangerous character."

"You've met him?"

"No! I stay away from people like that." Kelley's voice quavered and he stared down at his desk. "You'd have to be crazy to deal with a man like Branko. I'm not about to jeopardize my career by coming anywhere near him."

"Sounds like you might've been asked to do just that."

"Are you crazy? Why? Who'd ask me to associate with a thug like Branko?"

"That's what I'm trying to find out," I said. "Would make things a lot easier if somebody would tell the truth. Too much to expect, I guess." *Especially from politicians*, I thought.

"Look, Fontana, I've got other things on my mind right now. Maybe after the primary I can spare you more time." The interview was over as far as he was concerned.

"I'll be going. But I'll be back." I placed a hand on the doorknob, remembered something, and turned back to face him. "The night of the murder—"

"Fontana, I don't have—"

"Just hear me out. Could be helpful… to you, maybe."

"To me? I don't understand."

"The night you guys had your gay pub crawl showing us how much you like us, that's the night Brad and the others were murdered."

"What's that got to do with me?"

"Maybe nothing. I'm wondering if you remember Terrabito arriving late that night? That could be important."

"Terr… he was…, Let me think a minute that was a… a Friday, right?"

"Right." I watched his face.

"I remember now. We'd all been traveling in a group. Terrabito refuses to be seen with me and never likes arriving anywhere at the same time. So…." He rubbed his chin in a thoughtful gesture. I wasn't sure if he was thinking or posing.

"Coming back to you?"

"I remember Shuster hustling me out of one bar and into another until we finally arrived at your place—"

"It's not *my* place but go on…"

"Shuster got me there. I don't remember seeing Terrabito. Maybe he did get there after I did. Does that mean he was late?" Kelley could hardly suppress a smile. If he could spin this the right way, and backhandedly implicate Terrabito in something nefarious, he could maybe move up a point or two in the polls and give Terrabito the heave ho.

"It might," I said. "I'll let you know."

Walking out through the office, I felt Kelley's eyes on me. I'd left him with something potentially juicy. If I needed to talk to him again, he wouldn't keep me waiting.

My stomach growled as I walked back to the office but I needed to check on something before stopping for food.

Olga, still seated at her desk, tapped away at the keyboard.

"You must like the new office. You're here a lot more than ever."

"I am liking office, of course. I am liking Saturday money better," she smiled. I knew full well she'd never need another red cent, since her four husbands had left her more than well off.

"Got anything for me?"

"I am finding many things. Internet keeps no secrets." She looked at me as if warning me. "Is good to remembering this, *zaichik moy*."

"Did you find some of my secrets on the Internet?"

"No. Boss is safe. For now." She wore a slight smile for me.

"How about those land deals? Anything?"

"You are saying look for news. I am finding news." She handed me a huge sheaf of papers stuffed into an accordion folder.

"Thank you. You're a peach."

"Plum, peach. Is confusing."

I laughed.

"Boss is needing me later?"

"Boss is always needing you, Olga. You've done more than your share today. Besides, it's Saturday. Go out and enjoy the weather."

I took the file and went into my office like a kid with a new toy. I had no idea what Olga had found but at this point, just about anything would help. I almost didn't feel the stabs and needle points of pain my ribs sent out.

Filling my mug with what was left of the coffee, I sat at my desk. I heard Olga bustle around then heard the outer door slammed shut. I was alone with the papers and my thoughts.

For some reason I felt empty. Something lingered at the back of my mind, silent and without a name. I pushed it away. There'd be time enough for whatever it was later. Right now there was other business. If I were honest with myself, I'd admit there was always something else to do rather than explore those unknowns lurking just beyond my reach.

I slurped some coffee and pulled out the papers. Olga had printed tons of articles about different development projects. Our databases gave her access to newspaper files, industry news, and resources the general public didn't know or care about.

The first article concerned the struggle to clear properties for a combination mall and movie complex outside the downtown perimeter. Lots of homes and businesses had to be purchased, and people had to be relocated.

One article highlighted a couple of property owner holdouts who were made generous offers. One of them took the money but the other person died in a work related accident before he could do the same. His distant relations were given a smaller deal and took it. Interesting but not interesting enough.

The dozens of articles Olga had printed meant I'd spend the afternoon reading and making notes. Fourteen developments in the city and surrounding suburbs had generated press for one reason or another. It was more than I could manage on my own even in a few hours.

My stomach growled again. I'd have to move this show to another venue, which gave me an idea. I picked up the phone and tapped in a number.

"Clean Living. Luke speaking."

"All business even on a Saturday."

"What's going on, Marco? Missed you at dinner. I thought you'd be there. Even Xinhan asked for you."

"I'm sure he was just as happy I didn't show up," I said.

"You're jealous. I never thought I'd see that." Luke laughed.

"You have it all wrong, Mr. Guan. I'm just a keen observer of people."

"Call it whatever you want."

"Got some time for lunch and a little work?"

"For you? Of course," Luke said. "Will the French Canadian hunk be there?"

"You're like a dog with a bone. You clamp on and never let go."

"So, will he be there?"

"I'll call him. How's that? Can't promise anything, though I know he's eager to do any investigative work I can throw at him."

"Call and tell him your devastatingly attractive friend Luke will be there."

"Yes, sir. Anything else, sir? Shall I have the car sent around to pick you up?"

"I can handle getting there." Luke paused. "Exactly where am I meeting you?"

* * *

We settled on More Than Just Ice Cream since we could relax and talk without a lot of noise. I wasn't looking forward to calling Jean-Claude, but I'd promised. Dialing his number brought some things back into sharp focus.

Joseph R. G. DeMarco

Anton's question lingered in my mind. Worst of all, my failure to respond to Anton haunted me. After all the years of friendship, I couldn't find the words to tell him how I felt.

Jean-Claude's phone rang a few times before he answered.

"*Oui, allo,*" his voice was husky.

"Jean-Claude, still asleep?"

"Marco! It's you," he said. "Asleep? *Non*, I am doing the exercise. I'm dancing tonight and… you know how demanding they can be."

"You've got nothing to worry about."

"Nice for you to say that, but I see myself in the mirrors."

"Got some time for a little detective work?"

"Sure. You are serious? You need my help?"

"Yes. Serious. It's boring stuff but better than last time."

"You know I do not find this boring. It's exciting." Jean-Claude said.

"Don't get too excited just yet."

"Shall I come to your office"

I told him where we'd be meeting and hung up. Was I crazy asking for help from a man I considered a rival? Was I going out of my way to show I was a generous guy who didn't hold a grudge? Or was I punishing myself for allowing Jean-Claude to become a rival? It wasn't his fault, after all. When it came down to it, Jean-Claude was an innocent bystander. I'd let it all happen. Last night, I'd had it in my power to stop it with a word. Something had held me back.

I had deep feelings for Anton but they were overshadowed by my doubts about a relationship, any relationship. By my fears about the lasting nature of relationships. Everything was too uncertain for me to give him an answer, especially the answer he wanted to hear.

As I gathered the papers together, Galen popped into my thoughts. I don't know how he'd have handled the Jean-Claude situation. All I know is he'd have handled it. Period. It'd be settled and he'd move on. The same way he decided to disappear one day. His way of handling something. I still didn't know what that something was. The shadowy agency he worked for? A relationship I knew nothing about? When I found him, and I would, he'd have a lot to answer for. After we'd celebrated his return.

* * *

More Than Just Ice Cream was crowded—not unusual, it's one of the better spots in the heart of the gayborhood to eat— but I found a table in the corner and plunked my stuff down.

Bouncy, my favorite waiter, was on duty. I spied the mousy little server lurking in the background, every once in a while casting a furtive glance in my direction. But Bouncy's personality was too bright a light and everything else faded in comparison.

"What can I get you, stranger?" Bouncy smiled, shifting his weight from foot to foot as he waited. His light brown hair had a shiny, freshly washed look.

"Haven't seen you in a while either. New love interest keeping you under wraps?"

"I wish. School and a second job. And we deliver now, so I'm out on deliveries a lot," he said.

"That's new. And you didn't let me know, I'm hurt." I imagined opening the door to find Bouncy with a delivery for me.

"Limited delivery area, but I can make an exception in your case."

"I may place an order later." I winked. "How about some coffee while I wait."

"Meeting someone? Blind date?"

"More like a working lunch."

"Good," Bouncy said mysteriously and walked away, his flawless glutes moving in perfect rhythm.

Before he returned with my coffee, Jean-Claude entered, spotted me, and headed over to the table. I felt my muscles tense and warned myself to play nice.

"I appreciate this, Marco." Jean-Claude slid into the seat across from me, his hair still wet from showering, his muscle tee giving maximum exposure to his worked-out biceps. "I didn't think you would call me to help again."

"What gives you that idea?" I asked, knowing full well he clearly sensed my uneasiness.

Jean-Claude looked questions at me and tried smiling.

Bouncy cut the tension by arriving with my coffee and menus. "You all here now?" His gaze swept over Jean-Claude approvingly.

"One more and we'll be ready," I looked up as he smiled again and walked off.

"Ready for a boring afternoon?" I pulled a few articles from the folder. "There's a lot to read here."

"Like the last time?"

"Even more, and it's kind of complicated this time. Not just a list of names."

"Look at you guys, all business all the time," Luke said as he sat next to me. "Hi, Jean-Claude." Luke took one of the menus, but I knew he had it memorized.

"Glad you're here, this is gonna be quite a bit of work," I said.

"What've we got?" Luke asked eyeing the overstuffed folder.

Before I could explain, Bouncy made another appearance, this time standing next to me so his upper thigh pressed against my arm.

"You guys ready to order?"

"I'll have the burger," Jean-Claude said. "No bread, just meat."

Bouncy nodded and subtly moved his leg against my arm. "And for you?

"An egg white omelet with spinach and tomatoes," Luke said.

"Another healthy one. You only hang out with health nuts?" Bouncy sounded worried.

"Not all the time," I said.

"So, what'll you have," he asked. I felt his leg, warm and strong, as he seductively moved against my arm.

What I really wanted wasn't on the menu and there wouldn't be room on the table for Bouncy anyway. I gave his calf an unobtrusive squeeze and he pressed himself against me again. "The grilled chicken sandwich with sweet potato fries. And more coffee."

Bouncy took the menus and walked toward the kitchen.

"Seems pretty cozy." Luke said. "New fan?" He never missed a detail.

"Mutual admiration," I said. I thought about placing a home delivery order before I left. Something sweet, as a nightcap.

"Okay, killer," Luke said and winked. "So what's this work you need help with?"

I gave them a brief rundown on the developers and their political cronies. I asked them to read the articles and look for anything that stood out as odd or unusual about parcels of land or contracts. Making sure they knew to take notes, I handed them the fact sheets Olga had made.

"Anything might help. Names, types of businesses on the land to be developed, the original landowners, their families, how much they were offered by developers, holdouts against development. Anything like that," I said.

"How'd he rope you into this, Jean-Claude?" Luke asked.

"No. He did not have to force me. I want to do this. I want a career like Marco."

"Great job. Lousy pay, though," Luke said.

"Take these." I handed out highlighters and pens. "Highlight whatever you find that might have significance. Make notes too. When you finish with an article, put it in this." I placed a folder marked 'Read' on the empty chair next to Jean-Claude.

"No hints about what we should look for?" Luke asked.

"Can't say even if I knew. I wouldn't want to make you look for certain things and miss others."

"How will we—" Jean –Claude began.

"You'll know it when you see it. Trust me."

Bouncy brought our food. He leaned down close to my face when he set my plate on the table. I thought my lips might brush his cheek. Then I settled in to work. Customers came and went while we highlighted text and made notes. Neither Luke nor Jean-Claude spoke a word.

After an hour or so, we'd made more progress than I'd hoped. But the pile of documents was still large. I saw they'd made quite a few notes on each article and had to believe the answers I needed were there.

As I picked up another document, my cell phone rang. Caller ID said it was Anton.

"Finally decided to join us?" I was hoping he would. It could mean a bit of the ice between us had thawed.

"Marco, something's happened… Ty is missing."

"Missing? Have you—"

"I've tried everything. Can you meet me here?"

"On my way."

Luke and Jean-Claude looked up at me.

"Something's come up. I've gotta see what I can do."

"Okay. What about this work?" Luke asked.

"Can you two finish up?"

"Sure," Jean-Claude said.

"Luke, can you put the files on my desk when you're through? Have the key?"

"Right here." He jangled a key ring to prove it. "Shall I wait or…"

"Call me when you finish." I took out my wallet, placed a fifty on the table. "That should cover it and a nice tip. Gotta run."

Chapter 28

Anton stood waiting on the sidewalk in front of his building when I arrived.

"What's happened?"

"He's missing. Ty was here when I left this morning. Everything was the same as every morning."

"What makes you think he's missing? He could'a just gone out. Kid's got a life, right? Maybe he needed fresh air."

Anton handed me a slip of paper. "He left this."

The note read: *Thanks for taking care of me, Anton. I'll never forget how nice you've been. Tell Marco I can't do what he asks. I'll see you around.*

"Sounds like he doesn't intend on coming back. You see what I mean now?"

Anton said.

"Did he get any phone calls, any e-mails?"

"He never used the phone or the computer while I was at home. Who knows what he did when I went out." Anton paced, then stood in front of me again. "His cell phone goes straight to voicemail. I've left a dozen messages."

"How about his apartment?"

"He doesn't have a landline. I couldn't—"

"I have his landlady's number." Taking out my cell phone, I tapped a few keys, then waited.

"Who is it?" She was just as direct on the phone as in person.

"Marco Fontana, Mrs. Cellucci. Remember? The detective—"

"Oh, sure, sure. Hey, how's my little golden angel?" She'd answered my question before I could ask it.

"You haven't seen him?"

"Not since before you was here. Not since that monster hurt him."

"Oh, I was hoping you'd—"

"Did something happen to that kid? You're telling me something bad happened?"

"No, no, Mrs. Cellucci. Nothing bad," I said, hoping I was right. "We can't find him and he still needs bed rest."

"Musta gone out. He's an angel but he's still a kid. They go out."

"You're right. If you do see him, tell him to call Marco. It's important." She agreed and hung up.

"She hasn't seen Ty?" Anton asked.

"No, but that—"

"I called some of the dancers he's been friendly with," Anton said. "I called his family. I was very discreet."

"Got nowhere with them, right?"

"None of them have seen him. " Anton sounded defeated. "I hate to think he might've gone back to that creep."

"Eddie? We put him on a bus to the Middle-of-Nowhere, PA and he's not coming back."

"Eddie told you that?" Anton's eyes were steely. "People like Eddie lie. They lie about everything. I wouldn't be surprised if he's back and convinced Ty to meet him."

"Kevin said that Eddie's been calling every—"

"When's the last time you saw Kevin or asked him about Eddie's calls?"

"A couple of days," I said. "Kevin would've called if Eddie hadn't checked in."

"Call Kevin. Find out." Anton gripped my sleeve. "Please."

I dialed Kevin's number.

"Hey boss, what's up?"

"Ty's missing, Kev."

"Shit! What happened?"

"Has Eddie called in every day? From the same number?"

"Like clockwork. Latest was this morning. Why?" Kevin asked.

"Just wondering. We thought maybe he tried coming back for Ty."

"He does and he's mine. I been wanting to smash somebody like him for a long time."

"I'll help you if it comes to that. Right now we've gotta find Ty," I said. "Call you back when I know something."

"If Eddie hasn't missed calling in, where the hell did Ty get to?" Anton asked. "What happened to him?"

"I'll call a friend at the Department and see what he can do," I said.

"Don't they have rules about missing persons? Ty probably hasn't been gone long enough."

"Yeah, they've got rules. But even the tightest rules can be tweaked. Lemme see what my friend can do."

Anton looked at the entrance to his apartment building as if expecting Ty to saunter out. "Tell them... he's just a kid..."

"You gonna be okay?" I asked. Anton was close to the guys who worked for us. They were like his kids. Seeing Ty beaten was hard enough. "Can we go up to your place? Maybe I can find something that'll help us figure out where Ty is."

Anton looked at me as if this was a brilliant idea. "Why didn't I think of that?" His eyes brightened with the possibility of finding some odd clue that would give us a lead.

He led me into the building and up to his apartment. Though I'd been there a thousand times, I felt like a stranger. Like this place, and Anton himself, were new to me. Even Anton seemed shy and tentative.

"Take a good look around," Anton said. "Want some coffee or tea?"

"Sure, whatever you're having."

I went to the room were Ty had slept. The bed had been made and it didn't appear he'd left anything behind. Not that he had much with him when we brought him here. Still, I got on my hands and knees and searched under the bed. Nothing. Not even an errant dust bunny.

"The room's clean," I said, returning to the living room. "Doesn't even look like anyone other than you has been there."

"That's it, then?" Anton set two mugs of coffee on the table and took a seat on the couch.

I picked up a mug and debated whether or not to sit next to him or in one of the other chairs. Anton decided for me, glancing at me and then at the couch. I wanted to feel him next to me. I took him up on his offer and sat beside him.

"I'll call my police contacts. They'll help."

"You think he'll go back to Eddie, don't you?"

"It's possible. Maybe probable. He isn't convinced Eddie is bad for him."

"Why would he do that to himself? He's a vulnerable kid… not like some of the other dancers…they're stronger, tougher. You know I like them all equally… care about them…"

"Which is why they worship you," I said.

"Having Ty stay with me… taking care of him, keeping him safe… you know what I mean, Marco. It changed things. I guess I got attached. Like he was my kid."

"You did a good thing, Anton. I'm proud of you. Taking him in, spending all that time." I hesitated. "There's just so much anyone can do. Ty is who he is. He thinks he loves Eddie."

"Can't understand why he feels that way. Eddie's a scumbag."

"We'll find Ty. Assuming he wants to be found." I placed a hand on Anton's back and tried soothing him.

We sat that way for a while. Close together, sharing the silence. At some point, I moved to get my cell phone and told Anton I was calling Detective Shim.

He looked at me and blinked as if he'd been far away. I wondered what he'd been thinking. He placed a hand to my face and drew one finger across my lips. He looked so sad I nearly took him in my arms and hugged him. But I wasn't sure he wanted that.

* * *

The office was quiet when I got back. Olga had left and Luke hadn't yet returned with the papers. Not even a distant siren broke the stillness in the room. Solitude and silence were not exactly what I needed right then. Noise, music, voices. Anything but the thoughts I was thinking.

Almost on cue, tearing up the silence, Shim called to tell me he was on his way up to talk about Ty. In no time at all, I heard the elevator's signal and the sound of someone approaching.

"That was quick," I said as Shim opened the door.

"I was in the elevator when I called. Figured you wanted to get this done quick." He took a seat and pulled out his faithful notebook.

"I was hoping you could fast track this." I watched for a reaction.

"Hey, it's not like I have anything else to do. I've got cases coming out of my ears. I'm nowhere on the Vega case. And you're asking favors. I can do it all blindfolded."

"I'm digging up information as fast as I can. If I find Vega in there anywhere, I'll call you."

"So what's the missing persons case about?"

"Trouble is, he hasn't been missing long enough for you or the FBI to care." I spotted some of Olga's pastry on a plate near the coffee maker and went to get it. Shim followed me with his eyes. "Want one of these. Olga's a pro when it comes to pastry."

"Sure." He plucked one off the plate I held out to him. He sniffed at it before biting into it. "Pretty good."

"The kid's name is Ty. He's one of my dancers. He's in a bad relationship. Really bad. The guy beats him."

"I've worked cases like that."

"He stayed with my friend Anton after the latest beating. I thought I might get him to press charges…"

"He said 'No.' Right?" Shim had been on the job long enough to know that most abused lovers rarely ever testify. Their minds, their emotions are as battered as their bodies.

"Right. A few days later, he leaves Anton a thank you note and disappears."

"Back to the boyfriend?"

"Hope not, but… I kinda made sure the boyfriend wouldn't feel comfortable hanging around Philly anymore. At least I thought I did."

"The kid could've gone to meet him somewhere outside the city."

"That's my guess. His landlady hasn't seen him."

"What can I do?" Shim asked.

"If he goes back to that guy, I'm afraid Ty might not survive the next beating. I'm hoping you can track him down. Put out a bolo. Maybe get the Feds involved."

"You know I want to help…"

"Here comes the 'It Can't Be Done' excuse, right?"

"There's procedure…"

"What's the procedure when a kid's life is in danger?"

"I'm not saying I won't—"

Before he could finish, Luke opened the door and walked in. He caught my eye and smiled, then turned his charm on Shim. "Hey, nice to see you again," he said.

"Right, from lunch the other day."

"Hope I didn't interrupt anything," Luke said and wiggled his eyebrows.

Shim blushed. "N-no. We were talking about the case."

Luke brandished the file folders. "Speaking of which… I've got what you asked for, Marco. You're gonna want to see what we did." He placed the folder on my desk.

"I was just leaving, anyway," Shim said as he stood.

"Saved. Now you don't have to make any promises you can't keep." I looked him in the eye.

"I didn't say I wouldn't do anything. I can work around the protocols. Keep me posted if you hear from the kid. Let me know if anything comes up on the other case."

"You got it," I said. "Thanks. I owe *you* this time."

"I won't forget. That you can bet on," he said as he left.

"Alone at last." I gave Luke a smile. "What'd you and Jean-Claude find?"

Luke walked to the door of the conference room.

"Be easier if I spread things out on the table here."

"Gotcha." I followed him in. "You and Jean-Claude get along after I left?"

"Sure. Why wouldn't we?"

"Just asking."

"You never *just ask* anything. You always have a hidden agenda. Does the cute Detective know that about you?"

"He'll learn."

"Poor guy." Luke laughed.

"So I guess you got nowhere with Jean-Claude?"

Luke shook his head. "The boy is crazy about Anton. I didn't have the heart to say anything about you and—"

"Not sure there is a me and anybody," I said.

"Oh." Luke, characteristically, didn't ask for details. Instead he plopped folders onto the conference table and splayed out pages filled with notations. Then he sat in a chair and glanced over at me as if I were about to explode.

I took the seat next to him and peered at the pages.

"So, what've we got here?"

"These are the fact sheets you had on each development project," he said tapping each of them. "Take a look. See if there's anything similar between them."

I took a few minutes reviewing the sheets and felt Luke watching me. He fidgeted as he waited, but then he always was a little impatient, being quicker to grasp things than most people.

"Well?" he said. "Anything pop out at you?"

"Yeah," I mumbled as I stared at the pages, not believing what I saw. "Yeah, I see what you're saying. But... it's almost..."

"Unbelievable, right? Jean-Claude and I read for hours and made notes. When we finished we compared what we'd written and... it was... incredible."

"How many..." I did a quick count. "Ten different projects over a period of eight or ten years and... one, two..." I counted silently. "Five accidental deaths and two missing persons cases."

"All of them owned property the developers wanted."

I whistled. "All spread out nicely so no one ever thought about putting things together."

"They actually cleared the way by having these people killed?" Luke asked.

"Not that I'm the suspicious sort, but absolutely, hell yes! They had someone get rid of their problems for them."

"Next time someone wants to buy land I own, I'll remember this," Luke said and shuddered. "How can people do this?"

"They didn't do it all by their lonesome. They had help and I have a feeling I know who that was."

"That's no surprise but..." Luke hesitated. "What's it have to do with Brad's murder?"

"That's what I've got to figure out."

* * *

Luke left the office and I sat staring at the results of the search. Though the facts were laid out like beads on a string, I still couldn't prove a connection to the murders.

Someone knocking on the door jamb interrupted my thoughts. I looked up and saw a gaunt, angular young man dressed in cycling spandex and wearing a helmet. Unshaven, he stood awkwardly holding a box and a clipboard.

"Can I do something for you?"

"Package for M. Fontana. He around?"

"That's me." I held out my hand.

The messenger walked to my desk and held out the clipboard. "Sign the form." All charm and social skills, these bicycle messengers.

I took the clipboard and signed my name.

We exchanged clipboard for package and the skinny-assed cyclist strolled out the door without even a good-bye.

The box was plain cardboard sealed with packing tape and bearing an address label. No return address. Against my better judgment, I started opening the box. If it'd been a bomb, the cyclist wouldn't have gotten far with it. Could've been another type of bomb.

I held my breath and slipped off the tape. No explosion. No ticking clock.

Gingerly I lifted the flaps a bit and saw pink tissue paper. Opening the flaps all the way, I saw an envelope resting on fluffy pink tissue. Taking the envelope, I lifted the tissue.

I sucked in a breath when I saw it. A large multi-colored snake coiled on more pink tissue. Remaining motionless, I waited to see if it moved. It didn't.

Gently shaking the box, I watched the snake's body shift from one side to the other. It was dead.

I knew then, this was a gift from Ricky "Dead Snake" Sorba. The note he'd placed in the envelope read *Greetings. Think you can ruin my reputation? Think again. Wait'll you hear the series I'm doing. Calling it "Fag Private Investigaters and the Slut Boys Who Love Them." Got your interest? Tune in next week. All week. Hear all about yourself. See who gets ruined.* It was signed, *Ricky.*

I placed the note on my desk. I taped the box back up thinking I might show it to Shim. I needed to come up with a plan for the fanatic radio host.

I didn't care about him going after me. I could handle the smarmy bigot. It might even bring in some business. It sounded like Sorba was going to go after my friends, though.

I couldn't have that.

* * *

Sorba was a problem I didn't need right now, but I'd come up with something. I thought about that as I walked home. By the time I reached my apartment door, I'd worked out a bare bones solution.

A shower and a meal had to come first. I was due at Bubbles and needed to relax.

In the bedroom, I stripped off my clothes and was about to turn the shower on when the phone rang.

"Mr. Fontana?" The man at the front desk was new, and I didn't recognize his voice.

"Yes?"

"Front desk. Delivery for you."

"Delivery? I didn't…"

"Guy says it's the food you ordered at the restaurant this afternoon."

I had to think a minute. I hadn't ordered a thing. Then I remembered Bouncy mentioning the restaurant had started making deliveries.

"Mr. Fontana? Shall I let him up?"

"Sure."

In less than a minute, came a knock at the door. Throwing on a terrycloth robe, I opened the door.

"Delivery," Bouncy cooed, a cardboard box in his hands. "Thought you might like some *hot* food."

He didn't wait for an invitation, choosing instead to walk in.

"Nice place. But I knew it would be. Classy, like you." He placed the box on the coffee table and walked over to me. His hands slipped beneath the robe, and I felt them explore my body. Then he placed his arms around me and pulled me into a kiss.

His hair smelled of pine and mountain air. I held his face in my hands so I could look at him. He was boyish, and his big eyes made him seem more innocent than he was. I pulled him to me and we kissed again.

Maneuvering his hands around, he slipped the robe from my shoulders, as I undid his shirt.

He stepped back to look at me and smiled. "Ready for dinner?"

Chapter 29

Bouncy, whose name turned out to be Wes, stayed until I had to leave for Bubbles. I promised him I'd be ordering take out more often.

I reached Bubbles with plenty of time to set up the Saturday show, but my mind raced over the details we'd uncovered earlier. It was clear the developers, Wheeler, Berwick and others, were used to having things their way. What they couldn't buy, they took. For me there was no doubt the developers and their pet politicians had used "professional" services to make certain there were no obstacles in the path of their development schemes. Since some were acquainted with Branko, the logical conclusion was that he was the thug of choice to do their dirty work.

Branko was convicted on extortion charges centered around a land deal that his own fly-by-night company had structured. The victim of the scheme had been placed in witness protection along with a couple of others brave enough to tag Branko. Other charges had been dropped, at least one of which was murder. No witnesses, no evidence, no case.

It was an easy ride from extortion to murder. I was sure Branko had been the one the developers used in those cases we found in the articles. I had no proof, though.

There'd be little chance of making progress on a Saturday night. Besides, I wasn't yet sure which way to turn. Would anyone implicate Wheeler or others who'd been cozy with Branko? Wheeler was dead. Berwick was out of the country and out of reach. The other developers hid behind a wall of lawyers and Branko would be an idiot to implicate himself in anything.

I needed to find a way through the defensive wall. Someone would have to break and that wouldn't be easy.

On my way to Bubbles I'd put a call in to the photographer. Paranoid as he was, I didn't think I'd hear from him. If I did, I hoped he'd know who else Vega wanted him to photograph. That'd be something to go on.

"Hey, Marco!" Dale, front and center as usual, called to me as I entered Bubbles. The bar was half empty but it was early. I clapped Dale on the back and asked the bartender to comp him a drink.

"You're like Old Faithful. If I came in on a Saturday and you weren't here, things wouldn't be the same."

"As long as I can propel myself outta the house, I'm here!" Dale raised his glass in salute. "What's on tap tonight?"

I knew Dale had favorites among the dancers. I also knew three of them would be onstage later. "I should let it be a surprise," I teased.

"Not even a hint? C'mon, Marco. It's Dale. Don't make me bust. Still an hour before showtime."

"Just a hint. Remember the latest Full Moon show?" One of our most popular events. Bare buns with lots of up-close and personal time with the strippers made the customers delirious. The same three guys who'd be on tonight performed in that show.

"Ye-yeah…" Dale's eyebrows crunched together as he tried to remember. "Oh, shit! Yeah! I remember. Who was dancin' that night?"

"Nice try. I said you'd get a hint. That's what you got."

Dale smiled and went back to his drink.

I headed up to my office. I needed to plan and to decide whether or not to tell Shim about what we'd discovered in those articles. He only wanted solid information. What we'd found didn't prove much, yet. But it was a hell of a story on its own.

Anton was sitting at my desk and looked up at me when I opened the door.

"Hey." I felt as awkward as I had when I was fifteen.

"Hey, yourself. I wasn't sure you'd be in tonight."

"Wouldn't miss it. And I wouldn't leave you on your own."

"I thought you might want to let those ribs heal."

"I'm fine." I was about to thump my chest to prove it but thought better of it. "Takes more than that to keep me from seeing you... I mean... you know... helping you here. I don't like being an absentee owner."

"I'm glad you're here."

That sounded good. I walked over to the desk but Anton made no move to stand. Instead he spread out some papers on the desktop.

"I've been having scheduling problems and I thought you could resolve them."

"Sure," I said unable to keep the disappointment out of my voice.

"Did you talk to your police friend about Ty? I wondered if..."

"Talked to him after I saw you. He kinda echoed what you said about Ty not being missing all that long. And Ty did leave that note..."

"Because he leaves a note, they don't care? That's screwed up in so many ways."

"I'm not defending it, Anton. Don't shoot me for telling you what he said."

"Yeah, I know, but I don't like it."

"You said you had scheduling problems?" I moved closer and felt Anton tense as I brushed his shoulder with my thigh.

"With Ty gone and a couple of the other guys asking for different schedules, we don't have anyone for mid-week. That's—"

"Hey! Who the fuck let you up here?" The voice came from the hall just outside the office, stopping Anton mid-sentence.

Then another shout: "What's goin' on? I thought only..." The rest was muffled as he moved away.

"Lookin' good *papi*," the voice was familiar. Nina. She knocked on the door, waited a few seconds, then walked in. "*Jefe*, got some of that work you asked for." Nina sauntered over to my desk and waved a folder. "Anton. Where you been keeping yourself?"

"How'd you get up here, Nina?" I asked. "You charm your way past the bouncers?"

"Charm is my middle name, *jefe*. But you don't have anybody guardin' nothing. I came right up. Guess I scared the balls off some'a your dancers."

"Great," Anton said. "Maybe we need security cameras."

"Don't worry, *papi*. Hallie can install a security system. She's good."

"You're here alone a lot and the guys are… maybe we do need something," I said. "Tell Hallie to give me a call."

"Will do."

"You didn't have to come all the way here to deliver this. I'd've—"

"Don't flatter yourself, *jefe*. I like you, sure. But makin' special trips for you, I don't think so." Nina smiled sweetly. "I'm on my way to *Sisters*. So I thought I'd stop into to see my favorite private dick."

"I'll let you two lovebirds coo all on your own," Anton stood and gathered his papers.

"Don't leave on my account. Just gonna be a minute," Nina said.

"I've gotta get the guys together for the show. I should'a been out there fifteen minutes ago."

"Next time this big hunk comes down to my place, tag along. I don't get to see you much," Nina said.

Anton nodded, gave her a quick hug, and left.

"You two fighting?" Nina asked after a few seconds.

"I don't know what we are, Nina. We're not exactly fighting." We weren't getting along like we used to either, and I didn't know what the next step would be.

"Pretty cold in here if you ask me, *jefe*." She pretended to shiver.

"You said you got some hits on what I asked for?"

"I got something. Don't I always? It was kinda risky but for you… anything. Looks interesting, too." She placed papers from a folder on the desk.

"This what I think it is?" I said sliding a finger down columns of figures. Brad's name was at the top of each page.

"Your friend Brad's accounts and deposits to those accounts. Took in quite a bit and withdrew almost as much. Like we saw from the earlier search."

"I remember. Did you find out where the money came from?"

"Some of it." Pulling out a few more pages, she said, "A lot was cash deposits. Some were checks."

"Names?"

"There's the list," she said pointing to a particular page. "Looks like one of the big guns was a guy named Wheeler."

"He was an investor. That makes sense. The others were probably investors. No familiar names though." I'd have to look into them.

"Wish I had investors like that." Nina laughed.

"Not when you end up murdered, you don't."

"There were a few electronic transfers. All of them under the radar, meaning they weren't large enough to attract the attention of the Feds." She pointed to a list of numbers. "Just a numbered account."

"Dead end, huh?"

"Yeah, for anybody but me."

"You found a name?" I said. "Who is it?"

"You gotta come bail me out when they bash in my door and arrest me."

"Promise. You get the best bail money."

"I traced back the numbers through… ah, you don't wanna know all that, and it just makes me sound like more of a geek. I traced it, is all you gotta know. The name Shuster mean anything to you?"

"More than you know." I gave her a big bear hug which she accepted without complaint.

As soon as she left the office I dialed Shuster's number. It went to voicemail. "Shuster, call me when you get this. Something's up and you're right in the middle of it. If you don't want a scandal right before the primary make it quick."

* * *

I knew he'd get back to me, especially after I dropped the word "scandal." Until then, I needed to be onstage.

The bar was crowded, and the smell of stale beer wafted on the air. Better than stale cigarette smoke. Music thumped through the place energizing everyone. Eager patrons, some already clutching loads of dollar bills, huddled close to the stage as showtime approached.

I didn't see Anton at his usual station, so I wandered backstage. Cal and Junior, each of them in silky boxers which didn't hide much, oiled each other up so they'd glisten as they danced. I zigzagged between Turner and Guy, practicing a bump and grind for their routine, and noticed how much they enjoyed it. Other dancers jogged in place, bubble butts jiggling, packages bouncing. Surrounded by perfect bodies and knockout faces, I thought again how it never got old. All that fleshy temptation, every day, right under your nose, was a fantasy. You'd think the spell would wear off. It never did.

"Hey boss," Bruno said. "Lookin' for Anton?"

"How'd you guess?"

"He's back there with Jean-Claude, gettin' ready for the opening."

"Thanks, Bruno. You're gonna make a lot of money tonight," I said fingering his long silk scarf. The leather bomber jacket, white scarf, and creamy jodhpurs sinking into long black boots was a look that drove men wild. Of course, when he removed the costume, the audience usually went insane.

He grinned.

I found Anton helping Jean-Claude and a couple of others with their outfits at the back of the room. I noticed Anton's hand linger on Jean-Claude's shoulder and the way Jean-Claude looked at him. Something gripped me deep inside, but I couldn't afford to acknowledge it. Not yet.

"Ready to start?"

"We're set. Missing a guy, but we've got more than enough."

Sometimes dancers were no-shows. I figured it was their loss. No dancing meant no tips or house pay.

"I'll get out there and start things going." I walked away, still with that empty feeling inside. I shook it off.

Once I'd done my part, I decided it would be a good idea to mix with the crowd. Besides, I didn't want another awkward encounter in the office with Anton. Mingling with the patrons was what I needed.

Dale sat mesmerized by Bruno's performance. Talking to him would've been like sitting alone. Most of the other men seemed to be having a transcendental experience as they stared up at the dancers. Some of them probably were.

Walking outside I saw Kevin, the bouncer. "You hear from Eddie today?" I asked as he simultaneously checked IDs and searched out potential trouble in new arrivals.

"Called right on time. He sounded kinda funny but then he always sounds funny."

"I guess he didn't tell you if Ty was there?"

"Yeah, like a scumbucket abuser is ever gonna tell somebody that his punching bag is back with him."

"Maybe you're gonna have to take a train ride…"

"Sounds good to me. Just give me the word."

I clapped him on the shoulder. "Soon."

My cell phone rang and it sounded angry. When I saw the Caller ID, I saw it was Shuster.

"Fontana."

"You bastard." Shuster hissed the words. "How can you lay that on me and not tell me what you're talking about?"

"Slow down, cowboy. I'm doin' you a favor by givin' you this heads up. I didn't have to call at all."

"Says you. What's this all about?"

"Got time to meet now?"

"Of course I don't. But you've got me by the balls, so I'll make time."

* * *

The block was familiar. Apparently Shuster put out good money to prove he was a crackerjack political consultant. Had several offices and a staff doing his bidding. His center city place was in an old building on Lombard near Twentieth. Nice townhouses interspersed with buildings in need of work.

This time of night, all sorts of strangeness crawled the streets especially this close to South Street. The .38 in my shoulder holster felt like protection enough. I don't normally carry when I'm working at Bubbles, but after the past few nights, I'd decided a change of habit was in order.

Following Shuster's directions I entered a vestibule and faced a panel of call buttons. When I pressed the one he'd indicated, his voice crackled over the intercom.

"That you?" he asked.

"Depends on who you're expecting," I said.

"Can't be too careful, Fontana."

The jarring buzzer sounded and the door was unlatched.

Shuster's office took up the first floor. Empty at this hour, everything was silent, but you could see it was a slick operation. The building was in great shape and better than you'd expect for a political nightcrawler like Shuster.

I walked through a room of dimly lit cubicles and saw light spilling from a partially open door. Pushing the door in all the way, just in case one of Shuster's thugs was standing back of it, I entered keeping an eye out for anything strange. He appeared to be alone.

"What's this all about, Fontana?" Shuster's double chin wobbled with anger. "I don't have time to play games with you."

"You had time to play games with Brad."

"What're you talk....? We've been all over this. You pulling some kind of shakedown right before the primary?"

"We didn't cover the territory I just discovered, Shuster."

"There's nothing else. I told you everything. Brad was my masseur. That's it."

"Funny thing about the Internet. It never has memory loss and everything you think you're doing in secret might as well be plastered on a billboard over I-95."

"Are you telling me the little shit recorded my massage sessions?" Shuster's voice was strangled as he stood and pounded a fist on the desk.

"Nah. Brad wasn't like that. If you'd taken a little time to get to know him instead of using him, you'd have seen that."

"What the fuck are you talking about?" He leaned forward, propping himself with his knuckles on the desk. "You said you had something important. Now you say it's old news about Brad. I wish I'd never contacted the shit."

I stared at him a while, imagining how such a squat, arrogant butterball would look in an orange jumpsuit. "So, tell me, Shuster. Are you in the habit of paying ten grand for a massage?"

"Ten...?" Shuster looked confused for a moment then the anger returned. "What are you talking about? I paid his usual fee." Hand out palm up, he swept his arm around as if he were showing the room to a prospective buyer. "What I put into this office, does it look like I have much left over for a ten thousand dollar massage?"

"Looks like the classy nest of one of those things you see crawling the streets late at night. Doesn't matter what the place looks like. You paid Brad ten thousand dollars several times."

"You need to pay for serious psychiatric help."

"Records don't lie, Shuster. Especially bank records. You made several electronic transfers into Brad's accounts."

"Bullshit."

"Maybe you cut a few corners so you'd have the dough for a massage you'd never forget?"

"You're talking out of your hat, Fontana. I don't have that kind of money to throw around."

"Oh, I know, bucko. I know just how much you have. Which begs the question, where'd you get the money to lavish on Brad?"

"I'm telling you I didn't lavish any—"

"Save it, Shuster. I've got the records in black and white. I can have them printed in any color you want. It's gonna say the same thing in every color: you transferred money into Brad's accounts."

"You're bluffing. Trying to get me to admit to something I didn't do."

"I can have it in the hands of the press in an hour. You know how they crave juicy stories like this. The downfall of a political power player. You'll be a household name for a few minutes, then you'll sink into oblivion."

Shuster stared into the distance behind me and said nothing.

"So I'll ask again. Where'd you get the money and why'd you give it to Brad?"

"Don't you know?" Shuster snorted his contempt. "I thought the all-knowing Fontana and his Internet soothsayer knew everything."

"We're workin' on it, bucko. You can save us a lotta time if you tell me now."

Shuster's piggy little eyes flashed with a cold anger.

"Okay, then," I said and turned. "See you on the front page." I took a step toward the door.

"Hold on." Shuster suddenly sounded tired, drained of everything.

"Truth coming back to you?"

"Truth is I don't know what you're talking about."

"Here we go—"

"If the information you found looks like it came from me, then I'm being framed."

"Who'd frame you?"

"I make enemies. More than you can count on fingers and toes. In politics you've got to develop eyes on the back of your head and everywhere else. There are so many people who want things... money, favors, jobs, you name it."

"Me, I want answers. So, I'm askin' again, who'd blackmail you?"

"There are people who'd want to sink this campaign."

"Which, Kelley's or Nussbaum's? You work for both of those jokers."

"Kelley's campaign. He's running for the Senate. I just consult for Nussbaum. He's small potatoes. His House seat is a go nowhere position. Nobody cares who's in it." Shuster said.

"So you're sayin' Terrabito wants to wipe Kelley off the playing field?"

"Yes. His assistant Nolan is an underhanded player with a killer instinct."

"Kinda like you."

"Yeah, sure, whatever. Terrabito's not the only one. Wheeler hated Kelley. Who knows why, but he did. So did Berwick. That's practically the only thing Wheeler and Berwick agreed on."

"You used to work for Wheeler, right?"

"A few years, which is how I know his thinking. He wanted Terrabito to win the Senate seat. He probably saw the race tightening up and he had access to lots of things."

Shuster sounded sincere, but I'm not a trusting soul. Even if he was telling the truth, he wasn't telling the whole truth. My Italian blood wouldn't let me believe him.

"Who else wants Kelley to lose?"

"I don't know. Could be half a dozen people. You have to let me think about this before you shoot off your mouth to the press." His voice had faded to a dry hollow sound and he sat heavily in the chair behind his desk. Cradling his head in his hands he was silent.

"I half believe you, Shuster. But only half. Maybe you're right and somebody's framing you. So, why do I get the feeling you're not telling me everything?"

Shuster didn't answer.

"Tomorrow, Shuster. Figure out who else might want to pull you and Kelley down, and call me. I don't hear from you tomorrow, then bright and early Monday morning I'm headed to the Inky and the Daily News. They've got some sharks there who need a meal, and this is juicy stuff."

Chapter 30

I t wasn't easy believing Shuster was framed. Who'd benefit by putting him in a squeeze? If it looked like Shuster paid Brad lavish amounts, reporters would have a field day and Kelley would be out. Could be Shuster had kinky sexual things to hide and paid to keep Brad quiet. Could be he was making payments for Nolan. Or, it could be he was making payoffs on Kelley's behalf. Any way you cut it, that would kill Kelley's chances in the primary. If that was the motive, then Wheeler and Terrabito were back up on the suspect list. They both hated Kelley and wanted him to lose.

I was convinced that part of Shuster's story was a lie. Even if he was ignorant of the money transfers, which I doubted, he knew something he wasn't divulging. Which meant he was either covering for someone or protecting himself. One other possibility was that Shuster knew everything, the money transfers and more, but couldn't tell the truth because whoever dropped that money on Brad had some kind of hold over Shuster.

By the time I reached Bubbles my head was spinning with possibilities, and I needed a drink. I slipped through the doors just before closing and snagged a beer from one of the bartenders. The show had finished, customers filed out in a noisy unorganized way, and Stan's cleaning crew started their work.

I poked my head into the dressing room as I passed by but it was dark and empty. The guys usually left before the patrons for obvious reasons. Sometimes there were stragglers. Not tonight.

My office was equally empty and dark. Anton had probably left with the dancers. I flicked on the lights and sat in the chair. There was no muffled thumping of music from the bar, no teasing and shouting from guys in the dressing room, no laughter filtering up from the first floor. I felt totally alone and isolated. I hadn't expected Anton to wait, but somewhere deep down I wished he had.

I gulped down the beer, gathered Nina's papers and the rest of my things, then went down the stairs to exit through the bar where the crew was hard at work.

A bar is a strange place, if you think about it. Open every day, a home away from home for a lot of people, and nothing much in itself without them. Bubbles right now was an empty shell. Bring in the dancers and their fans, the bartenders, the bouncers, the barbacks, turn on the music and the lighting, and suddenly it was another world. Self-contained and, even if an incomplete world, Bubbles gave the appearance of being everything a guy needed for a while. A party, a place to forget, a place to be alone with his thoughts in the midst of a crowd.

A few of the cleaning crew waved as I walked past and I nodded, not in the mood for conversation. I walked out the door and headed home.

I was getting closer to figuring out what'd happened to Brad. Things were fuzzy though, and I needed clarity. Shuster was involved. I had to believe Branko was, too. How to connect them still escaped me.

It was difficult for me to believe Wheeler had anything to do with Brad's murder but if he had been involved, something had gone terribly wrong that night at the spa.

I walked through the doors to my building expecting to find Grace at the front desk, saw Carlos there instead. "How'd you get the late shift on a Saturday?"

"Emergency. Grace got sick or her kid or something. I'm on call this weekend. We all take turns. Just my luck."

"I know how you feel."

"Hey! Wait a minute, Mr. Fontana." His eyes lit up and he held out his hand like a stop sign.

"What's up, Carlos?"

"Somebody left a package for you. Hold on." He disappeared into the back room.

It wasn't Sorba's way to send more than one dead animal per person he was threatening. Maybe Matus and old Dusty Voice had left me some stomach turning warning in a box.

Carlos held a rectangular package in his hand. "Got it right here."

Wrapped in brown paper and tied around with twine, it reminded me of old fashioned parcels you'd see in old movies. When Carlos placed it in my hand, I realized it must be a book.

"Thanks, Carlos." I smiled and turned the package over inspecting it for markings. There were none.

"Gonna open that?"

"You remember who left this for me?"

"It was here before I came on tonight. Maybe one of the other guys remembers. You can ask 'em tomorrow." He eyed the package. "Leavin' anonymous packages like that is unusual."

I fiddled with the twine but the knot was unworkable.

"Got a scissors?"

He whipped out a pair of scissors so fast, I was astonished.

"Now we get to see what all the mystery is about." I cut the twine and slipped off the brown paper. It turned out to be three slim daybook-diaries for this and the two previous years.

"That's it?" Carlos seemed disappointed.

"You expected a magic lamp or something? A beautiful genie? I don't lead that kind of life, Carlos."

"You have a pretty exciting time, you ask me. I hoped it was something interesting."

"I'll let you know how interesting these are after I read them." I waved as I moved to the elevator bank.

I flipped through the books as the elevator took me to my floor. They were Wheeler's personal daybooks and there appeared to be a lot of entries. The person who'd left the package hadn't included a note, but I figured it was

Caragan. He'd been bothered by the implication that Wheeler was involved in something criminal. I had a feeling he'd keep searching for answers after our talk. Maybe he'd found something useful.

It was late but the idea of sleep had vanished as soon as I'd unwrapped the package and saw its contents. There was no way in hell I'd be able to set the books down then fall asleep not knowing what secrets they held. After slipping off my clothes, I padded around in my underwear making coffee and rummaging for something to snack on while I read.

A yellow legal pad, a couple of pens, and the daybooks lay on the table waiting as I plunked down the coffee and a croissant I'd forgotten about which had lost all its oomph.

Though I wanted to start with the weeks leading up to the murders, I knew the explanation for Wheeler's actions could lay in the months before that. There was no way to skip the earlier entries.

Flipping through, I noticed that Wheeler kept clipped but precise notes, except when it came to names. Sometimes he used initials instead of whole names.

In first daybook, Wheeler's notes held nothing unexpected. He'd made entries indicating his participation in community projects. I saw Xinhan's name mentioned several times in conjunction with Chinatown projects. Wheeler believed in Xinhan's ability and honesty. "He has my confidence. Steered other developers to him. Developers I trust."

Several months of entries were dedicated to the mundane business of dealing with contractors, local governments, developers, and politicians. In July of that year, things were different.

"The Chuffe Group will never get the Northern Liberties Tutto Mondo underway. Anders was furious at lunch. Two property owners refused Chuffe's offer. Every week's delay puts the project in jeopardy. Chuffe's funds will evaporate," Wheeler had written.

A week later, Wheeler wrote, "A. says they found the perfect compromise. The Tutto Mondo deal will happen. He offered to include me. I refused."

The next day: "Either The Chuffe Group is darkly lucky or something else is going on." He detailed the accidental death of one of the holdout owners and the capitulation of the other.

Two months later Wheeler mentions meeting "a beautiful young man. Has dreams of owning a spa." They'd apparently met at a business networking meeting which eventually developed into Connections, a once-a-month networking meeting. Brad had impressed him but there was no sign he'd intended to invest in the spa.

I slugged down some coffee and took a bite of the mushy croissant. Bleary-eyed, I continued reading. Wheeler mentioned Nussbaum, Terrabito, Kelley, and other politicians as being encouraging. After reading more of his notes, I understood that "encouraging" was Wheeler's word for politicians trading favors for contributions. That was all the first volume held.

Early in the next volume, Wheeler mentions using Brad's massage services, and noted each visit. Wheeler never hinted at anything remotely like sex in the sessions.

Other entries mentioned disagreements over methods with other development firms, chiefly Berwick, Inc. and The Chuffe Group. Wheeler didn't spell out the methods he referred to.

I ate the rest of the croissant and decided I needed more caffeine to finish reading the daybooks. Whether I'd make sense of them was something caffeine wouldn't help.

A couple of months into the next year, Wheeler indicated he'd decided to invest in Brad and the spa. "I must confess to being enamored. I know my assistant is more than enamored. Not entirely sure about Brad's business sense but he's a worthy person. This is an investment my heart wants even if my head doesn't agree. So be it."

That answered a few questions I had.

Wheeler had filled the February section with notations on developments around the Philly area and side notes on fellow developers. Few came off in a good light. The Chuffe Group was singled out as "unscrupulous and greedy." He considered Remy Berwick "untrustworthy but unavoidable." Wheeler mentioned meeting with two former employees, Shuster and Nolan. He didn't spell out what they'd met about but it looked like politics. Both of them vying for his political and financial support. Terrabito, Kelley, Clarke, even Mayor Stroup had come to visit Wheeler. Each with his hand out for a campaign contribution. Even in his private notes, Wheeler was too cagey to hint at the candidate he liked best.

Midway through the second volume, Wheeler made a note about projects stalled because of property disputes. "Our turn to sweat. Berwick is partnered with us. We won't take a financial bath alone."

He said property owners on three different projects were "being difficult." According to his notes, he was willing to make deals which would cost more. But not his partners. "Berwick refuses to spend more for the property." Wheeler noted that Berwick claimed he would find another solution. "Remy will go the political route. He thinks politicians are in his pocket and they think all of us are waiting to be used."

In May, Wheeler noted Berwick's suggestions. "Remy wants to bring the Branko Company in. I know about Branko. His concerns are not open and above board. He has a criminal mind and uses any means to get what he wants."

Several entries later: "Berwick is on notice that I will have nothing to do with Branko's company."

Reading Wheeler's notes gave me a different perspective on the man. He painted himself as the only one opposed to Berwick and other developers. Wheeler intimated that Berwick and the others resorted to "things I have no desire even to enumerate here."

That could mean anything but when you couple that with the number of "accidental" deaths found in those articles, and the association with Branko, it was easy to draw certain conclusions. Some developers were in bed with Branko, a man whose violent past they all knew about. The question nagging me was whether Wheeler had written the truth about himself or had made a false record to keep his reputation intact and avoid possible legal ramifications.

I massaged my temples, finished the coffee, and kept reading. The night closed in around me fogging up my mind but I had to finish.

September of that year, Wheeler made an interesting remark about Branko's arrest on extortion charges. "If they knew more," Wheeler had written, "they would bring more serious charges."

A few days after Branko's arrest, Berwick visited Wheeler. "He was alarmed. Branko threatened to reveal details of his relationships with the developers if he were to be convicted." Wheeler told Berwick he had nothing to fear since he, Wheeler, wasn't involved in anything. "Remy was furious. Insisted I had to help. Said I would regret not participating."

Wheeler didn't seem concerned. He mentioned warnings from other developers and noted, "Our political friends are feeling pressured as well. After all, we fund them. If the sources of campaign money are dirty, so are those who take that money."

Made sense. I still had to connect plenty of dots to get from that to Brad's murder.

I glanced at the clock in my kitchen as I made more coffee. Four in the morning was beginning to look like my new bedtime. I took the coffee to the table and picked up the final daybook covering Wheeler's last few months.

He continued noting visits to Brad's spa and said he was "delighted" with Brad's renovation plans. "I made the right decision after all."

Wheeler's notes on the desire to help others didn't seem contrived. The high regard in which he held people like Xinhan, Brad, Caragan, and a person he referred to only as "T" showed what seemed to be real interest in their welfare.

He didn't hold back on those he held in contempt, like Berwick. For some, like a man he called "D" he reserved comments that were both sad and angry at the same time, saying "D" was weak minded, easily used, and lacking confidence in his own abilities.

In March, Wheeler was approached by prosecutors to testify against Branko. "I gladly agreed. Foolishly dangerous, however, considering the reach of a man like Branko."

Maybe he was right about that.

Soon after, he mentioned someone else. "Hodding asked for my assistance. I told him about the prosecutors. He said I should not worry about them." That was certainly curious. He never mentions who the guy was or what help he enlisted.

As the trial got closer, Wheeler's notes were shorter. He spoke of collaborating with the prosecution but was worried about Hodding and "working at cross purposes." He never explained that.

According to his notes, neither Berwick nor any of the other developers would associate with him.

Wheeler's visits to Brad continued. After the last massage before the murders, Wheeler remarked, "The spa has been transformed. I can't believe Brad can afford these changes with only my investment."

That certainly made it seem Wheeler was unaware of the infusion of money from Shuster or anyone else. He could have been playing games with the notes he made to keep his image clean.

Wheeler eventually noted being dropped as a witness. "They say they no longer need me." He claims they never explained but he suspected they'd found out about Hodding.

Immediately after the trial ended in Branko's conviction, Wheeler mentions being approached by Peter Vega. "The journalist suspects the Branko jury was compromised."

It confirmed what the photographer had told me. Vega must have thought Wheeler knew something.

The day of the murders, Wheeler had two notes, the first said, "Met with Berwick and Terrabito. Frustrating!" The other was simple, "Meeting is set with journalist at Brad's spa."

Without details, Wheeler could have meant anything about Berwick and Terrabito.

His note about meeting Vega confirmed that Vega had been at the spa. It could either mean the spa was a location no one else would suspect or that Brad had some involvement in the jury tampering case. An easy conclusion since Brad had been on the jury. The money transfers now raised even more red flags. I'd have to find a direct connection between the cash and the jury. Then find out who was behind it.

On the other hand, Branko had been convicted. If the jury had been tampered with, whoever had been turned didn't follow instructions.

My mind was swimming in the deepest depths of the ocean. Four-thirty rolled around and coffee or no coffee, I could barely keep my eyes open. I made it to my bed and blacked out.

* * *

I heard a phone ringing and ran down unfamiliar halls, opened strange doors to gaze at rooms I didn't recognize. There were no phones in any of the rooms yet a phone kept up the insistent ring.

The sound seemed to come from another floor. When I saw a set of stairs, I started to climb. The landing at the top was enveloped by a darkness so complete I feared I would slip into nothingness if took another step.

About to move, I opened my eyes and blinked in the sunlight filtering into my bedroom. My mouth was cottony, my head pounded, and every muscle felt sore. Not to mention the set of kitchen knives still trapped behind my ribs. I forced myself to look at my alarm clock.

Ten-thirty. At least whoever it was let me get some sleep. Six hours wasn't much but it'd have to do. "Fontana," I slurred into the receiver.

"Still asleep, Marco?" Shim's voice wasn't the worst thing to wake up to.

"Nah, been drinking heavily since six this morning. That's why I sound this way." I closed my eyes against the sunlight and conjured up Shim's face. "Giuliani tell you I was a morning person? If she did, she lied."

"Just thought you might like a little information." The tease. He was good.

"Always in the market for information. Where are you?" I couldn't shake off the sleepiness.

"Actually I'm a block from your condo, I thought we could get coffee and compare notes."

"Come on up. The coffee's free and I'm in no shape to try looking bright and cheery in some café."

"You sure it's not an imposition?"

"If you don't mind seeing me unshaven, unshowered, and looking like an unmade bed…"

"I'll bring the coffee. Doesn't sound like you're in any condition to even boil water."

There wasn't much I could add about Vega's murder. My theory was he'd run into something lethal because he was investigating the jury tampering story. Did the police even know what Vega was working on? If they didn't, then I'd have a lot of explaining to do. Like, how did I come by all that information and why didn't I share? I could maybe bluff about the photographer but no way in hell could I tell Shim about getting Brad's financials. That would get Nina in a boatload of trouble and put me and her in the iron bar hotel.

Unless I solved the case first and threw Shim the credit. Then they wouldn't care how I did it and wouldn't ask.

By the time I'd gotten dressed, the phone rang.

"Front desk. Got a policeman here to see you."

"Sure, send him up."

Before long, Shim stood at the door, two huge cups of coffee and a bag of fragrant pastry in hand. I hadn't realized how hungry I was until that pastry reminded me.

"Come on in," I said.

Shim's jeans and PPD t-shirt, emphasized his worked-out pecs and muscular thighs in a way his suits never could.

"Hope you like your coffee with a little vanilla." He moved with graceful fluidity into the living room and placed everything on the coffee table.

"As long as it has caffeine." I sat on the couch. "That's my chief requirement."

Shim chose the chair to my left, facing the balcony. "Great view. You must feel like Zeus. Above it all."

"Never get tired of it, except when it rains and everything is dull gray." I took one of the coffees. "Then it's a drag on my mood."

"Sugar?"

"I kinda like the bitter taste," I said. "So what brings you here? And don't tell me you just happened to be in the neighborhood." I smiled.

"I *was* sort of in the neighborhood. The precinct is close by."

"They have casual dress Sundays now?"

"Okay, I came by on purpose."

I watched as his face flushed several shades of red but I silently waited for him to continue.

"Your missing persons case…" He hesitated.

"Yes?" Now he had my attention. "Has something turned up? Did you find…?" I didn't want to think about what they might've discovered.

"We haven't found anything. Kid didn't leave a trail. No credit cards came up. No ATM use. We don't even know if he's still in the city."

"Either the kid knows how to disappear or…."

"We checked that possibility, too." Shim said, his voice low. "Nothing matching his description."

"What about Harrisburg where Eddie's family lives?"

"Still waiting on that."

"I appreciate this, Dae."

"Your friend, what was his name, Anthony?"

"Anton. Name's Anton."

"Anton, yeah. He seemed upset so I thought you could let him know I haven't forgotten. Even if missing persons isn't my department."

"You could tell him in person, he'd like that. The dancers are sorta like his kids even if he's not much older than they are. He takes care of them. Something like this happens and he feels it."

"I thought you two were close and he might like to hear it from you."

"Yeah. Maybe…" I figured Anton wouldn't care who brought him the news. "If the news was better, Anton wouldn't care who told him."

"I've got the right people involved. They'll know what to do. I know how your friend must feel."

"Do you?" My tone was colder than I'd intended, but he reminded me that I should know how Anton was feeling and I hadn't said much to him about Ty.

"No…I guess…"

"Sorry I snapped, Dae. I've got a lot on my mind. Shouldn't take it out on a guy who brings me pastry in the morning." I smiled and ripped open the bag. "Having some?"

Shim reached for a powdered-sugar twisty thing that looked pretty good. I grabbed a vanilla frosted donut and as I lifted it to my mouth all I saw was several hours on the treadmill.

"Speaking of what's on your mind…" Shim looked me in the eye. "Have you gotten anywhere on the case?" He brushed powdered sugar from his jeans. Sometimes the simplest, most innocent action can be the sexiest.

"When we talked a while back, we mentioned the possibility that Vega was working on a jury tampering story, right?" I said.

"Think so but…"

"I've been trying to follow that lead. Among others."

"Get anywhere?"

"Truth?" I asked.

"What do you think?" Shim smirked.

"Truth is I feel like I'm skirting around the edge of the thing." That was sort of the truth.

"So, what've you got?" Shim asked then finished off the pastry he'd taken.

"I'm thinking it's strange that Vega and Wheeler show up at Brad's place on the same night."

"Maybe…" Shim said and I could almost see the wheels turning in his head. "Maybe not. Wheeler and Brad had a connection to the Branko trial. Stands to reason Vega might want to talk to them about the jury thing."

"So you're thinking Vega pumps them for information hoping they might know something he could run with. He was on a fishing expedition?" I asked. If I told him I had Brad's financials which made it seem, circumstantially, that Brad might have been the target juror, then Shim would have more to go on, and I'd be in cuffs. I had to continue playing dumb until I found another way to deal with this.

"That's what I'm saying. Vega probably didn't know much of anything. Was trying to squeeze information out of anyone he could find." Shim shook his head. "Whoever did this, I mean the Vega murder, whoever did it, was thorough. They left nothing. Not a shred of trace, not a witness, nothing."

"There's always something. You just don't see it yet."

"You're holding out on me, Marco. I can feel it. You like keeping people in the dark or what?"

"Me? I like bringing things out into the open."

"Unless I get a solid lead, this'll make my record look like crap."

"Look at it this way," I said. "When I solve the case and toss you the credit, you'll be a hero."

"Confident, aren't we?" Shim laughed then sipped some coffee. He relaxed back into the chair and gazed out the window. "It's not like all I've had were easy cases but this one's a bear. Giuliani dropped it in my lap quick. Think she knew it was impossible? She's—"

"She's not like that."

"*You're* defending *her*? She roasts you on a spit most of the time."

"She ever say that I was dishonest? Or that I didn't play fair? Or anything like that?"

"Well… no, I guess not. She certainly doesn't like you a whole lot."

"So, she's got no taste. But she's an honest cop who worked hard to get where she is. She hates me but everybody's got flaws. That's hers."

Shim chuckled and went back to staring out the window.

"Point is, she wouldn't give you this case if she didn't have confidence in you. She's not out to sink you."

✳ ✳ ✳

Shim hung around a while longer, slowly finishing his coffee and discussing the case. I'd debated telling him about Sorba's threat but decided to try something else before turning it over to the police.

After Shim left, I dialed Shuster's private number to see what he'd come up with.

"Shuster."

"Remember the deadline I gave you last night?"

"I… there hasn't been enough… you can't expect…" Shuster stammered.

"We need to talk. Now." I needed him off guard and unready.

"I can't. I've got campaign business. The primary's a week away—"

"My office. Twenty minutes. Don't be late."

I hung up before he could whimper once more, then hustled myself out of the apartment.

The best sort of cool Spring breezes and clear blue skies tempted people out of their homes. Sunday strollers moved languidly down the streets on their way to brunch or the gym or to sit in a café. I spotted an empty sidewalk table at the Village Brew and wanted to ditch work. Instead I trudged over to my office building.

Without Olga, the place was an empty shell. I walked through to my office, pulled some files on the case, and sat at my desk. If I was going to finesse information out of Shuster I needed a quick review.

As I read, I heard the elevator arrive, followed by the heavy sound of thumping footsteps. Shuster stomped into my office, flushed and angry.

"I'm here," he snapped. "What is it that couldn't wait?"

"You weren't being truthful last night," I bluffed.

"Truthful... are you crazy? I told you everything. You're the one jumped down my throat calling me a liar."

"Never used that word but since you opened the door... Why'd you lie to me?"

"I didn't." He seemed about to stomp his foot to punctuate his words, but he restrained himself.

"You know all about Brad's money. You know where it came from and why it was transferred into Brad's account." Bluffing sometimes works. Shuster knew more, I was sure of it. Maybe not as much as I hoped but more than he'd told me.

"What part of 'I don't know anything' don't you understand?"

"Guess I don't understand any of it. When it all shakes out, I'm gonna have documents detailing every tidbit of your financial life. People like Nussbaum, Terrabito, Kelley, and others like Josh Nolan, they're gonna be exposed to the sunlight, too. All because of you."

"If you've got the details why not use them now? Show me what you've found."

"That's not the way it works. I've got plenty but I want more. I need to know who killed Brad and Wheeler."

"Wheeler." He snorted. "Didn't your research come up with anything juicy about him? The old bastard wasn't as saintly as they say."

"Maybe, but he's dead. Wouldn't make sense, him having himself killed, now would it? He didn't have to funnel money to Brad secretly," I said. "So if you were thinking of pinning the murder on the dead guy, forget it. Nice try, though."

"So he was killed. Doesn't mean he didn't plan it all. Maybe he didn't plan well enough and he ends up in the wrong place at the wrong time. He could have framed me then accidentally got himself killed."

"Could be. Doesn't change the fact that you're hiding something. I'm thinking you're protecting somebody who's still among the living."

"Why would I protect somebody who framed me and is trying to sink my candidate's campaign? Why would I do that?"

"Who knows? Love? Maybe it was Nolan. Maybe you've got a thing for Nolan. He's a hot man. You worked together for years then went your separate ways. Maybe you still love the man. Maybe you love him more than you enjoy working for Kelley. I've seen the way you look at one another."

"This isn't high school. If I ever had a 'thing' as you put it, for Josh, that was in the past. He's straighter than straight. No matter how I felt, it could never have amounted to anything."

"Still, love's a powerful emotion. People kill over it. So, what's a little favor like funneling some money?"

"You forget that I have no idea money was transferred or why. If it happened, it was without my knowledge. It had to have been in and out of my account before I noticed it."

"I have some ideas about why you… excuse me… *someone*… would give Brad so much money."

"And that would be…?"

"What's the fun in *me* telling *you*? The idea is that you're gonna tell me and then I'll know if I was right," I said and leaned back in my chair. A ghost of a pain in my ribs sent a little shock through my body. "I know I'm right. I'm always right about these things."

Shuster said nothing. He stared at me as if his stare would be enough to knock me back through the wall and down several stories.

"Look, Shuster," I said and stood. "You don't have to tell me now. But you're gonna tell everybody sooner or later. Because at some point, I'm gonna take this information to the press and since I'm working with the police, they'll get the whole story, too."

"You don't have anything." He fumed silently, swaying as if he didn't know whether to stay or leave.

"Keep thinking that, bucko." I moved around to stand next to Shuster. Looking at him, I said, "Go on. Leave. You've got a campaign to run. Just remember this: I know."

Shuster turned and moved to the door.

"I don't have to let it all out of the bag for your campaign to take a hit," I said with a calm, even voice. "I'll let the press know money went through your account to that of a man who was later murdered. The media sharks'll do the rest. Believe me, I don't mind spreading chum in the water, if it'll help solve a case."

Without a word, he walked out of the office. I heard the elevator swallow him up. In a little while, all the ambient sounds settled like dust and everything was quiet.

I figured somebody had used Shuster as a go-between. Unfortunately other things I suspected had to be true. Brad was the juror who'd been tampered with. The money, coming when it did, was a clear sign. Shuster's involvement? That was something I hadn't worked out yet.

Everything flipped over and over in my mind. Sitting in the dense silence of my office wasn't helping. I needed noise and people and fresh air. Pulling myself away from the files, I left the office.

That seat I'd seen at The Village Brew was still vacant. I ordered coffee and claimed the seat. As I settled in with a newspaper, I realized I'd forgotten to call Anton. I speed dialed him.

"Hello." He sounded sleepy.

"I didn't wake you, did I?"

"No. What gives you that idea?"

"Just the way you sounded. Got a minute?"

"You have news about Ty?"

"That's what I'm calling about."

"That doesn't sound good. Is… is he…? Did they find him? I mean, is he all right?"

"They haven't found him, Anton. It's like he completely disappeared."

"What's this mean? They'll stop looking?"

"No. I think maybe this might kick it up a level."

"You think he went back to that creep? It's hard to stop thinking about Ty, you know? If he turns up hurt… somebody's gonna pay." Anton said.

"I won't lie to you, Anton. Never have and I'm not about to start."

"I know, Marco."

"There's a good possibility he intends to go back to Eddie. Where and how, I have no idea. I'm thinkin' it's the most probable thing."

"How could he do that?"

"You wanna get out of the house a while?"

"I was about to leave when you called." He sounded tired.

"How about some lunch? My treat…"

He was silent. Then he cleared his throat as if he were uncomfortable.

"Hey, it's no big deal. Thought I'd ask."

"Yeah, no… I've got some things I need to do, Marco. Maybe another time?"

"Sure. Another time. But I wanted to tell you something…"

"What?"

"It's… I want you to know I understand how you feel about Ty. I know how much you care about all the guys. And I'm sure you got even closer to Ty. I just want you to know I understand."

Anton was silent. He didn't have to say anything, I knew how he felt.

* * *

As soon as I went back to my paper, the cell phone rang.

"Fontana."

"It's Josh Nolan. If you can hustle over here, the Senator can talk to you now."

"Be right there."

It didn't take more than five minutes to get to the campaign office. The streets were on a quiet Sunday simmer. No buzz of excitement.

Pushing open the door, I found Nolan and Terrabito engaged in heated conversation. Both went silent as I approached.

"You called. I'm here."

Nolan half smiled then caught himself. "Senator, this is Marco…"

"I know who he is and what he wants."

I nodded at the man.

"I have no time to waste," he snapped. "I have no answers for you either."

"I haven't asked any questions yet."

"Whatever you're after, I don't know anything."

"Not even about the murder of one of your biggest backers?"

"A tragedy, of course." His tone changed. "I had nothing to do with it. You'll understand that we're in the middle of a campaign… and… things are difficult."

"Maybe. Three men are dead and I need answers."

"Three? But, I…"

"The night of the murders you arrived late to an event at Bubbles. When you did arrive, you were—"

"Talk to Tim Powell. He'll vouch for me. I was with him an hour before I went to that event."

"Funny. Pat Kelley, who was equally late, swears you came running in after him."

Terrabito shot a look at Nolan who glanced at me, his face distorted with confusion.

"The Senator is—"

"Let the Senator speak for himself." I didn't like brushing him off but it was necessary.

"I have nothing more to tell you," Terrabito said.

A short, icy staring match followed. The stone wall had gone up and that was that.

* * *

Back in my office I wondered why Terrabito had been so nervous. Sure, he was sinking in the polls. That makes candidates edgy. But there was something else.

I reviewed the files again, hoping something would pop out at me. As I read, I spotted Sorba's "gift" out of the corner of my eye. His threat had been all too real. I didn't care about what he'd try with me, but it sounded like he'd target Luke or Anton or someone else. I couldn't let that happen.

A preemptive strike would stop the turd.

I picked up the phone and dialed the All News All Now office.

"All News All Now. Leahy."

"A beautiful Sunday afternoon and you're tied to your desk?"

"This site doesn't run itself. Who is this?"

"Marco Fontana."

"Oh, the private dick. Got some news?"

"Matter of fact, I do. Maybe not what you were expecting but…" I told her the whole Sorba saga and said I could send the information if she wanted.

"It'll make a hell of a Monday front page, and I've been wanting to get something on that jerk for a while."

I hung up and e-mailed pages from Brad's appointment book with Sorba's complete client file including all his little peccadilloes and kinky secrets. I also sent photos of the dead snake and the threatening note it came with.

Outing someone was a tricky business, and I didn't always approve. A hypocrite like Sorba, who made his living bashing gays and others, was begging to be outed. So, I gave him what he asked for.

* * *

I went to Bubbles later where Jean-Claude helped to arrange the show for the night. As he left the office, my cell phone rang. Caller ID said it was Shuster.

"What's up, Shuster? Ready to talk?"

"That guy followed me again... you know... that one who—"

"Nothing much I can do. He's got you up his nose."

"You... you're refusing to help me?" He sounded genuinely angry.

"Don't you have some things to tell me, bucko? Remember the deadline?" I yawned.

"All right... all right, let's talk. I want to get this over with. You have time now?"

"It's nearly one in the morning, you sure you're allowed to stay up so late?"

"Meet me in half an hour," he said, his voice shaky.

"Same place?"

"No, too many eyes and ears. Let's meet somewhere else."

"What've you got in mind?" I knew he was planning something, he'd given in too easily. But I didn't have much choice. It was either meet him now or never get anywhere. Red flags popped up all over the place but I'd make sure I was prepared.

"I'm staying at a friend's condo near Twenty-fifth and Locust until the primary's over. I hate hotels."

"Of course, princess. You've got standards. Good thing you have swanky friends." Like I believed the story.

"This is a nice place. Quiet. They don't like trouble here."

"I'll be sure to behave. What's the address?"

He gave me the information I'd need and hung up.

As I left the bar, Jean-Claude assured me he'd keep things going.

I wanted to get to Shuster's early but I wasn't going anywhere without protection. I'd left my gun in the office. It was on the way and I'd still be able to get to the meeting place early. I didn't want to give Shuster much more time to prepare whatever surprise he had in store for me.

The building was quiet and I felt like a cat burglar. My .38 was just where I'd left it. As I turned to go, something told me to take along my extra. I pulled the ankle holster out of the drawer and strapped it on. My pants would keep it hidden. The back-up gun was ready and waiting. Lifting it out of the drawer, I slipped it into the ankle holster.

I'd be as ready as I could.

Chapter 31

I wore a light jacket which concealed the shoulder holster and walked a block out of the way to get used to the weight of the ankle gun. I hated carrying but there wasn't much choice. Shuster was up to something and I wasn't going in blind. He hadn't invited me over for a confessional session.

On my way to the meet-up at The Locust Tier, I gave Shim a buzz. I needed to tell someone where I'd be. Shim was the logical choice. I got his voicemail and told him I'd been called to a meeting with a possible lead, but there was something suspicious about it all. I opted to tell him less rather than more. Gave him the address and told him I'd call if I needed back up.

I strolled up Locust and around a dark, empty Rittenhouse Square. I tried visualizing what it must've been like forty or more years before when it'd been a prime cruising spot for gay men. Guys lounging on benches, or standing against the trees, waiting and wishing. That was all history.

Lots of people crisscrossed the streets. Restaurants slowly emptied out, cafés still buzzed, and I was walking headlong into an unknown situation. I usually had an escape plan but this time I couldn't, not knowing exactly where I'd be. I'd never visited The Locust Tier which put me at a severe disadvantage.

Around Nineteenth Street, things became less commercial. A blanket of quiet lay over the area. The closer I came to Twenty-fifth, the quieter and more expensive the neighborhood became. Yellow light filled a few windows here and there. In one or two, the silver-blue light of a TV flickered against the dark. At one-thirty in the morning, few people in this sedate precinct were awake.

I was alone. Even having called Shim, odds were there'd be no backup if something went wrong.

As I neared the dead-end corner of Twenty-fifth and Locust, I saw Shuster in the distance, standing in a pool of light created in the carport of The Locust Tier. He paced, occasionally looking at his watch.

"Get stood up?" I asked as I approached.

"Finally," Shuster huffed. "I thought you'd never get here."

"Right on time," I said. "Maybe you need a new watch."

"Maybe you need a watch period. It's almost two o'clock."

"I thought we were meeting in your friend's apartment." I suspected he'd try something like this.

"I decided it might be safer outside." Shuster fidgeted, his voice shook and he couldn't look me in the eye. "I've got a feeling the place is bugged."

"Yeah, can't be too careful." Now I knew he was scamming me. Who'd want to bug the guy? "So were do we talk? Out here on the apron?"

"No!" He stared at me wide-eyed. "You crazy? Somebody might see us. That guy… the one who followed me. He might spot us…"

"Would'a been safer in the apartment in that case." I waited for him to make a move.

"Let's walk. There's a park across the way." He pointed.

"Old Judy Garland Park." I laughed. "So you wanna play footsie with me in the bushes?" The "park" had been a poorly lit, trash-strewn, weedy area along both sides of railroad tracks next to the Schuylkill River. It'd served as a gay cruising ground for a long time. As soon as yuppies and others gentrified the area, complaints about the park rolled in, forcing the city to clean up part of the area, pave it, plant things nicer than weeds, and officially name it Schuylkill River Park. A large part of what the gay community used to call Judy Garland Park remained. The darkest and most dangerous area on the other side of the abandoned railroad tracks.

"Get real, Fontana." Shuster said, annoyed. "It'll be more private. No ears to hear."

"I got a better idea, bucko," I said.

"Like what?" Shuster looked at me, his eyes all squinty.

"Like we go to the apartment—"

"I just told you, I think it's bugged."

"Maybe I look dumb to you. Or, maybe you think you're smarter than you are. But I'm not buyin' the bug story. Got it?"

Shuster couldn't help himself and glanced at the park as if his plans had just been shot to hell. They had. He looked at me, then back at the park, then at me.

"So? What's it gonna be, Shuster? The apartment? Or you get to see yourself in the papers? Right before the primary, too. What is it they say, can't get too much free media, right?"

Shuster glowered.

"I'm gonna make sure they unload a shit load of free media on your ass."

"You can't do that," he whined.

"Oh, you're right. I can't." I paused, slapped my forehead with the palm of my hand. "No, wait! I *can*. And I will."

"I… this isn't what…"

"Listen, bucko, it's after two and I've got better things to do, like sleep. Talk or don't talk. Your call."

I decided to take his bluff and started walking away.

"Wait! Wait…" he said. "We'll do it your way. Just lemme make a call…"

"No calls, we go now or not at all."

"O-okay." He moved toward the entrance and the doors silently slid open.

We entered a cool, high style lobby with what looked like a river of light meandering through the ceiling. Mahogany and brass covered the surfaces, marble flooring, and a sweeping front desk curved and undulated through the lobby. At the far end of the desk a man sat, ramrod straight, curly-haired, and sternly gorgeous.

"Mr. Shuster," he said in a deep, throaty voice as he nodded.

Shuster smiled weakly. I looked the deskman in the eye, as if I'd been in the place a million times.

We rounded a corner and came to a bank of gleaming elevators. The elevator doors were like fun house mirrors. I saw a distorted view of me and Shuster waiting like misshapen cartoon characters.

A soft tone signaled the arrival of an elevator. We stepped into a luxurious carpeted car, with subdued lighting. Shuster pushed the button for fifteen and we were on our way. The closer we got, the edgier he became.

"Somethin' wrong, Shuster? You look like you ate something bad."

"N-no… j-just that I… I'm h-having second thoughts…"

"Thinking is good. But not if you're gonna get me all the way out here just to play games." I wondered if Nolan was waiting in the apartment. Had they hatched this plot together?

"You… you don't understand."

"I guess I'm gonna understand in a minute," I said as the elevator door opened and let us out into an elegantly plush corridor. Cool, sage-colored carpeting, beige walls, classy reproductions hung at regular intervals, expensive-looking sconces lighting the place like a palace.

Shuster said nothing. He moved forward robotically not looking back at me. When he came to the door for 15L, he stopped and pulled out a set of keys. His hands shook as he found the one he wanted.

After two or three trembling attempts, the key slipped into the lock and turned. The door opened and Shuster entered ahead of me. He cleared his throat loudly and made noise tossing his keys on a counter.

We moved into the oddly shaped living room. Large, expensively furnished with a long sofa and several side chairs, it felt like a movie set. Centered in one wall a fake fireplace sat dark. Another wall boasted gigantic windows overlooking the river. The opposite side of the room contained alcoves and nooks. One of the alcoves, nearly cut off from the main room, held a second sofa and small table. Another alcove housed a wet bar. You could host an army in this one room.

"All right, we're here," Shuster said in a too-loud voice. "Satisfied?"

I knew his chatter was meant for someone else stowed away in the apartment. Before I could say anything, I heard movement in another room. I tensed, slipped my hand under my jacket and on the gun, ready for what might come.

"You're back fast. Did you get rid of the dick?" The voice was familiar.

Pat Kelley appeared around a corner, drink in hand, sour look on his gray face. When he saw me, his eyes widened and his expression morphed from surprise to anger.

"What the fuck is *this*? I thought you said—"

"It's not… listen, Pat, I tried… I wanted to keep you out of this. Give you deniability." Shuster was pale. He looked drained and sounded tired.

"So you bring him right to me? That's your way of protecting me from this mess?"

"Kelley, what a surprise…" I said, then turned to Shuster. "This the answer you promised me? Kelley's the one?"

"What?" The look of alarm on Shuster's face was comical. "No! No! You've got it all wrong—"

"Have I? Whattayou say, Kelley? Am I mistaken about what your boy was gonna tell me?"

"I haven't the foggiest idea what he was going to tell you. He said he was going to help you with some case you're on. To stop you from making a splash in the papers with inaccurate information. I didn't want to know more."

"That's what Shuster told you?"

"Yes," Shuster said. "That's all. If I'd given him more details, he couldn't deny he knew what was going on. Naturally, I didn't tell him much." The panic remained plastered on Shuster's face but the color slowly returned.

"You're barking up this tree because Terrabito and his lapdog Nolan put you onto the scent, right?" Kelley snorted his contempt. "You're like a stupid bloodhound." He looked at me with disdain, sat on the long sofa in the center of the room, and drained his glass.

"Is that what you think? 'Cause I got a whole different idea…"

"Which is…?" Kelley held out his glass to Shuster. "Get me another."

Shuster hustled over, took the glass, and went to the alcove bar.

"Lookit how Shuster runs in circles for you. Gets drinks, makes underhanded deals, takes the fall if asked. Like the expendable political creature he is. So…" I turned to Shuster, still at the bar. "Doesn't surprise me you did the money transfer so nobody knew it came from Kelley. You hustle up drinks, contributors, sex partners. Whatever the little big man wants. Right?"

Shuster returned to Kelley with the refilled glass. "You're crazy Fontana." He placed the drink in Kelley's hand, then stood to the side. "Mr. Kelley had nothing to do with it."

"Not the way I see it." I filled in the blanks as I moved along but now that I was here, I knew I was right.

"Just what is it you see?" Kelley said.

"I don't have all the answers yet. That's one reason I agreed to meet tonight. Shuster promised to fill me in."

"I wasn't going to implicate Mr. Kelley, if that's what you thought."

"You didn't intend to, but that didn't work out. He's here and that makes me suspicious... Not too difficult to connect the dots leading to..."

"Josh Nolan." Shuster blurted out the name. "I did it for him. You were right. About me having a thing for him. I did. I still do. I can't say no to him and he uses that."

"That so?" I said. A bigger bucket of bullshit didn't exist, if you didn't count political speeches. "What was Nolan's reason for paying Brad Lopes?"

"He... uh... it was..."

"Maybe he wanted to keep the guy quiet," Kelley said. "Nolan's a closet case. Probably had a good time with this Brad then regretted it. Paid to stop him from ruining his career." Kelley's voice became more slurry with each sip of booze, but his eyes remained sharp and clear.

"Maybe, but I don't think so. That's not the way things happened."

"Why not?" Shuster was petulant. "Brad was desperate for money to renovate that spa. He told me he'd do anything to get it. He said he'd spoken to Nolan and was gonna spill the beans about having sex with Nolan."

"You know," I said. "You make it all sound plausible."

"Because it's true," Shuster insisted.

"Sounds right unless you truly know Brad and Nolan. See?"

"It's what happened."

"You're telling some of the truth, Shuster. Which always makes a lie sound good. But it's not the whole truth."

"Oh, tell us the whole truth, why don't you?" Kelley mumbled, staring into his drink.

"I'll do that. You're not gonna like it. Neither of you." I walked over to the sofa in the alcove and sat down forcing them to turn in my direction. I wanted them off balance. "You were right about one thing, Shuster."

"I was totally right."

"When you said Brad was desperate for money, you were telling the truth. He'd told you just how desperate he was, right?"

"We talked a few times."

"You talked a lot. Your name's all over Brad's appointment book. You should'a paid him rent, you were there so much."

Shuster was silent.

"Brad surely told you about his dreams which were bigger than the money Wheeler invested. Bigger than the cash he pulled in from his work."

"He was ambitious," Shuster said. "I admired that."

"You took advantage of his ambition."

"What're you talking about?"

"You were already in the middle of a situation with Branko, Berwick, and Wheeler and the politicians you work for. It was easy putting it all together from the bits and pieces you left."

"You're pulling things out of the air to build your case. It won't work."

"Stay with me and see." I stared at them. "When Brad told you he'd pulled jury duty and had to reschedule your massage, you probably quizzed him about the jury he was on… am I warm?"

"You're crazy. I told you—"

"Keep listenin', bucko," I said. "You knew Branko was going to trial."

"So what if we knew?" Kelley snapped.

"It was important because Branko threatened to reveal everything he knew about contracts you'd been involved with, about land developments, and about uncooperative property owners who'd had mysterious accidents. If he got convicted, he'd spill everything and you'd all be toast. Following me, guys?"

"You're crazy, Fontana," Shuster said without conviction.

"Once you told Kelley that Brad was a juror on Branko's trial, Kelley came up with the idea to corrupt Brad."

"You're a real storyteller you are," Kelley said.

"There's more. You got Shuster to convince Brad to vote 'Not Guilty' no matter what. Then you funneled money through Shuster to Brad. More money than the poor guy ever dreamed of. He couldn't resist and agreed to do what you'd asked. You thought you'd found the perfect way out. How's that so far?"

"Fanciful. Why would I fear this man Branko?" Kelley said.

"Konstantin Branko. You sent government contracts his way. And he did lots of favors for you and your contributors."

"Contracts? Listen carefully, Fontana. Here's a civics lesson: handling contracts is part of what we do in government. We make sure things get done. Contracts, projects, you name it. There are hundreds. I can't remember the name of every person I deal with."

"Even if you don't remember Branko's name, he remembered yours, Kelley."

"What's that supposed to mean?" Kelley's voice tightened. "Did Branko directly implicate me?"

"You're spinning a great fantasy, Fontana. That's all it is. The money had nothing to do with a jury," Shuster said. "I gave Brad the money for Nolan. To keep Brad from ruining Nolan."

"Sure you did."

"You said you had records. Bank records, right? Then you should be able to tell who it came from before I got it. It was Nolan's money."

"Funny thing about those records." I waited while Shuster squirmed. Kelley appeared lost in his glass of liquid gold. But I knew he was listening intently.

"What's funny? You found enough to implicate me, didn't you?"

"Right. We found records implicating you. *Only* you. The money didn't come from Nolan," I said. "His records are clean. He doesn't make that kinda money anyway."

"No… you must've missed something… I did it for Josh. He gave me the money…"

"You did it, but not for Nolan. You did it for Kelley and his friends."

"You've got no proof," Shuster hissed. "It's all speculation."

"It's more than speculation. Your boss and his cronies used you. They're letting you hang. They made sure the money can't be traced to them. The trace stops at you, bucko."

"You can't prove any of it—"

"What's the phrase? Leaving you to twist slowly in the wind? That's what they're doing."

"No!" Shuster shouted. "None of that is true. But... this must be..." Shuster's eyes brightened with whatever new thought was forming. "Somebody's paying you to make it look like the truth...Fontana, you're being paid to make me look bad..."

"Why would anyone do that? You're a nobody..."

"To smear Kelley's campaign. To make sure he loses the primary."

"You're way off, bucko. Kelley's using you and now he's—"

"He wouldn't do that. But Terrabito would or Nolan. How much are they paying you?"

"Think about it, Shuster. Whoever's behind this, they've concealed their involvement. They knew it would come to this, so they left you holding the bag."

"Bull," Shuster said, but he didn't sound so sure now.

"When all the shit comes down, it's gonna come down on you. Any idea what the sentence is for jury tampering?"

"More bullshit," Shuster's voice quavered.

"You'll be away a long—"

"Okay, okay... I've told you the truth. The money was a payment from Nolan to keep the masseur quiet. But let's play your game. Say there *was* jury tampering. I'm not saying there was, you understand..."

"You're a bigger fool than I imagined." Kelley said.

"No... what're you saying, Pat? Let's play his game for a minute. Trust me, Pat."

"Trust you? Look where it's got me..."

Ignoring Kelley, Shuster turned to me.

"There was jury tampering according to you."

"That's correct," I said, wondering where he was headed.

"So tell me, why didn't it work? A jury is usually rigged to get a not guilty verdict, right? So why did Branko get convicted?"

"I'll hazard a guess, that okay with you?"

"Guessing is all you've done so far. One more won't hurt." Shuster's confidence shone in his eyes.

"I'm guessing your bribe didn't work on Brad. He took the money but the poor guy was too honest to go through with it. So, Branko gets the orange jumpsuit and three meals a day courtesy of the taxpayers."

Shuster was quiet.

"Hey, I'll throw in another guess for free. Whaddaya say, Shuster?"

He glanced at Kelley then glared at me.

"My guess: Brad told you he'd pay back the money. That he needed time but he'd pay it back. Probably begged you, right?"

"You're way off… he was…" Shuster mumbled.

"Brad trusted you. Right? I mean, you were a long time client."

"I…"

"So long, in fact, he considered you a friend. I'll bet you counted him as a friend. Or, maybe you wanted more than a friendship?"

"I… we… we were close…"

"What happened? If you liked him, why'd you use him? If you were friends?"

"It wasn't like that. I wanted to help him."

"By putting him in danger?"

"Wheeler gave him so much money. Brad was dazzled. How could I compete? I couldn't give him much of anything. Then… then this…"

"Shut the fuck up, Shuster. Shut up or I'll—"

"Don't listen to him, Shuster. Just tell me… you've been wanting to tell someone."

"This… this opportunity comes along, and I can give Brad money. All he hadda do was…"

"But he couldn't. You made him beg you to take the money back. Made him beg. A person you had feelings for. You made him grovel. It's disgusting. You're disgusting, Shuster."

Shuster stared at the carpet. "H-he… Brad was soft… he… I shouldn't—"

"Shut up!" Kelley, suddenly alert, stood and turned to Shuster. "Shut up or—"

"Yeah, shut up, Shuster. So they can put you away for murder in addition to jury tampering. Listen to your boss. He's got your best interests at heart."

Shuster glanced from me to Kelley then back again.

"M-murder? What... I didn't murder anyone..."

"Might as well have. As soon as you put that cash into Brad's hands, he was as good as dead if he didn't play ball."

"I... it wasn't like that... Pat said... Tell him, Pat... tell him!"

Before Kelley could open his mouth, someone pounded on the door. Kelley froze. Shuster went wide-eyed with fear.

"It... it must be..."

The pounding got louder.

"Who?" Kelley demanded.

"H-him... must be... I f-forgot... he w-was waiting..."

I *knew* I'd been right. Whoever was at the door had probably been left waiting in Judy Garland Park. Now he was here wanting to know why.

"Open the door, you stupid fuck," Kelley shouted. "Before all the neighbors take a look and see that thug. How did he get in anyway?"

Shuster hesitated, stepped back then forward, then started toward the door. The pounding made Shuster flinch as he walked. Hand on the doorknob, he hesitated again.

I stayed in the alcove, hidden from the view of anyone not in the center of the living room. I pulled my gun from the shoulder holster knowing I could watch and listen from this position.

The door opened. I heard someone rush in, and Shuster grunted as if he'd been pushed, hard.

"Wha'the fuck you guys doin' up here?" The voice was way too familiar. Brought back memories of a recent car ride. Matus.

"W-we..." Shuster started to speak.

"Asshole detective didn't showing up? You are leaving me standing in park and not telling me he is no show?"

"Get out, Matus... you've got to leave... he's—"

"Tell me why you are leaving me standing in filthy park..."

I flattened myself against the wall, moved so I could see a piece of the room, and took the safety off the gun.

"No... Fontana didn't want to... he wouldn't fall for it..."

"You are telling me he is here? In apartment?"

From my vantage point, I saw Matus barge into the room, brandishing his gun.

He spotted me as he moved. I trained my gun on him.

"Asshole detective." Matus spat out the words.

I kept my gun on him.

"You need more lessons from Matus, huh?" He pointed his gun at me and waved me into the main room.

I didn't move.

"You are stubborn like pig." Matus moved toward Shuster, roughly pushed the frightened man into a chair then held the gun to Shuster's head. "Put gun on floor or I make hole in head of fat man."

I stayed where I was, gun pointed at Matus.

"Fontana!" Shuster screamed. "Listen to him. He's... he's... he'll do it. He doesn't care."

"Listen to fat man. He is speaking truth. I *don't* care," Matus said and smacked Shuster on the head with his gun.

"Fontana! Please..." Shuster yelped.

I tossed my handgun to the floor. The weight of the gun strapped to my ankle reassured me.

"Kick gun to me."

Giving the gun a kick I watched it slide off toward the right, nowhere near Matus.

"Asshole plays games."

"I tossed the gun, now leave him alone," I said.

Matus pushed Shuster aside roughly and laughed as Shuster scrambled toward the wall.

"Tell your boss he's got a problem now," Kelley said, his voice shaky. "A real problem."

"I am telling no one no such things," said Matus. "You are making problem going away. Or I will make you going away. Like I am making other problems disappear."

"Fontana knows everything," Shuster blurted. "He knows."

"Shut your mouth," Kelley said.

"No. Talk, fat man! How does he know?"

"He knows. He's smart." Shuster said. "He put things together."

"No. You have told him. This is how he is knowing. Boss will not be happy man."

"I said nothing," Shuster complained. "Nothing. He guessed about the money. He knows we bribed that juror—"

"Little fag? At filthy spa? You are telling him this?"

"No!"

"You are telling him is Branko's money?"

Shuster was silent.

"Don't say another word, Shuster," Kelley snapped.

"How could I tell him that?" Shuster put out a hand to steady himself. He wobbled as if he were about to faint.

"Shut your mouth," Kelley said.

"Why should I? Think Fontana won't find out it was *your* money I gave to Brad? Money you got from Branko. He'd find out sooner or later."

Matus looked at each of us in turn, unsure what he should do. He pointed his gun first at Shuster, then me, then Kelley.

"Why'd you do it, Shuster?" I said, keeping an eye on Matus.

"Branko said he'd ruin all of them if he was convicted. Fixing the jury was his price for silence."

"You're a useless fool," Kelley said.

"It's true then... what Fontana said... you were going to let me take the fall for you...?"

"You don't know anything," Kelley said.

"Boss will not like mess—"

"Should've thought about that when you killed Brad." I said. All of it was clear now, I knew what'd happened.

"Fag should keep promise. He is taking money and not keeping promise."

"So you murdered him and Wheeler and Vega."

"Fag betrays us, others are knowing too much."

"What happens now, Matus?" Kelley said as if they were old buds.

"Someone must be paying. Detective knows too much. Fat man cannot keep mouth shut."

"I'm calling the police..." Shuster said, not moving an inch.

"Go on. Call police. They will be finding dead fat man and Matus will be gone."

Shuster eyed the phone just out of his reach. "I won't say a word, Matus. Not a word." He made a slight, almost involuntary, move toward the phone.

"Do not move!" Matus shouted, aiming at Shuster.

Shuster seemed dazed. As if he hadn't heard Matus. He stepped closer to the phone.

Matus was riveted on Shuster.

"Stop! Now!" Matus shouted at Shuster. He paid me no attention, certain I was unarmed.

"Don't do this, Matus." I said as calmly as I could.

Matus kept his eyes on Shuster. He didn't notice when I bent down to slip the gun from my ankle holster.

Stubbornly, Shuster put a hand out toward the phone.

Matus got off two quick rounds. The sound muffled by the silencer. I heard Shuster hit the floor with a dull thud.

I concentrated on Matus.

Turning toward me, he noticed my gun. Eyes wide, Matus squeezed the trigger.

Without thinking, I fired twice. Hit him square in the chest both times. He stumbled back with the force of the shot, an ugly grimace on his face. His body shuddered as he fell.

Everything was still.

Moving cautiously toward him, I kicked the gun out of his hand. I knelt over him and placed a finger to his neck. There was no pulse. His expression had relaxed into peacefulness. A scar across one cheek was the only flaw in an otherwise handsome face. He was a cruel, angry man who'd been used by others as nothing more than a tool. It was all in that face.

You never forget the faces and this one would be no different, no matter how savage he might've been. I'd taken a life and I would never be able to forget that.

It was then I felt the pain. Matus had nailed my arm with his last shot. Ignoring the wound, I moved to where Shuster and Kelley lay.

Shuster had been hit in the head and was gone, his blood spattered everywhere.

Kelley lay on the sofa, bleeding like a pig from a shoulder wound. Lucky bastard would make it. I wanted him to pull through just so he could stand trial for Brad's murder. I'd make sure that happened.

My left arm blazed with pain now, blood seeped through my jacket, ran down over my hand and onto the white carpet. I staggered back to the sofa and sat down, placing the gun near my leg. I pulled my cell phone from my pocket but before I could open the thing, it began to ring.

It was Shim.

Chapter 32

I left the voting booth and maneuvered my way out of the polling place through knots of poll workers and candidate surrogates waving papers and flyers as voters entered. Some of them stared at me as if they thought they should know me. They'd probably seen my face on TV during coverage of Kelley's arrest and the political melee that followed. He was ruined and several others teetered on the brink. I wasn't happy about the attention I'd gotten but playing with politicians has its down side. On the other hand, one striking dark-haired guy working the polls gave me a look that made me want to rip off my sling and get back to normal quick. Instead I tossed him a wink, and he smiled.

The only thing I felt about my vote was that it seemed anticlimactic. The act itself was easy, even with my arm in a sling. Doesn't take much effort to push little buttons and place your fate in some stranger's hands. I'd never trusted politicians much, and Kelley made me certain I was right. My default position was the best position: Trust no one. That's how I was raised and how I continued to operate.

It was anybody's guess how many people would still vote for Kelley even after being arrested and forced to drop out of the race. Dead men had won elections in Philly, so Kelley would probably get some votes.

Terrabito should be happy since I'd given him the gift of running unopposed. I was actually glad after I'd been told that both he and Wheeler had been working with the FBI to build a stronger case against Branko. Turns out Wheeler was close to being the saint people thought he was.

Before I knew it I was back home. I paused before going in, enjoying the breeze, the sunshine, and the feeling that I'd put a particularly bad case behind me. Losing a friend had been rough and everything I'd found out about him had made things worse.

Somehow, closing the case didn't seem like enough and left me feeling I had more to do before I'd be satisfied. There were loose ends I hadn't tied up. Yet.

Lost in thought, I swept through the automatic doors and walked into the lobby.

"Hey, Mr. Fontana," Carlos called out from behind the front desk. He was always more formal with other people around. "Got another package for you." Disappearing around a corner, he reappeared almost immediately with a large box wrapped in shiny green foil. There was a card attached.

"Thanks, Carlos. You see who left this for me?"

"Messenger service," he said. "Saw you on TV again. Guess you got cases comin' out of your as… ears, huh?"

"More than I can handle, Carlos. Wanna be a detective?"

"No way, man. Look at you, arm in a sling. Not me." He smiled. "Anyway, you got it all covered, right?"

I smiled as I moved toward the elevator. I wanted to pull the foil paper off the package but thought I should wait until I was home. Never knew what might be inside. Maybe another snake. A live one this time.

In the elevator, I did tear open the card. It read: "You kept your word, Marco. I guess I owe you at least a drink. Until then, this'll have to do. Giuliani still says I should be careful around you. But I don't have to take her advice all the time." It was signed "Shim."

I rattled the box. A soft sound and the feeling of something sloshing back and forth inside. As soon as the elevator reached my floor, I walked quickly to my door and entered my apartment.

Once inside I ripped off the foil and opened the box. A dark blue Philly PD tee-shirt lay folded next to a Police Department baseball cap. There was nothing that could be misinterpreted as romantic in Shim's gift. Except the fact of the gift itself. Not a very macho cop-like gesture, if you ask me. I smiled and pulled the tee-shirt out of the box. It was soft and just the right size, which told me Shim had been more than a little observant. I put it all aside and went to the kitchen.

Pulling a bottle of water out of the fridge, I placed my cell phone on the kitchen counter, and walked out onto the balcony. I shut the door behind effectively cutting off the telephones. My arm throbbed when I bumped it against the door. The pain medication usually did its job, but once in a while, my arm reminded me the gunshot wound was worse than I'd thought when it happened. It'd be good as new eventually.

I plunked the plastic bottle down on the weathered teak table I kept forgetting to oil. That'd come back to bite me when it fell apart. I figured another few days wouldn't matter.

Looking out over the city helped. It was soothing, even healing. No matter what happened there was a certain peace in that sleepy landscape, and I allowed it to soak into my spirit. The river sparkled as it drifted along, while trees were greening up all around. Puffy clouds eased across the brilliant blue sky. Things were placid, lazy, composed, as if nothing could even make a ripple across the calm surface of the city.

I knew better, and the pain in my arm told me I knew better. Evil things had happened, lives had been lost, careers destroyed. People were affected forever. The peaceful cityscape had changed in subtle ways that couldn't be fully understood from a distance.

People, good people, were missing from the streets below. Brad, Wheeler, and Vega were dead. Even Shuster, the poor dupe, was gone. All for what? They'd pursued dreams in ways that eventually put them in jeopardy. You can't put your dreams on hold, I guess, but you can't let them kill you, either. At least Brad, Wheeler, and Vega had died following their own path. Shuster had been a tool of politicians. Maybe he had dreams of his own but he was trapped doing the bidding of others and smothering his own desires. I actually felt sorry for him. But he'd snared Brad in a lethal scheme and had used Brad's own dreams against him. I couldn't forget that.

I couldn't forget a lot of things. Ty was still missing. Neither the police nor any of my contacts could locate him. Wherever he'd tucked himself away, he didn't want to be found. I hoped he hadn't gone back to Eddie and maybe gotten himself killed. I wouldn't forget about finding Ty. Anton wouldn't let me forget. One way or another, we'd find him.

I added that to the several mysteries I hadn't been able to solve yet. Like Max Gibson, another ghost in the wind. He'd made Brad's life miserable for a while and was doing it again to someone else. I couldn't let that pass unnoticed.

There were changes shaping things for me, too, and I couldn't help thinking about the possibilities. I wondered where Anton was at that moment, and if I could put things right between us eventually. Luke was out there, too. His skyscraping condo building close to the river's edge, shimmered in the Spring sun, reminding me that Xinhan was a person who might make our world a little different.

Detective Shim had made me realize how lucky I was in a lot of ways. At least I knew who I was, or thought I did. Shim was on the verge of making sense of the feelings he had. I could see that every time I looked into his eyes. He'd figure it out soon, I was sure. When he did, he'd have the potential to change the equation for me, too. I might like that.

Cases like Brad's always made me look back at the past, which inevitably had me thinking about Galen. My old friend. He was out there somewhere, and I needed to find him. Something was missing in my life, and I had this notion Galen knew what it was and could tell me how to find it. He knew me better than I knew myself. I couldn't even find *him*. Not yet. I wasn't about to stop looking, though.

In the meantime, I listened to my own thoughts and lived with the new ghosts that came with every case, joining the crowd of others I'd gathered. I tried blanking my mind but it was impossible. Faces floated up in my memory, voices whispered in my ear, and there was no avoiding them.

I itched to get back to work and tackle the pile of messages Olga must have placed on my desk. I needed a new case. I'd had enough of recuperation, it was time to move forward again. I gulped down the water, slid open the door, and went to the kitchen for my cell phone. There were people waiting.

About the Author

Joseph R.G. DeMarco lives and writes in Philadelphia and Montréal. Several of his stories have been anthologized in the *Quickies* series published by Arsenal Pulp Press, in *Men Seeking Men* (Painted Leaf Press) and in *Charmed Lives* (Lethe Press). His essays have been published in anthologies including *Gay Life, Hey Paisan!, We Are Everywhere, BlackMen WhiteMen, Men's Lives, Paws and Reflect, The International Encyclopedia of Marriage and Famiyl, the Encyclopedia of Men and Masculinites,* and *The Gay and Lesbian Review Worldwide* among others.

He has also written extensively for the gay/lesbian press and was a correspondent for *The Advocate, In Touch, Gaysweek.* His work has been featured in *The New York Native,* the *Philadelphia Gay News* (PGN), *Gay Community News, The Philadelphia Inquirer, Chroma,* and a number of other publications.

In 1983, his PGN article "Gay Racism" was awarded the prize for excellence in feature writing by the Gay Press Association and was anthologized in *We Are Everywhere, Black Men, White Men,* and *Men's Lives.*

He was Editor-in-Chief of *The Weekly Gayzette;* Editor-in-Chief of *New Gay Life,* and has been an editor or contributing editor for a number of publications including *Il Don Gennaro,* and *Gaysweek.* Currently his is the Editor-in-Chief of *Mysterical-E* (www.mystericale.com) an online mystery magazine.

One of his greatest loves is mystery (all kinds) but he also has an abiding interest in alternate history, speculative fiction, young adult fiction, vampires, werewolves, science fiction, the supernatural, mythology, and more.

You can learn more at www.josephdemarco.com and at www.abodyonpine.com

CPSIA information can be obtained at www.ICGtesting.com
Printed in the USA

235551LV00004B/1/P